MAXWELL'S MASK

When Deena Harrison was eleven she set fire to the toilet block of Leighford High School. She threw Ollie Wendell down the science lab stairs when she was twelve, but she could sing and act, so the headmaster kept her on. The autumn she came down from Oxford, Leighford High had a crisis in the drama department and the *Little Shop of Horrors* was in danger of closing down. So Deena came back – and people started dying. Oh, just tragic accidents of course – minor health and safety issues really. It took Mad Max, Deena's old Head of Sixth, to find out who was killing the company...

MAXWELL'S MASK

Maxwell's Mask

by

M. J. Trow

Magna Large Print Books
Long Preston, North Yorkshire,
BD23 4ND, England.

British Library Cataloguing in Publication Data.

Trow, M. J.
    Maxwell's mask.

    A catalogue record of this book is
    available from the British Library

    ISBN   978-0-7505-2821-4

First published in Great Britain in 2005 by Allison & Busby Limited

Copyright © 2005 by M. J. Trow

Cover illustration © BrightonStudios.com

The moral right of the author has been asserted

Published in Large Print 2008 by arrangement with
Allison & Busby Ltd.

Magna Large Print is an imprint of Library Magna Books Ltd.

Printed and bound in Great Britain by
T.J. (International) Ltd., Cornwall, PL28 8RW

For Michael

Chapter One

They came in ones and twos under the over-hanging arch of willow, solemn, silent; the only noise the crunch of their feet on the gravel.

She watched them from the window as they picked their way in the lengthening shadows. Three or four she recognised, fellow travellers to the Other Side. The others were new to her; anxious faces taking in the dark granite mass of the old vicarage, wondering what they had come to, where they were going. No one made eye contact, no one spoke. She had told them to leave their cars on the road. And all they were to bring with them was one special item, something unique, something to remind them of their dead.

'I am Rowena,' she said and held out a hand.

The tall, angular man who took it was about to swap names, but she checked him with a soft finger to her lips.

'No,' she purred, tracing her fingers for a moment over his knuckles and the back of his hand. 'No names.' She looked up at him, frowning. 'You are in great pain, aren't you?' she said.

For a moment, the tall man didn't know whether to laugh or cry. He just nodded, feeling a serenity he hadn't known for months. 'Pass along,' Rowena said softly. 'The first door on your right. All will be well, she's waiting for you.'

She caught the hand of the next one, a frail lady

9

in a plastic pac-a-mac they hadn't made in forty years. 'Rowena,' she smiled. And Rowena smiled too and held her soft cheek for a moment. She leant closer, whispering into the woman's good ear. 'He's been in touch,' she said. 'He still loves you very much.' And a little sob broke from the old lady as she tottered by, on her way to her usual seat.

'Welcome.' Rowena caught the next two simultaneously, one by the left hand, the other the right. 'There will be news,' she promised. 'Tonight.' And the pair, a bald, bespectacled man and his nearly as bald and bespectacled wife, gripped each other tightly before moving through the door.

'Please,' Rowena held the arm of the next, a girl of perhaps twenty with a mass of red hair and a tangle of black, beaded clothes. 'Don't be afraid. There's nothing to fear from the Other Side, my dear. Only This Side holds its terrors. Please take a seat in the room on the right.'

To the last but one, a sour woman whose greying hair was tied in a wispy bun, Rowena said, 'So you came back. I knew you would. You won't be disappointed, believe me. Your chair is by the fireplace.'

It was the last one that caused Rowena to check herself. As she took the gaunt woman's hand and felt her cold jewellery, she was troubled. Something akin to panic gripped her and she didn't know why. 'We haven't met,' Rowena said. 'And yet we have.'

'Our paths have crossed,' the woman said. Her accent was ... odd. Eastern European, perhaps. Foreign, certainly. But her gaze was steady. As though she'd seen all this before. Done all this before. But not here. Not in Rowena's home.

'Please go through,' she said.

'I know,' the foreign woman said. 'The room on the right. And any chair but the one with its back to the window.'

'That's my chair,' Rowena nodded, more uneasy than ever now. When they were all assembled, the unlikely company sitting rigid on their dining chairs in the room lit only by a small fire and the gathering dusk through the window, Rowena lit an oil lamp. Her face flared with the taper and the light spread its warm glow from the glass chimney. She placed it in the centre of the table and sat down, her back to the window as the strange, gaunt woman had predicted. No one knew quite where to look or whether to speak. All except the gaunt woman, and she was staring at Rowena the whole time.

'Please,' Rowena said. 'Place your precious things on the table, around the lamp. And please, no talking. We need peace now. Peace and focus.' One by one, the sad little trinkets came out. A rosary. A book of Keats' poems. A yellow glove. A little cross made of raffia. A tattered teddy bear, its ears ripped, one eye gone. A fountain pen, green-swirled and brass. The gaunt woman merely placed a business card; it read Magda Lupescu.

Rowena saw it and blinked. Her heart skipped a beat. Skipped several beats. Then she took a deep breath and closed her eyes. No one moved. No one, except Rowena, appeared to be breathing.

'There is a man,' she said, her back rigid, her

11

upper body rocking gently from side to side. 'He is standing by the fire.'

They all turned except Magda Lupescu, who remained motionless, her eyes fixed on Rowena the whole time.

'Is it Alphie?' the old lady asked, unable to see anyone there at all.

Rowena swayed more violently. 'No,' she said, frowning, listening, trying to catch the garbled snatches of conversation that were out there on the ethereal wind from the Other Side. 'No. Not Alphie. He's ... oh, dear.' She was frowning harder now, her breathing ragged, erratic. 'Oh, God, no. He's going to die. He's going to pass over.'

'Who is it, dear?' The old lady was desperate to know.

'He's tall, dark.' Rowena was squinting to see him in the gloom of her dark drawing room. 'Not handsome exactly, but he has a certain ... roguish charm. His name is... I can't quite make it out. What's that? He's talking to me, but I can't quite ... Maxwell. That's it. His name is Maxwell. And he's going to die.'

Chapter Two

'*Try to remember the kind of September when you were a young and callow fellow...*' Peter Maxwell chuckled to himself. That was a long time ago, in the Granta days when he had wandered the Cam with his scarf around his neck, brothel-creepers on his feet and dear old Frank Stenton's *Anglo-Saxon England* bulging out of his rucksack. If anyone had said to him, in those dear, dead days, 'What do you want to be when you grow up?' he'd have said, 'I want to make historical films,' – to be Steven Spielberg before they invented Steven Spielberg. Oh, and win a Nobel Prize for Literature and settle into an old leather chair as Emeritus Professor of History at St Oldfarts' College and watch generations of Young Turks, just like he had been, wandering the Cam with copies of Sir Peter Maxwell bulging from their rucksacks. And when he got to feeling old, he'd up and drown himself in a lake of Southern Comfort.

And how much of all that had come to pass, now that it was a different September all these years later? And dreams had faded with the summer?

'Deena Harrison.'

The voice made him turn from the window, overlooking the plane trees that dotted the car park where colleagues were colliding with children

13

to beat them to the school gates. 'Holy Mother of God. Now there's a blast from the past.'

'Sorry, Max, you were miles away.'

'I was, Sylv,' the Great Man confessed. 'Lamenting my lost youth. And now you bring me another lost youth. What's she done? Burnt down Brasenose? Pushed a professor off Tom Tower? I wouldn't expect much less.' He knew perfectly well that Deena Harrison hadn't gone to Brasenose with its legendary doorknocker, or Christ Church, over which the seven-ton bell called Great Tom loomed. It was just that Peter Maxwell was a sucker for alliteration.

'We had a date for coffee,' Sylv reminded him.

'God, it's Thursday.' He slapped his forehead and kicked the flimsy Consortium furniture in mock fury. 'How could I have been so remiss? One lump or two?' He desperately tried to find a clean mug on the grisly surface of his second-hand office fridge.

'Why do you buy those bloody things?' she asked him. 'By the time they've dissolved, I'm on to my third repetitive strain injury of the morning. And that's just the staff. God, my feet.'

Sylvia Matthews was the school nurse, the Florence Nightingale of Leighford High, forbidden by EU law to do nearly everything that nurses once did, like giving out tablets and driving kids to hospital. But then, EU law was doing its best to make life impossible for everybody. Peter Maxwell hadn't been allowed to touch a stick of chalk since 1978. And the last time he'd hit a child that nice Mr Baldwin was at Number Ten and somebody pinched the Lindbergh baby.

14

Sylvia sat down heavily at the end of another Leighford day. The roar and clatter of eleven hundred children leaving the building like it was the Towering Inferno had long ago died to a distant drone. The horde would be on its way to the High Street by now to shoplift for England. Nervous proprietors were already erecting shutters and flicking up 'Closed' signs. The odd miscreant was still skulking in the corners of the school where the CCTV didn't reach, probably plotting tonight's little sortie to wreck the Geography Department's weather Thingee perched invitingly on the flat roof four storeys up. Better brought-up children would have put their intrepidity to better use, like tackling K2 or whichever is the dodgiest face of the Eiger. A solitary child wandered the otherwise deserted Quad below Maxwell's office, carrying the front wheel of his bike; the rest of the contraption had mysteriously vanished about half past three.

'Deena Harrison?' Peter Maxwell was being mother, sniffing the milk carton as he automatically did, for fear. King Cholera wasn't exactly back in Leighford, but every other nasty had been spread far and wide by the National Health Service.

'She's back.'

'That would be right,' Maxwell nodded. 'Went up to Oxford three years ago. She'll have graduated.'

'Yes, but I mean she's back here, in school.'

'Ah, the lure of the old place.' He passed her a steaming mug. 'They just can't stay away.'

'Max, we're talking about Deena Harrison.'

15

Sylvia looked at the man. The walk was slightly more plodding these days and he took the stairs two at a time now rather than his erstwhile three. The hair was wilder, wirier, greyer, but the eyes were as dark and bright – and sad – as ever. Peter Maxwell had been Head of Sixth Form at Leighford High for as long as anyone could remember. He had long ago leapt that generational hurdle which saw him teaching the children of the children he had taught. One day – and it wouldn't be long now – some kid would say ''Ere, sir, you taught my granddad.' And on that day, Peter Maxwell had promised himself, he would take the loaded Webley Mark IV from his desk and put a bullet in his own brain.

'Deena Harrison,' Sylvia persisted. 'You must remember her rap sheet?'

Maxwell sat opposite her on his swivel, the one luxury he allowed himself in the inner sanctum that was the office of the Head of Sixth Form. 'Oh, I do,' he nodded, scalding his lip on the coffee. 'Let's see. In her first year here she set fire to the toilet block.'

'Wanted to see what happens when you put a lighter to toilet paper,' Sylvia recollected the girl's excuse.

'Nothing wrong with that,' Maxwell winked. 'Healthy spirit of enquiry, that was all. What did happen when she put a lighter to toilet paper?'

'A couple of grand's worth of damage and two months of the loo in my sick bay being used like a public convenience.'

'Tsk, tsk,' Maxwell shook his head.

'Then there was Ollie Wendell.'

16

'Oh, yes,' Maxwell smiled at the memory of the snot-nosed kid. 'Mind you, he had it coming.'

'Max,' Sylvia sat upright. 'Deena threw him down the stairs in the Science Block.'

'Now, we only have Ollie's word for that.' Maxwell wagged a pinko-liberal finger at her. He who had no pinko-liberal digits of any kind.

'Don't give me that. John Anstruther was on duty that break-time if I remember. Got there seconds later and Deena was giggling at the top of the stairs while Ollie was spark out at the bottom. Could have killed him.'

'That was the point, Sylv. Any one of us could have killed Ollie Wendell. My money was always on John Anstruther. Physics teacher. No rapport with kids. "Got there seconds later" indeed!'

She looked around her. 'If you had any cushions on this bloody awful settee of yours, I'd throw one at you. You know as well as I do the girl belonged in a straitjacket.'

'Ah, but the voice, Sylv, the voice. She made Charlotte Church sound like ... someone who can't sing. Damned good actress too. That's why Legs kept her on. Invoked all sorts of inclusion clauses and EU equal opportunities initiatives and she stayed. She came good in the end.'

'Legs' was James Diamond, Leighford's Head-teacher, named by Maxwell for the fictional gangster in the film of the same name. Oddly enough, that very poster was stretched on the wall above Maxwell's desk, the darkly handsome Ray Danton smouldering coldly at the camera. In his more exasperated moments, Maxwell threw darts at it; pretty unfair on Ray Danton

17

and not half painful enough for James Diamond.

'Don't tell me you're applauding a decision made by Diamond?' Sylvia couldn't believe it. Perhaps the man was unwell.

'Wash your mouth out, Nurse Matthews,' Maxwell bridled. 'Legs got lucky, that was all. If we'd had Ted Bundy, Jeffrey Dahmer and Aileen Wournos at Leighford, Legs would have made them a Special Needs group and told them they needn't wear uniform or go to lessons. It's just that Deena grew up. She was fine in the Sixth Form.'

'The Water Fight in '01?'

Maxwell screwed his face up. 'Too close to call. I had Roger Morris in the frame for that one.' Maxwell always had Roger Morris in the frame. He had 'fall-guy' written all over him.

'Morris was a patsy,' Sylvia corrected him. 'Deena was behind it. Trust me. And what about the Millennium fireworks?'

'Ah, that was quite beautiful in its own way.' The Great Man smiled at the memory of it. Beautiful in a Somme sort of way.

Sylvia stopped in mid-gulp. 'Max, I can see the *Advertiser's* headline now. "Arson at Leighford. Rocket attack on Sixth Form block".'

'Yes, and if you also remember the small print, the *Advertiser's* reporter even speculated an IRA connection. Say what you like, those Catherine wheels were quite enchanting.'

'Except that they were pinned to the back door of every house in the bloody neighbourhood. The phone was ringing off the hook with complaints.'

'That's right,' Maxwell remembered. 'Thingees

One and Two on the switchboard both went home crying on two consecutive days. Funny how when kids go on the rampage it's always the school's fault and never the parents'.'

'Deena,' Sylvia announced triumphantly.

'You see, Sylv,' Maxwell leaned back in the swivel, clasping his hands across his waistcoat, 'we, in this great democracy of ours, need a little thing called proof. In a court of law...'

'Max!' Sylvia stood up. 'You're impossible. And...' she pointed a finger at him, 'like all men, you'll forgive a lot for a pretty face and a pair of sparkling eyes. That girl was trouble. And she still is. Thanks for the coffee.' She put the mug back for him, but pointedly didn't offer to wash up. 'You have a nice evening, now.'

'You too, Nursie.' He patted the pile of exercise books on the desk beside him, just a little reminder of the gulf of devotion that separated their worlds. 'Love to Guy.'

'And to Jacquie.' Sylvia ignored his body language. Maxwell had a heart of gold, but he'd rather have his liver torn out than mark a book. 'How is she, by the way?'

'Well, morning sickness has given way to an appallingly healthy aura. She's pink and breezy and really quite nauseating, especially at five in the morning when I'm trying to get my beauty sleep. I hear this distant hum, bit like the Zulu approaching Rorke's Drift. It's Jacquie, totally unable to resist the urge to hoover in the lounge. Oh, and she's rather soppy at the moment, bursting into tears all the time.'

Sylvia laughed, 'That's what pregnancy will do

19

to you every time.'

'God, is she pregnant?' Maxwell looked aghast. 'How did that happen?'

She threw a metaphorical cushion at him and was on her way.

The rain set in early that night, sweeping from the west across the South Downs, bouncing off the coloured lights that swung and dangled across the High Street and the Front, soaking the hoardings that proclaimed that Freddie and the Dreamers were playing the pier back in July and a Perry Como tribute band was going to wow everybody early in October. The dark headland that was the Shingle was a shapeless mass that melted into the great grey ghost of the sea as Peter Maxwell stared out from his skylight.

Any stray bird, winging homeward in the driving rain after a hard day's worming, would have been struck by the odd sight on the dry side of the glass. Peter Maxwell was standing in the loft of 38 Columbine, his home now for the best part of twenty years, a Crimean officer's pill box cap at a rakish angle on his barbed-wire hair and a glass of Southern Comfort in his left hand. In his right hand was a paintbrush, a little clump of sable that had never been anywhere near a squirrel. Under the fierce glare of the lamp and the modeller's magnifying glass on the table in front of him, his latest acquisition was taking shape. Private William Pennington of the 11th Prince Albert's Own Hussars sat his bay nonchalantly, waiting, in his own plastic, fifty-four millimetre sort of way, for the balloon to go up.

20

Across the room from Maxwell's modelling table lay Maxwell's pride and joy, his lifetime's work. Four hundred and sixteen soldiers of Lord Cardigan's Light Brigade were drawn up at the safe end of the Valley of Death, waiting for the Noble Yachtsman to give the order to 'Walk, March, Trot'. Maxwell had been putting this collection together forever. Other men fished, played football, went down the pub. Peter Maxwell collected, glued, painted and adapted model soldiers. It was, he supposed in his darker moments, an addiction of sorts. But he remained resolutely in denial, refusing to go to the monthly Modellers Anonymous meetings they held in Tottingleigh Village Hall, where sad middle-aged men sat in corners and tried to come to terms with their problem. 'I am Peter Maxwell and I'm a Modeller.'

Maxwell sat back down, flicking the gloss black onto Pennington's sabretache and the slings that secured it to his sword belt.

'Well, you've just got to start listening, Count,' he murmured without looking up. 'Because I've told you all this already. William Henry Pennington had served in the Merchant Navy before enlisting in the 11th ... well, it was the nicer uniform, I suppose. Dublin, that's where he joined up. What the hell was he doing there?'

The Count had no answer. That was partly because he didn't give a rat's arse and partly because he was an eleven-year-old neutered tom cat.

'Bit of a smartarse, this one. Survived the charge, thanks to a kindly old TSM in the 8th,

21

and went on to become an actor. Wowed old Gladstone with his Hamlet, apparently. Became the Grand Old Man's "favourite tragedian" – and I quote. But then, Gladstone also believed he could answer the Irish Question – Gladstone, that is, not Pennington. You going out tonight?'

The Count stretched, yawning, just to show his Master his superior set of gnashers, sharp as needles and twice as deadly.

'Yeah, I know,' Maxwell nodded, glancing up for the first time. 'Was the Pope a member of the Hitler Youth? Well, you've got to remember, Count, there's a lady of the house, now. It's not just you, me and most of the Light Brigade any-more. You come in quietly, closing the cat flap behind you, and you do not, repeat, *not* bring back any little chums, especially chums that will become a late-night snack for you later. The Memsahib doesn't go a bundle on things that go squelch in the night. Get it? Got it? Good.'

Count Metternich straightened, totally un-impressed by Maxwell's immaculate take-off of Danny Kaye, and checked his nose was still there with the tip of his tongue. He slid down from the pouffe he had made his own, all fleas and claw marks, and swayed gracefully towards the trap door. He paused to munch something that had wriggled out of his forearm fur and lashed his tail twice in Maxwell's direction.

'You're right,' Maxwell sighed. 'I have been putting off Thirteen Bee's attempts to explain *Volksgemeinschaft* for too long. Time to beard the beasts in their lair.'

He padded down the attic stairs behind the cat,

22

avoiding the creaking one four from the bottom. In the dim light, he saw his Jacquie curled up under the covers and he caught Metternich in mid-air as the black and white bastard was about to leap onto the duvet beside her, just for jolly.

'He's OK, Max,' she murmured, half asleep. 'Let him stay.'

'Sorry, heart of hearts,' Maxwell said. 'House rules. I don't rip voles apart with my teeth or play football with pygmy shrews' intestines – the Count doesn't sleep on the bed. Savvy?' He breathed a whisper into the cat's twitchy ear. Briefly, Metternich considered twisting out of the Great Man's grip and demolishing his face with a timely claw-swipe. Then the better side of his nature took over and he broke wind with deafening silence in his master's hand. It had much the same effect and Maxwell dropped him like a hot cat. The Count bounced off the carpet and took the stairs three at a time. Mercifully for all of them, the Great Outdoors was calling.

'I didn't mean to wake you up, darling,' Maxwell said.

'What time is it?' Jacquie was half sitting up, trying to focus on the clock, and trying to release her nightie before it strangled her.

'Half-ten,' he told her. 'Now, back to sleep, young lady. I won't be long.'

'Marking?' she slurred turning to face him. Whatever Sylvia Matthews thought, Maxwell did actually do some from time to time.

'The teacher's curse,' he nodded. 'Hate it or hate it, it goes with the territory.' He patted her shoulder and made for the stairs.

'Max,' Jacquie was sitting up now, or at least on her elbows. 'Are you sure you're all right about this?'

'Oh, I've been marking for a long time now, Jacks. I think I'll manage.'

'I'm not talking about that,' she said. 'As well you know. I'm talking about this. Us. Me moving in with you.'

He crossed back to the bed and sat in the curve made by her knees. 'We tossed a coin,' he reminded her.

She reached out in the semi-darkness to find his cheek. 'I don't think that was a very adult way to settle things.'

He chuckled. 'It was your place or mine,' he said. 'We can't bring up a baby in two houses three miles apart. Night time feeds would be a bitch.'

'I know,' she said, 'But ... well, you're such a...'

'Bastard?' He was being helpful.

'I was going to say bachelor, but yes, that too.'

But Peter Maxwell had not always been a bachelor. In the darkest recesses of his wallet lay the battered photographic evidence to prove it. A beautiful woman. A lovely child. His first family. In a car on a wet road. A long, long time ago. The wrong time. The wrong place. Dead On Arrival. He looked at the girl in his bed. His new family, complete with bump. Another little girl to replace his Debbie? Perhaps. They'd both turned away during the necessary scans. Leighford General's Maternity Unit knew the sex of Maxwell's and Jacquie's unborn child, but the doting parents didn't have a clue. It was how they wanted it.

'No,' he said, stroking her hair. 'I've been a bachelor for long enough.' And he kissed her. 'Now, go to sleep, Woman Policeman Carpenter. Abyssinia.'

Woman Policeman Carpenter. She still loved it when he called her that. And as she listened to his footfalls padding down the stairs, she heard again the laughter and the ragging at the party they'd thrown at the nick as she took her maternity leave of them.

'Come back and see us, Jacquie,' the guv'nor had said. And she thought, just for a moment, she'd seen him smile. But it was probably just the champagne or a trick of the light.

'The lengths some people will go to to avoid night-shift!'

'Who's going to make the fucking tea now?'

And she heard herself chuckling as sleep crept over her, and their faces faded into dreams.

If he'd been perfectly honest, Gordon Goodacre would have admitted that he'd never really liked the Arquebus. It had been derelict for years, part of a row of abandoned warehouses that ribboned the twisting path of the Leigh, searching, as rivers will, for the sea. Arts Council grants and Regeneration money had turned it into a theatre and the great and good of West Sussex had patronised various productions and the place began its new life as a centre of dramatic excellence.

Gordon wasn't a thesp. Matilda, she was the one. Her Eleanor of Aquitaine in *The Lion in Winter* had been legendary; people said they'd never seen anything like her Yentl – but that went

25

without saying. Gordon was a personnel manager by day. But by night, to keep Matilda quiet, he worked on sets at the Arquebus.

'What can Gordon do?' someone on the committee had asked Matilda. And Matilda, usually so voluble, had been stuck for an answer. 'He can paint,' she had said, in a sudden burst of desperation. And so here he was, that Thursday night, painting. Or at least, he was about to. Leighford High School were taking their *Little Shop of Horrors* on tour and the first whistle-stop was the Arquebus. But the Arquebus had just mounted *Waiting for Godot* and every flat in the place needed a lick of paint. Yes, it was nearly eleven. Yes, Gordon had been there since seven. Yes, it was bucketing down outside. But he still had...

There it was again. That noise. What was it? Gordon Goodacre tried to rationalise it. In the half-light of this once-derelict building he didn't like. Not the rain, certainly. That was coming down hard enough, but it was recognisable, rhythmic, pounding the reeded skylights overhead. This was ... well, if Gordon was asked to pinpoint it ... it sounded like something heavy being dragged. Then a sigh. Not quite human. Not quite real.

'Is anybody there?' Gordon straightened from the black paint pots at his feet.

There was silence now. Then the dragging sound again. And the sigh. Not once. But twice. And a sound of falling. He couldn't think of a better way to describe it. As though something was hurtling through the air to end with a snap. A creak, like a foot on a stair. Or the tension of a rope.

'Look, who's there? What do you think you're playing at?'

Gordon had let himself in. He had locked the doors behind him. The keys were in his overalls pocket now. If this was that stupid bastard Ashley... He walked to centre stage, where the light formed a pool of liquid blue. He glared out into the silent, empty seats of the auditorium. The house lights were full on. Only the area under the balcony was in shadow and there was nobody there.

Gordon turned, first this way, then that. It was over there. Towards the Green Room. But somehow higher. As if there was a walkway. But there wasn't a walkway, not anymore.

'Look,' his voice boomed out in the stillness. 'I've had enough of this.'

They say you don't hear the bomb that blows you to pieces. You don't see the bullet that bores through your chest. The one with your name on it is not the one you can read. So it was with Gordon Goodacre. And the ladder he didn't notice. Until it was too late.

Chapter Three

'Deena Hamilton, Max.'

Was this how it was? Maxwell wondered. When the Last Trump came and that Great Headmaster in the sky called you to account? Was it just a series of déjà vu's and endless reminders of Kids You Love To Hate? Any minute now, he'd be hearing of Wayne 'The Farter' Bryson, who could clear classrooms; Wonky Wadham, on whom nature had played a cruel trick; James 'Hell Boy' Gardner – all of them locked in an eternal detention in the Classroom That Time Forgot.

But he shook himself free of it. It was Friday morning – albeit the 13th – and a far from great headmaster sat across the desk from him. James 'Legs' Diamond had a degree, it was rumoured, in Biology, but after that all serious links with education were broken irrevocably and he had become senior management, worrying about initiatives, league tables, specialist status, that hellish group the Learning Skills Council and all the other gobbledegook that had knocked Peter Maxwell's legs from under him over the last four hundred years. All he really wanted to do was to teach some History and nobody would let him.

'Lovely girl, Headmaster,' Diamond's Head of Sixth Form smiled.

For a moment, a look of panic and incomprehension swept over Diamond's face. His problem

– one of many, it had to be said – was that he never knew when Maxwell was joking.

'She was here yesterday, at Leighford.'

'So I believe,' Maxwell nodded, fully able at his age to put the concepts of 'here' and 'Leighford' together. 'I was, of course, mortified that she didn't pop in to see me.'

'You?' Diamond blinked.

There were times – many, many times – when Peter Maxwell had such withering scorn for Legs Diamond that he couldn't be bothered to answer him. He'd left Assemblies, staff meetings, working lunches, all for fear that he might lose his cool and put one on his headmaster. It was a terrible, but all too excusable crime, principicide.

'I was her Year Head for two years, Headmaster – though I grant you, there were times when it seemed longer. I like to think I did my bit in getting her into Oxford.'

'Oh, indeed.'

'We haven't had too many, have we?' Maxwell saw an irresistible chink in his headmaster's less-than-proof armour. 'Oxbridge successes, I mean? Let's see, the last one, before Deena, was Clive Moon. PPP, if memory serves.'

'It's not the be-all and end-all, you know.' Diamond smiled awkwardly, never, in these sparring sessions with Peter Maxwell, knowing where the next attack was coming from. Truth be told, he'd forgotten what PPP stood for and he wanted to move on.

'Indeed not,' Maxwell asserted. 'Clive went to Merton, Oxford, when he should have gone to Jesus, Cambridge.'

'No, I meant ... there are other universities.'

'Are there, Headmaster? Do tell.' He glanced at his watch. 'Four minutes till the balloon goes up, Headmaster. Nine Eff Two. I must needs set up my Powerpoint presentation on factory reform.'

'Powerpoint, Max?' Diamond sat back in amazement. 'Er ... good. Good. I'm impressed.' Like everyone else at Leighford, James Diamond assumed that Peter Maxwell had stumbled out of Jurassic Park.

'Of course you are,' Maxwell beamed. 'So ... er ... Deena?'

'Oh, yes.' Diamond pulled himself together in the corner of the bland office where school successes in Young Enterprise and Engineering Challenge shone proudly on the wall. 'She came to help out, with the show, I mean.'

'The show,' Maxwell repeated, as if the word was new to him.

'*Little Shop of Horrors*,' Diamond reminded him. 'We're putting it on at the Arquebus in October.'

'Excellent,' Maxwell nodded. 'Thanks for the word. I shall book my ticket.'

'Well, actually, Max, it's a little more complicated than that.'

'Oh?'

Diamond had seen that eyebrow rise before and he didn't like it. It was like a cobra spreading its hood, a tiger stalking in the tall grass. 'Well, as you know, we were unable to appoint an Expressive Arts Supremo, so Angela Carmichael was having to cope on her own – well, with a little help from the Music Department, of course.'

'Of course.' Peter Maxwell knew exactly how

little that help was. The Head of Music, Geraint Horsenell, was a good chum and a realist. But he was not a man you'd want beside you – or indeed anywhere near you – in a shipwreck.

'Well, unfortunately, Angela's having complications, with the pregnancy, I mean. She's off for the foreseeable future.'

'Oh.' This time, Maxwell's concern was genuine. Angela Carmichael was a nice woman. And his Jacquie was pregnant too...

'So Deena's arrival was a godsend.'

Maxwell frowned. Not for the first time, the machinations of what Diamond laughingly called a mind left him perplexed, confused. The Demon Headmaster was sometimes not of this earth. 'It was?'

'Well, she's got a degree in Dramatic Arts, Max – from, you hinted at it yourself, one of the best universities in the country. She's at a loose end *and* she worked on the production up at Oxford.'

'But she's not a teacher, Headmaster.'

'No.' Diamond squirmed in his plastic, County -bought swivel. He toyed momentarily with trying to climb inside his laptop for safety. 'That's right. And that's where you come in.'

'Where I come in? What, sort of ... enter stage fright?'

The muscles along Diamond's jaw flexed and rippled. This man was so infuriating, so bloody obtuse. But there had been times, and not so very long ago, when he literally owed Maxwell his career. There was no going back now. He was staring into the Abyss. 'I can employ Deena, but only on a part-time, untrained teacher salary.

31

She'll need someone ... experienced. An old hand, so to speak.'

'Out of the question,' Maxwell said and was on his feet. 'Nine Eff Two, Headmaster. That Power-point won't wait.'

'Max,' Diamond was standing too, edging round his desk, trying to head Maxwell off at the pass. 'Max, I know this is an imposition, but unless you can work it, we'll have to cancel.'

Maxwell paused in the doorway. 'If you're attempting to blackmail me, Headmaster...'

'No, for God's sake, Max. You've done this before.'

'Not for years.'

'You were a legendary Cyrano, I understand, before my time?'

The Head of Sixth Form nodded. Everything was before Diamond's time, really. 'Passing competent,' he said, 'even if I say so myself. Depardieu was on the blower asking for a few hints as his own modest effort went into production.'

'And didn't you do Macbeth?'

'Scottish fight arranger only,' Maxwell corrected him. 'And all that was a long time ago, Head-master – when the Scottish play was still current affairs.'

'All right,' Diamond relented, with a heartfelt sigh. 'It'll have to be Dierdre. Have a good morn-ing, Max.' And he slunk back behind his desk.

'What?' The Great Man had turned, like the Hell-hound he was, in the head's doorway.

'I said "Have a good..."'

'Before that.'

'Oh, well, if you don't feel you can do it, it'll

32

have to be Dierdre Lessing.'

Maxwell had crossed Diamond's office in three strides, his knuckles on the man's desk, taking the weight of his arms. 'You know,' he growled, his face inches from his headteacher's, 'you're getting pretty good at this. I'll have to watch my step.'

Slowly, Diamond's face melted into a smile. He'd have to mark this on his calendar. Friday the 13th – the Day He Put One Over On Peter Maxwell. 'Thanks, Max,' he said. 'I knew I could count on you.'

The bell shattered the moment and Maxwell regained his composure. 'No cover lessons for the duration of the rehearsal time. A late start every Thursday. And a personal chauffeur called Les.'

But wheeling and dealing humour and pinching lines from telly ads was lost on James Diamond. Maxwell saw himself out. 'Bugger,' he said just before he closed the door. 'No time to set up Powerpoint now. It'll just have to be talk and chalk for Nine Eff. God, I just hate being so old-fashioned. Heigh-ho!'

'I just can't believe the bastard did it,' Maxwell was saying, snug in the confines of 38 Columbine. 'I'm getting slow.'

'But Dierdre would have been a disaster.'

'Exactly. But you've got to hand it to Legs. He knew exactly which buttons to press. He's been going to *realpolitik* classes again.'

'I thought you gave those.'

'Ah, Woman Policeman,' he smiled, stroking her arm. 'You know how to lift a man when he's down. I only give biennial masterclasses. Low life like Legs aren't invited. Some bastard must have published my stuff on the Internet, whatever that is.'

She freshened his drink as the glow brightened behind the plastic coal of his electric fire. 'How is Dierdre this term?'

'Same as she is every term,' he hissed as the amber nectar of his Southern Comfort hit his tonsils. 'Like the Marie Celeste in full sail. Responsible for every evil in the world from Hoodies to Global Colding. She ate a peripatetic music teacher last week.'

She snuggled closer to him, curled up as they were on his settee. 'You didn't tell me you'd played Cyrano de Bergerac.'

'Oh, yes.' He let his head loll back and closed his eyes. 'Beat the long-nosed bastard in straight sets. Mind you, they were different days. We all seemed to have so much more time then. Putting in twenty-eight hours a day wasn't only possible, it was fun. Old Bill Vintner was head at Leighford. And it was a...' he checked to see the coast was clear and that they were alone, 'grammar school.' He whispered it; the education that dared not speak its name. 'Lovely old boy, was Bill.' The fire-glow and the Southern Comfort and the warm woman were beginning to get to Peter Maxwell. He was in memory mode. 'Claimed to have ridden up San Juan Hill with Teddy Roosevelt.'

Jacquie Carpenter loved Peter Maxwell with every fibre of her being, but there were times when she didn't have the faintest idea what he was talking about. This was one of them. 'But he didn't?' she asked tentatively.

He looked at her. What a love. So much to learn. So little time. Bit like Year Ten, really. 'No,' he said, kindly. 'But I wouldn't be at all surprised to learn it was Senlac Hill with William the Conqueror.'

She was on safe ground now and slapped his drinking hand, just for good measure. William she'd heard of. Senlac Hill, Mad Max had had her wandering all over, not six months before. 'So, when do you start?' she asked.

'Well, Monday, I suppose. I must admit, it'll be intriguing to tread the boards again. But, I ask you, *Little Shop of Horrors* – what's that about?'

'Well,' she put down her coffee mug and adjusted the protuberance in front of her. 'There was this flower shop in downtown...'

'Oh, ha!' he snorted. 'I mean, why couldn't it have been Ibsen, or Chekhov, or, Heaven forfend, the Bard?'

'Because nobody'd go,' she told him. 'At least this way you'll get an audience. If somebody's little Johnny was playing Uncle Vanya, not even little Johnny's mum would turn up. As it is, no doubt you've got a thousand girlies anxious to strut their stuff – all their mums will be there. So will the dads, having an illicit shufty at their daughters' friends fol-derols...'

'Disgusting,' snarled Maxwell.

'And the geeks will be there to see how you do Audrey.'

'Audrey?'

'The man-eating plant. God, Max, I thought

you were kidding about not knowing what the show is about.'

'I am, dear girl, I am. You seem very clued up about it.'

'Did it in Year Eleven, didn't I? And before you ask, yes, that was a long time ago.'

'Well, the Arquebus doesn't know what's going to hit it.'

'The Arquebus?'

'The theatre. Along Quay Street.'

'Yes, I know. Why there?'

'Well, it's Angela Carmichael's idea, apparently. Theatre in the Community or something crappy. We don't use the Hall and invite the locals to come to us. No, that's far too boring and obvious. We go to them. Sort of mountain and Mohammed.'

'There was an accident there last night.'

'At the Arquebus?'

'Hm. Fatal, actually.'

'Really?' He sat up a little, and looked her in the grey, sparkling eyes. 'Have you been listening in to Police Wireless again?' he asked, the eyebrow of disapproval threatening his hairline.

'Jane Blaisedell called round this morning. You know, just to see how I was.'

'How are you?' He looked down at her, attentive, solicitous, taking the mick.

'Piss off and listen,' she insisted. It was one of Jacquie's stranger stage directions, but Maxwell let it pass. 'Somebody was killed, working on the set.'

'Anybody we know?'

'Gordon Goodacre. Didn't ring any bells with me.'

'God, yes.' Maxwell was frowning.

'Did you know him?'

He moved a little way away from her and held up his fingers in the sign of the cross. 'Put those lighted matches down, Woman Policeman. I know nothing.'

'Seriously.'

'Seriously, no. But I have had the pleasure of *Mrs* Goodacre – and not, mercifully, in the Biblical sense. She'll love this.'

'Max!' she squeaked. 'That's not very nice.'

'Sorry, no,' he checked himself. 'No, it's tragic. But Matilda Goodacre is the original Drama Queen. I remember her wailing in the High Street when we ratified the Maastricht Treaty. Fine sentiments, of course; just a little over the top. What happened?'

'Oh, carelessness, I suppose,' Jacquie shrugged. 'Jane said Goodacre had been working late on the scenery and a ladder had slipped. Fractured his skull.' Jacquie looked up at him suddenly, struck by a thought. '*You'll* be careful out there, won't you, Mr Maxwell?'

He smiled. 'Careful,' he said, 'is my middle name.'

'It's a little late for you, Henry,' the man in the white coat said. He checked his watch. 'Come to think of it, it's a little late for me.'

'Sorry, Jim.' DCI Henry Hall emerged in the pool of light that flooded the stainless steel heart of the mortuary at Leighford General. In *Morse* or *Midsomer Murders* those places were always dark, mysterious, like the doings that were investigated in them. In reality, they were neon-stripped, chemical-coated, like slightly upmarket abattoirs. 'I was just on my way home.'

Jim Astley chuckled, the bow tie wobbling under the once-firm chin. 'If you're going to get all busier-than-thou on me, I'm out of here now. In the comparative stakes, pathologists' hours versus policemen's, I'm not sure which one of us would come up smelling of roses. I was off to the George. Time for a quick one?'

Jim Astley didn't offer to buy a round often. He had too many Porsches to run, his wife's habit to control and probably Scottish blood in his veins a few generations back. So it hurt like hell for Henry Hall to have to pass it up. 'Not tonight, I'm afraid. I was wondering if you'd made any progress with Gordon Goodacre.'

Astley hauled off his coat at the end of another long day, throwing it vaguely at some hooks. 'You know what they say,' he said, 'about miracles taking longer?'

'Sorry,' Hall shrugged. He and Astley went back a few years. They'd come to know each other pretty well. Astley was a vain prig whose orifice housed the rising sun. Long years ago he'd opted for that branch of medicine where the patients don't talk back. And in these litigious days, he was increasingly grateful for that. Hall was an unfathomable bastard, the consummate professional with no smiling muscles at all, a thinking machine in a grey three-piece who hid his hard eyes behind curiously opaque glasses. Jacquie Carpenter had never seen another pair like them. Hall could see out; no one could see in. What else was there to know?

'I can confirm my preliminary verdict.' Astley hunted for his coat in the bowels of his office off the morgue, realising again what a slob his assistant Donald was. 'The skull was fractured in two places, both occipital, by a blunt instrument, viz and to wit, a ladder. Death would have been virtually instantaneous. Routine one, this, Henry. Unless...'

'Unless?'

Astley pushed the man gently aside so that he could close the door and lock it. 'Unless your nose tells you something else.'

'Should it?' Hall was as impassive as ever. He let other people do the sniffing around. The wait was usually worth it.

'It's half past nine, Henry,' Astley told him. 'You're a Detective Chief Inspector and it's Friday. A man died last night at about eleven o'clock in what has all the appearances of a tragic, but not unusual, accident — shall I quote you the ladder death stats? So why the interest? Unless...'

There was a slight twitch to one side of Henry Hall's mouth. It would be the nearest he was likely to come to a smile, at least this side of Christmas. 'You're right, Jim,' he said. 'I don't get out enough. Love to Marjorie.'

'And to Margaret. A bientôt, Chief Inspector.'

Peter Maxwell went to the Arquebus Theatre that night. He saddled his bike, White Surrey, named for the charger of England's most maligned king, Richard III (Henry VII did it, by the way), and pedalled through the mizzle over the Flyover and down the maze of streets that led to the Quay.

The building itself still retained an exterior that spoke of grander days, when Leighford had been a minor port on the south coast and sugar and rum and slaves and molasses had come creaking in under full sail with the smell of hemp and tar. The old pulley was still there, high above its column of doors on four storeys and the forecourt where timber was piled and manifests checked now housed the ghastly new glass entrance-way.

Maxwell remembered the Arquebus as a row of warehouses, derelict, rat-infested, open to the weather and the winos. In a glass case by the front door, a rather long-in-the-tooth Matilda Good-acre smiled at him, wearing a ludicrous wimple *à la* the redoubtable Eleanor of Aquitaine. Other faces, the grave old plodders and gay young friskers of Leighford's am dram community, he didn't know. He tethered White Surrey to some railings with his trusty padlock – this *was* downtown Leighford of a Monday night, after all, and you couldn't be too careful. Then he pushed the glass door and he was in, his damp feet on plush red carpet in the refurbished atrium. Dim lights revealed the ticket office and the stairs curving to left and right. As he read the notices, he heard the rain start with a vengeance, bouncing on the glass roof of the portico and running like tears down the high windows.

'Hello. Oh, it's cats and dogs out there!' The wrinkled little woman in the Fifties pac-a-mac shook her tousled hair in the doorway. 'You are?'

'A little drier than you, it seems. Luckily, it was fine when I arrived. I'm Peter Maxwell.' He held

40

out a hand.

She took it in the bird-like, fragile way that women do, limp and not quite real. 'Maxwell. Maxwell. Now, I know that name. *Ring of Bright Water* chappie. Any relation?'

'Er ... I don't think so.'

'Probably just as well. That whole episode put the cause of wildlife back by a generation, I always thought. I'm Martita Winchcombe, the Arquebus Treasurer. Are you the new lighting man?'

'No, I'm afraid not. I'm with Leighford High.'

'Oh.' The Treasurer's face fell a little. 'Can I be frank, Mr Maxwell?' The old girl wrestled to close her umbrella.

'Please,' the Head of Sixth Form suggested. A woman with dentures as ill fitting as hers surely had the right to be anybody she wanted to be.

'Well, children nowadays are a pretty unruly bunch, aren't they? I mean, I'm sure they mean well, but their manners...'

'Ah, sign of the times, I fear, Ms Winchcombe.'

'Miss,' she corrected him tartly. 'Miss Winch-combe.'

Yes; Maxwell thought it might be.

'And I have to say that teacher person, what's her name? Mrs Carbuncle?'

'Carmichael.'

'Yes, I knew it was some sort of car. Heart's not in it. Too self-absorbed if you catch my drift.'

'You mean pregnant?'

Miss Winchcombe looked up at the man. The bow tie, the tweed jacket. Seemed acceptable enough. And that, surely, was the scarf of one of the more reputable universities around his neck?

Still, you heard such stories about teachers these days. 'That's not a word we bandied about in my youth,' she told him crisply.

'Quite,' Maxwell nodded, straight-faced. How old was this woman? 'Well, Mrs Carmichael has had to bow out, as it were, from this production.'

'Oh, so you're her replacement?' She peered at him more closely. 'I thought there was another girl I met. Oh well... I suppose you'll do. Come on up.'

'Thank you.' Maxwell followed her up the velvet-carpeted stairs as the old girl flicked lights on in all directions. On the first half-landing, she stopped. New-smelling parquet floors led off in what seemed all directions, some ending in closed doors, others extending around the auditorium to culminate in gantries with lanterns and cables and all the other inexplicable gadgetry of theatre land. 'Wait,' she all but shrieked. 'How did you get in?'

'Through the door,' he told her slowly, as though feeling his way through a trick question.

'I see. Well that must mean Patrick's around somewhere. Was that *your* bicycle I almost fell over outside?'

'Probably,' Maxwell confessed. 'Whitish frame? Two wheels? Racing basket?'

'I didn't look that closely. Ah, Patrick. There you are.'

Ahead of them on the upper landing, at the end of one of the narrow, darker corridors, a large crimson man in a cravat was carrying a large bundle of scripts.

'This is Mr Marple. He's producing the

musical whatnot.'

'Not exactly,' Maxwell said, but the old girl was already dripping her way to the next landing, rattling keys as she went and opening doors, apparently at random.

'You'll have to forgive Martita,' said the crimson man. 'She was Treasurer here when this place was still an indigo warehouse or whatever it was. Patrick Collinson. I'm Theatre Secretary, moonlighting from the day job. And you're not the producer.'

'No,' Maxwell chuckled. 'And I'm not Mr Marple, either. Maxwell. Peter Maxwell.' He shook the man's hand.

'You're from Leighford High, aren't you?' Collinson pointed at him. 'I caught your Spartacus lecture at the Historical Association last year. Masterly.'

'That's very kind.'

'Look, you'll have to forgive us. I'm afraid there's no rehearsal tonight.'

'Really?' Maxwell frowned. Legs had sold him a pup yet again. Perhaps his assumption of a Monday start was a little premature.

'Cancelled at the last minute. We had a bereavement last Thursday.'

'A bereavement?' Maxwell had long ago learnt not to let anything slip he heard from Jacquie via police sources.

'Down there,' Collinson pointed to the dimly lit stage, below them and to his right. 'Gordon Goodacre, poor chap. He was working on the set and a ladder fell on him. Couldn't have known what hit him.'

43

'Will the production go ahead?' Maxwell asked.

'Lord, yes.' Collinson ushered the man along the corridor and down again to the back of the auditorium. 'Matilda insisted on it.'

'Matilda?'

'Confusing, isn't it? Martita, Matilda. Worse last year; we had a Martina as well, but mercifully she moved to Glossop.'

Maxwell breathed a sigh of relief.

'No, Matilda is Gordon's wife – widow, I suppose now. She's Chairperson for the duration. Life and soul of the Arquebus Committee. She's called an Extraordinary Meeting tonight which is why Martita and I are here. Ashley'll be along presently and the whole motley crew.'

'Well, I'll take my leave...' Maxwell said.

'Nonsense!' Collinson insisted. 'Now you're here, you might as well meet everybody. You are going to be part of the family for a while, after all.'

'Well, all right.' They both heard the rain thundering on the skylights. 'It's a filthy night... If you're sure I won't be intruding.'

'Dear boy, think nothing of it. Come and have a coffee. I'd offer you something stronger, but we're only licensed during runs. You look like a b and s man.' Collinson looked him up and down.

'Southern Comfort.' Maxwell knew the mantra from his AA days.

'Good lad.'

Collinson led him into the newer part of the theatre. Maxwell had seen the odd production at the Arquebus. He'd been dragged, against his will, to see *The Boyfriend* and had nodded off in *Death of a Salesman.* He'd left *A Streetcar Named Desire* at half time; they were showing *The Quatermass Experiment* on the telly and he'd forgotten to set his timer; a man had his standards, when all is said and done. But this was a part of the building he'd never seen before. Some schizophrenic architect had had a field day with the Arquebus. The stage, auditorium and foyer were pure Grand Guignol, with a proscenium more arch than Eddie Izzard. But the Green Room, rehearsal units and offices were Nineties Noir, all harsh light, dark brickwork and stark angles. Bewildering.

'Take a pew, Mr Maxwell. May I call you Peter?'

'Max will do.'

'Max it is.'

The door swung open behind them. 'Well, well.' Collinson's beam froze like a rictus. 'Dan Bartlett. Artistic Director. This is Peter Maxwell.'

In a weaker light, Dan Bartlett could have passed for a rather seedy Bill Nighy. His dark hair hung floppily over his forehead and ears and he wore a long coat over a crisp white shirt and a pair of leather trousers. His skin was the colour of David Dickinson and you just knew the tan was courtesy of the sunbed at Chez Paul, the beauty parlour in Wellington Road. He had an empty pizza box under his arm.

'From Leighford High.' Maxwell shook the man's hand.

'You're working on this disaster, are you?' Bartlett asked. Emerging into the light, he looked like Nosferatu.

'Not that bad, surely?' Maxwell tried to lighten

45

the moment.

'If you've only just joined, then you'll find out soon enough. What time is this thing likely to wind up, Patrick? I've another engagement.'

'How long is a piece of string, old boy.' Collinson was hunting in MFI-fronted cupboards, looking for coffee. 'I thought Ashley was going to lay all the refreshments out.' He raised his eyes heavenwards and tutted. 'You just can't get the staff. Same for you, I expect, Max, at the High School?'

'Don't get me started on that one.'

'Christ, it's pissing down.' Another new arrival crashed his way into the Board Room. This man was about a thousand years younger than anyone Maxwell had met so far. His thick thatch of hair curled over his upright collar and he dripped onto the cord carpet. There was a hint of corpulence about the man, although he was wrapped against the elements and it was difficult to tell.

'Ashley,' Collinson put out another cup. 'We're honoured. This is Peter Maxwell, overseeing Leighford's production. Our Theatre Manager, Ashley Wilkes.'

'Ashley...?' Maxwell paused before he took the man's hand.

'Yes, I know.' The Theatre Manager raised his head in an acknowledgement born of years of resentment. 'My mother had this thing for Leslie Howard. Please don't tell me you're a film buff, Mr Maxwell.'

'I dabble,' Maxwell shrugged. 'And don't worry. My mother was frightened by the burning of Atlanta while she was carrying me. Just as well,

46

or I'd have been called Vivien.'

'Matilda, darling!' Bartlett was on his feet, all gush and concern, like Old Faithful. Everybody who had found a seat was on their feet, standing awkwardly as though at a wake. Matilda Goodacre was as statuesque as Maxwell remembered her from her Maastricht days. The years had been kind – she clearly had a self-portrait in the attic – and the rain appeared not to have touched her at all.

'Daniel.' She was all ice, from the purse of her lips to the tips of her shoes. He kissed the air somewhere near her cheek in time-honoured theatrical tradition.

'How are you, m'dear?' Collinson fussed, helping her off with her coat and looking the epitome of concern.

'About the same as last night, Patrick.' She accepted the chair young Ashley had slid back for her. 'Who's this?'

'Peter Maxwell.' He held out his hand. 'From Leighford High.'

'Ah, yes, you're with the schoolchildren, aren't you?'

It had been Maxwell's lot for rather a long time now. 'Please accept my condolences, Mrs Goodacre,' he said.

'Thank you, Mr Maxwell.' She wriggled to accommodate her ample self in the steel-framed chair. Usually at Committee Meetings she spent the first ten minutes complaining loudly about the monstrosities of modern living; but tonight it seemed less than appropriate. 'And I do appreciate it. Now, listen to me, all of you.' She clasped

47

her expression-filled hands in front of her and waited for their full attention. Even in grief – especially in grief – Matilda Goodacre loved to be centre stage. 'I am touched by your concern, and I realise how awkward all this is. Last Thursday night, in what we can only call an Act of God, my darling husband...' her voice caught for a moment as she made her way, like a spoon through treacle, through what was clearly a well rehearsed speech, '...my darling husband, Gordon, met his untimely end. It is, of course, tragic, and I alone must come to terms with it as best I can. But Gordon would not want us sitting here, moping. The Arquebus was his life – as it is mine.'

Hear, hear's rumbled through the room.

'He would want us to carry on,' Matilda carried on. 'Hence tonight's little get together. I am glad you are here, Mr Maxwell. You represent the future.'

This was a first. To most people, Maxwell represented the past.

'We all look forward to the *Little Shop of Horrors*. And after that Ernie Ferguson is giving us his *Everything in the Garden*.'

'Jesus!' The heartfelt moan came from Dan Bartlett, but everyone else ignored him.

'So!' Matilda Goodacre straightened her megalithic shoulders. 'Patrick. Do we have an agenda?'

'Indeed, Matilda,' and Collinson broke off his coffee-making duties to lay a sheaf of papers before each of them, Maxwell excepted.

'Do we have a Treasurer tonight?' Madame Chairman asked.

'Oh, Lord,' Collinson sighed. 'Yes, Martita's

here somewhere. You know what she's like.'

Matilda waved the air with all the grace of somebody or other's last Duchess. 'We'll fill her in later. Feel free to chip in, Mr Maxwell, as we go. Any apologies – other than Gordon's of course.'

For the next hour and a half, Peter Maxwell learned anew why they called such places Board Rooms. After this, he vowed he'd never snore in a staff meeting again and the games of Bollocks Bingo he'd initiated so often were now strictly reserved for addresses by the Chairman of Governors. So it was with an air of immense gratitude that he said his good-nights and shuffled downstairs to the foyer, grateful to feel his feet again and longing for the wind in his face.

'Psst!' Noises stage left. Maxwell halted on his way down the plush corridor.

'Miss Winchcombe?' he peered at the wizened face half hidden in the shadows.

'It's Mr Maxwell, isn't it?' she said, frowning at him and glancing left and right in quick succession.

'It is,' he nodded, secretly grateful for the reminder.

'I misheard earlier.' She huddled him into a confined space behind a pillar, for all the world as if they were playing sardines. 'But now it all fits into place. You're the teacher who solves murders, aren't you?'

'Well … it's never really been put quite like that…'

'I've seen you in the paper. In the *Leighford Advertiser*. You're a sort of Sherlock Holmes, aren't you? A consulting detective.'

49

'Miss Winchcombe,' Maxwell chuckled. 'You mustn't believe all you read in the papers, especially...'

'Mr Maxwell,' she said solemnly. 'Gordon Goodacre didn't die in an accident. Someone killed him. Deliberately, I mean.'

'Martita!'

They both froze at the sound of her name.

'There you are.' Dan Bartlett flashed into the half light, peering around the pillar. 'We've been looking for you. Come along, Matilda and Patrick need your Treasurer's Report.' He checked his watch. 'Treasurer's Reports are always delivered at eight-thirty, you know that,' he said patronisingly. He took the old lady firmly by the elbow, then half turned. 'Sorry about that, Mr Maxwell,' he whispered. 'Few accounts short of a ledger, I'm afraid. Good luck with that ... effort you're doing.'

And Maxwell forced open the front door of the theatre, glad for the sting of the rain and the comforting ridge of White Surrey's saddle under his buttocks. Miss Winchcombe might not know the difference between a raven and a writing desk, but he did ... didn't he?

Chapter Four

'Murder, she said.'

'Max, you've been wrestling with this all night; give it a rest.'

He was actually wrestling with his bow tie at that hour of the morning, a half-eaten round of toast left languishing on a surface he couldn't quite call to mind.

'What did Jane Blaisedell say again – about Gordon Goodacre, I mean?'

It was morning in the Maxwell household, in a little town house on a quiet estate on the edge of a sleepy seaside town on the south coast. A teacher and his partner were talking about killing again. Nothing odd about that.

Jacquie sighed and passed him his cycle clips, undress, officers for the use of. 'It was just a freak accident, that was all. These things happen.'

Maxwell looked at the pregnant woman who shared his house, his thoughts, his life. Her he trusted; her he loved. Jane Blaisedell? Well, Jane Blaisedell was another kettle of fish altogether. Maxwell would die rather than admit it, but Jacquie's bestest new friend in all the world was just a little on the limited side. And she had an edge about her that he didn't altogether like. 'I suppose they do,' he sighed in retaliation.

He snapped on the cycle clips over the turn-ups of his countryman's trousers, hauled the bright

Jesus scarf around his neck and took a final slurp of coffee.

'Toast?' she reminded him.

'Of course.' He clicked his fingers and drew himself to attention, raising his cup aloft. 'How remiss of me. To the prince over the water.' It was an immaculate John Laurie for all the sun was still struggling over the yardarm and Maxwell hadn't finished gargling yet. 'Don't wait up, heart.'

'Max, what time will you be home, for God's sake? It's Tuesday.' Even a non-teacher knew that schools didn't have meetings on Tuesdays. There were very strict professional association rules about that.

'So it is. Half past four of the clock, with a prevailing wind.'

She waddled closer to him, planting a kiss on the end of his nose. 'You have a nice day, you mad old buffer.'

'I'll give it my best shot,' he smiled, cradling her cheeks in both hands. 'Oh, darling. Could you drop my green trousers in to the dry cleaners? Oh, and put that ad in the *Advertiser*, there's a good girl. Oh, no chance of paella tonight, I suppose? And for God's sake take it easy – you're expecting, remember.'

'Yes.' She rolled her eyes at him. 'It's called working for two. On yer bike, Peter Maxwell.'

But Peter Maxwell didn't get on his bike. Not quite then. Because, having checked the mail for little tiny bills and realising yet again that he wasn't earning enough, he wheeled Surrey to the verge of Columbine and who should be inspecting her Michaelmas daisies there but the redoubtable neighbour whom Peter Maxwell loved as himself – well, nearly.

'Mrs Troubridge.' He raised his battered hat.

'Good morning, Mr Maxwell.' The old girl waved her Speedy Weedy at him. 'Isn't this glorious after all that rain?'

Indeed it was. If wheezy young John Keats had wanted a better morning to fire off his mellow fruitfulness line, he couldn't have found one. The last wasps of the summer that had died droned in the privet, looking for one last kill before autumn claimed them; miserable, psychotic bastards. Across the grass that rolled away from Columbine to the Flyover and the sea, a thousand spiders had woven their gossamer carpet and it shimmered like so much silver in the pale morning sun.

'Heavenly,' he said, propping himself against Surrey's crossbar. 'I believe I met a friend of yours last night,' he fished.

'Really?' Most of Mrs Troubridge's friends were no longer of this world, it had to be said.

'Martita Winchcombe.'

Mrs Troubridge's face fell. 'Oh. Her.'

Maxwell was good at body language. The fact that his neighbour had just hacked off a late rose with her hook-billed pruner was perhaps a *slightly* less challenging message than usual.

'Not a friend, then?'

'Martita Winchcombe and I have not spoken since the January of 1946. I'd rather not go into details, Mr Maxwell; let's just say it involved Mr Troubridge and a loose Venetian blind. I don't think I need say more.'

'Er ... indeed not, Mrs Troubridge. That pretty

53

well sums it up, I feel sure. It's just that ... well, in the light of what you've told me, I suspect that my next question will be a little redundant.'

'Question?'

'Well, would you say,' Maxwell was choosing his words carefully, 'that Miss Winchcombe's judgement is sound?'

'Redundant because we haven't spoken in sixty years? Yes, I can see your point. However,' the old girl folded her pruner with a finality that was awful, 'Martita Winchcombe was mad as a tree when she was twenty. What she must be like now, I can't begin to imagine. Mr Maxwell, did she tell you she was a friend of mine?'

'Not in as many words, no. I just assumed, you and she being of an age...'

'How dare you!' Mrs Troubridge bridled. 'Martita Winchcombe is three years my senior. Surely that must be obvious, even...' she pulled herself up to her full five feet one, 'to a man.'

'Of course,' Maxwell frowned. 'It was very bad light in the Arquebus.'

'Oh, she's still there, is she? Interfering busybody. Oh,' she lightened. 'Do forgive me, Mr Maxwell. You've pressed the wrong button, I fear, this morning.'

'My mistake, Mrs Troubridge.' He doffed his hat again. 'Well, I must away and make the lives of a lot of children really wretched.'

'Jolly good!' she smiled beatifically, a boon as she was to denture manufacturers.

And he swung into the saddle of Surrey and was gone, pedalling like a thing possessed, his wild scarf flung behind him.

The day named after the great god Tiw had not gone well. An over-reacting Bernard Ryan, Deputy Headteacher without portfolio, or aptitude or talent, had called the police to a Year Nine cat fight. It was all claws and handbags and in the good old days a single cuff round the ear would have settled it. Maxwell had been at a Curriculum Managers' meeting all morning and by half-ten had lost the will to live; and he still had the pleasure of Deena Harrison later that evening.

He sat for a moment in the relative quiet of his office in the Sixth Form Block, watching the dust gathering on his spider plant and fitfully dozing with a cup of coffee perched on his chest. From the walls around him, those he had loved looked fondly down. Marlene Dietrich was showing him her frillies in *The Blue Angel;* Mary Astor was proving she had *White Shoulders;* the bell was clearly tolling, not for Maxwell, but for Gary Cooper and Ingrid Bergman; and just to remind him of his day job, a kid with a red face and terrifying white eyes was one of the *Children of the Damned.* How well he knew them.

'Sorry, Mr Maxwell.' The door crashed back and an apparition in a green overall stood there, fag in one hand, the invention of the late head of the FBI in the other. 'Only if I don't do you now, that bloody supervisor'll be on my back again. Bosses, eh? Ain't they the bane of yer bleedin' life? How's that young lady of yours? Any day now, ain't it? Must get on.' And the hoover roared into life as Maxwell meticulously answered her questions one by one. He hadn't actually realised that Mrs B had the hots for him and that she was driven by lust as well as duty; or that she engaged in exotic Eastern sex with her line manager in the cleaning department.

'Tcha!' he snorted. 'Indeed they are. She's fine, thanks, Mrs B. November, actually. Yes, I'm sure you must. No rest for the wicked.'

But Mrs B was already well into her rendition of extracts from *Les Mis* and, what with the hoover, didn't hear a word of it. He was on his way to rinse his cup when he all but collided with a girl in the corridor.

'Deena?'

'Mr Maxwell.' The hair was different. Frizzed rather than straight. As if she had just stepped from the shower. She'd lost a few pounds too, although it wasn't in Peter Maxwell's nature to stare too long and hard at the nubile bodies of his ex-students. Not, anyway, when somebody might be looking. She held out a firm hand to grip his. 'Mr Diamond told me you'd be working with me.'

'Did he now?'

'Oh, I'm so pleased,' she beamed, her dark eyes as bright as he remembered them. 'It'll be like old times.'

'Great.'

'I'll be *so* grateful to learn from you.'

He laughed. 'My dear girl. A-level History was a long time ago. You're a red carnation woman now, unless I miss my guess.'

'A red ... oh, yes, yes, of course.'

'As I understand it,' Maxwell swept on, 'you're

56

in the driving seat now. I'm just tagging along for legal reasons.'

'Now, now.' She wagged a finger at him. 'I've heard things about you.'

'Ah, none of those are true,' Maxwell assured her. 'I've burnt all the negatives.'

'Your Cyrano,' she said. 'Not a dry eye in the house.'

'My Cyrano?' he repeated. 'You weren't a twinkle in your father's eye when I did that.'

'It's in the blood,' she assured him. 'Like falling off a bike. You never forget.'

There was rather an over-richness of metaphor there for Maxwell's taste, but then, the girl had gone to Oxford; you couldn't expect too much.

'I just popped in to apologise for last night. The last minute rehearsal cancellation, I mean. The Arquebus big-wigs had some sort of committee meeting and I didn't have a chance to get a message to you.'

'So I believe,' he sighed.

'Tonight, though. Half-seven, if that's OK?'

'Half-seven would be fine.'

'I'd offer to pick you up – still got old Surrey, I hope?'

'My trusty steed,' he smiled. 'Oh, yes. She's got a few years in her yet.'

'Well, my car's off the road at the moment. Soon as it's fixed though... Look, this is *awfully* good of you.'

'No, no,' he assured her. 'It's good of *you*. The production would have fallen apart without your stepping in.'

'Well, I felt *so* sorry for Mrs Carmichael. Are

things all right? I mean, as all right as they can be? With her baby, I mean?'

'I believe so,' he told her.

'Good.' She flashed him her broadest smile. 'Well, till tonight, then.'

'Looking forward to it.'

And she was gone, tripping gaily through Mrs B's crisp packet collection on her way out.

Peter Maxwell watched her go, with the old bounce he remembered and then some. It was odd about ex-students now that nobody called them Old Boys or Old Girls. Some of them were strangers whose faces were the same but whose lives had moved on. As if they were husks of their former selves, inhabiting familiar bodies but with souls and experiences and memories that were far away. Others couldn't keep away, like those sad people who haunt the superhighways of Friends Reunited. 'Hi, I'm still mad as a skunk and Party Animal. Oh, by the way, I've had three divorces, six kids, a prison sentence for fraud and am currently living on my own. Would *love* to hear from the Old Gang.' Still others had changed beyond recognition – mice who scurried along corridors were now men and women of the world, with firm handshakes and steely gazes. And Deena? Well, Deena seemed the same as ever.

Anthony Wetta was of Cypriot extraction via the Balls Pond Road. His family had been shunted down to Leighford, to that spur of protected family housing they'd built off the already vast and sprawling Barlichway Estate, to make a fresh start in life. Anthony's big brother, Charalambos, collected ASBOs like most people collected other people's chewing gum on their soles. Anthony's dad was inside, although how much pleasure he actually gave Her Majesty was a moot point.

'Bed,' the hiss came from the privet. 'Can you see anything?'

'Shut the fuck up,' Anthony hissed back. 'I'm thinking.' And for that, the boy needed silence. He checked his position. He was ... what ... a hundred metres from the road? Two? The place was big and he couldn't see any lights. He checked his watch in the fitful moonlight, the one he'd liberated from the KwikiMart by the bus station. Pity he hadn't liberated some batteries for it really. The time said '88'. Still, it must be past eleven. They were still rolling out of the Moon and Sixpence down the road, but the landlord there was one of Anthony's 'uncles' and his time-keeping was not as immaculate as it might be.

'Bed.'

'Stuff me sideways.' Anthony leapt a mile in his hedge hideaway, shaking the foliage and ducking down again. 'If I was *this* much older,' he whispered, holding his thumb and forefinger close together, 'I'd've had a fuckin' connery there. You're supposed to stay over the other side. We're casing the joint.'

'But I can't see anything.'

Anthony looked at his partner in crime. George Lemon looked even more stupid in the moonlight than he did under a neon strip getting a good letting off from Mr Diamond. The word bovine was unknown to Anthony – he just thought George looked like a cow. Just as large, but nothing like as useful.

'All right,' the master-cracksman whispered, taking George resolutely by the horns. 'We go left.'

'What if they've got dogs?' George had been to Literacy and Numeracy classes. He'd been around.

'Then we'll hear the bloody barking, won't we? And you and I'll make a bleedin' world record getting back to the gate. If I'd known you was this windy, I'd have asked Jazzer.'

'Jazzer's a prick.' Clearly, George had been to Psychology hour too.

'Yeah, well he ain't the only one. Now, pull yourself together. You told me you'd done this hundreds of times.'

'Yeah, well,' George whined. 'Maybe not hundreds.'

'Well you're doing it now,' Anthony assured him. 'Keep low and follow me.'

'What we looking for?'

'Jewellery. Cash. Credit cards. Nothing heavy. Nothing marked. There's an old lady lives here. Now either she'll sleep through a fuckin' earthquake or she'll be wide awake wandering about in the kitchen, muttering the bollocks they do. Just like my bleedin' granny.'

'But it's late,' George pointed out. 'She ain't gonna buy that meter reader bit.'

'You know, George, Mad Max is right about you. If I had a quid for every time he says, "Mr Lemon, you're not concentrating", I wouldn't be reduced to turning over this old lady's gaff tonight. We're fourteen, for fuck's sake! How

60

many fourteen-year-old meter readers do you know? I was merely regaling you with stories of my uncle Anastas and his MO back in London. Anyway, he *was* a meter reader. No need for fake ID and bullshit there. Here we go.'

Like the natural he was, Anthony was gone across the gravel, his trainers padding like cat prints as he bounced off the porch wall, and he melted into the shadows. George was altogether slower, bulkier, but he made it in record time. Together, the likely lads skirted the lounge window. No lights and the curtains were drawn.

'Yurghh!' whispered George. 'Snail shit.'

'Yeah, you getta lotta that in people's gardens. Occupational hazard, that is. You tooled up?'

'You what?'

Peter Maxwell didn't know it, but Anthony Wetta was a lot like him really. Born out of his time and with a passion – albeit as yet unrealised – for old movies. When the mood took him, he could recite the screenplays of *The Italian Job* and *The Long Good Friday* by heart.

'Are you carrying an object of metal for breaking into places like this?' It was like a foreign language.

'No,' said George.

'You're fucking useless, you,' Anthony assured his friend. 'Keep up.'

And the lither lad was gone, scuttling through the foliage like a rat up a pipe. This side of the house looked even more deserted than the front, but the cloud cover was breaking now and the privet came to an abrupt stop. Nothing ahead but moon and lawn. Not a good combination for those of the larcenous persuasion.

'Who did you say lived here?' George hissed, trying to keep his hoodie out of his mouth, and his heart in more or less the right place.

'I dunno. Some old trout. She lives alone, though. Look,' Anthony pointed. 'There's the kitchen door. Waddya think?'

'What about?' George had never been asked the merits of gentrified Victorian architecture before. He was a bit stumped for an answer, to be honest.

'I mean, shall we make a run for it? Try the door and if no go, hit them bushes on the far side.'

''Ere, Bed, we're not going on the roof, are we?' George asked in sudden horror. 'I mean the ground floor's one thing. But I dunno about the roof. I get funny on the pier sometimes.'

'Yeah, I know, George,' Anthony nodded, frowning at the lad and the embarrassed memories that came flooding back. 'You wait here. If I can see a way in, I'll give you a signal.'

'What signal?' George gripped his oppo's arm. This was all getting just a little heavy for him now.

'I'll do this,' Anthony waved frantically. 'Got it?'

A nod. As good as a wink to a blind horse, Anthony supposed, and anyway, that looked like it was all he was going to get. 'Right, then.'

If truth were told, Anthony was quietly shitting himself, as teenage boys will when their macho bravado has placed them in impossible positions. His hands felt like lead and his knees like water. His throat was bricky-dry and his heart was pounding an inch or two above his Adam's apple. But he wasn't letting George see any of this.

Crouching like a hidden tiger, he suddenly sprang into the moonlight, a black shadow against the pale yellow brick of the house.

George couldn't see what happened next, but Bed seemed to stop, check himself as though in disbelief and turn back to his chum. 'Fuck me!' George heard himself whispering. The door was opening. Bed was in the fucking house. It was George's turn to feel the thumping in his chest. This was beginning to freak him out. Bed had bragged how he could break into anywhere, take out any lock ever made. Had George seen *Gone in Sixty Seconds*, Bed had asked him. Well, Bed could do that to houses.

From the darkness of the kitchen, Bed's arm was summoning his sidekick. Too late to turn back now. Bed would think George was chicken if he didn't cross that grass. Worse, he'd *tell* everybody he was. Time for some decisive action. All right, so he slipped. Fell over on the bloody gravel, didn't he? But never mind. He was up again and running, like a fucking greyhound. He who always had a sick note signed by 'George's Mum' so he couldn't do PE up at the school. He was like a fucking greyhound.

The greyhound skidded to a halt at the door and felt himself yanked down in the darkness.

'Give your eyes time,' Anthony ordered through clenched teeth. 'They'll become clematised in a minute and you'll be able to see stuff. All right?'

'How d'you do that, Bed?' George couldn't help but let his admiration show.

'Do what?'

'Open the bloody door.'

'Skill,' Anthony shrugged. 'Now. Are you starting to see what I am?'

'What?' George was peering through the gloom. 'What are you?'

'No, Nutbar. I mean, can you see what I can see?'

'It's a kitchen.'

'Yeah, I know it's a fucking kitchen, George. But if you and me's gonna make a living out of this, we've gotta get the feel of a place. Point one,' Anthony was holding his thumb upright, 'No dogs. Otherwise,' he raised his head, scenting the air, 'we'd smell 'em. And they'd smell us.'

'I can only smell old lady,' George sniffed.

'That's good, George. That's very good. Using your old factory organs now, mate. No cats either.'

'No smell?'

Anthony tapped the door behind them with his heel. 'No cat flap. What else?'

'Um...'

'No burglar alarm, George.' Anthony had thought of everything. 'Otherwise, there'd be flashing lights, ringing bells and a fucking army of Old Bill tramping all over the place.'

'Wadda we do now?'

'Now, old son,' Anthony peered along the line of work surfaces, gleaming in the moonlight that streamed in through the window over the sink and the glass in the door behind him. 'We see where the old girl keeps her stash.'

'What? You mean she smokes stuff?'

'Put these on,' Anthony sighed. It was like wading through treacle.

'What are these?'

Anthony paused for a moment. This couldn't be happening. 'They're gloves, George. Like the ones you had when you was a kid. Remember? They had no fingers in 'em and your mum tied 'em together up your sleeves, in case you lost 'em. *But,*' he pressed his button nose close to his friend's, 'you lose 'em 'ere, mate, and you're talking about a stretch in Parkhurst.'

'Gettaway,' George demurred, but he made sure the gloves fitted tightly even so.

Anthony slithered across the floor, moving noiselessly forward until he reached the open archway that led into the hall. George was with him as the two boys stood up. It was darker here, much darker, and the only light came from a small window above the front door; the one Anthony had tried – the one that was locked. The underfoot sensation here was soft – carpet. There was a sound, too, the steady, deadly ticking of a grandfather clock. George had seen them on *Flog It.* Worth a few bob. Even so, he prayed that Bed wouldn't decide to nip off with that under their respective arms.

'What's that?' George was pointing to what looked like a small bundle of clothes at the foot of the stairs.

'Crafty old tart,' Anthony chuckled in a hushed sort of way. 'Burglar alarm.'

'You what?' George's heart stopped beating for a second.

'It's what old people do to protect themselves. Can't afford a real alarm, so they put piles of crap in corridors, hoping we'll fall over it. Only, they

65

ain't dealing with a pair of mugs 'ere, y'know. Go on, then.'

'What?'

'Climb over it.'

'What? You mean we're going upstairs?'

'Well, that's where old ladies stash their stuff, ain't it?' Anthony could only wonder anew at George's naïveté. 'They're shit scared of being burgled, so they take all their valuables to bed with them.'

'I'm not going into some old cow's bedroom,' George announced horrified. 'You didn't say nothing about that.'

'You won't have to,' Anthony reassured him. 'That sort of job you leave to the professionals.' And he patted his own chest, in a modest sort of way.

'I dunno,' George dithered.

'Oh, for fuck's sake,' and Anthony took the lead. He grabbed the banister with his right hand, twisting himself over the heaped clothes and landing neatly on the fourth or fifth stair. What an athlete. George, it must be said, was less secure. He approached from a bad angle, too low to the ground, and missed his footing. His right foot missed the stair completely and his left got entangled in the bedclothes. As he thudded down to the hall floor, Anthony flattened himself against the wall, ready to leap down and do a runner. He hadn't expected the old duck's improvised burglar trap to be so effective.

As for George, he was undergoing an entirely different experience and one that he'd remember for the rest of his life. Wrapped in the bundle of clothes was an old woman. She was cold. And for one brief, appalling moment, George had looked straight into her dead eyes.

Chapter Five

'I thought you ought to hear this, Mr Maxwell.' When Nurse Sylvia Matthews used a colleague's surname, there was clearly trouble in the wind. Or there was a kid in the vicinity. This time, it was both.

Maxwell took in Nursie's room. When he was a kid himself and Andrew Bonar Law was at Number Ten, this sort of place was called the San. Chaps would end up there after too many hours under a fierce July sun at the wicket or crocked up after a pummelling in the scrum. He ended up there once when somebody tried to throw a gym bench at him. Now, it was all morning-after pills and cosy, anti-suicide chats. Sylvia Matthews had her special Mr Maxwell's-Been-Horrid-To-Me chair. Other than that, the place was scrupulously clean and Spartan and simple. In a plastic-covered chair in the far corner was one of the simplest of them all. George Lemon.

'George isn't feeling too well this morning, Mr Maxwell,' Sylvia said.

'Oh dear.' Maxwell's sincerity had barely reached room temperature.

'George,' Nursie sat down next to the boy. 'Tell Mr Maxwell what you told me.'

George's usually bovine face had an odd look about it this morning, a different one altogether from that caused by the prospect of double

French before lunch. If Maxwell didn't know better, he'd swear the lad had been crying. 'I seen something last night,' George muttered. 'I didn't like it. I couldn't sleep thinking about it.'

George lived on the Barlichway. This could have been anything. Drug abuse. Gangland slaying. Visit by a prospective UKIP candidate. Maxwell braced himself. 'What was it, George?' He perched on the end of Nursie's bed, lolling back to ease the moment and to give the boy plenty of space.

'It was an old lady,' he mumbled. 'She was dead.'

Maxwell looked at Sylvia. Both of them had been here before.

'Where was this, George?' the Head of Sixth Form asked.

'Bottom of the stairs. I thought it was just a pile of old clothes. Bed said...'

'Whoa, whoa.' Maxwell reined the boy in. 'Let's back up a little bit there, George. Bottom of the stairs, where?'

'In a house.'

Maxwell nodded. This was a kind of progress.

'I dunno where.' George sensed somehow that his explanation lacked a certain something. In History lessons, Mad Max usually wanted to know what evidence he'd got. It was all becoming horribly relevant now.

'All right.' Maxwell had given Torquemada a few tips in his day and any fan of Python knew that nobody expected the Spanish Inquisition. He slipped his trusty thumbscrews back in his pocket and changed tack. 'What time was this, George? Do you remember?'

'Haven't got a watch,' the boy told him, the red-rimmed eyes never making contact with anything other than the floor and occasionally Nurse Matthew's feet.

'About, then,' Maxwell shrugged. 'About what time was it?'

'Eleven. Twelve.'

'OK. Not your house, then.' Maxwell was feeling his way, leading the clearly terrified boy through it. His voice was soft and gentle. 'Not Granny or the lodger at the bottom of the stairs?'

George looked at him. These teachers were supposed to be clever, for fuck's sake. What would an old lady be doing in his own house, dead at the bottom of the stairs? The Lemons didn't have a lodger. And his granny was only forty-seven. For his part, the Head of Sixth Form had seen George's CAT scores. He had the IQ of a cat.

'I dunno whose house it was,' the boy volunteered.

'Well,' Maxwell had no choice now but to grasp the nettle. 'What were you doing there, George? In somebody else's house at eleven or twelve o'clock at night?'

He saw the boy's eyes flicker for a second. 'I dunno,' he said.

'Come on, George,' Maxwell said softly, holding up a hand as he noticed Sylvia about to intervene. 'You can do better than that.'

'I dunno,' George insisted, getting louder. 'I get confused.'

'What about Bed?' Maxwell asked. 'Shall I ask him?'

'Who?'

'Bed,' Maxwell repeated. 'A minute ago, you said "Bed said". I didn't catch the rest.'

'No, I never!' George was looking at him now, for the first time, the fear in his eyes turning to hostility, panic.

The sound of silence.

'All right, Nurse Matthews.' Maxwell broke the moment and leapt to his feet, bored with the whole charade, tired of the game. 'Call the police, will you? Whatever this is, it's out of our hands now.'

'All right!' George was on his feet, trembling, crying, the words tumbling from him in a torrent. 'Me and Bed broke into a place last night. There was a dead old lady in the hall. I fell over her... On her...' and he collapsed in a quivering heap on the ample chest of Nurse Matthews. A goodly percentage of Leighford's alumni had been there before him.

Maxwell waited while she calmed him down, patting his distressing hair, passing him tissues and giving him strict, no nonsense orders about blowing his nose. He sat down and waited until George had composed himself.

'We didn't kill her, Mr Maxwell,' the boy said, his lip quivering. 'She was already dead. Bed reckoned she'd fallen downstairs.'

'I'm sure he's right, George,' Maxwell told him. 'But we can't just leave her there, can we? What if she's got no friends? No family? We need to sort this out. Maybe then you can get some sleep.'

'But I don't know where it is,' George whined.

Maxwell looked at Sylvia, acting, as he usually did, on impulse. 'Can you take me there, George?

71

You and Bed?'

'Not Bed,' George shouted. 'He'd fucking kill me ... er ... I mean he'd kill me. I shouldn't have said anything.'

'No, George.' Sylvia wrapped an arm around him. 'You should have. It's great that you have.'

'What's your problem, George?' Maxwell asked, matching her female softness with his macho masculinity. 'You'd make three of Bed. You could sort him out easily.'

'It ain't him,' George explained. 'It's his brothers. They're built like brick shithouses ... er ... toilets.'

'All right,' Maxwell said. 'Just you and me, then.'

George looked at the man, blinking. He was ... what? Eighty-three, eighty-four? Wearing that poncy bow tie and those tweedy old togs. What *did* he look like? And what would it do to George's street cred to be seen with him? 'I dunno,' he said.

Maxwell shrugged and leaned back with his head on the wall and his arms folded. 'It's the Old Bill then,' and he reached across for the phone.

'OK, OK!' George shouted. 'But you ain't coming round my house. I'll never live it down.'

Maxwell chuckled. 'Don't worry, George. I won't lower the tone of the neighbourhood. What shall we say? Ten o'clock? The Old Spike?'

George looked from one to the other – the kind, almost beautiful face of the School Nurse, her blue eyes smiling at him. And the lived-in, unfathomable face of the Head of Sixth Form. He was going out on a date with Mad Max. What, he wondered a little before his fifteenth

72

birthday, was the world coming to?

'This is not sensible, Max,' Jacquie warned, sliding the salt across the kitchen table.

'A three-egg omelette? Oh, come on, heart of hearts. They still had rationing when I was a shaver. I was forty-two before the threat of nuclear war receded, give or take a Middle Eastern megalomaniac or two. Give me a break, will you? It's one of my civil liberties to be able to take responsibility for my own cholesterol. Can I have survived all that and not cope with three eggs?'

'I am talking,' she said archly, 'as well you know, about your little escapade tonight. The implications don't bear thinking about.'

'Ordinarily, no,' Maxwell agreed, tucking in to the excellent little Spanish number Jacquie had rustled up. 'But I know enough about kids to realise that we won't get anything out of George Lemon beyond the time of day because he's terrified of the Cypriot connection.'

'Have you spoken to Anthony Wetta?'

'Bed? No. I gave George my word. Besides, Bed's an altogether tougher nut to crack. Oh, I could do it, of course, given Skeffington's Gyves or the Duke of Exeter's Daughter. But either of those little torture gadgets would play merry Hamlet with the concept of political correctness. And anyway, think of the mess... I'm not sure the rack would fit in my classroom.'

'I'm thinking of you,' she told him. Jacquie always was. They'd known each other now for nearly ten years. She'd been a struggling DC in those days, smoking too much, drinking ditto.

73

They'd found a body at the Red House – and it was one of Maxwell's Sixth Form, one of His Own. Oddly, she couldn't remember the first time she'd actually seen him. And Christopher Marlowe was wrong with all that tosh about love at first sight. Peter Maxwell grew on you, like an old warm jumper she'd grown to like, to love and now, could not live without, its warmth and softness holding her, caressing her, keeping her – sometimes – together.

He reached across and patted her hand. 'I know,' he smiled. 'We'll be careful out there.' They both remembered *Hill Street Blues* on the telly, with its flaky cops working out of a Precinct from Hell and the kindly old sergeant's message to his people as they went out to face the mean streets. It packed more of a punch than dear old George Dixon's 'Mind 'ow you go' and 'Look after dear ol' Mum', but essentially it said the same.

'If this turns out to be genuine,' Maxwell said, 'the dead woman, I mean, what'll your people do to George Lemon?'

'He won't get much more than a caution,' Jacquie told him. 'First offence and – apparently – nothing taken. Anthony Wetta, now... Well, I'm afraid he's on file already.'

'Yes,' Maxwell sighed. 'I thought he might be.' And he put his fingers in the corners of his mouth. 'Cracking eggs, Grommit,' he croaked, in a near-perfect Peter Sallis.

There was no moon that night to light their way. Only clouds scudding darkly, threatening rain for the morning. He kissed her at the car door and jogged up the hill that led to the Old Spike. Jacquie shook her head. She didn't approve of what he was doing, with all her training and experience. Maxwell should have passed George Lemon and his night terrors over to the police this morning. Come to think of it, Sylvia Matthews should. She knew perfectly well that telling Max anything like this was like waving a red rag at a bull. Mixing her metaphors madly, she knew that all anyone had to do was wind him up and let him go. On the other hand, she couldn't help chuckling. The man she loved, the Cambridge historian, all tweeds and college scarf and elbow patches and bow tie, was jogging up the hill on the edge of the Dam in trainers, jeans and a hoodie. He was, indeed, a funny age.

The Old Spike wasn't a spike at all any more than there had ever been a dam on the open stretch of gorse-strewn headland that went by that name. It was one of those things that just grew up with time, those myriad factettes about places that no one remembered. The Spike, they said, was a beacon from the Armada, when nervous Englishmen scanned the horizon for the huge and deadly Spanish sails, dripping with Catholic symbols and glittering with gilt. Others said it went back much further, to the time when flaxen-haired Saxons watched the mists of another September, long ago, when William the Bastard's Normans rode the high seas. Only Peter Maxwell seemed to know that it was actually a Napoleonic early warning system as the Leighford Fencibles manned their posts and tried desperately, in that long tense summer of 1804, to

75

learn one end of a musket from another. Now it was just a twisted tangle of metal, a rusting monstrosity the local council kept meaning to take down. It was a health and safety issue and might upset our near neighbours, the French.

'Jesus!' George Lemon couldn't believe his eyes. Mad Max was madder than anyone realised. The old git was in fancy dress, lolling against the base of the Spike like something out of *Shaun of the Dead*.

'Evening, George.'

'Mr Maxwell,' the lad managed.

'Got your bearings, then?'

George thought they were things that whizzed round in his bike gears. He wasn't going to enjoy tonight. Together, the unlikely pair retraced the steps the lads had taken the previous night. From the Spike, they took one of the dozen or so bike trails that criss-crossed the Dam, dipping down into the oak-treed hollow where Bud cans nestled among the nettles and marked the last resting place of a Morrison's trolley. A thick length of rope with a tyre tied to its free end hung strangely silent and still from a high oak branch. Then they were out on Sycamore Grove, keeping to the shadows at George's request. He had family in this street; he was sure Mr Maxwell understood.

As they swung left into Martingale Crescent, George's resolve left him and he stopped dead. 'I thought it was,' he said, waving an uncertain arm ahead. 'That's the place. On the corner.'

'That Victorian place?' Maxwell realised he'd asked a question too far. 'That big house with the bushes?'

George nodded. 'I can't do this, Mr Maxwell,' he blurted suddenly. 'I can't go back in. What if she's still there?'

'I expect she will be, George,' Maxwell told him. 'That's why we're here; remember?'

George remembered. But he didn't want to remember. He backed off into the privet that lined the pavement, then turned and fled, years of pasta and chips taking their toll long before he reached the darkness of the Dam again. Ahead was the Barlichway and home and a return of the nightmares before the cops came calling. And Maxwell didn't chase him. Time was when he would have done, but then time was when he wouldn't have got involved in things like this anyway. Perhaps it was all too weird. Perhaps it was time to hang up his board-marker and shuffle off to that great Staff Room in the sky. But not yet awhile; he had a few jobs to do first.

The house was solid, unimaginative, pale yellow in daylight, an even paler grey by night. Dark rhododendrons ringed it and a tall cedar guarded the scruffy lawns. The summer had been long and hot and it had taken its toll on the untended gardens of old ladies. He crossed the weedy gravel, feeling it springy underfoot, and tried the porch door. Locked. He put his nose to the stained glass and looked through. He couldn't make out much. There was another door ahead of him, more solid, opulent with a fanlight that read *Dundee*. An old umbrella lay furled in a cane stand to his right and an ancient pair of green wellies to his left. He pulled the hood more securely over his hair and trotted around to the right, past the bushes and onto the rear lawn. Here was a smaller door, glass-panelled, and it was wide open.

His hand reached into the hoodie pocket for his mobile, the one Jacquie insisted he carry. He was already late in using it. As soon as he'd found the house, he'd promised her, he'd ring. She'd contact the station and the ambulance service and the wheels of officialdom would grind into action. Except that he wasn't *absolutely* sure that this was the house. He only had George Lemon's word for that and remembering George's recent and memorable interpretation of why the eighteenth-century penal system was called the Bloody Code, that didn't say a lot really. He needed more proof.

The kitchen in which he now stood had been modernised several times since someone had built the place back in the days of Empire. Its work surfaces were gleaming Formica and the torch beam stabbed into dark recesses, highlighting cobwebbed corners and an already-growing mustiness. All the way from the Spike, Maxwell had been coaxing more information out of George Lemon. He knew the boys had gone in by the back door into the kitchen, but after that it got a little vague and George had clammed up.

The torch lit the way as Maxwell took the single step that led into the hall. He could understand why the boy had got the jitters. There was an indefinable *something* about this house, a sense of disquiet. It was the sort of place where, just for a second, yet always, you sensed there was something at your elbow. He heard the clock chime and the torch beam flashed back at him from its dull glass face. Half past ten. If the

78

occupier was an old lady, she'd probably be in bed by now. And a forgetful old lady might leave the back door open. Then again...

He saw the 'then again' at the bottom of the staircase and shone his torch on the bundle of clothes. He held his breath in the way he imagined George Lemon had done and he knelt down to confirm his suspicions.

'Jesus,' he whispered through clenched teeth as first a gnarled hand and then a head of wild, white hair flopped out of the blanket. The place, he suddenly knew, was freezing cold, for all the mild, dry night outside. It was like a tomb. This time he had the mobile in his hand.

'Jacquie.'

She was glad to hear his voice; a signal this nonsense was over. 'Where are you?'

'Martingale Crescent,' he told her. 'A house called Dundee. Big Victorian place on the bend, you can't miss it.'

'Are you all right, Max?' she asked.

'Yes,' he told her, not sure if that strictly was true. 'You'd better give your lads a call. It's Martita Winchcombe and she's dead as a doornail.'

It was a little before two when they got round to him. Peter Maxwell had been sitting in Leighford Police Station for the best part of two hours. Pretty little Jane Blaisedell, Jacquie's friend, had nipped in as often as she could, bringing him tea and a couple of Jammie Dodgers. What she couldn't give him was any information – and that was what he wanted most.

'Mr Maxwell, I am Detective Chief Inspector

Hall. For the record and for the tape, this is Detective Sergeant O'Connell.'

Maxwell looked at them. Henry Hall was a bland bastard, his small, sharp eyes forever hidden behind blank lenses, his jaw firm, his manner serious. O'Connell Maxwell had never seen before, although Jacquie had talked about him from time to time before she'd gone on maternity leave. He had a shock of dark auburn hair and a skin ravaged by the terminal acne that is sometimes the downside of puberty. Maxwell had yet to work out what the upside was.

'Mr O'Connell.' Maxwell reached out a hand. The detective sergeant sat impassive on the other side of the desk. Maxwell drew the hand back. 'Henry,' he smiled. 'How the hell are you?'

'I'm well, Mr Maxwell,' the DCI told him. 'Could you just tell us what you were doing in Miss Winchcombe's house this evening.'

'Snooping,' Maxwell said. He'd done this before, more times than young O'Connell had had hot dinners, he expected. Ever since the Red House, when he'd been in the frame for murder, he had or had not been helping the police with their enquiries, depending on your point of view.

'Would you care to clarify that?' O'Connell frowned, jotting down notes as the interview went, despite the fact that the tape was whirring. He and Maxwell did not go back any way at all and in the space of two minutes the Head of Sixth Form had managed to get right up the detective sergeant's nose.

Maxwell thought only butter was clarified, but he'd been flippant with the police before and it rarely paid off. 'Acting on information received,' he said.

'Are you taking the piss?' O'Connell wanted to know.

'I think,' Hall stepped in quickly, 'this kind of phraseology is Mr Maxwell's idea of a joke.'

'Thank you, Henry, yes. I went to the house to verify what we all now, tragically, know – that Martita Winchcombe was dead.'

'And why should you assume she was?' O'Connell asked.

Maxwell looked at them both. He'd gone a long way to avoid what he knew he had to say next, but he had to say it all the same. 'One of my lads was trying to burgle the place. He stumbled, quite literally, across the body.'

'One of your lads?' O'Connell took him up on it, frowning. 'Up at the school?'

Maxwell nodded. 'Year Ten,' he said.

O'Connell's scowl turned to a grin as he glanced at Hall. 'Knew it would be,' he said.

'Ah,' Maxwell smiled. 'The Year Group from Hell. Have you ever got chalk under your finger-nails, sergeant?'

'If you mean, have I ever done any teaching, no thanks. But I was in Year Ten myself once. I remember...' but the look from both the other men in the room made him shut up. 'We'll need a name, of course,' he said.

'I was hoping...'

'Mr Maxwell, you know the score,' Hall reminded him. Heads of Sixth Form might choose to turn a blind eye from time to time; Detective Chief Inspectors didn't have that luxury.

'Yes, of course,' Maxwell sighed. 'George Lemon. I can get you his address tomorrow. There was another lad involved, albeit only by hearsay – Anthony Wetta.'

'Oh, yeah,' O'Connell grunted. 'Comes from a long line of gentlefolk up the East End way. Who says crime doesn't run in the family?'

'I still don't see your involvement.' Henry Hall had tangled with Peter Maxwell before. He was the Saint, he was the Toff, he was Lord Peter Wimsey, he was the Four Just Men all rolled into one. Unfortunately, this bastard was real.

'George was traumatised by finding the old girl dead,' Maxwell explained. 'Reluctantly, he told me the gist. But George is not the brightest card in the pack. He couldn't remember exactly where the house was. He's not the sort to volunteer information to you gentlemen, despite the fact that at Leighford High we teach Citizenship and are constantly extolling the virtues of an honest, upright life, so I reasoned the only way to find her was to get him to take me to the place in question.'

'But he wasn't with you when we arrived,' O'Connell reasoned.

'Did a runner,' Maxwell shrugged. 'I told you – he was traumatised. I don't know how I'd have reacted falling over a corpse at fourteen.'

'Did you know the deceased?' O'Connell asked.

'Yes,' Maxwell said.

'Yes?' Henry Hall looked up. For a moment, Maxwell was sure he saw the devious bastard's eyes flicker behind his rimless glasses, but it may have been the subdued lighting and the lateness of the hour.

'Perhaps "knew" is too strong a word,' Maxwell said. 'We'd met.'

'In what context?' Hall wanted to know.

'At the theatre – the Arquebus. I'm working there on a show with some of our kids. I understand Miss Winchcombe was the Treasurer.'

'Was she now?' O'Connell was scribbling away furiously.

'May I ask, Chief Inspector,' Maxwell said, 'whether Miss Winchcombe met her death by natural causes?'

'She fell downstairs, Max.' Jacquie was pouring coffee for them both, that grey, dull Thursday morning. 'Isn't that what Henry said?'

'Henry,' he fished in the fridge for the milk, 'wasn't saying anything.'

'Oh, you know what he's like,' she said. 'Tighter than a gnat's chuff. You didn't expect him to give anything away, surely?'

'No, I suppose not. Do we have any chocolate digestives, light o' love – or are we in divorce discussions already?'

'Third shelf,' she directed him, squeezing herself into the kitchen chair. 'No, back. That's it. Behind the muesli. Jane was more forthcoming.'

'Ah,' he sat down opposite her. 'I hoped she would be. Didn't want to disturb you last night when I got in so late, but it's high time some bean-spilling went on. Say on, oracle mine.'

'Max,' Jacquie looked at him. 'Miss Winchcombe was an old lady. Unsteady on her pins.

Jane said there were a helluva lot of empties in her rubbish. She'd probably gone one over the eight, lost her footing at the top of the stairs and wallop. Broken neck.'

'That was the cause of death?'

'Well, we won't know for sure, of course, until Jim Astley's done his stuff, but it seems likely. Jane's seen it all before.'

'And has she seen a corpse wrap itself in blankets?'

'How do you mean?'

'I mean, we have to rely in this situation on the less than spectacular witness skills of one George Lemon, who could thick for England, and one Anthony 'Bed' Wetta, known associate of every gang since Robin Hood and his Merry Men. George must have fallen over the old girl to come face to face with her as he seems to have done. I doubt whether a casual glance at a bundle of cloth would have *quite* so unhinged him as the sight apparently did. So George probably rearranged the blankets, at least by accident. God knows what Anthony's involvement was and, ashamed though I am to confess it, I may have been instrumental in a little fabric dislodgement myself.'

'Old people frequently wrap themselves in blankets,' Jacquie said, sipping her coffee. 'Was it cold in the house?'

'Like a tomb,' Maxwell nodded.

'Well, there you are. Huge great place like Dundee, living on a pension. She can't afford to heat it, so she wraps herself in an extra layer one night. Gets a bit tanked up and a loose stair

84

carpet and gravity do the rest.'

Maxwell looked into his love's cool, grey eyes. Was *anybody* out there listening to him? 'The old girl was *wrapped*, Jacquie. Having fallen downstairs. Someone had carefully arranged the body – it doesn't just happen that way. And then there's Gordon Goodacre,' he said. 'Friend of the Arquebus, hit by a flying ladder on stage. Martita Winchcombe, Treasurer of the Arquebus, leaps, blanket-shrouded, to her death at the bottom of her stairs. Let me introduce you to a phrase that may not be in police procedural vocabulary – bloody enormous coincidence.'

Even routine departures have to be investigated. That's what SOCO are for. Scenes of Crime Officers. Men and women. Old ones, new ones, some as big as your head. Giles Finch-Friezely sounded like he'd stumbled out of a PG Wodehouse novel, a Drone lost in the corridors of time. In fact he'd gone to a bog-standard comprehensive not unlike the one in which Peter Maxwell was squandering the last remaining years of his sanity and he'd got the scars to prove how awful it was in that situation to be saddled with a name like his. He'd toyed with doing the deed poll thing but, as he was built like a brick shithouse, had gone for the quicker option and battered seven bells out of anybody who so much as sniggered.

That Thursday morning, while Peter Maxwell was pedalling White Surrey over the Flyover on his way to another dazzling day of intellectual cut and thrust, Finch-Friezely was crouching on the stairs of Martita Winchcombe's house at Dundee, on the curve of Martingale Crescent.

'Bugger me,' he muttered to himself, peering at the wallpaper and then at the banisters on the other side. 'Blu-tack.'

Chapter Six

'Mrs Shiva.'

A long silence. Then...

'Mrs Shiva?'

'Oh, for God's sake!' A dark brown voice shattered the moment. Deena was not having a good evening. And if she didn't, nobody else did either. Like a whirlwind in the trees, like a deluge on the dykes, she tore up the central aisle, script in one hand, soul in the other.

'Mr Mushnik,' she turned to the hapless fat lad playing the flower shop proprietor. 'What are you?'

'Sorry?'

She looked into his dark, slightly mystified eyes. 'Apart from being a talentless little shit, of course.'

Mr Mushnik was actually Dominic Reynolds. He had been the only lad in Year Nine who had auditioned for *Willy Wonka,* so, almost by default, he had become a male lead in every one of Leighford High's productions since. Anyway, Dominic had a quiet sense of pride. If you're doing A-level Theatre Studies, you should put your money where your mouth is. Get up on stage and act. And that, deep down, was all Deena was asking him to do.

Even so, the lesson came hard and the lad stood there, jaw open. Mrs Carmichael had never spoken to him like this.

'You are a Jewish shopkeeper in downtown Nowheresville. You only have a tiny coterie of clients – Mrs Shiva is one such – and you have yet to fully grasp the enormity of Audrey II's money-making capacity. You're ... what ... fifty-five? Sixty? Your parents came over, before you were born, to Ellis Island, from some ghastly Eastern European existence. Let's try some method here, can we, and forget we're from a bog-standard comprehensive in Leighford? OK with you?'

Before Mr Mushnik had time to forget anything, Deena had wheeled to Seymour. She narrowed her eyes, hands on hips, bristling with attitude. 'There are nerds,' she growled, 'and there are nerds. At the moment, Seymour dear, you have all the believability of that bloody cardboard flower.'

'But in the film...'

'We're not doing the fucking film!' she screamed at him. 'And Rick Moranis you ain't.'

No, he wasn't Rick Moranis. He was Alan Eldridge, an up-himself ex-private schoolboy whose parents had fallen on hard times and been forced to send him to that sink of mediocrity that was Leighford High. He could do a pretty good Bronx while carrying a tune in a bucket and Mrs Carmichael was running out of options.

'Boys and girls!' The familiar voice made them all turn. A silhouette in cycle clips filled the doorway that led to the auditorium. The light was behind him, but the hat, the scarf, the *presence*. Who else could it be? The Cavalry had arrived. There was a warmth in that voice, a comfort.

Sally Spall as Audrey I nearly burst into tears. But then, she'd been doing that since Year Seven. Sally was a tiny flower of a thing with freckles, a lisp and a little, pointed chin. She could have been born to play the downtrodden, single-brain-celled florist kicked around by her mad psycho dentist boyfriend. No problems for Angela Carmichael there.

'Mr Maxwell,' Deena's smile was serene from centre stage. 'Lovely. Come on, then, people.' She clapped her hands around the script. 'From the top. We have an audience tonight.'

He waited until she reached the back row then hauled off his hat and scarf and sat beside her in the darkened theatre. 'Problems?' he asked, as the cast went through their paces, improvising with cardboard boxes as furniture.

'No,' she trilled. *Au contraire.* They're very good, aren't they?'

'I think so. How's Dominic settling in?'

'Dominic?'

'Mr Mushnik.'

'Oh, excellent,' she said quickly. 'Bags of motivation.'

'Angela Carmichael was a bit worried about him. Rather flat, apparently.'

'No, not at all,' Deena assured him. 'I was just congratulating him on his delivery.'

'Fine. Benny?' Maxwell had the skill of all teachers – conducting an apparently innocuous conversation while actually spotting delinquents skulking at all points of the compass. He motioned a lad across to him. Benny was dressed in black, trailing leads and looking very techie.

'Mr Maxwell?'

'I realise you're something terribly important in the Woofers and Tweeters Department, but get in touch with your feminine side, would you, and make your old Head of Sixth Form a cup of coffee, there's a good Key Grip.'

Benny had been Leighford High's general factotum for years. Rumour had it he was thirty-eight and they'd kept him on just for productions. Nobody knew exactly what he did on a daily basis. There was talk of Social and Health Care AVCE, but that was only talk. *Real* men didn't take subjects like that and real schools didn't teach it. Whatever, Benny seemed to live in the little room behind the stage at school and seemed forever to be fine-tuning the PA. He tugged his forelock and trudged off in search of a kitchen. 'That'll be no problem at all, Mr M,' he winked.

'Is it true, Mr Maxwell?' Deena asked as the action resumed on stage and flower shop customers came in droves from the wings to gawp at Audrey II, looking at the moment spectacularly like a badly-painted stage prop.

'Is what true?'

'That a man died over there? About where Seymour is standing now.'

'I believe so,' Maxwell said. 'Does that bother you?'

'Me?' She turned to him in the half-light. 'God, no. I've been in haunted places before.'

'Haunted?' Maxwell chuckled. 'What makes you think the Arquebus is haunted?'

She looked at him for a moment, a weird

90

enigmatic light in her dark, sparkling eyes. 'Oh, I know it is,' she said. 'Audrey,' and she was on her feet. 'Excuse me, Mr Maxwell. Audrey, can we try that again? That crossing bit? It was excellent, darling, excellent, but it needs just a teensy bit of timing. Seymour?'

Maxwell sat back and watched. He had to admit it: Deena Harrison was good. He remembered her Mary Magdalene in *Superstar*, her Maid of Orleans in *St Joan*. OK, so you didn't turn your back. But that *was* a long time ago – the mischievousness of youth, little more. And on stage, what a presence! Now she was driving another cast on, as Maxwell had in years gone by. What a Roxanne she would have made to his Cyrano. And he let it all wash over him as Benny brought his coffee and Deena transformed a handful of quite limited kids into smooth-moving, harmony-singing Sixties kitsch. Of course, he reasoned in a less than euphoric moment, it would be radically different when Geraint Horsenell came on board. Heads of Music would roll along with his drums.

'Right, everybody,' Deena called the cast to order. 'Well done tonight. Work on that shoulder thing, Mr Mushnik. Let's have more awe when we see the plant for the first time. Tomorrow night, please,' she consulted her clipboard. 'Principals at seven, please. Audrey, Seymour and the Dentist. The rest of you guys, words, words, words. You don't know 'em; Mr Maxwell can't hear 'em.'

'It's my age,' Maxwell yelled back.

'Eh?' Benny shuffled past under a step-ladder.

91

'I'll do the jokes, Barber,' Maxwell reminded him. 'And for God's sake, be careful with that thing.'

That thing exercised Peter Maxwell's mind long after the kids had gone home. They left the premises, in knots, gaggles or clumps, depending on their taste. Seymour and Mushnik were off to the Vine, masters as they both were in the art of fake ID, to drown their sorrows and bitch about Deena. Audrey was swept up by her boyfriend, a bit of rough her parents detested; even though he wasn't a dentist, it did seem a little like life imitating art. The extras just seemed to vanish into the dark of the September night, flower shop frequenters and down-and-outs and radio DJs and the line-up of chorus girls. Maxwell would have offered to give Deena a lift home, but that would have meant his crossbar and all sorts of articles, not just in the *Advertiser* but in the *Smut on Sunday,* and not a few probing questions in the Crown Court. The night air, she said, would do her good. She had rather a lot on her mind at the moment. That Maxwell didn't doubt and he took the opportunity to tread the boards himself.

He checked out Benny's ladder in the silence of the theatre, propped and silent against the back wall. He ran his finger over the three or four that rested there with it. Cold, aluminium rungs and steel safety chains. He put his weight on each of them. Two of them gave a little way, one moved several inches. The others didn't move at all.

'Mr Maxwell?' The voice made him turn. For a

moment he couldn't see anyone, because all the house lights werc full on, then a figure sauntered out from under the dark of the balcony.

'Mr Bartlett, isn't it?' The Head of Sixth Form crossed to the apron, talking to the Artistic Director.

'I was just about to lock up. It's half past ten.'

'Yes, of course, I'm sorry. I was miles away.'

'No, you weren't,' Bartlett smiled up at him, keys in hand. 'You were wondering how it was possible for one of those to fall on poor old Gordon.'

'Sorry,' Maxwell confessed. 'A macabre turn of mind, I'm afraid.'

'The chains weren't in place,' Bartlett told him. 'They should have been. And they weren't.'

'Whose responsibility was that?' Maxwell asked, coming down the steps stage right.

Bartlett wagged a finger at him. 'Ah, the blame culture,' he sighed. 'Everything has to be somebody's fault, doesn't it?'

'I didn't mean...'

Bartlett shook his head. 'No, I'm sure you didn't. The Theatre Manager is Ashley Wilkes,' he said. 'Health and Safety issues rest with him. Want to cast the first stone?'

Not a million miles away from the Arquebus, as the moon risked the odd visit from behind the scudding clouds, two policemen sat in Leighford nick. The place, within and without, was the same as police stations everywhere – Thirties-ghastly, replacing its rather homely Victorian predecessor with the blue lamp outside it; that was now a trendy wine bar. It had no personality, no presence. It was square and it was there – a depressing combination, really. One of the men was a double-barrelled SOCO with shoulders like tallboys; the other was DCI Henry Hall. Both of them had long ago given up their private lives.

'From the top then, Giles.'

'Well, I must confess, guv,' the earnest lad told him, 'I nearly missed it. Two treads down from the landing at the Winchcombe house. Blu-tack on both sides. It was less clear on the banister base oddly enough, more obvious on the wallpaper; got sort of caught in the knobbly bits.'

'What does this tell us?' Hall was playing stupid policeman tonight.

'What's Blu-tack for, I asked myself.'

'And what did you reply?' Hall hadn't got *all* night.

'Putting up posters, notes, whatever.'

'And?'

'And who puts up posters four inches above a stair riser?'

'Go on.'

'The Blu-tack was obviously the residue of larger bits – quite large blobs, I'd say, judging by what was left. They were in an exact line with each other.'

'Which told you what?'

'A tripwire. Somebody had placed a tripwire two stairs below the landing. Even in daylight, it's not likely the old girl would have seen it.'

'All right,' Hall nodded, peering into the steam of his coffee cup. 'Let's brainstorm. Martita

Winchcombe is a spinster lady. Lives alone.'

'Has a niece,' Finch-Friezely was flicking through his pocket book. 'A Mrs Elliot.'

'I've got people working on that. She's next of kin and she's been informed. Lives in West Bromwich and is not exactly hurrying down.'

'Worth a bob or two, though, I shouldn't wonder,' Finch-Friezely reflected. 'The old girl.'

'We're working on that too,' Hall assured him. 'You've been to the place. Seems a little run down. Central heating on the blink. If she's worth anything, she's not spending it on the house.'

'What time of death have we got?' the lad asked.

'Astley thinks about nine or ten on Tuesday night. The boy from Leighford High fell over her just over twenty-four hours later.'

'I checked the lights,' the DC told his boss. 'If Astley's right about the time, she'd already be in bed, I guess. Certainly she was wearing her nightie and dressing gown and was wrapped in a blanket. How cold was it Tuesday night?'

'Seventy-plus years cold,' Hall told him. 'In old people, it's nothing to do with the weather.'

'Right. So Miss Winchcombe was in bed. She gets up. Why? Call of nature?'

'Disturbed by something,' Hall preferred. 'If somebody stretched a wire across the stairs, they might want to stay around to see that it worked.'

'You think they were in the house all along?'

'It's possible. You and I might have seen the wire immediately, but even if not, it's possible to step over it, walk right through it. What have you boys got on the prints?'

'Usual partials all over the place,' the SOCO man said. 'I don't think anybody realises the sheer number of fingerprint details in the average house.'

'Put in for overtime,' Hall said impassively. He didn't like whingers and didn't care who knew it. 'So, she walks along the landing. Her bedroom was ... where?' He checked the rough plans another of the SOCO team had sketched for him. 'Second door on the left as you look from the top of the stairs. Where's the light switch?'

'Top of the stairs.' Finch-Friezely craned his neck to decipher his colleague's doodles. 'That would have operated two bulbs, one on the landing and one in the hall.'

'And when we got there?'

'No lights on at all.'

'So?' Hall was used to masterclasses like this, piecing together the jigsaw of a life.

'So she either didn't put the lights on at all...'

'Unlikely,' Hall reasoned.

'Or someone came along afterwards and switched them off.'

'Not realising,' Hall finished the thought, 'that we'd know the time of death was at night. The old girl's night attire would give it away, though. So what *was* that all about?'

'Beats me, guv,' the lad confessed.

Hall leaned back in his chair. 'She goes downstairs, not merely to the bathroom which is along the landing, and she trips. Falls down ... what ... twelve stairs?'

'Fifteen.' Finch-Friezely had counted them.

'Breaking her neck at the bottom. No doubt Jim Astley will be more precise, but that's the long and short of it.'

'Are we talking Incident Room, then, guv? Full blown inquiry?'

Hall sighed. It looked like things were going that way. 'Full blown, yes,' he said. 'But no Incident Room. If we make too much of this, we'll have every old duck this side of Brighton screaming "Boston Strangler". Softly, softly, I think, on this one, Giles.'

'Qui bono?' Peter Maxwell let his head loll back on the pillow that Thursday night, not a million miles away from Leighford nick.

'Hmm?' Jacquie was dozing beside him. He had watched her Jackie Collins drop towards her bump several times already.

'Qui bono?' he repeated. 'Dear old Marcus Tullius Cicero, the greatest advocate in Roman history. He was the first lawyer to pose the question in a murder trial. 'Who gains?" Who gains from the deaths of Gordon Goodacre and Martita Winchcombe?'

'Max,' Jacquie struggled out of her sleep. 'Are you *sure* they're linked? Come to think of it, are you sure they're murders at all?'

'Come on, Jacquie. You and I have been around this kind of thing for all the time we've known each other. I've never trusted statistics in my life. Me and old Dizzy – you know, "Lies, damned lies and statistics".' Jacquie knew. She'd heard Maxwell quote the late Prime Minister often enough. 'But when two people from the same theatre troupe die within a couple of days of each other, I smell skulduggery.'

'A falling ladder,' Jacquie reminded him. 'It can happen. I told you...'

'I know.' He turned to her. 'You can quote me the stats. But I told you, I don't believe in them.'

Jacquie sighed, sticking to logic, sticking to reality. 'As far as we know, the old girl fell downstairs.'

He propped himself up on one elbow, staring into her sleepy face, the little freckles peppering her ski-jump nose. 'You ... er ... don't fancy a visit to Leighford nick, do you? You know, just to say "hi" and show 'em your predicament.'

'And ask them the score on the death of Martita Winchcombe? No, I don't. This isn't just an interest of yours, is it, Max? It's a bloody obsession.'

'Well, I just thought...'

But Jacquie was already singing loudly, her pillow over her head.

'There's a Mrs Elliot to see you, guv.' Dave Walters was the desk man that morning, a grumpy old git with dyspepsia and a martyr, on and off, to sciatica too. Who says you can't have the lot? An Indian summer had settled on the south coast and the sun dazzled on the cars parked beyond the grimy glass. Leighford nick was one of the few still open in Tony Blair's England and Sergeant Dave Walters one of that vanishing breed of men, a boy in blue. It wouldn't be too long before Sir David Attenborough was discovering the shy woodland creature in some

98

woodland somewhere and doing a survival special on them. He could even call it *Blue Planet Two*.

'Right.' Walters unpressed the intercom. 'Detective Chief Inspector Hall is on his way down, madam. If you'd take a seat.'

She did. Around the walls of the waiting room, posters warned of rabies and wondered whether anyone had seen a particularly unprepossessing adolescent, last known in Southampton. It occurred to Fiona Elliot this was someone she'd rather not see, especially after dark. Still others asked, rather belatedly, whether you'd locked your car because there were thieves about. Of course there were; this was a police station. Dave Walters hadn't left his Ginsters more than three feet from his elbow in ten years.

'Mrs Elliot?' A tall man in a three-piece suit put his head around the door. 'I'm DCI Hall. This is DC Blaisedell.' He pointed to the short, dark-haired woman beside him. 'Won't you come through?'

Fiona Elliot had never been in a police station before. It was cold, clinical, for all the sun sparkled outside. Spider plants reflected the woman's touch and the woman walking with her now seemed pleasant enough. She was ... late twenties, perhaps early thirties and her clothes looked too big for her. The DCI held the door open for them both. Then they were sitting in Interview Room Two. Fiona had seen this sort of place before, on the telly. There was always a two-way mirror along one wall, with either Trevor Eve or David Jason standing behind it. Come to think of it, Trevor Eve was always shouting at his oppos in ludicrously dark corners and David Jason was filling his face in the nick canteen. This place was nothing like that. The light was bright and artificial, the room without windows and every wall was painted an acidic green. The only gadget in the room appeared to be a tape-recorder and that wasn't switched on.

'First,' Hall started the ball rolling, 'can we say how very sorry we are about your aunt. And to thank you for coming in so promptly.' When the moment called for it, Henry Hall could lie for England.

'Thank you,' she said. Fiona Elliot was a bulky woman, utterly unlike the frail, bird-like corpse lying on one of Jim Astley's slabs in a cold corner of Leighford morgue. She was attractive in a matter-of-fact sort of way, with a steady gaze that was quite compelling. 'I'd like to see my aunt.'

'Of course,' Hall nodded. 'DC Blaisedell will arrange that. In the meantime, if I could just ask you some questions.'

She nodded.

'We are making the assumption that your aunt lived alone?'

'That's right. She had for years.'

'And had she always lived in Leighford?'

'She was born in that house, Chief Inspector. Rather fitting, in a way, that she died in it.'

'Indeed?'

'My aunt had a hatred of hospitals,' Fiona told them. 'She once told me she'd put an end to herself rather than go into one.' She looked at them both, the skinny, pretty girl and the bland, expressionless DCI. 'Is that what happened?' she asked, unable to read the body language. 'Suicide?'

Jane Blaisedell looked at Hall. He was the guv'nor, in the hot seat. Questions like that she left to the top brass.

'Mrs Elliot,' Hall leaned forward across his desk. 'We think your aunt may have been the victim of foul play.'

She blinked. This wasn't happening. This was for other people. *Crimewatch,* news items, the Discovery Channel. 'Do you mean murder?' she asked.

Hall nodded.

'My God.'

'I'm sorry.'

Jane Blaisedell braced herself to react. For all she was only twenty-six, she'd been here before, too many times already. Some victims' relatives fainted away like a lily at bedtime. Others, in insane denial, refused to accept it; the police were lying; it was all some ghastly mistake, a macabre joke. Was Beadle about? Others cried uncontrollably, sobbing as their bodies shook and reality dawned. Somebody's mother. Somebody's son. Still others were like Fiona Elliot.

'What are you doing about it?' she wanted to know. She was calm, matter of fact, precise. But her voice was ice in the cool of that Interview Room.

'Making our enquiries,' Hall assured her. 'That's why I need to ask you some questions.'

But Fiona Elliot was on her feet. 'Later, there are things that will need to be done,' she said. 'Now, I want to see my aunt.'

101

Hall nodded at his DC. 'Very well,' he said, standing too. 'I daresay it'll wait.'

After all, he told himself as the women left, Martita Winchcombe wasn't going anywhere.

Chapter Seven

Jane Blaisedell had never intended becoming a copper. Her dad had been one, with the Met, but he'd been invalided out after a particularly insane night at Broadwater Farm, when mobs roamed the streets and petrol bombs exploded into the night. Jane had seen what that had cost the man – the nights when he paced the bedroom all night; the days he spent slumped in a chair. It wasn't the surface wounds – they'd heal. It was the deep ones, the ones that scarred his soul.

It had just happened, that was all – both because of her dad and in spite of him – and so here she was, the tough little girl from the banks of the Thames who had crossed the tracks; crossed them because that was the only place to be.

'Fag?' She passed a ciggie to the scrawny, snub-nosed lad in front of her.

'Nah, I don't,' he said.

'Liar,' she laughed. 'Your fingers are browner than Hitler's jacket. You just don't want to take anything that might resemble a freebie from a copper. Am I right or am I right?'

'You're not from round here, are you?' he asked her.

'The East.' She lit up and blew smoke sky-wards. 'Deptford. Know it?'

'Nah,' he shook his head. 'I don't know south of

the river.'

'You?'

'Paddington.'

'Thought I recognised it,' she smiled. 'The lilt. Bed, they call you, don't they?'

'Some do,' he shrugged. 'Friends.'

'Well, then.' The WPC leaned back, cradling her knee with both hands, the ciggie curling smoke on the lip of the ashtray alongside her. 'I'd better make it Anthony, hadn't I? I'm not going to bullshit you with all that think-of-me-as-your-big-sister crap. We're coming at life from different sides, you and me. Fair enough?'

'Fair enough,' Anthony agreed.

'Tell me about the Winchcombe house.'

'Where?'

She looked at him. His look said it all. The cherub nose and brown thatch, the bright, dark eyes darting everywhere. Jane had seen dozens of Anthony Wettas, perhaps hundreds of them. Contempt for authority was written all over them, they had a natural aptitude for it. And no amount of family rehab was going to change them. All that was different was the playground – the game was the same.

He looked at her. She was pretty enough – for a copper, of course. Most of the filth he'd come across – and that was quite a long list by now – had been big blokes, with shoulders like high-rise buildings. The women had been dogs. This one was a bit different. A bit street-wise, offering him a fag an' all.

'Don't waste my time, Anthony. An old lady is dead.'

'It wasn't me,' the lad assured her quickly.

'Yeah,' she nodded, leaning forward and folding her arms. 'And that's not a very convincing Bart Simpson, is it?'

His eyes flickered as his surroundings hit and a thought occurred to him. 'Ain't you supposed to have a tape running? And where's my brief? My social worker?' Anthony Wetta knew the score; he'd been around.

'Same place your hope is, Anthony,' she told him. 'Gone. Tell me about the old lady.'

They were sitting together in a part of Leighford nick that was due for demolition and it was raining. The giant drops bounced off the leaking skylights and dripped into a plastic bowl crookedly placed in the corner. A brighter boy than Anthony would have realised there was something odd about this – no second copper, no support. There again, no rubber hoses, either. His dad had told him, on the few occasions he'd seen his dad, that all coppers used these. They worked on yer feet first, where it didn't show. That was why, when he was arrested and brought to the nick, he'd carefully chosen a pair of socks that said it all. On the sole of one was "Fuck" and on the other was "Off ". He hoped he'd put them on the right feet – a spoonerism wouldn't have been half so effective.

'What old lady?'

Jane picked up her cigarette, fighting the urge to stick it up the little shit's angelic nose. 'Look, Anthony, George has talked, OK? We know it all anyway.'

'You don't know squit,' the boy assured her.

'Sure we do. It was all your idea. George is as green as goose-shit. He wouldn't have had the bottle to break into the house without you. He says you hit her.'

'What?'

'The old girl – Miss Winchcombe. She woke up, didn't she? While the pair of you were crashing about downstairs, she heard you. What did you use? Poker? Rolling pin?'

'I never touched her,' Anthony shouted. 'George is a lying shit.'

'No, he's not, Anthony.' Jane took a long drag on the ciggie. 'You are. He hasn't got the imagination. If he says it happened, it happened. I was just hoping you could tell us something which means we don't throw away the key in your case, that's all.'

'She was already dead,' Anthony insisted.

'Yeah,' Jane laughed. 'And I'm Arnold Fucking Schwarzenegger.' She stood up, scraping the chair back. 'Five to ten in a Young Offenders Institution,' she said, deadly serious now. 'After that? Well, you're bound to have pissed somebody off in there, so it'll be the big boys' prison then.' She looked hard at him. 'I know some old poofs in there will just love you.'

For a moment, she saw his eyes widen, his lips quiver. The old lag, the hard man, was gone. And in his place sat a little boy, alone, vulnerable and very frightened. 'What do you want to know?' he asked.

She sat down and this time he took the out-stretched ciggie. 'The truth,' she said.

'Mr Wilkes?' Peter Maxwell called through into the lamp-lit office at the Arquebus. It was in that new part of the theatre, the one that was all glass and breeze blocks and had won some sort of award.

'Mr Maxwell.' The Theatre Manager glanced up. 'I was just about to lock up. Have you finished – the rehearsal, I mean?'

'Yes, thank you. I wondered if I might have a word.'

'Of course. Time for a night cap?'

'That's very civilised. White, please. Two sugars.' Maxwell was grateful to collapse into a chair. It had been a long day and an even longer evening. David Balham had gone down with something and Maxwell was the only spare body to squeeze into the unutterable cardboard interior of Audrey II. By the end of the rehearsal, Maxwell felt less like a man-eating plant and more like the contents of a parcel, kicked from pillar to post by courtesy of those careful gentlemen in the Royal Mail.

Wilkes looked oddly at the man. 'I meant a night cap,' he said and hooked open his desk drawer with an expert, suede-capped toe. He hauled out a half-empty bottle of Scotch and a couple of glasses that flashed their cut facets in the half-light.

'Even better,' Maxwell beamed. 'Just one sugar with that.' And he already had to adjust his position to relieve the cramp in his leg.

'What can I do for you?' Wilkes poured and passed him the glass.

'Gordon Goodacre,' Maxwell said.

'What about him?'

'Don't you find it all rather odd?' Maxwell asked. Ashley Wilkes was of an indeterminate age. Anything between twenty-five and forty, with a mane of mousy hair. He had an odd, expressionless face with small, sharp grey eyes that seemed not to miss a trick. Out of his bulky topcoat, he was actually quite scrawny.

'Odd?'

'Gordon Goodacre and Martita Winchcombe,' the Head of Sixth Form said, savouring the Scotch. 'Both dead inside three days of each other.'

'Not really,' Wilkes slurped, turning in his swivel to switch off his computer. 'Gordon's death was an appalling accident. As was Martita's, but she *was* an old lady, living on her own. Literally an accident waiting to happen, I should have thought.'

'How long have you been Theatre Manager?' Maxwell asked him.

'Nearly four years now,' Wilkes told him.

'And before that?'

'I was an outreach worker for the National Youth Theatre; London mostly, but the odd provincial gig. Look, Mr Maxwell, why all these questions?'

'I'm sorry,' Maxwell chuckled. 'A natural curiosity, I'm afraid. My better half's in the police.'

'Is she?'

'Sort of matrimonial hybrid, I suppose. Other couples talk about interior decorating, shopping, the garden. We ruminate over great serial killers of our time.'

'Are you seriously suggesting that either of them – both of them – were murdered?' Wilkes was frowning at him.

'I really don't know. Like I said, I'm intrigued.'

'All right,' Wilkes said. 'Come down to the proscenium with me, will you?' And he led the way. Down the open-plan stairs they went, their feet thudding in unison on the treads, past posters of performances past, until they reached the plush, Arts Council-sponsored carpet. 'I found Gordon's body, you know.'

'I didn't,' Maxwell said. 'Did you know him well?'

'Gordon?' Wilkes sauntered down the central aisle, making for the stage. 'No, he was something of a cipher, I'm afraid, although it sounds unkind to say so now. Matilda – she wore the pants in the family. Gordon just did odd jobs around the place to keep her sweet, I think. I've been at the sharp end of Matilda Goodacre's tongue-lashing; believe me, it isn't fun. Here.'

The pair were standing centre stage now, in front of the great burgundy backdrop of curtains that masked the rear wall of the stage. 'Gordon was lying just here.'

'Which way?' Maxwell asked. He'd stood on the site of sudden death before. It made the hairs on the back of his neck crawl every time.

'Um,' Wilkes had to think for a moment to get it right. 'This way.' He crouched. 'His head was over here. Feet a little further back. There was ... quite a bit of blood.'

'From the head?'

Wilkes nodded. 'Skull smashed,' he said. 'He

109

couldn't really have known what hit him.'

'What did?'

Wilkes straightened up, fumbled in the join of the curtains and hauled one of them back a little. 'A ladder. Or more precisely, two of them. Only one, the longer one, actually hit him, but the police I spoke to thought the weight of the shorter had bought the longer down with it.'

'They were ... what? Free-standing?' Maxwell was running his hand over the chains and padlocks that held the ladders in place.

'Mr Maxwell,' Wilkes said solemnly. 'Back in my office I've got Health and Safety qualifications as long as your arm. All that's hunky dory, but if people choose not to follow instructions ... what can you do?'

'And that's what Gordon did?' Maxwell checked. 'Chose not to follow instructions?'

'Must have,' Wilkes shrugged. 'When I came in to open up the next morning...'

'The door was open?'

'... No, locked. The point is that only one of the chains was in place. The other was dangling, the padlock lying on the ground. Gordon must have been using the others earlier and either forgot to re-padlock or was hit before he'd finished.'

'What did you do?' Maxwell wanted to know.

'Called an ambulance,' Wilkes told him. 'Silly, really. It was an absolutely pointless thing to do. The paramedics were marvellous. Of course, by that time Gordon had been dead for at least ten hours. I blame myself entirely.'

'No, no,' Maxwell said. 'I'm sure no one is pointing the finger at you.'

'Who did Martita Winchcombe warn you against?' the Theatre Manager asked.

'I'm sorry?' There was a change in the atmosphere at that moment, a certain coldness that Maxwell couldn't quite explain.

'Come off it, Mr Maxwell. I've been up front with you. How about a bit of honesty in exchange?'

'Like what?'

Wilkes squared to his man. This arrogant son-of-a-bitch needed taking down a couple of pegs. 'Dan Bartlett told me she'd been talking to you on the night she died. What was all that about?'

'That?' Maxwell smiled. 'That was our mutual fascination for Double Entry Bookkeeping.'

It was already Saturday morning when DCI Henry Hall finally called it September 22. He let his specs fall to the paperwork cluttering his desk and rubbed his eyes. On the corner where his woodwork still showed through, a smiling family looked lovingly at him. His eldest boy was gone now, through the labyrinthine ways of life, a struggling lawyer. Little Greg was treading that thin line that separated the men from the boys they taught and was starting his PGCE course at Portsmouth. Jack was discovering that girls were rather more fun than football, especially in the back row of the Screen De Luxe. And Margaret? He broke the habit of a lifetime and smiled in the secrecy of his solitude as he looked at her loving face. She was Margaret. Let that be enough.

'Guv?'

The voice made him lose the smile and snap on

the specs. It reminded Jane Blaisedell of the late Christopher Reeve playing Clark Kent. And Henry Hall, she mused, probably had as much to hide as the inept, awkward schmuck who was really Superman.

'Jane?' He peered over his rimless glasses to catch the face in the shadows beyond the desk-top. 'Haven't you got a home to go to?'

'I'm on my way, guv. Just thought I'd fill you in on Anthony Wetta.'

'Who?'

'The lad with George Lemon in the break-in to the Winchcombe house.'

'Oh, yes. Park yourself. What did you get?'

She sat down opposite her boss, her neck aching from reading her VDU screen for what seemed like forever. 'The back door was open.'

'Was it now?'

'Our problem is we don't know how meticulous the old girl was. Did she habitually leave the door open? Was this a one-off? Or did somebody have a key and forget to lock up after they killed her?'

'What kind of person,' Hall was talking to himself really, 'goes to the lengths of stringing a wire or whatever across the stairs and then not only leaves Blu-tack evidence behind, but ruins the whole accident effect by leaving the door open? Locking it then would have put us off the scent rather more. How did you get the lad to talk?'

'Usual,' she smiled. 'Matches under the finger-nails and twenty hours solid of past Eurovision Song Contest videos.'

The levity was wasted on Hall.

112

'We had a mutual exchange of views,' Jane said, realising that flippancy was no way forward. 'He's going to be in and out of somebody else's property all his life, but he's no killer. He's quite a nice kid, actually.'

'No doubt that's what the magistrate's court'll decide too, after the social reports and the school... Goes to Leighford High, doesn't he?'

'On and off,' Jane told him. She'd seen the boy's attendance record, those nasty little electronic printouts that Maxwell loved so much.

'Do you happen to know,' Hall asked, hiding, as always, behind the blankness of his lenses, 'who his History teacher is?'

'Mad Max!' Jane Blaisedell called through her open window.

The Great Man half turned, peering through the driving rain into the interior of the girl's four-by-four. 'Was I speeding, Woman Policeman?' he asked.

'No, no, sir.' She did a pretty mean George Dixon for a female who wasn't even a twinkle in her dad's eye when *that* particular copper walked Dock Green. 'As long as you're pushing that thing, most of us are quite safe. 'Course, I'm not all that happy about your rear reflector.'

'Nobody ever is,' Maxwell shook his head. 'It has, I have to admit, blighted my life.'

'For Christ's sake, Max, get in. Shove that rust heap in the back. You must be soaked.'

'There, there,' Maxwell stroked Surrey's dripping framework as he hoisted the bike onto the rear seat. 'The nasty lady didn't mean it. You just

113

lie there for a bit, get your breath back. We'll have a nice cup of cocoa later.' And he hopped in alongside Jane Blaisedell, Jacquie's friend.

'Mad as a tree.' She shook her head as he fumbled for the seat belt.

'Kind,' muttered Maxwell, 'kind. How goes it in the world of Mohocs, Coney Catchers and Cosh Boys, girl in blue?'

She slammed the vehicle into gear. 'I don't know how Jacquie puts up with you,' she said. 'I'd have had you committed bloody years ago.'

'Ah, but she can't find the paperwork.' Maxwell tapped the side of his nose.

'How is that woman of yours?' she asked, as they snarled towards the Flyover. 'And how dare you stay out so late? Been on the tiles like that damned cat of yours?'

'Do you know Mrs B?' Maxwell asked her. 'Does for me up at the school and at home now that the Mem can't see her toes any more. She's prone to asking me questions in batches. I answer in similar vein; so, here goes: Bonny as all get out. I got a puncture somewhere along Bracken Avenue. The only tiles I've ever been on are those in my own kitchen, thank you very much. And as for my cat, he has had no meaningful love life since 1996 when I shelled out a fortune to an overpaid veterinary surgeon to dampen his ardour somewhat, using two bricks. What's the score on the Winchcombe murder?'

She crashed her gears, whether by accident or design he couldn't tell. Jacquie often did the same, but that was usually when he was getting to her and her composure was slipping. Jane

114

Blaisedell was an altogether tougher proposition.

'The DCI was asking after you tonight.' She ignored his fishing expedition.

'Really? Henry?' Maxwell smiled in the darkness. 'How sweet. Long time no see,' he lied. 'How is the old upholder of public morals?'

'Infuriating as ever,' Jane told him. 'And what makes you think the Winchcombe death is murder? The *Advertiser* didn't say so.'

'The *Advertiser* didn't say tiddly squat,' Maxwell said. 'Because even an outrageous, muckraking rag like that can't print what you don't tell them.'

'I ask again,' Jane said, drumming her fingers on the steering wheel at the slowness of the traffic lights. 'What makes you think the old girl was murdered?' Jane Blaisedell's middle name was persistence.

'Call it ... male intuition,' Maxwell said.

'Bollocks!' Jane snorted. 'I hope you're not pestering Jacquie with all this.'

'Now, would I?' Maxwell spread his arms for agony and loss. She flashed him an old-fashioned look he pretended to miss in the bad light.

'The DCI told me *specifically* not to talk to you,' Jane said. 'In fact, he went further. He said if I was to happen upon you with a puncture by the roadside, I was to drive my vehicle at and over you, reversing for good measure. I, of course, told him I couldn't do that.'

'Really?' Maxwell chuckled. 'Why, pray, Woman Policeman?'

'Because, beyond all the laws of reason and good taste, you're shacked up with my bestest friend in all the world. And it wouldn't be fair to her.'

'You say the nicest things,' he laughed.

And then they were there, the four-by-four grumbling alongside the kerb at Columbine. 'Get out,' she said cheerily. 'And don't forget that thing in the back.'

'Ssh, Surrey, ssh.' Maxwell stroked the handle-bars as he lifted the injured thing out of the back. He turned at the wound down window. 'Thanks a million, Jane.'

'You're welcome, you mad old bastard.'

But his hand held the rising window. 'We are talking murder, aren't we?'

Her face twisted into a smile. How long had Jacquie faced this? The disingenuous smile, those sad, gorgeous eyes? What, as Homer Simpson frequently asked rhetorically, are you going to do?

'Oh, yes,' she told him. 'That we are.' And he watched her tail-lights twinkle out of sight through the rain.

She sat cross-legged in the blaze of candles in the otherwise darkened room. She breathed in the scent, the smoke and let her hands hang loose, upturned on her naked knees. There was a jolt. A bump. A scrape as though something heavy hit wooden floorboards and the candle flames guttered.

There was a sigh, half-human, half-not. And a word. She listened carefully, cocking her head to one side, trying to catch it if it came again. It sounded like ... but it couldn't be ... it sounded like 'Murder'.

Chapter Eight

'Well, Donald.' Jim Astley hauled the green cap off his head and what was left of his hair sprang upwards. 'Give me a masterclass in geriatric passing over.'

The heavy rain had driven Astley off the golf course late that Saturday morning. Had it not been for the weather, the inside of Leighford General's morgue would not have seen him in a month of Saturdays. As it was, no need to overtax himself. He was getting a bit long in the tooth for this job, rummaging about in dead people's insides all day. At least, as some Roman had observed a long time ago, the dead don't bite.

'Run of the mill,' his assistant said, checking his notes and the naked, operated-on body that lay before him. 'Half the conditions known to man, anything from osteoporosis on down.'

'Except?' Astley sank into a chair, resting his glasses above his hairline.

'Except this.' Donald had been Astley's mortuary assistant now for years. He was bright and efficient in a paramedic sort of way; simply couldn't handle the pressure of being the man who made the decisions, called the shots. He was also the victim of too much linguine and found it a little difficult, if truth were told, to bend over bodies these days.

'Go on.' Astley was resting his head against the

wall, his eyes closed, his still-gloved hands clasped in his lap. He wasn't sleeping these nights. He and Mrs Astley hadn't shared a bedroom for years, still less a bed. Even so, her nocturnal rambles kept him awake too often as she rummaged in the empties, engaging in wild, hooting conversations in which she revelled the night away with imaginary companions. The Romans had a name for that too – *delirium tremens*. He knew he should have her committed, but there was still a tiny remnant of compassion in Jim Astley and he couldn't go through with it. The papers were in his study at home, second drawer on the left in his desk. One day ... one day.

'Cause of death is a dislocated vertebra,' Donald said, looking again at the odd angle of the neck above Astley's neat Y-shaped scalpel work.

'Consistent with?'

'Consistent with a fall,' Donald said. 'There are no contusions on the skin.' He felt the scrawny neck with podgy, rubber fingers. 'Nothing to suggest a scrap. No sign of finger-marks or ligature that might cause a break.'

'So?'

'So...' Donald checked his notes again, the mortal remains of Martita Winchcombe reflected in each of his glasses lenses, as if Nature had doubled death in some bizarre cloning experiment. 'She fell down stairs.'

'Bravo, Donald.' Astley clapped his gloved hands with mocking softness. 'Thank God for police reports, eh? Look at her ankles, man.'

'Ankles?' Donald was confused. He thought he

118

was doing pretty well, really, all things considered. Violent death didn't come his way often, not in sleepy Leighford. He didn't want to be a full-blown pathologist, but he didn't want to be found wanting either. 'Ah.'

'Are you on the Damascus Road yet, Donald?' Astley asked. 'Any blinding flashes of divine inspiration?'

'Horizontal abrasions.' Donald had indeed seen the light. 'On both shins.'

'From which you conclude?'

Damn. Conclusions. Decisions. Not Donald's forte. These were the moments he hated. 'Trip wire?' he ventured.

'Bugger me sideways!' Astley opened his eyes and Donald hoped that wasn't an order. 'Spot on. It's in the police report, of course.'

'It is?' Donald blinked, riffling the pages on his clipboard. 'Where?'

'Here.' Astley picked up the single sheet on his desk and waved it at him. 'Well, you didn't think I'd leave it there, did you? That would make life far too easy. I wanted you to work for your money today. Yes, it's routine, all right.' He crossed to the body and stood alongside Donald. 'Routine murder. Some sharp-eyed SOCO noticed Blutack on each side of the stairs. He guessed – rightly – that the Blu-tack held wire, strung across said stairs. It was high enough that the old girl wasn't likely to step over it and low enough for her not to notice it. You and I would have crashed through it, ripping it from the Blu-tack, muttering something along the lines of "What the fuck was that?" and gone on our merry way.

119

But Martita Winchcombe was seventy-nine and not that nimble on her pins. As you say – half the conditions known to man.'

He smiled down at the peaceful, sleeping, grey face of the old lady, the top of her cranium missing. 'So, whoever did this to you, Martita, old thing, knew quite a bit about you, didn't they? They even wrapped you in a blanket. Why was that, I wonder? Did they think you'd catch cold? And they took away the wire, the murder weapon, but they left the Blu-tack traces.' And he broke into an old song totally unknown to Donald. 'A set of stairs that bears some Blu-tack traces.' Yep, the old boy was losing it, all right.

Astley straightened and looked at his oppo. 'Know what Henry Hall's looking for here, Donald?'

The fat man had given his decision for the day. He'd roll over for this one. He shook his head.

'A beginner,' Astley told him. 'A novice. Somebody who makes mistakes. And somebody with a peculiar streak of compassion that could land them in the slammer for the rest of their natural.'

He looked up at the grey, frosted skylight overhead. 'Clean up here, will you? I think the rain's easing off.'

'So what have we got?' the DCI wanted to know. Still no Incident Room. Still a wish not to frighten the natives. No panic in the streets. While Jim Astley braved the dying drizzle to get to the golf course and Donald put Miss Winchcombe away before trotting round to KFC for a Bargain

Bucket, Henry Hall was marshalling his troops in downtown Leighford, within a walk of the sea.

'Murder, by person or persons unknown.' DC Gavin Henslow chanced his arm. Someone had to open the bidding. Gavin Henslow was actually a bright young copper, but like all bright young people in any walk of life, he came across as a pain in the arse. Everybody knew that Henry Hall was university, fast-track, smartarsed, but he was also the guv'nor and that made it different. Henslow was still wet behind the ears, the ink not dry on his warrant card. Nobody intended to make life easy for him.

'All right, Gavin.' Hall sat stolidly behind the front desk as his team had collected in front of him; all the usual suspects. 'That'll do for the coroner's court. I think here at Leighford CID we need a *little* more.'

'Suspect knows the victim.' It was Jane Blaisedell's turn. She sat in front of her VDU, her shoulders aching, her eyes feeling like gooseberries.

'How do we know that?' Hall was putting them through their paces.

'No sign of a break-in,' Giles Finch-Friezely came back, leaning forward in his chair, sipping a ghastly canteen coffee.

'Not even when Batman and Robin tried to stage one.'

A chuckle ran round the room. The Batman that was Anthony Wetta had been in and out of Interview Rooms various at the nick so often in the last few months, DS Bill Robbins had considered charging the little bastard rent. It was

121

Robbins who held the floor now. 'Where are we on prints, guv?' Robbins was Tweedledum to Dave Walters' Tweedledee. In a bad light they could have passed for brothers, except that Robbins wore the suit and Walters didn't. They'd both cut their teeth back in the Miners' Strike, when King Arthur took on Queen Margaret and the result had been a foregone conclusion. And they were both, Tweedledum and Tweedledee, looking forward to imminent retirement. You could do that in these great forty-three police services of ours. Life was a bitch, but they let you out early for good behaviour.

'Giles?' The guv'nor had been on advanced courses in deflection. There were times when the buck had to stop with him. Today was not one of them.

'Well,' he sighed. 'That's proving something of a long process, Sarge. We've eliminated the old lady's, of course, and the lads who found her – although they seem to have remembered halfway through to put their gloves on. Apart from that, we've got butchers and bakers and candlestick makers. Apparently, Miss Winchcombe had a friend who shopped on line for her, so deliveries came to the house.'

'Was she a recluse, then?' Henslow had been to university and a relatively good school and liked using his extensive vocabulary. It wasn't Leighford High.

'Certainly not,' Hall said, swivelling a little to look at the blown-up photo of the dead woman on the screen behind him. 'She went out for coffee most days. Maisie's in the High Street. She

122

took the odd walk along the Front and even on Willow Bay when the place wasn't too crowded. She was a stalwart at the Arquebus Theatre; Treasurer on their committee.'

'Any motive there, guv?' Jane asked.

'Bill?' Hall's superlative deflection yet again.

'We're looking into it,' the DS told the smoke-filled room. 'But Treasurer is only a figure of speech, really. I spoke to...' he checked his notebook, '... a Mr Wilkes who manages the place. He said the last time she handled any money was about 1983. Ever since then, she's just sorted out cloakroom tickets and moved things of a light nature from A to B. I think we can assume she wasn't behind the Brinks-Mat.'

Guffaws all round.

'Somebody,' Hall damped the levity down, 'went to the lengths of putting a wire across the stairs in her home. Jim Astley gives us a possible time of death as Tuesday night, somewhere between nine and twelve. Anybody been to the house that day?'

'Tesco's delivery late morning.' Jane Blaisedell had been on this one. 'Delivery man checks out. Pure as the driven himself and the old girl probably went up and down the stairs half a dozen times after he left. He was in the house for less than five minutes according to a bloke painting his house next door and helped her put the shopping away. She was in fine spirits and his known movements match his time sheet exactly.'

'Did anybody else call?' Hall asked. 'Afternoon, evening?'

'Somebody around three,' Jane told him. 'The

near neighbour, a Mrs Grannum, heard feet on the gravel and the old girl telling whoever it was to go away because she was watching *Murder She Wrote*.'

'Very apposite,' Hall noted, wondering silently where Jessica Fletcher was at times like these. 'But I think we're talking after dark here. Anybody know what time Miss Winchcombe went to bed?'

Exchanged looks. Shuffles. The odd phone ringing in a corner. Nobody did. It was just one of those little ironies in life. An old spinster, living alone, with no one to mark her comings and goings. No one to mark her passing. Or was there?

'Right,' Hall said. 'Jane, as of tomorrow I want you all over the late Martita Winchcombe like teenage acne. Concentrate on the niece, Fiona Elliot. I want to know the old lady's friends and enemies – especially her enemies. Anybody she'd spoken to recently. At the theatre, in the coffee shop, anywhere. Check out this friend who shops on line for her. Above all – and Gavin, this one's yours – I want her bank details. What's the house worth? How much has she got stashed away – and who gets it? The dogs' home or...'

'The Arquebus Theatre.'

The sudden chill in the room could have left frost on the cut glasses and their companion decanter.

'Say that again.' Fiona Elliot was sitting bolt upright in the offices of Digby, Lassiter and Lassiter along Quay Street. She was lucky to be there at all, in that place and at that hour. It was late on Saturday afternoon and the premises were normally closed. Old Mr Lassiter refused to open up for anyone, no matter how insistent. But young Mr Lassiter was rather more of a soft touch and his social conscience had driven him, along with his vintage Daimler, in to work at an unlikely hour. The size of his fee would, of course, have to reflect this fact.

Young Mr Lassiter had a lot to live up to. His great grandfather had founded the firm way back when, when some solicitors still accepted sides of beef in lieu of cash payment. His great grandfather had represented Madame Fahmi, the wronged and abused wife of an Egyptian nasty into whose brain she finally placed a well-deserved bullet. His grandfather, by contrast, tried to defend one Neville Heath, an utter boundah and cad who specialised in torturing young women while pretending to be an RAF officer. Some the Lassiter family won; some it lost.

'I'm afraid there's no doubt, Mrs Elliot.' Young Mr Lassiter was shaking his head. 'Your late aunt's will is very clear. The sale of her house at Martingale Crescent and all its contents, as well as two ISAs to the value of eighteen thousand pounds and a bank draft of nearly three hundred, all goes to the theatre which, and I quote, "I have loved all my adult life".'

'Outrageous,' the woman grunted. Roger Lassiter swore he could see the steam hissing from her ears. 'She has been coerced.'

'Mrs Elliot.' The young Mr Lassiter may have had a social conscience, but a pussy cat he was not. 'This last will and testament was drawn up by my father. It is accurate, I assure you, and there was no coercion involved.'

'Is there no codicil?' she snapped.

'Nothing,' the barrister told her.

'When is it dated?' Fiona Elliot demanded to know.

'The third of December, 2003,' he told her. 'See for yourself.'

'I don't doubt your end of this wretched business, Mr Lassiter. What I do doubt – highly – is that this decision was made of her own free will. You do know she should have been committed, don't you?'

'Well,' Lassiter leaned back in his leather chair, sighing. 'Which one of us can say hand on heart that we are fully sane?'

'*I* can,' she assured him, standing up suddenly. 'Is there any way I can contest this?'

'Legally, no,' Lassiter said. 'Oh, yes, you can go through the motions, of course, but it would be a delaying tactic only. Hate myself for saying it though I do, my father does not make mistakes.'

'Well, someone has,' Fiona Elliot growled. 'The person who has come between me and my rightful inheritance. And let me assure you, I have ways of finding out who that person is.'

'You have? How?'

'That,' the woman looked at him levelly, 'is entirely my business. But the information will, so to speak, come from the horse's mouth.'

Private William Pennington's face wore an anxious look in the glare of the modelling lamp, later that night. He was an actor, Maxwell reasoned, a

126

sensitive soul who probably worried more than most. All morning, Cardigan's Light Brigade had waited for the off. And now, here it was, in the form of that cocky bastard Captain Nolan with his flash uniform and his leopard skin flounces. He was supposed to be a staff officer, for God's sake, not some clown in fancy dress.

'So, there it is, Count.' Maxwell dipped his brush into the white spirit and laid the theatrical private down on his back, alongside the plastic hoofs of his horse. 'Ashley Wilkes didn't know Gordon Goodacre very well, could think of no reason why anyone should want to kill him and had no idea who might have tampered with the ladders.'

The black and white beast twitched his left ear, his yellow eyes watching the mad old bugger closely. Why did it always smell so awful up here under the eaves? And why did he only wear that ridiculous cap when he had that wooden and fur thing in his hand? In a quiet moment, when the old bugger wasn't there, Metternich had snuck up on that wooden thing, smelt the fur in a hopeful, meal-in-a-moment sort of way and recoiled in shock and horror as powerful chemicals tore through his nostrils. Still, the old bugger provided the hard, crunchy, scrummy stuff in his bowl every day downstairs, so he couldn't be all bad. What *was* he talking about now?

'I get the impression our Mr Wilkes is watching his back,' Maxwell went on, sliding the magnifying glass on its stand to one side. 'After all, he *is* Theatre Manager. The cock-up with the ladders *was*, technically, his fault, wasn't it? I mean,

127

directly or indirectly, in this great blame-culture society of ours, Mr Wilkes has a helluva lot of can to carry.' He reached for his Southern Comfort, but the glass was empty. 'It's your shout, I believe.'

'Jacquie!' Jane Blaisedell was already in her four-by-four the next morning, ready for the off. 'How the hell are you?' The day was bright and crisp, the slight hint of frost that had laced 38 Columbine's front lawn long gone by now, leaving a seasonal dew in its wake.

'Fishing,' the woman told her straight.

'Do you fancy a bevy?' Jane asked her. 'What with the baby and all?'

'He's Peter Maxwell's, isn't he?' Jacquie asked, climbing in and belting up as best she could. She was belting up for two now.

'Is that just a rhetorical question?' Jane asked. 'Sorry,' she laughed. 'Just joking. How is the old reprobate?'

'Nosey,' Jacquie said as Jane swung the wheel onto the main road.

'I know. I made the mistake of giving him a lift the other night. Did he tell you?'

'He did,' Jacquie nodded. 'I must say you were particularly loose of lip.'

'Was I?' Jane frowned. 'You can go off people, you know. I thought I was being helpful.'

'Jane,' Jacquie said. 'I love the man dearly, but he *does* have this habit of sticking his nose in...'

'Somebody'll break it for him one day,' Jane warned. 'Look, I don't fancy the Ferret. How about an early lunch up at the Clarendon?'

'Max is doing his Gary Rhodes bit in the kitchen,' Jacquie smiled. 'Although he calls it his Philip Harbin, whoever he was. Won't be ready for yonks, though, so I'll sit and watch you eat yours. Pick at the odd roaster, you know, bit of crackling, the merest suggestion of glazed carrots.'

'What's Max doing?'

'Egg and chips.'

'Ah, the delights of wedded bliss,' Jane laughed.

'Not exactly wedded,' Jacquie waggled a ring-less finger at her. 'Talking of which, how's the ever-gorgeous Michael?'

Jane beamed archly as the four-by-four shot a red light. 'So what did you want to know about Martita Winchcombe?'

'Well, I wasn't going to waddle into Leighford nick,' said Jacquie as his kitchen clock showed two-thirty, 'make small talk about booties, matinée jackets and baby sick and somehow bring the conversation round to current murder cases. Give my colleagues *some* credit, Max; they wouldn't have bought it. The last time Dave Walters saw a baby he was looking in a mirror forty-five years ago and if Henry Hall *did* father those three kids, he's well and truly beyond that now. As for Gavin Henslow, he's still a baby himself...'

'Fair enough.' He shovelled two eggs expertly onto her plate. 'So what did you do?'

'Talked to Jane Blaisedell, woman to woman, as she munched her way through the Carvery at the Clarendon. And I mean, the Carvery. All of it. God, that woman can eat. How come she's only five feet and a perfect ten?'

'She's made a pact with Lucifer,' Maxwell told her, straight-faced. 'Picture in the attic. No shadow. No reflection. The whole nine yards. Red sauce, I suppose?'

She nodded beatifically. 'And brown.'

'God save us!'

Pregnancy was a brilliant cover for delinquent behaviour and they both knew it. He sat down opposite her and watched her tuck in. 'You didn't have any, then? Of Jane's lunch, I mean?'

She looked at him for a moment. 'Nah!' she said. It didn't fool either of them.

'So what did you learn?' He delicately reached for a little salt and a glass of invigorating tap water.

'You do realise, Max,' she said in all earnestness, 'that *none* of this – absolutely none of it – must get back to the nick. This isn't my little old career we're talking about – God knows I've risked that often enough. We're talking about Jane's. She's new at Leighford and I don't know how Henry rates her.'

'Discretion, dear heart,' he held the flat of his right hand over his own, 'is my middle name. Anyway, Jane has been wonderfully indiscreet with me already.'

'Oh?' she arched an eyebrow in the way she'd seen him do. 'Anything I should know about, due to my slight indisposition?'

'She told me Martita Winchcombe was murdered.'

'Oh, that.'

'How are the chips?' he said, through a mouthful of his own.

130

'Divine,' she assured him. 'You do a mean chip, Peter Maxwell.'

'It was touch and go when I was a lad,' he told her, 'whether I'd go to Cambridge or the Tante Marie. I often feel I lost my calling there somewhere.'

'Believe me,' she reached for her tea. 'You didn't.'

'So, what of the Treasurer of the Arquebus?'

'Tripwire across the stairs.'

'Nasty. When?'

'Tuesday night. Astley estimates between nine and twelve.'

'So when Bed and George found her...'

'She'd been dead for about twenty-four hours or just over.'

'Rigor on its way out?'

'I *am* having my lunch, Max,' she reminded him.

'So am I.' He spread his arms wide. 'I still feel like a bit of a shit shopping those two; George especially. What did you say they'll get?'

'Time off for good behaviour,' Jacquie told him. 'George has no form at all and there'll be an army of social workers and child psychologists all over Anthony telling us how society has let him down and offering him holidays in the Seychelles, courtesy of the tax payer. I don't know about you, but I can't sleep sometimes because of it.'

Maxwell tutted and shook his head. 'So young, so cynical,' he said. 'And you about to be the mother of my baby.'

'Jane'll be coming to talk to you tomorrow.'

'Will she? Why?'

'You were one of the last people to talk to the old girl – at the theatre.'

'Well, it was hardly a conversation,' Maxwell shrugged. 'Wait a minute – tomorrow's Monday.'

She reached across and patted his cheek. 'Not just a pretty face,' she smiled, adding a little more brown sauce.

'No, I mean ... is she coming to school?'

'Of course,' Jacquie smiled. 'Maximum disruption. Rattle you, annoy your colleagues, intrigue the kids. It's what we do, we upholders of the law, Max, you know that. You wouldn't have us any other way. Pass that ketchup, will you? I've still got a couple of chips left. Anything for pud?'

Chapter Nine

'So,' Dan Bartlett leaned back in the snug of the Volunteer, one of the more upmarket watering holes that Leighford now boasted as part of its Regeneration scheme. 'Tell me about Oxford.'

'Oh, Lord,' Deena Harrison snorted, toying with her ciggie and Long Slow Screw. 'I'd rather put all that behind me.'

'Really? Some people dine out on Oxbridge. Take that Maxwell fellow, for instance. Still wears the bloody scarf, though he must have been an undergraduate when they opened the place.'

'Max?' Deena smiled. 'He's an old sweetie. It was under his auspices I tried for Oxford in the first place. Trust me, he's one of the good guys.'

'If you say so. I'm afraid I can't see it, myself.'

'Where did you go?'

Dan Bartlett extended his longish neck still further. 'Rose Bruford,' he said.

Deena smiled. Further comment seemed superfluous. 'Oxford was so twelve months ago,' she said. 'Full of pretentious people all trying to outdo each other. Pitiful, really.'

'Hmm,' Bartlett nodded. 'Rose Bruford was like that. Luvvies to a man.'

Now, if truth were told, Deena Harrison had Dan Bartlett down for a luvvie. He wore a dark crocheted scarf of ludicrous length, a long leather coat and a silly peaked cap which made him look like a cross between a poor man's Tom Baker out of one of the far too many reincarnations of Dr Who and Roman Polanski in his Sixties heyday.

'How long have you been at the Arquebus?'

'Oh, my dear,' Bartlett raised both eyebrows. 'For ever. Whatever you do with your life, don't end up in am dram. It's fatal.'

'It certainly seems to be,' she said. 'What with Mr Goodacre and that nice old Miss Winchcombe.'

Bartlett's smile could have curdled milk. 'My dear,' he hissed, 'nice has nothing to do with it. She was a venomous old toad who made the lives of several perfectly pleasant people Hell on earth. I wouldn't have wished her dead, of course, but I can't help thinking the curve of the stairs did us all a favour.'

He squeezed himself nearer to her on the pretext of people pushing past to the bar and that gave him a better angle to gaze at her cleavage.

'What about Mr Goodacre?' Deena asked, fully aware of Bartlett's line of vision. 'Was he horrible too?'

'Gordon?' Bartlett sipped his g'n't with an elegance learned of too many play launches and not enough plays. 'Hardly knew him. But you know yourself, theatres are dangerous places.'

His arm had crept along the back of her seat. She noticed it, let him know she'd noticed it and smiled. 'You're right,' she said. 'They can be. Well,' she checked her watch, 'I'd better be getting home.'

'Home?' Bartlett repeated. 'Surely not. The night is young.'

'Can we go on somewhere?' she asked, looking up a little breathlessly into his mahogany tanned face.

'What had you in mind?' he asked. Dan Bartlett was on familiar territory. The old charm hardly ever failed. Even so, this one did seem a trifle easy to get.

She licked her lips and jutted her breasts at him, cocking her head to one side. 'How about your place?' she asked and ran her hand obligingly over his crotch.

Bartlett swallowed hard, thinking how lucky the girl was. 'Er ... yes. Yes, of course.' And he necked his g'n't in one. 'Fancy a pizza on the way?'

'No.' She barely recognised it as her own voice at first. 'No, I don't want to go there. Not there. You can't make me.'

There were shadows on the wall. A man's voice. Then a woman's. A sigh, slow, long drawn out. From nowhere a light flashed across her eyes, sharp, white, blinding. She screamed. And then the darkness.

'Tell me about Charles Stuart, then, Jason.'

The sound, again, of silence. It was Tuesday morning. Lesson One. Aitch Four was Maxwell's classroom. Posters of Adi Hitler and Joe Stalin, those old chums well known to every secondary school child in the land in the twenty-first century, decorated the walls. There was a world map, too, on the grounds that Geography teaching had failed generations of children abysmally and nobody but Maxwell knew where anywhere was any more. There was a picture of Nelson walking

135

down some steps; another one of Isambard Kingdom Brunel smoking a cheroot, with his hands on his lapels, looking pretty damn smug and self-made in front of the anchor chains of the Great Eastern. Even Winston Churchill, God rot him, was up there. There was no sign of Mahatma Gandhi or Nelson Mandela. That was because Peter Maxwell was teaching British History at the moment and had forgotten to take down Adi and Joe. In Maxwell's classes, you left your political correctness, along with your pointless baseball cap and idiotic skateboard, at the door.

Jason took all this in through tunnel vision. None of the pictures was helping at all. Why, why, why, he wondered, and not for the first time, did Mad Max pick on him? That dick-nose Carter hadn't been listening either, so it couldn't have been that. That tart Joanne was texting under the desk like a maniac, so that couldn't have been the reason either. No, it was just pure, old-fashioned picking on, that's why he did it.

'He was a king,' Jason offered.

The Great Man hovered at his elbow, looming over him like the sword of Damocles Jason knew nothing about. 'Spot on, my old Argonaut. I don't suppose you remember his number at all?'

'Er...'

'Sir! Sir!' Lobelia's hand was in the air again. Maxwell – and indeed the rest of Eight Eff Four – didn't know why she didn't just keep it up permanently, perhaps in a splint. But Mad Max wasn't looking for answers; he was looking for attention. Not because, like most of the little horrors in their seats in Aitch Four, he was a

136

sociopath and misfit who craved it, but because he had that long ago discredited idea that it was his job, nay his duty, to thump some learning into their empty heads.

'So, what are we talking about, Mr Carter?' Mad Max could spin on his heel for England and Charlie Carter was caught in mid-daydream. Maxwell lifted the *Biking* magazine from the child's lap. 'Ah, a counterfactual hypothesis, I see, in that it has precisely nothing to do with History. Just so that your civil liberties aren't infringed, I will refrain from tearing this up before your very eyes, Charles. You will, nevertheless, not see it until the end of the day – and that only if you report to my office to collect it.'

'Yes, Mr Maxwell.' Charlie Carter was secretly seething. It was only Lesson One and he had another five to go without his *Biking* mag. Could he survive?

'And what have we here?' Maxwell had whirled again, like the Dervish he was, and held out his hand for Joanne's mobile phone. At first, she toyed with stashing it away, but the mad old bastard would only tip her upside down until it fell out onto the floor, so she meekly passed it to him. 'Just as I thought,' the Great Man nodded. "I go fm a cptble to an incptble cwn, wh no dstbnce can b, no distbnce in th wld." Excellent, Joanne. A text version of Charles I's last words from the scaffold, delivered at the king's palace of Whitehall on January 30 1649. How imaginative of you.' He closed to her, invading her privacy, scaring the bejazus out of her. 'You will, never-theless, have to live without this gadget for the rest of the week.'

'The week?' Joanne was incensed. 'But you only took Carter's magazine for the day.'

'I can read a *Biking* mag in a day,' Maxwell explained. 'It'll take me five to work out how this little gizmo works. And it's all about punishment fitting the crime, my pet. Give me an innocent, healthy, boyish *Biking* mag any day of the week over one of these instruments of Satan.' As usual, nobody knew what he was talking about.

There was a knock at the door. It was the one he'd been expecting. Paul Moss, Maxwell's long-suffering Head of History, stood there, all newly-spiked hair and corduroy jacket. Paul was a bit of a cipher really. Oh, he was fine on target setting and lesson dynamics and group hugs, but if anybody wanted to know any History, they went to Peter Maxwell. 'Mr Maxwell, you have a visitor.'

'Ah, yes. Mr Moss, I shouldn't be long. Could you hold the front line here for me, please? Lobelia over there has the lowdown on King Charles I and why he managed, over a fifteen-year period, to piss off just about everybody in England.' He beamed at the class as he reached the door. 'And I *shall* be asking questions again when I return,' he said. He winked at Moss and bounded down the corridor, past the fluttering notices of September, the reminders that ski-trip money was overdue and that Afterbirth were performing at the Stag on Naughties Night. That was one Maxwell was determined not to miss.

A short, freckled, dark-haired detective stood inside his office, fairly gobsmacked by the sheer wealth of film postery around the walls.

'Jane.' He reached down to kiss her hand. 'How lovely to see you.'

'Cut the crap, Max,' she scowled, allowing the physicality only on sufferance. 'This is official.'

'You know,' he smiled, 'I could have done with you in my Joe Stalin re-enactment lesson last week. The uniform's wrong, but the attitude's spot on.' He made for the kettle. 'Are you officially allowed to have a cup of coffee?'

'No, thanks. When did you last see Martita Winchcombe?'

'Er...' he invited her to sit down on the excruciating County furniture and flopped onto his own chair. 'The night before she died, I suppose. That would be last Monday.'

'Where was this?' Jane had her notebook poised. She was an attractive woman, with her coal-black hair and large, brown eyes. She seemed to have a broom up her arse this morning however, a reminder of how a woman can turn on a sixpence, whatever that used to be.

'At the Arquebus Theatre,' Maxwell told her.

'What did she say? As exactly as you can.'

'Look ... Jane,' Maxwell could see the end of his tether looming. '...the other day you were sweetness and light. You kindly gave me a lift, asked after Jacquie. You were even moderately indiscreet in confiding that Martita was murdered. I live with your best friend, Goddammit.'

'What point are you trying to make, Max? I'm just doing my job,' she said.

He stood up. 'So am I,' he said. 'It's called teaching. And you're keeping me from it.'

'All right.' Her voice checked him at the door.

'All right. I'm sorry. I'm being... Look, this is a little difficult. You were possibly one of the last people to see her alive.'

Maxwell relented. Everybody was a little on edge this morning. What with murder and Eight Eff Four ... come to think of it, those terms did tend to blend a little. He wandered to the settee and sat close to his interrogator. 'Let's start again, then,' he said. 'What do you need?'

'What do you remember about your conversation? Did anything strike you as odd?'

He of the total recall kicked into action. 'Well, she introduced herself. We did the British thing and whinged about the weather. As soon as she realised that I taught within these hallowed portals, her demeanour changed completely. She didn't approve of children, or indeed anybody much under seventy. She was a little mutt, if I remember rightly. It was only a fleeting chat at best, but...'

'Yes?' Even for her tender years, Jane Blaisedell was good at nuances, inflections, dots. She was like Jacquie Carpenter through a funny mirror; one of those they used to have down on the Front before electronic gamesmanship took over and people only laughed if electronic blood spurted all over the screen.

'Well, all this was on the way into the theatre. I spent the best part of twenty years sitting through a committee meeting and met her again on the way out.'

'You mean she wasn't in the meeting?'

'No. I assumed she had other fish to fry. I was just leaving the Arquebus when she collared me.

Told me she knew me from the *Advertiser's* always-inaccurate stories as something of a sleuth.'

Jane Blaisedell's face said it all.

'Yes, yes.' He caught it. 'I know. None of my business. Civilians keep out. I know the drill. Anyway, she told me that Gordon Goodacre's death wasn't an accident. She said that someone killed him.'

'Did she say who?' Jane couldn't believe her job could be *this* simple.

'No, we were interrupted at that point and the world moved on. I had a sou'westerly to face cycling home.'

'But it got you snooping anyway?'

Maxwell shrugged. 'You know me,' he said. 'Can't keep an incorrigibly, morbidly macabre man down.'

'Who interrupted you?' Jane wanted to know. She still wasn't smiling.

'The theatre's Artistic Director, Dan Bartlett.'

The Artistic Director, Dan Bartlett, lay on the floor in his sprawling bungalow on the edge of Tottingleigh, where the South Downs began and suburbia ended. He was stark naked and stiff as a board and SOCO men in white coats and masks flitted around him like extras in a Sci-fi film. One of them was Jim Astley and he was secretly wishing he hadn't overdone it on the golf course the other day because he was kneeling down and his sciatica was killing him.

'This is a weird one, Henry,' he nodded as the familiar square face of the DCI appeared around the door. 'Electrocution.'

'Talk me through it.' Hall had Tom O'Connell at his elbow that Wednesday morning, mechanically going through the note-taking. Giles Finch-Friezely was still in the van outside, swapping his day clothes for the SOCO whites. Cameras were flashing, measurements being taken. Men dabbed paint brushes on door frames, window catches. Others scraped samples from carpets. Nobody had been told yet to dig over the garden, but the spades were ready in the van, just in case.

'Worst case I ever saw was on a golf course, funnily enough,' Astley said, grunting to stand up again. 'Some chap killed by lightning. You'd swear he'd been through some kind of shredder. Half his hair was gone and his skin and muscles were torn to pieces. Even his arms were fractured. Green-stick cracks all the way down the humerus, radius and ulna. Damnedest thing I ever saw. And the smell! Well, you can't describe it.'

'Yes,' Hall held up his hand. 'Thank you for your breadth of experience, Doctor. Let's deal with the here and now, shall we?'

'Well, as you can see, nothing like as bad.'

Dan Bartlett's left leg was black up to the groin, his foot charred across the sole, and his hands were raised in some ghastly, frantic dance to escape the pain. His eyes were wide open, glazed and dull and his back was arched. But it was his face that held Henry Hall's attention and he'd see it throughout many a sleepless night to come. Just another to add to his collection. Dan Bartlett's lips were peeled back from his bared teeth and he grinned like a deranged Cheshire cat.

'There's your culprit,' a SOCO man said,

142

pointing to the scorched carpet between the dead man's feet. 'Faulty wiring. If I had a quid...'

The SOCO was right. An electric cable lay exposed where the team had peeled away the carpet with its ghastly swirls of blue and grey. 'Routine, then?' Hall straightened to look at the man in the white hood. Bob Hartley. On loan from Sussex University.

'Routine my arse,' Hartley said. 'Look at that cable again. You don't get fraying like that from ordinary wear and tear. Look here.'

Hall did. There were tiny shavings of plastic and wire in the fibres of the underlay and scattered on the floorboards. 'You only get this sort of thing if you go at it with a Stanley knife. I think we can assume somebody didn't like Mr Bartlett.'

'If you must know, I despised him with every fibre of my being.' Carole Bartlett was not a woman to mince words. Her lips were tight, a living version of her dead husband's, and she sat bolt upright in Henry Hall's second Interview Room in the nick at downtown Leighford. It was a grey, dismal Wednesday afternoon in Tony Blair's England and Henry Hall was trying, not for the first time, to piece together a life. The woman was tall, probably more scrawny now than when Dan Bartlett had married her, but she carried herself well and had a rather haughty way with her, underlined by a habit of looking people up and down with a withering scorn. Her clothes were far too young for her and she had a rather tarty air.

'You found the body?'

Hall was sitting alongside Jane Blaisedell,

143

quietly wishing, as he'd found himself doing ever more frequently over the last few weeks, that she was Jacquie Carpenter. Oh, Jane was doing a good job, certainly. She'd make a decent DS in twenty or twenty-five years, but with Jacquie ... well, there was an indefinable something.

Carole Bartlett nodded. 'It was horrible,' she shuddered. 'Quite horrible.'

'But I thought you said...' Jane began, confirming anew why Henry Hall wished she was Jacquie.

'I know what I said,' the widow snapped. 'But I did once share a life with that man, a bed. If it weren't for the way of things, we'd have shared children too. And anyway, even if I'd never seen him before, finding a naked corpse in that revolting position is not one of the moments in life I shall look back on and cherish.'

'The way of things?' Hall liked to leave no stone unturned and was a past master at spotting important adverbial clauses.

She looked at him, blinking in a blind fury born of life's little injustices. What did he know? A mere man? She wasn't going to share her innermost secrets with him. 'Let's just say there were ... complications. Medical, I mean.'

'Him or you?' Jane cut to the chase.

'Hah!' the woman snorted. 'No, there was nothing wrong with Daniel's "wedding tackle", as he so grotesquely put it. And put it he did, wherever and whenever he could. The whole of the south coast is probably littered with his bastards.' She composed herself as, the venom subsided. 'My ex-husband was a serial philanderer, Chief

Inspector, and he liked them young. Obsessed with tottie and pizza – oh, and the time, of course, but above all, himself.'

'The time?' Hall frowned.

'Anal.' Carole Bartlett threw her hands in the air. 'Utterly anal. Everything had to be done just so. Breakfast 7.40, lunch 1.15, bath time...'

'Ten-thirty,' Hall said.

'Close,' she said. 'Ten-fifteen, actually, unless of course there was some tart in there with him.'

'You still keep the name Bartlett,' Hall observed.

'As I kept the family home and the Porsche. Daniel was not only unutterably vain and self-obsessed, he was also loaded. After I found him in bed with some revolting little chorus line member in 2001, I gave him his marching orders and took him to the cleaners. Not mixing too many metaphors, am I, for you?' she snapped at Jane, busily taking notes.

The policeman thought of smiling. Jane did not.

'As long as I was still Mrs Bartlett, I was a constant reminder to him. A thorn in his side. The alimony was very satisfying.'

'You went to see him earlier today?' Hall clarified.

'I did,' Carole said.

'Was this a regular thing?'

'Certainly not. I'd come for the Sheridan.'

'The Sheridan?'

'Daniel came from old money, Chief Inspector. Apart from poncing around on stage and being "creative" as he called it behind the scenes, he never actually did a hand's turn in his life. His

145

grandfather was something out in Kenya before the blacks took over. Among the old boy's souvenirs was an original copy of Richard Brinsley Sheridan's *School for Scandal*. Oh, hopelessly overrated and unfunny now, I'll grant you, but in the right auction worth several times the salary of this gel here.'

Jane looked at her flatly, but knew better, in the DCI's presence, than to respond.

'I fancied a few weeks in the Seychelles and decided to fund it via the Sheridan. Sotheby's would have been more than interested.'

'Would have been?'

'It wasn't there.'

'I'm sorry, Mrs Bartlett.' Hall was frowning behind the blank specs, more than a little confused. 'Can you talk me through the events of this morning – in as much detail as you can.'

Carole Bartlett sighed, as if all this was slightly irritating, rather than the shock of her life. 'Very well. I got to Daniel's wretched little bungalow at about nine-thirty, perhaps ten; I'm not sure.'

'You have a key?'

'Of course. But I never used it if he was there. In case I caught him in some degrading situation. He wouldn't have minded about that, of course. All part of his appalling arrogance. "Look at me, I can still pull, while you're a dried up..." Well, whenever I had to go there, I'd ring the bell first.'

'As you did this morning?' Hall checked.

'Indeed. Of course, there was no answer. So I let myself in.'

'And then?' It was Jane's turn to move the story on.

'I assumed he was out. As I presume you know, the garage is separate from the house and I wouldn't have known whether the car was there or not. I went straight to the lounge, looking for the Sheridan.'

'Which is why the place looked a little ... shall we say ... done over?' Hall had noticed that before his SOCO team's work confirmed it.

'If you mean by your vulgar police parlance, disturbed, yes. The Sheridan, when I saw it last, was on the highest shelf to the left of the fire-place. I "did over" the rest of the room, but to no avail. So I tried the study.'

'The study.' Hall was remembering the layout of the Bartlett bungalow as best he could, but the SOCO photographs and diagrams hadn't come through yet.

'To the right as you leave the lounge,' Carole reminded him.

'Right. And the book wasn't there either?'

'No. I was about to try the first bedroom – his – when I found him.'

Hall shuffled a little. 'I realise this is difficult for you, Mrs Bartlett, but I wonder...'

She closed her eyes, but whether to obliterate the worst of her memories or to focus on them, neither Hall nor Jane could tell. 'He was lying with his feet towards me. They were black. Or at least, one of them was. He was totally naked, but there was a towel under his body. His back was arched, I remember, like a coat hanger. It was ... quite grotesque.' She turned away sharply, as though something out of the window had caught her attention.

'What did you do?' Hall took her away from the moment.

'I called the police. You people.'

'Did you use your husband's phone or your mobile?'

'I don't carry mobiles, Chief Inspector,' she told him. 'Ghastly, intrusive things. I used Daniel's land line.'

'And you waited?'

'Yes. But while I was waiting, I checked the bedrooms, both of them, for the Sheridan. Absolutely no sign.'

Jane looked at Hall and he at her. He could see her shoulders square, the muscles in her jaw ridge. He moved quickly to defuse the situation. The cold-hearted bitch had just found the body of her ex-husband and went on calmly looking for a book. Why not have a coffee and watch some day-time television?

'So you believe the book has been stolen?' he asked.

'I assume so,' Carole Bartlett shrugged.

'Who knew about it?' Hall asked. 'Apart from you, obviously.'

'God knows. Daniel was notoriously tight with money, except when it came to entertaining his lady friends. But he was also appallingly up himself. You noticed the photos, I suppose?'

'Photos?' Hall repeated.

'In his lounge. Daniel with Larry Olivier. Daniel with Kenneth Branagh. Daniel licking every orifice of Dame Judi Dench. He was nauseating, Chief Inspector. It's no wonder someone killed him.'

It was Hall's turn to shift in his seat. 'You think your husband was murdered?' he asked.

'Chief Inspector,' she said. 'I was in that ghastly piece of ribbon development breeze-blockage for nearly an hour after your people arrived. "Could you just wait in here for a moment, madam?"' – it was a passably good DS Walters. 'Those idiots in white overalls have inescapably loud voices and precious little respect. For all they knew, my late husband and I were hopelessly in love and they virtually had their casual, matter-of-fact scene of crime conversations all around me.'

'I'm sorry,' Hall apologised on behalf of his SOCO team. 'I'll have a word.'

'You do that,' she nodded. 'And when you find the individual who did this, do two things for me, will you? Get my Sheridan back off him and give him a medal.'

'A police person?' Dierdre Lessing wanted confirmation. She was the Senior Mistress at Leighford High, now Assistant Headteacher i/c Special Needs and Student Services, and she came from Hell as far as Peter Maxwell was concerned.

'A woman,' Bernard Ryan, the Deputy Head, affirmed. Ryan was a chinless wonder promoted way above his capabilities. If they'd left him to teach Business Studies, he might just have coped. As it was, well...

'Talking to Maxwell?'

'Took him out of his lesson, apparently.'

'But he's living with one, isn't he? Policewoman, I mean.'

149

'I believe he is.'

'Disgusting!' Dierdre snarled. 'So what's he up to now, Bernard? It's no good. He'll have to go.'

Chapter Ten

'Look, we've got a bloody show to put on in three weeks. Is this some sort of joke?'

Deena Harrison was in full flow that evening as in the sky above the auditorium of the Arquebus, the clouds built in the darkness to the east. Here on the ground, her long-suffering cast tried yet again to get it right.

'Feed me!' a vaguely Afro-Caribbean voice rumbled from inside the cardboard and resin creation that was Audrey II, the man-eating plant. David Balham wasn't a bad actor as far as projection went. And his singing voice was OK too, in a tune-in-a-bucket sort of way. It was just that he couldn't move. Puberty had hit him hard three years earlier and he had difficulty controlling his feet after that. There was probably a Syndrome to cover it, but Angela Carmichael didn't have time for any of that. So she put him in Audrey II as a damage limitation exercise. The line tonight was rather more John Inman than James Earl Jones and Deena couldn't let it pass.

'Jesus Christ!' she shrieked, fists clenched at her sides, back like a ramrod, eyes flashing in the reflected light of the stage. 'You've just got to cope with that thing, David. I'm not asking for the moon. Just coming in on cue would be nice. Again!'

Maxwell was about to intervene, as he had

151

often been about to intervene in the last few days. He hadn't remembered Deena being this feisty. On the contrary, she'd always been rather sweet, engaging. Trust her? No. Like her? Yes, most people did. But this was a different Deena, one driven by ... who knew what? But Maxwell had barely risen to his feet in the fifth row back to suggest taking five so that everybody could cool off when a shaken-looking Patrick Collinson came thundering down the aisle. His normally crimson face had an odd pallor about it and he stepped nervously up on stage.

'Ashley.' He was talking to the man in the sound box upstairs at first, then, 'Everybody. I hate to interrupt, but can you gather round?' His voice was coming and going as he moved in and out of mike range. The girl chorus, The Tendrils, came down from their perches, Seymour and Audrey I broke their awkward clinch and Mr Mushnik appeared from behind a stand of aspidistras. A slightly asphyxiated head popped out, gratefully, from the fronds of Audrey II; David Balham could breathe again. Deena stood with her arms folded waiting for the old git to make his point and get off. She knew of old the acerbity of the *Advertiser's* reviewer. This show wouldn't be ready and he'd tear them to shreds. "Lacklustre", "brave", "under-rehearsed" – this was the best they could hope for.

'What's the matter, Patrick?' Ashley Wilkes' voice boomed over the p.a. and the assembled cast saw his silhouette against the glass.

'It's Dan,' Collinson flustered, trying to focus on the silhouette's face, hovering in the lighting

152

box. 'Dan Bartlett. He's dead.'

'I'm sorry, Max, I'm not very good company, I'm afraid.'

Patrick Collinson sat slumped in the snug of the Vine. Unlike the Volunteer, this place was not Regenerated. Picture Moe's from the Simpsons, with Fifties butcher shop sawdust on the floor and a jukebox that still played *A Horse With No Name* and you've got part of the idea. From his seat beside Collinson, Peter Maxwell could see three under-age drinkers. He'd do his duty in that context presently, but now he had more pressing matters. 'I didn't expect a cabaret,' he told the Secretary. 'You just looked like you needed a drink, that's all.'

'Look,' Collinson muttered. 'I shouldn't have done that, made that stupid, over-the-top announcement in front of your kids. It wasn't fair. Will that girl be all right?'

'Sally Spall? She'll be fine. The wailing wasn't really connected with your news in fact. It's a tough call being Audrey and her boyfriend's just dumped her. Last straw, I'm afraid. Although I understand her parents are over the parrot about it.'

'Last straw for Dan, certainly,' and Collinson gulped his brandy.

'My shout.' Maxwell waved at the barman. It was rather an imperious gesture for the infant end of the twenty-first century, but Dave Wakeham, appearing tonight on pints and optics, reckoned the Great Man. He had, after all, single-handedly, got him a Grade C in GCSE History. Greater love

153

hath no History teacher. 'Same again, Dave.' And the shots were forthcoming.

'Is he all right, Mr Maxwell?' the lad asked, jerking his head in the direction of the Arquebus' secretary. 'I've seen blokes his colour before. Usually before they drop dead of a heart attack. Gives the place a bit of a bad name, you know.'

'He'll be OK,' Maxwell said, using the Americanism he detested so that Dave could follow the conversation. 'Had some bad news tonight, that's all.'

'The pork scratchings are on special offer.' The barman was well in tune with the finer things in life.

'Joy,' Maxwell beamed. 'A bit later, eh?' and the lad left. Maxwell turned to the matter in hand. 'Do you know what happened?'

'To Dan?' Collinson tried to compose himself. 'Electrocuted,' he said, shaking his head in disbelief. 'It's just incredible. A worn cable, or something. What's happening, Maxwell?'

The Head of Sixth Form didn't know. But he knew a woman who might.

'Nothing from Jane, then?' Maxwell was stirring his cocoa.

'Contrary to public opinion,' Jacquie put her knitting down, that quaint old, half-forgotten pastime that women rediscover when they're pregnant, 'women do not dash to the nearest mobile and indulge in idle speculation.'

'Don't give me that,' he laughed. 'Jane Blaisedell could goss for England.'

'Well, I don't,' and it was all of three seconds

154

before both of them exploded into uncontrollable laughter, Jacquie's bump wobbling along with her. Clearly, it had the measure of its parents already.

'Mind you,' Maxwell said, 'she was off hooks with me this morning.'

'You didn't tell me that.'

'My dear girl, since casting the last of my pearls before the Gadarene swine, I have attended a two hour staff development meeting (whatever that means), cooked my own supper while you were at breathing classes, clipped the back hedge and sewn my left arm back on. This is the first chance I've had to sit down.'

'Tut tut,' Jacquie shook her head, smiling. 'You housewives.'

'How did the breathing go?' he asked. 'Seriously.'

'Fine,' she told him. 'No problems. Everything going according to plan – swimmingly, in fact. Sonny Jim spends most of our time doing the butterfly stroke, by the feel of it.'

He reached over and patted Jacquie's bump.

'Let's not change the subject.' She knocked his hand gently away. 'Jane Blaisedell.'

'Wanted to know,' Maxwell carefully blew the skin off his cocoa, 'the last words of Martita Winchcombe.'

'Which you, of course, Mister Memory, were able to reel off.'

'In a manner of speaking,' Maxwell told her in all modesty. 'But what I didn't say was that people generally regarded the old duck as a few scenes short of an act. Dan Bartlett certainly...'

'But Dan Bartlett's dead,' Jacquie didn't need to remind him.

'And Mrs Troubridge is of like opinion. Have you seen her lately?'

'Have I?' Jacquie rolled her eyes, rearranging herself on the sofa, placing a cushion just so, so that she could feel her back again. 'She harangued me for nearly an hour this morning on how it wasn't good for people "in my condition" – it sounded like leprosy – not to have a husband.'

'I hope you retaliated,' Maxwell retorted. 'Even I am forced to concede that this is the twenty-first century.'

'Max, to the Mrs Troubridges of this world a partner is someone you play bridge with.'

'And to the Mr Maxwells, come to think of it,' he told her. 'She didn't give you her love life, did she, instalment by instalment?'

'She did,' Jacquie sighed. 'Although it was so full of euphemisms I wasn't quite sure what she was talking about. "Let's just say, my dear, that Mr Troubridge bought a ticket and got off half-way". By the time she got to Ventnor on her honeymoon, I'd lost the will to live.'

'Ah,' he sucked his teeth. 'Now we'll never know.'

'What's going on, Max?' she asked him.

He looked at her, face wreathed in cocoa steam. 'In what respect, heart of hearts?'

'At the theatre.'

He sat bolt upright, slamming the cocoa down on the coffee table and pretending to shake her. 'I asked you that!' he screamed quietly.

'No, you didn't,' she protested, laughing. 'You

156

asked me if I'd heard from Jane. Not at all the same animal.'

'Does maternity leave relieve you of your Peel-ite oath, Woman Policeman? Never to divulge to folks outside the Force any juicy titbits of goss that come your way in the course of your inquiries?'

'No,' she said flatly. 'And we've had this conversation, maternity leave or not, ever since I've known you.'

'So, let's get this straight, then.' Maxwell lolled back, arms folded. 'You can pick my brains, poor befuddled creatures that they are, but you won't tell me anything. Is that how this works?'

'Something like that,' she nodded. 'Bringing to mind clichés like "Ve vill ask ze questions" and so on.'

'No dice.'

'Oh, come on, Max.' She hauled on his arm, pulling him backwards and forwards. 'Come on. I'll do the supper.'

'Too bloody right,' he told her. He was working for three now.

'And the coffee tomorrow. You can have a lie-in.'

He looked are her, sensing a ground-breaking arrangement in the wind. 'You teach Nine Aitch Three the significance of the Corn Laws lesson four tomorrow and you might have a deal.'

'Bollocks!' she snorted.

'It's only because you can't!' he whined in a perfect Private Pike from *Dad's Army*. 'Isn't it, Uncle Arthur? Isn't it? Isn't it?'

She hit him around the head with a cushion. It

would have to do until science found a permanent cure. 'Fact for fact,' she suggested. 'How about it?'

He looked at her through narrowed eyes. 'Well...'

'I'll still do the coffee in the morning.' She was driving a hard bargain, but he'd see the wisdom of it as the alarm went off and he could afford the luxury of rolling over and saying 'Sod it!'

'Done!' he said and shook her hand smartly. 'Three deaths in connection with the Arquebus theatre.'

'But only one *at* the Theatre.'

'The first,' he nodded. 'Gordon Goodacre. What do we know?'

'Ladder fell on him. Apparently accident.'

'That's *so* unsatisfactory, Jacks,' he slapped his knee. 'Working alone like that. No witnesses. No forensics. Nothing. Just something going bump in the night.'

'You can't get over that, can you?' She shook her head.

'What if it's the key?' he asked her. 'What if the other two deaths hinge on that one?'

'With the theatre being the link.'

Maxwell nodded. 'I asked Graham Costigan, the Head of Maths, what were the odds of three people from one organisation dying in the space of ten days of each other. Know what he said?'

Jacquie shook her head.

'"Fucked if I know,"' Maxwell quoted. '"I'm just a Maths teacher." It's Archimedes, Mandelbrot and Fermat all over again. Say what you like, comprehensives just can't get the staff.'

'But you think the odds are unlikely?'

'Don't you?' he frowned. What sort of woman was he shacking up with here?

'Yes,' she frowned back, echoing his posture. 'Yes, I do.'

'All right. Let's backtrack. What do we know about Goodacre?'

'Got a dragon for a wife.'

'Yes. Eleanor of Aquitaine meets Lady Macbeth. And?'

'He helped out at the theatre, presumably in fear of said wife.'

'What are you saying?' Maxwell asked, retrieving his cocoa again, 'that *she* killed him?'

'You've met her,' Jacquie shrugged. 'Is she the type?'

Maxwell laughed. 'Don't get me on stereotyping,' he said. 'But, yes, I think she's capable. On the other hand, I get the impression she'd rather call him out and demolish his skull with a pickaxe, toe to toe. There's nothing clandestine about Matilda Goodacre. She'd do it, then call the police, conduct her own defence, get off and write a best-selling play about it, with her in the title role, of course.'

'Death two, then.' Jacquie moved them both on.

'Martita Winchcombe. Had enemies.'

'Really?' Jacquie narrowed her eyes. 'Who?'

'The person who wired her stairs, for one. Our next door neighbour, perhaps.'

'Mrs T?' Jacquie snorted. 'Never in a million years.'

'Jealousy, my dear.' He patted her wrist. 'The

159

old green eye. A motive at least.'

'What, that rubbish about Mr Troubridge and the Venetian blind?'

'It made my eyes water,' Maxwell confessed.

'How long's he been dead?'

'Mr Troubridge? God knows. Before I moved in, certainly. Got to be thirty years.'

'Rather a long time to fester, then, isn't it?' Jacquie asked.

'Ah,' Maxwell smiled. 'Revenge is a dish best served cold.'

'Cold, yes,' Jacquie agreed. 'But not put in the freezer, taken out and defrosted.'

'Martita wanted to consult me,' Maxwell said.

Jacquie leaned back, clasping her hands over the new life inside her. 'So that's it!' she said.

'Sorry?'

'That's what all this is about. She came across La Mancha to engage your trusty lance and Rosinante. And you just can't resist saddling up, can you? Going for those bloody windmills again.'

He leaned across and kissed her. 'You wouldn't have me any other way,' he smiled.

'Maybe yes, maybe no,' she told him.

'Which brings us to murder three.'

'Let me rein you in there, Don Quixote.' She wagged a finger at him. 'I'll grant you Martita Winchcombe was murder. Jane said the SOCO evidence was overwhelming. The jury's still out on Goodacre. And as for Dan Bartlett ... who knows?'

'Jane Bloody Blaisedell, for one!' Maxwell told her, as their conversation came full circle. 'And this, in the parlance of Fifties cinema, is where I

160

came in.'

'I've got to tread softly here, Max,' she told him.

'Of course, sweetstuff,' he beamed. 'I understand. But do at least *tread*, there's a good girl. Shall I tell you something odd?'

'What's that?'

'When I had my last conversation with Martita Winchcombe, on the night she died, it was Dan Bartlett who interrupted us.'

'So?'

'So, until earlier tonight, I sort of had the late Artistic Director in the frame. He seemed anxious to shut the old girl up, warn me off, dismissing her as barking. Perhaps, I thought, he wanted to shut her up permanently.'

'Then he upped and died,' Jacquie said.

'Precisely,' Maxwell nodded, half talking to himself. 'Now why would he do a thing like that?'

'Who's on last movements?' DCI Hall wanted to know. That Wednesday morning saw a tired and tetchy Incident Room. Henry Hall had had no choice now but to create one and they'd moved out of the overcrowded nick, lock, stock and computer system, to Tottingleigh. Yes, the public would murmur; yes, some might over-react; but *some* might just provide answers.

'That's me, guv.' Tom O'Connell was still wrestling with his tuna mayo wrap, which he felt he'd better ditch in preference to spraying everybody with its contents. He lunged for his notepad, buried under piles of bumph. 'We've got an approximate time of death from Dr Astley of ten

161

to ten-thirty. Bartlett was found by his wife the next morning, i.e. twenty-four hours ago. We know from Ashley Wilkes, the Theatre Manager, that Bartlett was at the Arquebus the previous day, i.e. the one in question.'

Jane Blaisedell leaned across to an oppo at her elbow. 'Remind me how he made DS again,' she hissed in an aside.

'What time was that?' Hall wanted it narrowed down so that the whiteboard made sense.

'Er... Half-two,' O'Connell confirmed. 'He and Wilkes were going over plans for a possible theatre extension that's in the consultative stage.'

'Is that a general erection,' Jane whispered, 'or something specific?'

'Just the two of them?' Hall asked.

'Um...' O'Connell was double-checking. Didn't want to get it wrong in front of the DCI. 'Mrs Goodacre joined them at one point. That was somewhere around four. She stayed for an hour, then left. The meeting between Wilkes and Bartlett broke up about six.'

'What then?'

'Wilkes knocked off for the night and left Bartlett to oversee the rehearsal.'

'What rehearsal?' Hall was putting them through their paces.

'*Little Shop of Horrors*, Leighford High School,' the DS told him.

'What time was that?'

'Er ... rehearsal began at seven, finished a little before nine.'

'Who was on that?' Hall scanned the murder team ranged before him, faces he knew, men and

162

women he trusted.

'That's me, guv,' Gavin Henslow admitted. 'I spoke to the producer. A woman called Deena Harrison. She said the rehearsal finished at eight-fifty and they all went home. Bartlett was still in the theatre, as far as she knew, when they left.'

'And Peter Maxwell?' Hall felt he had no choice but to ask.

'Guv?' Henslow felt a little out of the loop on this, fast-track graduate or not.

'Peter Maxwell,' Hall sighed with the air of a man worn down by the cares of the world. 'Head of Sixth Form at Leighford High.'

Ripples of comment ran round the room and Hall let it happen. He did catch the phrase 'interfering bastard' a few times. 'I understand he's keeping an eye on rehearsals.' He looked straight at Jane Blaisedell, when it came to Maxwell his right hand woman. 'Did you talk to him, Gavin?'

'Er … no, guv; sorry.'

Many people had been sorry they hadn't talked to Peter Maxwell and some of them wore blue uniforms. 'Follow it up,' Hall ordered. 'What about the cast?'

'Kids,' Henslow shrugged. 'The couple I spoke to didn't seem to understand the question. There was a … Sally Spall. Downtrodden little thing with a lisp. Um … Alan Eldridge – he plays Seymour…'

'Yes, I don't think we need the entire programme notes here, Gavin,' Hall interrupted to the accompaniment of sniggers. 'Did any of them tell you anything relevant to Bartlett?'

'No, sir,' Henslow admitted. 'Not a sausage.'

'Go into Leighford High tomorrow,' Hall said. 'Jane, go with him. I want exact confirmation of Bartlett's movements on the day he died. He was a stickler for timings. Should be easy to chronicle. Giles, the dead man's computer?'

Finch-Friezely blew outward at the memory of the task he'd been on for what seemed the last twenty-four hours solid. 'Vast amount of luvvie stuff,' he told the Incident Room. 'Old Vic, National Youth Theatre, begging letters to Kevin Spacey, Tim Rice, the Arts Council.'

'Anything private?'

'Er ... thirty-eight unidentified females in regular or casual correspondence via his emails.'

'We have names?'

'Of a sort,' Finch-Friezely snorted. 'Dimples springs to mind. Cuddlekins, Lash La Rue. I think we can assume the late Mr Bartlett lived life to the full.' That the team could still raise chuckles was a good sign.

'They'll need to be checked out,' Hall said. 'Especially in the light of testimony from his ex-wife.'

'Helluva lot of femmes to cherchez, guv,' Finch-Friezely whinged.

'Welcome to Murder Squad, sonny,' Hall nodded, having heard it all before. He wasn't a man interested in moans or requests for over-time. He seemed to remember having a family once. 'Bill, what have we got on the man's bunga-low, apart from dodgy electrics?'

'Signs of female visitation,' DS Robbins said. 'And recent. He had at least one visitor on the evening he died.'

'Do we know who?'

Robbins shook his head. 'No.'

'Prints?'

'Uh-huh. Saliva on a glass.'

'That's all?'

'At the moment.'

'Bedroom?'

'His bed hadn't been slept in. SOCO are still working on the sheets, but we're not hopeful.'

'Right.' Hall was scanning the whiteboard now, looking at the chain of events, the circumstantial links that marked a man's passing. 'So the last time Bartlett was seen by more than one person was at the Arquebus at shortly before nine. Presumably he drove home in that his car was in his garage; and he had a female visitor at some time after that who took at least one drink. No evidence of sex.'

'Probably did it on top of the wardrobe,' was Giles Finch-Friezely's suggestion. Everyone looked at him a little oddly. Perhaps that was the way your mind worked when you had a double-barrelled name at a comprehensive.

'We know from Astley,' Hall swept on, 'that Bartlett was dripping wet when he died – in fact, it was a combination of water and shredded cable that killed him. The bath was full of cold water, which was presumably hot when he left it on his way to meet his maker.'

Jane Blaisedell looked up at the guv'nor. He wasn't usually so poetic.

'Calm Me, guv,' Finch-Friezely said. Everyone looked at him again. 'It's the stuff in the bath,' he explained quickly. 'Relaxing foam.'

165

'Did he have a little duck too?' Henslow grinned. Guffaws all round.

'People, people,' Hall's quiet, sensible voice brought them back into line; men who were tired, women who were wilting. 'We're missing something here. Why did Dan Bartlett get out of the bath, having got in?'

'Somebody at the door?' DS Robbins suggested.

'Perhaps,' Hall nodded, slowly.

'Somebody on the phone,' Jane Blaisedell volunteered.

'Right.' Hall leaned forward, supporting his weight with his hands on the cluttered desk. 'Has anybody checked Dan Bartlett's phone?'

Nobody had.

Time for action.

Kick ass.

Chapter Eleven

In the beginning, God made Chief Constables. Whether He made them in His own image was difficult to say, but that was more or less how Derek Slater saw it. But then, as he *was* Chief Constable, he would, wouldn't he?

Henry Hall wasn't so sure, especially that Wednesday as the purple clouds over Winchester gathered and rolled, the glittering bars of dying sun between them like a cosy, electric fire you remembered always burning at your granny's. The point was that Hall had been at the joint Hampshire/West Sussex Police Service Symposium now for the best part of six hours. It was, as usual, all about targets and community relations and PR and ethnic sensitivity. Nobody mentioned the cops and the robbers at all. It seemed more like a fortnight had passed by the time it was his turn to sit across the Chief Constabularian desk and look the man in the face.

It was the silver braid you saw first, as with all senior policemen, contrasting with the battleship grey habitually worn by the DCI. Then, Hall's attention was drawn to the curious centre parting and the small, dark, dancing eyes. Every move was precision, every mannerism choreographed. Derek Slater had nervous breakdown written all over him.

'To cases, Henry,' he said, shuffling papers like

a fastidious faro dealer and peering over his impossibly antiquated pince-nez. 'This business at the Arquebus in Leighford. What progress?'

'Well, sir,' Hall was the picture of unflappable immobility. 'I'm not sure the link is as obvious as it seems.'

'Oh? And what do you think the link is?'

Henry Hall, had he been a flippant man, would have said it was a mobile phone shop. Peter Maxwell, had he been asked, would have said it was a pro-Nazi organisation in Thirties England. Horses for courses. Neither quip crossed the Chief Constable's desk. 'The theatre itself, sir.'

'Uh-huh,' Slater nodded, as though Hall was outlining the various theories of the origin of the universe. 'Say on.'

'Gordon Goodacre dies in the theatre.' Hall felt he'd better guide the man. It had probably been a long time since he'd been directly involved in a case at all, still less a murder. 'Actually on stage. Martita Winchcombe was the place's Treasurer. Daniel Bartlett was its Artistic Director. I don't really see how I can be clearer.'

'No.' Slater cleared his throat. 'Quite. Quite.'

'Now, we could be looking at some sort of conspiracy...' and as soon as the words left Henry Hall's lips, he regretted them.

'Ah, so you're a conspirationist, are you, Henry?' Slater's slightly twisted smile seemed smarmier than ever.

'If you mean, can more than one person be involved in the commission of a crime, indubitably. Burke and Hare, Leopold and Loeb, Craig and Bentley.'

168

'That's *folie à deux*, surely?' Slater was anxious to outsmart his longest-serving DCI and Henry Hall had a killer to catch. Neither of them had time for the niceties of criminal history.

'It is possible that there is some common ground relating to the theatre we haven't uncovered yet. We're still checking the books, for example.'

'Miss Winchcombe's?'

'Not exactly. She was Treasurer only in a nominal sense by virtue of her long association with the place. The finances are actually handled by a committee spearheaded by Ashley Wilkes, the Manager. They are regulated by the expertise of the theatre's secretary, Patrick Collinson, in that he is a Chartered Accountant.'

'Anything untoward there?'

'As I said, sir, we're still checking. You know how long financial checks can take.'

Slater nodded wisely, but Henry Hall knew men like him. Peter Maxwell believed Hall to be a copper of the new school, all graduate and fast-track and smart alecry. By comparison with men like Slater, Hall was Dixon of Dock Green meets Inspector Lestrade.

'What's known about these victims?' the Chief Constable wanted to know. 'Anything in their background?'

'Again, sir, it's under way. A murder enquiry is a slow business.'

'And three murder enquiries three times as slow, eh?' Rosters. Timesheets. Expenses. Those things were bread and butter to Slater. He'd long forgotten, if he ever knew, the human cost of murder.

Hall shrugged.

'Your report casts doubt on the first one. No evidence of murder at all.'

'That's right. No doubts about the others, though. And they're definitely linked.'

'How so?'

'Similar MO,' Hall told him. 'Both Martita Winchcombe and Daniel Bartlett died in their homes, both as a result of an apparent accident. And both, incidentally, quite sloppy.'

'So we're not talking about a hit man, here? A contract killing?'

'No, sir. Definitely not.'

'So what are we talking about?'

Hall twisted a little in his chair. Squirming might have to come later. 'I'm not sure yet,' he said. 'Let's just say I'm keeping an open mind.'

The Chief Constable leaned back in the large swivel obliging tax-payers had bought for him. He had an odd look on his face. 'Are you?' he beamed. 'You don't know how glad I am to hear you say that.'

'Really?' Hall's eyebrows appeared over his glasses' rim. He was beginning to smell a rodent.

The Chief Constable slid a business card across his desk and got up and strolled to the window. He gazed down on the well-kept lawns that fell away from police HQ and the knots of coppers, in and out of uniform, waiting in the car park at the end of a long day. When he turned back, Henry Hall sat there open-mouthed.

'A psychic consultant?' he said.

Slater sat back down. 'Don't knock it till you've tried it,' he said. 'Modern policing, Henry. No barriers. No frontiers. Pushing the limits. Testing the water. We've worked inside the system. Dammit, we *are* the system.' He got off his soap box and relaxed, the little pulse in his neck subsiding. 'And we're not getting results, are we? What have we been hearing all day, from both Services, West Sussex and Hampshire? The public don't trust us. The public don't like us. We're not getting results. Henry,' he leaned towards his man. 'We're not getting closure.'

What a ghastly word, Henry Hall thought. Peter Maxwell would have had a fit.

'And you think this will help?'

'It's been done, Henry,' Slater frowned. 'It's a proven aid. I've just come back from the States. No less than eighty-one police authorities use psychic investigation as routine. So does the FBI.'

And the Pinkertons, no doubt, thought Hall, but perhaps this wasn't the place to say so.

'Think about it, Henry,' Slater urged. 'There was a time when DNA was rubbished by the police service. Fingerprints; Hell, there was a time when unless a man was caught red-handed, there'd be no prosecution at all. I want that open mind of yours on this.'

'So you're suggesting I try this ... Magda Lupescu.'

Slater frowned, leaning back in his chair to remind Hall of the operational gulf between them. 'I'm not suggesting, Henry,' he said. 'I'm ordering it.'

That was the morning they came for Peter Maxwell, in a body. Like Father Gapon leading his thousands to the Winter Palace on Bloody Sunday long, long ago in the snow of a tragic year, Dominic Reynolds thudded down the mezzanine corridor on his way to the Great Man's office. Mad Max was Head of Sixth Form, like Nicholas II was the Father of All the Russias. He would understand. Behind Reynolds trooped his cast of thousands – Sally Spall of the broken heart, who played Audrey; Andy Grant as the mad dentist; Sian Golding, Woman in Shop; Alan Eldridge, geekier than Seymour; David Baiham, colliding with the corridor corners; and all of the Tendrils, without a rara or a beehive in sight.

Unlike Tsar Nicholas back at the Winter Palace, Mad Max was at home. His number two, Helen Maitland, not unused to trouble herself, beat a tactical retreat and let her Lord and Master deal with this one. She was a good woman, was Helen. Large and white, hence her nickname, the Fridge. Maxwell could rely on her in a crisis. But she'd spread herself a little thin recently – let Max take the heat for a bit. And he'd seen it all in his time – the Shorts Issue, the Skirt Length Controversy, the Smoking Room Remonstrance, the Mobile Phone Texting Civil Liberties Debate. He'd fielded them all with a mixture of bonhomie, cold reason, wheedling and, it had to be said, a long time ago, a couple of cuffs round the ear. That was the way with Enlightened Despots. And they didn't come much more enlightened, or more despotic, than Peter Maxwell.

'So,' Maxwell settled into his chair as they all squeezed into his office. 'Who's going to bell the cat?'

172

'Sir?' Benny Barker spoke from the back. Maxwell hadn't even seen him come in.

'Who's doing the talking?' It was pure Humphrey Bogart but no one in the room was old enough to realise.

Sally nudged Dominic. 'Go on,' she hissed in one of her best stage asides.

'It's Miss Harrison, sir,' the plump lad said. 'Deena. She's impossible.'

Maxwell had seen this building for some time and the appearance of the disgruntled mob didn't surprise him in the least. He was just glad they weren't wielding scythes and pitchforks and grumbling *à bas les aristos*. 'Go on,' he said.

"Well, she's mad, Mr Maxwell.' Sally couldn't simply stand there while Dominic lost his bottle. She had to strike a blow for womankind. Alan looked geekier than ever and if there was ever a moment that proved how miscast Andy was as the psycho dentist, this was it.

'So am I, Sally,' Maxwell smiled.

'Ah, yes, but ... no, but, I mean...' Sally blushed bright crimson. 'No, I mean you're...'

'Mad nor-nor-west,' Maxwell helped her out, although the Bardic quotation was sadly lost on the A-level Theatre student. 'Good of you to notice.'

'She's a nutter, sir,' Benny chimed in. 'Mr Maxwell, may I speak freely?'

Maxwell spread his arms in a beatific gesture. This was the twenty-first century. Titles had been abolished and women had the vote. The end of civilisation.

'She's a fuckin' nutter.'

173

Some of the demonstrators froze. Others grinned sheepishly. All of them watched Maxwell. What would the Great Man do? They'd all heard since Year Seven that he once hung a kid from the school flagpole for swearing. And some of them believed it.

'Come off the fence, now, Benny,' Maxwell growled with a smile in his voice. 'Let's analyse this, my children. Spread yourselves.'

One by one they found chairs or arms of chairs or corners of carpets, sitting at the Great Man's knee. 'Let's see. You want Mrs Carmichael back, right?'

There were nods and grunts and 'hear, hear's' in all directions. Benny whistled. 'And you want the smoking ban lifted and a bar in the Common Room and free contraception and the abolition of exams and... Anybody catching my drift, yet?'

They all were, but nobody said so.

'But if we said you could smoke, some of you wouldn't want to and there'd be howls of complaint about passive smoking and you'd upset the government initiatives of that nice Mr Blair. If we put a bar in the Common Room, Benny, you'd whinge about the price and Sian, you wouldn't like the pork scratchings. Rijiura,' he singled out a Tendril, 'it would be against your religion and you'd be torn by impossible peer pressure. If we gave out free contraception, there'd be naughty fumblings in dark corners ... sorry, even more naughty fumblings than there are now...'

A ripple of laughter.

'And if we abolished exams, how would we decide who were the chiefs and who were the

174

Indians? We'd be consigning you to a lifetime of filling shelves at Tesco's – oh, no offence, Dominic.'

The Mr Mushnik of Leighford High grinned. Many was the bottle of Southern Comfort he'd passed obligingly to Mr Maxwell on his trolley runs.

'That's not the real world, people,' Maxwell told them, looking into each and every disappointed face. 'I could have a word with Mr Diamond and I could probably persuade him to dispense with Miss Harrison's services. And then what? You'd have no show. Nothing. Mrs Carmichael's just not well enough. If she knew what you guys were going through now, she'd jump through hoops to come back; you know she would.'

Some of them nodded. All of them agreed.

'And she might just lose her baby. *That's* the real world.'

The grumblers had stopped grumbling, the back row element a rabble no more. They knew he was right. Bugger Mad Max. He was *always* right.

'OK,' Maxwell had done it again. 'Guys? OK?' The Americanisation of Emily was extending to Peter. 'So Deena shouts at you. Why?' He held up his hand. 'No, Benny, she's not a fucking nutter. Sally, you miss a note. What does Deena do?'

'Calls me useless.' The girl looked close to tears, lisping more than ever.

Maxwell nodded. 'Andy, you miss your entry cue. What happens?'

'She bawls me out,' the scrawny dentist said. 'In front of everybody.'

175

Maxwell nodded again. 'Tendrils, the dance routine goes haywire. Deena's reaction?'

They looked at each other, unsure, unsettled, looking for an answer.

'She's cross with us,' Tina Morgan suggested.

'Right. Now see it from Deena's point of view. She's not much older than you. And she doesn't know any of you. She's got a helluva job on and she's doing it out of the goodness of her heart. To help Mrs Carmichael. To help her old school. To help you. Nobody's paying her very much and it must seem, about now, to be a bit of a thankless task. Sally, you don't miss notes. You sing like an angel – I know, I've heard you. Get it right next time. Andy, you've trod the boards before – your Sweeney Todd was legendary; what's with missing cues? Tendrils, how much rehearsal time do you need? Remember *Grease?*'

They all did.

'It was magic,' he told them. 'Four nights and four standing ovations. You can do this, everybody. *I* know it. *You* know it. *Deena* knows it. That's why she's riding you hard. If you were really useless, do you think for one moment she'd say so? Remember, before you judge Deena, walk a mile in her shoes. Then, when you judge her, you're a mile away *and* you've got her shoes.'

The sniggers rose and grew into open guffaws and hysterics. It wasn't original, but it got the team back onside again. 'And if you'd enjoy wearing Deena Harrison's shoes, Benny, I'd rather not know about it. All right?'

They laughed again.

'Now, get out of here. I've got to do the near-impossible and teach Year Seven some history and you have got a show to put on!'

He waited until they'd gone, their steps lighter, their faces brighter with smiles. They were chattering in the corridor, laughing. When the door had closed, he reached for his phone.

'Thingee?' It was, as far as he was concerned, the name of the girl on the school switchboard. 'Have we got a number for Deena Harrison? I need a word.'

'A psychic what?' Margaret Hall couldn't believe her ears. Over the years, she'd seen her husband come home with some pretty cranky initiatives, psychobabble dreamed up by a Whitehall think tank only marginally in touch with reality. But this...

She was already in bed when Henry thudded up the stairs. He'd ignored her note on the kitchen table, the one that told him the outside tap was leaking again and there was shepherd's pie in the fridge. He reached over in the soft lamplight and kissed her forehead.

'Didn't think you'd still be awake,' he said, hauling off his tie.

'And miss your psychic consultant announcement? Not a bit of it.' She yawned and fumbled with the bedside clock. 'Oh, God.'

'Tell me about it.' Hall sat next to her and let his shoes thud to the floor.

'What are you going to do?' Margaret struggled to sit up, her nightie ruched under her. She and Henry had shared a life now for a long time. He was a quiet man, close – some would say secretive. If he mentioned things at nearly two in the morning, it was because they worried him.

'Well,' Hall peeled off his socks and flexed his toes for the first time in hours. Conferences! What crap! 'I could embrace the whole initiative in the visionary spirit in which it is offered.'

'Christ, Henry,' Margaret frowned. 'That's very management of you. What'll you really do?'

He turned and in the confines of their bedroom, in the dim light of their bedroom lamp, in the company of his wife, his companion of a mile, he risked a smile. 'I'll give it to the only one of my team who won't piss themselves with laughter and chuck the woman's findings in the nearest bin. I'll give it to Jane Blaisedell.'

'Mrs Lupescu?' A fresh-faced detective stood in the elegant doorway.

'Yes.'

'I'm Jane Blaisedell.' She flashed the inevitable warrant card. 'Leighford CID. My guv'nor suggested we had a chat.'

Magda Lupescu could have been anything between thirty and late fifties. She was a gaunt woman with a riot of dark, ringleted hair and a sallow complexion. She was dressed in a crisp, white, man's shirt and tight jeans with a broad belt of silver filigree.

'Your guv'nor is Detective Chief Inspector Hall?' The accent was slight, the words slow and deliberate.

Suppressing the urge to giggle and say 'You must be psychic', Jane just nodded. Magda showed her into one of those opulent flats that front onto the sea at Brighton, once the drawing room of a fashionable Regency family when the house was all one and new and frothing with guests and bobbing servants. Its owners had strolled in the Steyne around the corner and bowed or curtseyed to the fleeting plumpness that was HRH the Prince Regent. Now, the house's rooms were sublet microcosms of a different time, peopled by stockbrokers, publishers – and at least one psychic consultant.

'My God!' Jane Blaisedell stood in Magda Lupescu's hall. Huge black and white drawings of a young girl smiled back at her from every wall.

'She was Gary Gilmore's wife,' Magda told her. 'You know the case?'

Jane did. Gilmore was the psycho who shot people indiscriminately in Utah back in the Seventies in lieu of the girl who smiled down from Magda's white walls. On Death Row he had demanded his own death by firing squad and only achieved his ambition after months of wrangling with the pinko-liberal do-gooders who wanted to save his life. 'It was a little before my time,' she said.

'Mine too,' Magda said, leaving Jane none the wiser as to the woman's real age. 'Can I get you a drink?'

'Er … no, thanks,' Jane smiled. 'Duty and all that.'

Magda flashed her an odd look. She invited the detective to sit on a cream-coloured sofa buried under scatter cushions. Charles Manson stared maniacally at her from the far wall, a swastika on his forehead and hatred in his eyes. Beyond the fireplace, John Reginald Christie stood in his garden at 10 Rillington Place, his wife beside him, unknown corpses at his feet. She was in the garden; he was in a graveyard.

'I don't know that one,' Jane said, pointing to an anonymous little man in a Homburg and grey suit, standing just to the left of a table lamp.

'Peter Kurtin,' Magda said, lighting a cigarette. She offered one to Jane, who declined. 'Of course,' the consultant smiled, 'You're on duty. Kurtin was the monster of Düsseldorf, one of those social misfits who gave Weimar Germany such a bad name.'

'Are you German?' Jane was still trying to place the accent.

'Romanian,' Magda corrected her. 'A long time ago.'

'Tell me ... Ms Lupescu. Why...?'

'The pictures?' She blew smoke to the high, plastered ceiling. 'A reminder,' she said. 'Know thine enemy. Oh, these are the worst of them, of course. And I'm glad to say I've never met anyone on their plane of sheer evil. But it's only a matter of scale.'

'It is?'

Magda looked hard at the girl. 'How can I help you?' she asked.

'Well,' Jane rummaged in her bag for the paperwork. 'You came highly recommended by my ultimate boss, the Chief Constable.'

No response.

'Mr Slater. His suggestion was that you might be able to shed some light...'

Suddenly, the gaunt woman lunged forward.

180

She snatched Jane's bag and held it tight to her chest, then smelt it, then let it go. 'Why didn't you like your uncle?' she asked.

'What?' Jane sat there, frozen.

'Your uncle ... Tony, was it?'

Jane's eyes swivelled. She licked her lips which were suddenly bricky dry. She was nodding slowly, scared of where this was going.

'He used to come to visit sometimes, didn't he?' Magda went on with a relentlessness that was unnerving. 'In the house at Leopard's Leap.'

'How...?' the girl was frowning, rattled now in a world she didn't understand.

'He touched you, didn't he?' Magda asked. 'You were ... what ... nine? Ten? You never told anybody.'

Jane had already frozen. Now she wanted to cry. She wanted to scream. No one had known about that. No one but her and Uncle Tony. And Uncle Tony was dead.

Magda Lupescu was leaning towards her, gazing steadily into her eyes, handing back the trailing strap of Jane's discarded bag. 'It *is* only a matter of scale,' she said softly. 'Charlie Manson, Gary Gilmore, Peter Kurtin, whoever you're looking for. You deal in death in your business from time to time, Detective Blaisedell. I deal in it all the time. Now, again, how can I help you?'

There was a light. There was always a light. It never went out. When she finally went to sleep, it was burning. When she woke up, it was burning still.

Chapter Twelve

'Two weeks in, then, Deena,' Maxwell smiled. 'How do you think it's going?'

The girl gave a brittle, slightly bitter laugh. 'You tell me, Mr Maxwell. I suspect you've done more of this than I have.'

'Ah, but never at OUDS,' he chuckled.

'Footlights, surely?' Deena always gave as good as she got.

'I *may* have given a rendition or two. I was the retired colonel in Agatha Christie's *A Decimalisation of Vertically Challenged People of Ethnic Persuasion* when it was still called *Ten Little Niggers*.'

'And that's not all,' she said. 'I bumped into Sylvia Matthews the other day.'

'Really?'

'She told me your Cyrano was to die for.'

'Ah,' he laughed. 'Had to be mine, really. I was the only one who had an artificial nose. Along with the leg, of course. You don't think ... you don't think you're pushing the kiddywinkies a bit hard?'

'Ah.' Her smile froze. 'There've been complaints.' Always quick on the uptake was Deena.

'Not complaints, exactly,' he told her. 'Concerns. I was going to ring you, but I thought I'd wait until after tonight's rehearsal.'

She looked at him, sitting opposite the Great Man on the hard, uncomfortable chairs on the

Arquebus stage. 'Can we get out of here?' she asked. 'I'm beginning to feel like I've moved in.'

'Of course,' he laughed. 'Deena, this is not the type of question a teacher should be asking a student, even an ex-student, but can I buy you a drink?'

'I thought you'd never ask,' she said.

'Mr Wilkes!' Maxwell was on his feet, trying to locate the sound and lighting box in the semi-darkness.

'Mr Maxwell?' a disembodied voice boomed around the auditorium.

'We're off now, thanks.'

'OK,' Wilkes answered. 'See you Monday night.'

The rain had eased off by the time Deena Harrison and Peter Maxwell left the theatre. The Arquebus rose black and oddly derelict against the purple of the late September night. They walked side by side, Deena clutching a sod-off great knitted bag full of scripts and whatever women carry in their sod-off knitted bags, Maxwell wheeling the faithful Surrey, purring at his side as they took the curve of the pedestrianised bit by the river.

'I'll ease off,' she promised him in the context of rehearsals. 'I just get a bit ... well ... intense, I suppose. Ever since Mum and Dad...'

Maxwell looked at her. 'Mum and Dad?'

'They were killed, Mr Maxwell. Head-on crash. Three years ago.'

'Deena,' he stopped the bike and turned to face her. 'I am so sorry. I had no idea. I thought they had moved away.'

183

She shrugged. 'That's what most people think. When something like that happens, you're devastated at first. Can't understand it. Can't come to terms. Then, you feel numb. As if nothing matters. Nothing at all. Not career. Not relationships. Nothing. You come out of that, eventually, and everybody treats you like a leper. "I am so sorry", they say. But it's just words, isn't it?'

Maxwell opened his mouth to say something, but it would only have been to say sorry for saying sorry and that was so flat, so wrong. Neither could he say 'I know how you feel', because the strange thing was that he did, but he couldn't tell her that. He remembered the devastation all too well. A Saturday afternoon in a wild and wet March, long years ago, but it could have been yesterday A grim-faced copper standing at his front door, miles from here, and a WPC behind him. 'Mr Maxwell?' He didn't really hear the rest. No, he couldn't understand it either. His wife was a damned good driver, better than him; focused, sensible, careful. And no, he couldn't come to terms. For weeks afterwards – or was it months – he'd hear her key in the lock, hear her singing in the bath, rattling cups in the kitchen. Smell the soft, impossibly smooth back of his baby's neck as the tears rolled and fell. And nothing mattered, nothing at all. People said he should have been a Head in two or three years, something big in County Hall, or, for God's sake, running a Cambridge college with a K for good measure. And people had loved him, or at least they told him they did. He couldn't quite remember them now. Their names and their

184

faces blurred. 'For I was nothing to him and he was the World to me.' He had, indeed, come out of that eventually, but not for him the rest of what Deena was talking about. He couldn't bear the kind eyes, the quiet sympathy, the pats on the back and the pale Christians muttering that it was all right because his loved ones were with God. So he'd left. Got a new job. Emerged like an imago from the pupa of his pain, crusty before his time. He put the O in Over-the-Top, wore bow ties and battered hats and growled in Latin at the uncomprehending, bewildered children in his care. He bought himself a tatty old bike, White Surrey of blessed memory and he never sat behind the wheel of a car again. That was something Deena hadn't mentioned. Hadn't mentioned, perhaps, because she'd never felt it. Guilt. Because Peter Maxwell should have been driving that wet, wild Saturday in March. *He* should have picked up his little girl from that party, not his wife. If only, if only ... he looked into the deep, dark eyes of the girl with him, hoping that, at least, she'd been spared that.

'Do you want to talk about it?' he asked.

She nodded, the tears near. 'Mr Maxwell, I don't feel like a drink tonight. Can we just ... stay here?'

It wasn't the most elegant of settings, under the roar of the Flyover, where the river curved and the ducks settled down on its banks for the night. 'Sure,' he said, and parked Surrey on the grassy slope, where it was dry. She climbed the ramp of concrete that took them out of the weather and sat down, cradling her knees with both arms and

185

resting her chin on her tattered jeans.

'It was my first year at Corpus Christi,' she said, staring ahead where the dull purple of the sky lit the water in myriad rippling reflections. 'My college mother came to my room late one night. She told me my parents were dead. But I knew already.'

'Sixth sense?' he asked, easing himself down beside her.

'No,' she said slowly. 'My Dad told me.'

'Your Dad?' Maxwell wasn't quite following this.

'I believe it's what they call in parapsychology a death visitant.'

Maxwell said nothing.

'It's the corny old line, isn't it?' she said, still staring at the darkening waters. 'I saw a ghost and sure enough, I learned later that at that very moment, my father died. Load of old bollocks, I always thought. Though, in my case, it's true.'

'Tell me,' he said.

'I wasn't feeling too good,' she said, focusing on events, trying to get them straight in her mind. 'It was a Sunday and we'd all been to a Valentine's bash the night before. I guess it was the same in your day, Mr Maxwell, at Cambridge?'

'No, no,' he assured her. 'We were all teetotal at Jesus in those days. Honey still for tea was about as exciting as it got.'

She managed a smile. Mad Max was good at that, coaxing happiness out of the sad, smiles from the tears. 'I was pretty hungover, lying on my bed when, quite suddenly, I felt cold. I thought at first it was just the morning after the night before. Somebody'd spiked the punch and I felt like shit as the day wore on. Then, there was Daddy. Just standing there, in that baggy old jumper I'd knitted for him in my gap year. I remember thinking – how did he get in? I hadn't heard the door go and he certainly hadn't knocked. I...' she struggled to get the memory straight. 'I remember saying to him, "What are you doing here, Dad?" Ever the original, that's me. "You're supposed to be going on holiday. Why...?" He just smiled and said, "Just checking, sweetheart. Just checking you're all right." Just like that. As if...'

The tears shook her body and she buried her face in her knees. Maxwell reached out and cradled her in his arms, holding her tight. He'd been here before, with sobbing girls whose lives lay in ruins. Girls whose boyfriends had left them; girls whose girlfriends had left them. Girls who had failed their exams; girls who were pregnant. Girls who were hopelessly hooked on drugs. The father in him always wanted to hold them, hug them, kiss away their tears, make everything all right. The teacher in him knew the risk he was taking – the professional suicide of the closed office or classroom door, the unpredictability of females scorned, the rampant prurience of the national press. It had never stopped him. It wouldn't stop him now. And besides, the relationship was different. Deena wasn't a student any more. She was a woman grown. And Jacquie would understand. He buried his face in her hair and kissed it gently.

'They never did get to go on holiday,' Deena

said, holding up her head, suddenly. 'My college mother got the details from the Dean who got it from the police. They'd been on the M25 on their way to Gatwick. An artic came off the slipway The car...' and she burst into uncontrollable sobs again, nuzzling against his cheek. When she lifted her face again, her soft mouth was slightly open and the tears ran silver alongside it. He smiled and wiped them away, but that wasn't enough. She kissed him, softly at first, like the frightened little girl she was, the little girl whose daddy had come to say goodbye. Then, it turned into something else. And she closed to him, swinging her knees sideways, so that she could hold him too and her tongue pressed against his lips.

'Deena,' he pulled away gently. 'Deena, it's all right.'

She pulled back too, head up, sniffing sharply, changing direction, putting her demons back in the box. 'So, yes, Mr Maxwell,' she said. 'I guess I'm too hard on people now. Instant rejection, sudden death – it'll do that to you. You know I was engaged?'

'You were?'

She nodded, finishing his tear-wiping job with the back of her hand. 'His name was Alex. He was nice, really. We might have made a go of it. But after Mum and Dad ... well, I just couldn't get it together any more. Perhaps one day...' and she smiled at him through her tears.

'Oh, yes,' he nodded, smiling broadly. 'You've a helluva lot to offer, Deena Harrison,' he told her. 'One day soon.'

She screwed up her face and shrugged. 'That's

why the Arquebus doesn't bother me.'

'The rehearsals?'

'No, the ghosts.'

'The ghosts?'

'Oh, I'm sorry,' She rummaged in her big knitted bag for a tissue. 'I think you either feel these things or you don't. The Arquebus is haunted all right. As soon as I went there, I knew. It starts with a sort of ... tingling ... hairs on the back of your neck sort of stuff. There's a particularly nasty cold spot at the back of the stage.'

'That's where Gordon Goodacre died,' Maxwell muttered, staring at her.

'Was it?' she asked. 'Well, I didn't join the theatre until a couple of days after that and nobody seems to want to talk about it.'

'Have you ... heard anything?' he asked. 'Seen anything?'

Deena was laughing now. 'Mr Maxwell,' she said. 'Don't be afraid of it. "There are more things in Heaven and Earth, Horatio, than are dreamed of in your philosophy." And I always thought *you* were only mad Nor' by Nor'West.'

'Very perceptive, my dear.' It was his turn to laugh now. 'We're not going to have a philosophical debate, are we? Sitting on a bloody uncomfortable heap of concrete between the Flyover and the river on a dark and dismal Leighford night?'

'Which would you rather?' she asked, her voice hard and tight suddenly. 'A philosophical debate or a fuck?'

'Er ... I think you should know, Miss Harrison,' he said softly, 'I am a partnered man. And I think

189

you'd be disappointed.'

Her face, cold and pale in the half shadows, softened into a smile. 'Just checking,' she said. 'Who's the lucky woman?'

'Jacquie Carpenter,' he told her. 'She's a Woman Policeman.'

'Good for you,' Deena said. 'When I was at Leighford, we all thought you and Sylvia Matthews were an item.'

Sylvia Matthews. One of those who had loved Maxwell when Maxwell had not yet rediscovered love.

'Others of us, of course,' she scrabbled to her feet, 'thought you gay as a wagon-load of monkeys.'

'Ah,' he stood up with her. 'I'm like Cleopatra,' he said. '"Custom cannot stale my infinite variety".' He stepped back to negotiate the slope and collect White Surrey And he felt her hand on his arm. Slowly, she reached up and kissed him, just a peck on the cheek.

'Thank you, Mad Max,' she said.

'Why, honey-chile,' he gave her his best Steppin' Fetchit from the black stereotype films of the Thirties. 'It ain't hardly nothing. Whatchu thankin' me for?'

'For being mad,' she said. 'We'll have that philosophical debate one day. Now I've got a bus to catch.' And she was running away from him, sod-off bag bouncing on her hip. 'And I'll be nice to the kids,' she promised to the Leighford night. 'And there *are* such things as ghosts. I'll prove it to you.'

DCI Hall had dragged his feet on this one. In the past, when he was a young DI in charge of his first case, he'd rushed to set up Incident Rooms, hold press conferences, engage Joe Public's help while at the same time reassuring himself that all was well and that Henry Hall was in his Heaven.

But press conferences could backfire, public support vanish like the sea mists that rolled in over Leighford's beaches at this time of year. It was a chill, grey Saturday morning as September was thinking of turning into October and, not for the first time, the late Mr Keats had got it wrong. The season wasn't very fruitful and it sure as hell wasn't mellow.

A barrage of microphones faced the DCI and Henry Hall had never felt so alone at one of these. The Baum Hotel had done the honours; tea, coffee and water was provided and the bar was open. There were even trays of vol-au-vents and bits of cheese and pineapple on sticks. For those of the paparazzi who led less frenetic lives than their colleagues or who took the gastronomic delights of their calling more seriously, luncheon was provided at one-thirty, as if the 'eon' referred to the quality of the meal, rather than the time it took to be served.

Henry Hall had held dozens, nay, scores of these. The reason he felt so alone was that the Chief Constable, no less, had leaked to an expectant and breathless media lobby the information about the divine help he had enlisted.

'*Guardian*, Mr Hall,' a Young Turk called. 'Could I just paraphrase the great Mr McEnroe and say "you cannot be serious"?' Guffaws all round and cameras flashed to catch the DCI's facial reaction to perfection. There was none, of course. It was as though someone had asked him to pass the salt.

'We intend to leave no stone unturned,' he told the *Guardian*'s man.

'I don't think platitudes will cut the mustard, Chief Inspector,' somebody else called. 'I've got a whole file of Constabulary clichés like that on my laptop already.' More laughter.

'Three people are dead,' Hall felt it necessary to remind the entourage. In the world of the cynic, reporters left everybody else for dead.

'Have you established a tangible link yet, Chief Inspector?' the *Telegraph* wanted to know.

'Other than all three of the deceased have links with the Arquebus Theatre, no.'

'Mr Hall.' It was Tom Lederer of the *Leighford Advertiser*. Rumour had it he'd been kicked off the *Sun* by Rupert Murdoch himself for being too nasty. 'Are you saying that there's something sinister about our local theatre? And if so, why haven't you closed it down?'

Hall waited until the chorus of assent died away. 'I have no reason to,' he said. 'We continue to believe at this stage that the only death at the theatre, that of Gordon Goodacre, was nothing more than a tragic accident...'

'Oh, come off it, Chief Inspector,' the *Mail* man broke in. 'We're not going to start trading the statistics of coincidence here, but what are the odds, for God's sake?'

'Can we cut to the chase, Chief Inspector?' the *Telegraph*'s representative chipped in. 'Who is this clairvoyant and what's his role, exactly?'

Again, the beleaguered policeman waited for the derision to die down. 'We are not talking about clairvoyance, ladies and gentlemen,' he said squarely, the lenses of his glasses reflecting their cameras. 'The West Sussex police service does not go in for Madame Zsa Zsa and a reading of tea leaves.'

Hoots of laughter. This was descending into a circus.

'You're going more for the runes, are you, Chief Inspector? Or a spot of spirit writing? The old planchette?'

Hall was on his feet. 'People,' he said calmly. 'Someone is out there who knows what happened to Martita Winchcombe and Daniel Bartlett. It may be someone who sat by you on the train this morning; someone you let past on the pedestrian crossing. Perhaps it's even someone you had breakfast with or are going to have lunch with. When you've let that sobering thought sink in a little, perhaps you'll all use your considerable talents to help me catch a killer. Good morning.'

He ignored the barrage of questions, the flashing lights, the stumbling over camera bags and sound booms, and marched swiftly into the Ballin's foyer. Jane Blaisedell was standing there with a gaunt-looking woman alongside her.

'And that, Detective Constable,' Hall said to her as he brushed past without breaking his stride, 'is how not to run a press conference. Mark it well.'

'Deena Harrison believes in ghosts,' Maxwell muttered.

'Ghosts?' Jacquie was handing him his elevenses – milky coffee and a four-finger KitKat, a dying breed specially flown in from KitKatland for the connoisseur.

'Spirits,' Maxwell sighed. 'Phantasms. Death visitants.'

'Well, you said she was a nutter.'

Maxwell looked at the other half of his soul over the top of the pince-nez he had taken to wearing for close work. 'I hope I didn't put it quite so bluntly, sunshine of my life.'

'No, indeed.' She humoured him. 'Your exact words were "Deena Harrison is as mad as a partridge." I don't remember that feathered link on my behavioural psychology course.'

He smiled at her. The steam from the coffee frosted his glasses and for a fleeting moment he looked like Henry Hall, Jacquie's once-and-future boss. He took them off, realising he could find his coffee without them after all. 'I didn't ask to share my life with a smartarse,' he said. Secretly, he was delighted. Jacquie was turning into him. Younger, certainly, far more attractive in a girly sort of way, but him nonetheless. Soon, they'd be calling her Mad Maxine down at the supermarket. Joy!

'What did she say?'

'Said her father came to visit her at university – on the day he was killed in a car crash.'

'Oh, Max.' She put her coffee down. 'Oh, my darling, I'm sorry.' She put her arms around his neck and looked deep into those sad, dark eyes. 'She didn't ... well, she didn't go into details, did she?' Jacquie knew what pain her man had gone through. She'd been no more than a baby at the

194

time, but ever since she'd known him, she knew that Maxwell had ghosts of his own. Sometimes, she'd seen them, the faded, grey photos in his wallet, carried near to his heart. She dared not hope to replace the beautiful, dark-haired woman in that photograph, but perhaps the life inside her might one day hold its place alongside the little girl with her mother.

'She wanted to talk,' he said. 'She needed to.'

'And you?' Jacquie put her face close to his. 'Did you need to listen?'

'Perhaps,' he said softly, kissing the tip of her nose. 'Perhaps I did.'

Chapter Thirteen

'What's she doing now?' Ashley Wilkes hissed to Jane Blaisedell at the back of the auditorium.

'Mr Wilkes!' she hissed back. 'If you persist in these interruptions, I shall have to ask you to leave.'

'This is a theatre, policewoman, not an extension of your bloody Incident Room.' Wilkes was a patient man. But his theatre had come into disrepute recently. He felt fingers pointed at him wherever he went over Gordon Goodacre and the whole place felt like an endless crime scene. It was like doing *An Inspector Calls* forever.

Jane had no time to take the awkward bastard out. 'Jane. Over here.' Magda Lupescu stood stock still centre stage right, looking up, her elegant hands posed theatrically on her pointed chin. Jane scowled at Wilkes and pounded off down the gentle, carpeted slope of the central aisle. She found herself climbing the steps and standing downstage of the strange woman.

'Something?' she asked.

Magda's eyes were closed, one foot pointing downward on tip-toe. 'How old was Gordon Goodacre?' she asked.

'Fifty-seven,' Jane told her. She'd gone over the man's life often enough in the last couple of weeks.

'He had a bad heart.'

'Did he?' Jane didn't remember that from the details of Astley's post-mortem and she didn't have her notes with her. Magda gasped, spinning fast on the flat heel, frowning into the shadows of the wings. 'He heard something. Over there.' She was striding across the stage now, her heels clacking on the boards. She stopped abruptly, shuddering. 'Here,' she said loudly. She looked up suddenly and followed something with her eyes. Jane looked up too, but there was nothing there. Nothing but lanterns and the tangled cables that always festooned theatre ceilings. Then, quieter, Magda said, 'He died here.'

Jane was nodding. 'That's right.' She hadn't seen the body *in situ*, but she'd studied the SOCO photographs and diagrams minutely.

Magda was looking backwards and forwards, then up into the tangle of cables and gantries and lights overhead again. 'He was afraid,' she said softly. 'When he died, Gordon Goodacre was afraid.'

'Of what?' Jane asked, eyes wide.

Magda seemed to come to, as though out of a trance. She smiled darkly at the raven-haired girl. 'Perhaps of that.' She pointed to the largest incarnation of Audrey II lying in sections behind the tabs, its tendrils stretched across the apron, where a grateful, exhausted David Balham had left it. 'After all, it eats people, doesn't it?'

From his skylight world, Peter Maxwell could see the lights twinkling out on the Shingle, the dark spur of land that jutted out to sea like the black carcass of some huge, stranded whale. He'd lost

197

track of time painting the tiny crimson vandyking around the sheepskin of Private Pennington's horse. His mind wandered at times like these, when he could switch off from the cares of the world. And when he switched off, the Great Man's thoughts turned, inevitably, to murder.

'Well, frankly, Count,' he muttered to the cat lolling on the upturned linen basket in the corner. 'I'd expected rather more. What do you think of Scenario One – the Jacob's Ladder theory?'

Metternich twitched his left ear and stared Maxwell down. He'd need more advance notice than this for God's sake. He had a whole night's hunting to plan. And then, there was the sortie into Mrs Troubridge's rubbish... Did this man have no sense of priorities at all?

'Gordon Goodacre is still a blank canvas.' His master was putting it all together, slumping down in his modelling chair again and tilting the gold-laced pill box over his eyes. He locked his fingers behind his head and swivelled. 'I don't even know yet what the man did for a living, still less for a dying. I think it's fair to say he didn't exactly wear the pants in the Goodacre family, however. I get the distinct impression that Matilda, his good lady, has that privilege and, indeed, distinc-tion. So what do we know?'

Clearly, the Count was from Barcelona. He knew nothing.

'Gordon was apparently alone in the theatre on the night in question and fell foul of a ladder. Did it fall or was it pushed? Catch!' He suddenly hurled a cushion at the cat, the one he used when his back had given up the ghost completely.

198

Metternich dodged aside and pirouetted off to a perch high up, where Maxwell's many battered suitcases lay in the semi-darkness of his attic.

'Exactly' Maxwell loved it when a plan came together. 'If you know something's coming at you, you get out of the way, don't you? Now, admittedly, at his advanced age, I think it's probably true to say that Gordon Goodacre didn't have your lightning reflexes – no, now don't be modest, Count; you know it's true. But that ladder is nearly twenty feet long – I know, I've seen it. Damn, I wish I'd listened in those Physics lessons all those years ago when I was doodling obscenities in my homework book. There must be a ratio for the length of time it takes a ladder to fall from the vertical to the horizontal, pinning an unsuspecting set painter beneath it. But,' he picked up his glass of Southern Comfort and pointed a finger at Metternich, 'there's no ratio known to man that explains how such a ladder can slip its chains without human agency at the very time that said set painter is passing under it. Who stood to gain?' He echoed the great Cicero again, in English this time for the benefit of the cat, who, let's face it, had little Latin and no Greek. 'Matilda Goodacre, if she cleans up financially. Or maybe she just hated the old man's guts. *Cherchez la femme*, Count? Can it be that simple?'

Maxwell was warming to his theme now, or was it the Southern Comfort kicking in? 'How long had they been married, I wonder? Twenty years? Thirty? More? Things irritate, don't they? The way he sucked his dentures, picked his feet, farted in the bath – all those little endearments which

199

wear thin as time itself wears on. Did she finally snap, old Matilda? Oh, of course, she could have gone for him with the bread knife, the poker, the wasp killer in the shed, but all that would have tied her in, wouldn't it? You know Henry Hall, Count – he'd have had her on Leighford's Death Row before you could say "Where are my bollocks?" – No, don't look for them now.'

But it was too late. The cat had jack-knifed, as felines do, and was munching the fur perilously close to where his testicles had once been housed.

'So she had to kill him away from *chez ons*. Even so, the Arquebus seems a little near to home, too, to be honest. Anyhoo,' he took a swig of the amber nectar before inspecting his paintwork's drying time, 'Scenario Two...'

'Max!' It was Jacquie calling from two floors below. 'Max, can you come down?'

In the lounge on the first floor, Jane Blaisedell stood with her back to where a blazing log fire would have been if 38 Columbine hadn't been built by a four-year-old chimpanzee with acne. She was clutching a large glass of Maxwell's Southern Comfort. A very large glass.

'I think you'd better hear this,' Jacquie said, passing him another, unaware that he already had one simmering upstairs.

He took it, winking at Jane. 'I'm not driving, Woman Policeman,' he said. 'To what do we owe the pleasure?'

The girl sat down on Maxwell's settee, Jacquie next to her for moral support. Maxwell took the chair opposite. Jane had always been, if truth were told, just a little in awe of Peter Maxwell.

200

People didn't call him Mad Max for nothing. And Jane always felt a bit like a little girl in her Headteacher's office when she saw him, for all the forthright spade-calling she tried to do.

'Look,' she said firmly, fortified by one giant slug for mankind. 'I know I shouldn't have come here, but I've seen things today… Jesus, Jacquie,' and she swigged again, her face contorting as the liquor hit her tonsils. 'The guv'nor's called in a psychic.'

Jacquie and Maxwell looked at each other. 'What?' She popped the question first, laughing.

'Her name is Magda Lupescu,' Jane said. And she wasn't laughing at all. 'I've seen her in action.'

Jacquie was frowning now, putting her Pellegrino on the hearth. 'I've known Henry Hall for the best part of ten years now,' she said, 'and never, in all that time…'

'It's not the DCI,' Jane said, staring at the carpet. 'It's from the top floor – the Chief Constable.'

'Waste of bloody space!' Jacquie growled.

'Tsk, tsk,' Maxwell shook his head. 'Such disloyalty' But then he didn't know David Slater at all. 'What have you seen, Jane?'

'What?' She blinked at him, her eyes flicking up to his face from the carpet.

'You said you'd seen things today,' Maxwell reminded her. 'What things?'

She looked steadily at him for a moment, then looked away, lip trembling, fumbling for the right words. 'We went to the theatre,' she said, 'to the Arquebus. She picked out the precise spot where Gordon Goodacre died – not just the stage, mind, but the *exact* place. As if it had been

201

marked with a cross.'

'She'd seen the crime scene photos.' Jacquie, ever the realist, offered a sensible solution.

'No.' Jane was adamant. 'No, she hadn't. That's just it. She refused to see them. Henry told me to give her every help, any paperwork she wanted. She took nothing. Didn't even open the file. Christ, Jacquie. She *knew*. And about Uncle Tony...'

'Who?' Maxwell asked. This wasn't a name he'd come across at the Arquebus. Uncle Vanya, yes; Uncle Tony, no.

'Nobody,' Jane said quickly. 'It's not important. Let's just say this woman's for real.'

'Where's she from?' Jacquie asked.

'London. Although she's living in Brighton at the minute. She's been involved with the Met before now. Half a dozen European forces. Apparently, they think highly of her at Quantico.'

'So who did it?' Maxwell asked. Quantico was just a place that was vaguely suspicious of the whackier exploits of Scully and Mulder; and where Clarice Starling ran through dark woods before chatting to Hannibal Lecter. None of it seemed very real, somehow.

'Hmm?' Jane was far away.

'Who killed Gordon Goodacre? That's the bottom line, isn't it? How she gets there is irrelevant. Except of course that none of it is acceptable in a court of law.'

'She ... she *became* Gordon,' Jane said, emptying her glass with a shudder.

'How do you mean?' Jacquie was lost.

Jane blurted it out as if she could only bear to

say it once. 'She stood on the spot where Good-acre died and she started talking in a man's voice. "Who's there?" she said. "What do you think you're playing at?" And her face ... oh, God,' and the girl ran her hands down her pale, sweating cheeks.

'What about it?' Jacquie's own voice was shaky now.

Jane half turned to her. 'It... I don't know. She ... she actually *looked* like Gordon Goodacre.'

Instinctively, Jacquie's hand snaked out, not to Jane, but to Maxwell. Fear was climbing her spine, spreading across her shoulders, tightening her jaw and making her skin crawl.

'You knew Gordon?' Maxwell asked Jane.

The policewoman shook her head. 'I've only seen the photos from the morgue,' she whispered. 'But that's how she looked. Shadows around her eyes, like ... just like a corpse. Christ, I think I'm going to throw up.'

'Jacquie,' Maxwell said softly. 'Some black coffee, darling, please. Jane, look at me.' He leaned forward and took both her clammy hands in his. 'Here. Up here.' And she tried to focus on him. 'Breathe in. That's it. Gently, now. And out. That's the way.'

Jacquie was in the kitchen, clattering the kettle, spooning the coffee. She'd seen shock before, they all had. And they all knew how to cope with it. But no one was better than Mad Max in mad moments like these.

'All right?' Maxwell slowly relaxed the pressure on the girl's hands and held her face in both his. 'Jane, are you all right?'

She nodded.

'How did you know this psychic sounded like Goodacre?' he asked.

'What?'

'You said she spoke in a man's voice. Was that Goodacre's voice? You'd never heard his voice, surely?'

'That's right,' she said. 'That's right. But the theatre manager, Ashley Wilkes, he was standing next to me. And he said "That's him, Jesus, that's him". Jack, I can't do this any more.'

Jacquie was back with the black coffee in record time and sat down next to her colleague, patting her arm and cradling her shoulder. 'Talk to Henry,' she advised. 'This is putting you under a lot of strain. You don't need this.'

'I don't understand it,' Jane said, the tears near now. 'That's the problem. I can take the corpses, the mutilations, the heartbreak of the bereaved. All that goes with the job, doesn't it? Like a bloody warrant card and a night stick and a cold cup of tea. But this ... I ... I just can't work out how she does it. And it scares me, Jacquie. Max. It scares me.'

Saturday night. And Henry Hall had nobody. He sat alone at his desk, the lamp illuminating the scattered papers in front of him and the light bouncing back from his glasses, as always. He whipped them off suddenly and rubbed his tired eyes. Day Twelve of a double – or was it a triple? – murder enquiry. And he knew all too well what they said. If you hadn't solved it by Day Four, perhaps you'd never solve it.

He looked up to see Tom O'Connell standing there. 'Detective Sergeant,' he said. 'I thought you'd gone home.'

'What, and miss out on all the overtime, guv?' The sandy-haired sergeant crashed into a chair. He went far enough back with Henry Hall to risk a line like that.

'Read the Lupescu report?' Hall asked him.

O'Connell nodded.

'And?'

'Well...' the detective sergeant was being just a little cagey.

'Come on, Tom.' Hall flicked his glasses back on. 'I've known you now, man and boy, for the best part of three years. That's forever in our business. No bullshit. What do you think?'

'I think it's bollocks, guv.'

'Well,' Hall sighed. 'Thank you for your candour, at least.'

'I mean, what's it all about? Some nutter with a ouija board goes down to the theatre and starts talking in tongues. Do you reckon Jane's all right, guv?'

'I'm sure it's a perfectly accurate reflection of what happened,' Hall said. 'Why?'

'Have you seen Jane? Since this morning, I mean?'

'No.' Hall frowned, sensing an undercurrent here. 'No, she emailed this to me.' He lifted a four-page dossier from his desk. 'Is there something I should know?'

'Well, I saw her at the station late this afternoon,' O'Connell told him. 'White as a bloody sheet. Looked to me like...'

'What is it, Tom?' Hall leaned back, giving the man time, giving him space.

'Guv, I don't want to land the kid in it.'

The DCI shrugged. 'This is between you and me, Tom,' he said, indicating the empty room. 'Nobody else here.'

'Well, I'd say she'd had a few. Her voice was shaky and just a tad slurred.'

'What time did you say this was?'

'Five-ish, half past, maybe.'

Hall checked the report again. 'And she'd gone to the theatre with Magda Lupescu this morning. Did she say where she'd been in the meantime?'

'Working on the report, I guess, guv. But she wasn't working here or I'd have seen her. I've been on the Winchcombe woman's last known movements for most of the day'

Hall nodded. 'Did she say where she was going?' he asked. 'Home, I hope.'

'No, guv,' O'Connell said seriously. 'She said she was going to see Jacquie Carpenter.'

'Did she now?' Hall's face hadn't changed at all.

O'Connell nodded. 'And doesn't that mean Peter Maxwell?'

It was Hall's turn to nod. It *always* meant Peter Maxwell. Every time he turned his back.

She wandered down a narrow corridor. It was dark and the only light came from its end. Everything seemed far away. As though, at one moment, she might reach out and hold the light in the palm of her hand. Then, it was gone again. Not one light, but many. Not many, but the same one. Repeated and repeated, again and again. And the noise. She hadn't noticed the noise before. It was a gentle sound, caressing like the lapping of water. And the smell came again as it always did, a rising tide of nausea that filled her throat and coated her parched lips. And the solitude. That was the all-defining emotion at times like these. The feeling of being totally, unutterably alone.

'Mr Maxwell?' The woman was old enough to be Florence Nightingale. 'Do you intend to be present at the birth?'

'Yes, Middie Prentice, I do.'

The woman frowned. Her lips pursed like an old pea pod. 'Why are you calling me that?'

'I'm sorry,' Maxwell shrugged. 'It's just that it says Prentice here on your desk. I naturally assumed...'

'Not that,' she interrupted him. 'That ... what is it, Middie thing?'

'Oh, it's Puritan-speak,' Maxwell beamed. 'In the seventeenth century Mrs was Goodwife, or Goodey for short. You're a Midwife, so Middie for short. No offence, I hope. Just my idea of levity, to lighten the moment.'

'You'll have to forgive him, Mrs Prentice.' Jacquie thought it was time to step in, for all their sakes. 'He's a historian.'

'Is he?' The midwife looked the man up and down as if the term had more in keeping with paedophilia. 'Well, I'm afraid we don't do the hot water and towels thing any more. And positively *no* cigars in the theatre. You'll have to gown up, of course.'

207

'Of course,' Maxwell nodded solemnly. 'Will my old Jesus one do? I mean, I can get it dry cleaned, if you like.'

Jacquie flipped her handbag strap quickly so that it stung his hand under the midwife's desk.

'Have you had any home visits yet?' the woman asked.

'No,' Jacquie said, smiling serenely in an effort to counter the idiocy of the father of her unborn child. 'One was due in August, but there was a kerfuffle. You said you'd rearrange.'

'Yes, of course we will.' Mrs Prentice scanned her ledger. 'It says here you are a teacher, Mr Maxwell?'

'Does it?' He craned round to read the line.

'So, if somebody called, say on Wednesday, you'd be at school, would you?'

'I think you can take that as a racing certainty,' Maxwell said.

'Good.' The midwife slammed the book shut. 'Wednesday it is, then.'

Chapter Fourteen

'What do you make of it all, Patrick?' Peter Maxwell was getting outside a large Southern Comfort. It was Patrick Collinson's shout. And they were in the Vine again. The place was a bit like the Trenches really. You hated it, but you just couldn't help going back.

'My dear boy, I am at a loss. Gordon was such a lovely man.'

'So I believe,' Maxwell nodded, feeling the amber nectar coat his tonsils. 'Did *nobody* have a bad word to say for him?'

'Well,' Collinson shrugged. 'I suppose the thing is none of us knew him very well. He was always Matilda's other half, as it were. It sounds rather cruel, but Matilda's other quarter would have been more accurate. You know the sun fish, Max?'

The Head of Sixth Form was pretty sure it used to be on the menu at Leighford High before the world turned Green and they'd banned chips and chocolate, along with Southern Comfort, the staples of society. 'Not intimately,' he admitted.

'The female sun fish is huge, omniscient and omnipotent, not unlike our Matilda. The male is tiny, insignificant. It attaches itself to the female during mating and there it stays, anchored until it shrivels and dies. Isn't that ghastly?'

'It brings tears to the eyes, certainly,' Maxwell nodded.

'And it's not an *exactly* apposite analogy. Not really. Bit unkind to poor old Gordon, who I'm sure had his moments. May I ask why the particular interest, Max?'

'Some people say I am morbidly curious, Patrick,' Maxwell confided in a low, conspiratorial voice. 'Others,' and he was thinking of Henry Hall and his boys in blue, 'think I'm a pain in the arse. The bottom line?' He tossed a peanut skyward and caught it expertly in his teeth. He was as gobsmacked as Collinson that he could do that, but he didn't let it show. 'The bottom line is that while rehearsals for the *Little Shop of Horrors* are running at the Arquebus, I am sort of *in loco parentis* for the horrors from Leighford High. And people are dying around them, Patrick. The parental backlash hasn't started yet, but it will. What can you tell me about Martita Winchcombe?'

'Ah,' Collinson beamed. 'Much maligned was old Martita. Oh, potty as a shepherd's pie, of course, but I'd grown quite fond of her over the years.'

'You'd known her long?'

'Oh, let's see.' Collinson was wrestling mentally with the maths of it all. 'Must be nearly twenty years. I got involved with the Arquebus when it was that ghastly Methodist chapel place on Godolphin Street.'

'I remember,' Maxwell smiled. 'I saw *Sweeney Todd* there.'

'Did you?' Collinson enthused. 'That was my first production; as secretary, I mean. That awful old humbug Edward Royce was in the lead, wasn't he? Claimed he knew Olivier. I mean, please.'

'And Martita was already there then?' Maxwell wanted to keep his man in the nearly here and now. People were dying – and not like Edward Royce used to, centre stage, every night.

'She was. Very much the heart of the place, in fact. She really had her finger on the financial pulse in those days. More recently, of course ... well, it was rather emeritus, to be honest. Nobody had the heart to kick the old girl out. Although I believe Dan Bartlett wanted to.'

'Did he now?' Maxwell asked, cradling his drink in both hands in their corner of the snug. 'What makes you say that?' There was a roar from the pin-ball machine in the far corner. Clearly, Tommy was in again.

'Max,' Collinson smiled benignly. 'How often did you meet Dan?'

'I don't know,' Maxwell shrugged. 'A couple of times, I suppose. Why?'

'What impression did you form?'

'Er ... well, that's a little difficult. He was a bit ... arrogant, I suppose.'

Collinson snorted into his Scotch. 'Well, that's the understatement of the decade. How many people do you think we meet in our lifetimes, Max? Thousands, surely.'

'Yes, I suppose so,' the Head of Sixth Form agreed.

'Well, in all those thousands, I don't think I've ever met anyone quite so detested as Dan Bartlett. You're not a fan of *Murder She Wrote*, are you? Dear old Angela Lansbury as Jessica

Fletcher from Cabot Cove?'

'Ah, daytime television.' Maxwell glazed over in a perfect Homer Simpson, drool forming on his open lips. 'Sadly, in a busy world...' He shook himself free of it.

'Oh, quite, quite.' Collinson understood. 'The point is that every week, Jessica meets an absolute stinker who is so repellent that *everybody* wants to kill him – or her. One of these days, it'll be Jessica herself.'

'So, such a one was Daniel Bartlett?' Maxwell asked.

'I'm afraid so.'

'Any particular motive?' Maxwell chased it.

Collinson sighed. 'Does that still count?' he asked.

'MMO,' Maxwell flicked three fingers in the air. 'The Holy Trinity of violent death – motive, means, opportunity. Yep, it still counts.'

'It's just that these days people are killed for looking funny at other people, aren't they? Trainers, mobile phones, Koranic differences. It's all gone rather pear-shaped, don't you think?'

'If the world was a pear tree, that wouldn't matter, would it?' Maxwell smiled. And Collinson gave him an old-fashioned look. There was no doubt about it – Peter Maxwell didn't get out enough.

'Let me understand this, Max.' Bernard Ryan may have been the First Deputy at Leighford High School, but he'd also been Maxwell's whipping boy cum sparring partner for more years than either of them cared to remember. Time was

212

when Ryan had been earmarked for promotion – von Ryan's Express as the ever-filmic Maxwell put it – but then reality had dawned and it became obvious he was always going to be third spear-bearer. He invariably lost his clashes with Maxwell and took his punishment like a man. 'You want to go to the funeral of someone you never met, just to pay your respects.'

'It's a vital PR exercise, Bernard.' Maxwell perched on the Deputy's desk, swinging his off-the-ground left foot to some irritating tune he couldn't get out of his head.

'Come again?' Dierdre Lessing was Bernard Ryan's hatchet woman. The scary thing was that when Legs Diamond was away, these two were directly responsible for the education of nearly eleven hundred children. Pray God their parents never found out.

Maxwell had been holding his mirrored shield in front of him to face Dierdre for years. The serpents writhed around her head and her terrible eyes glowered at him. He was patience itself. 'PR,' he said, slowly. 'Public relations – and not, as you might think from my legendary Politics Enrichment lessons of last year, Proportional Representation.'

'You've lost me, Max,' Dierdre snapped, irritated by the man beyond measure. What was new?

'I know,' Maxwell beamed. Dierdre Lessing had been a handsome woman once, but years of bitterness had etched themselves into her pores, carving furrows over her glacier face, contrasting oddly with the serpents that coiled from her hair. 'One more time, then,' he said to them both, as though Seven Eff Three didn't quite get that bit about Existentialism. 'Leighford High School – the institution to which you and I, colleagues both, are shackled for life – is putting on a musical extravaganza called *Little Shop of Horrors*. We are using the services of a local theatre, the Arquebus...'

'Max!' Dierdre snapped, the snakes twisting and hissing at him.

'I'll cut to the chase,' the Movie Man said. 'This afternoon, at half past one, they're burying Gordon Goodacre, who worked as a volunteer at said theatre. Since I am consulting director in the absence of Angela Carmichael, I thought it would be a nice gesture if I attended his passing.'

'What are you really after, you ghoul?' Dierdre wanted to know.

Even Bernard was taken aback. 'Dierdre, I don't think...'

'Perhaps it's time you did, Bernard,' she hissed, along with her snakes.

He ignored her. 'What'll you be missing, Max?'

He smiled broadly at the Senior Mistress.' Why, Dierdre, of course.' And he kissed the air alongside her. 'Thirteen Bee.' His smile vanished. 'No cover required.' And he'd reached the door. 'I was merely being civil, Senior Managers,' he scowled. 'Next time, it's a bad back and no more Mr Nice Guy.'

'What are we going to do about him?' Dierdre wanted to know.

'You were a *little* harsh, Dierdre,' Bernard chided her.

'Men!' she growled and stormed out of the

214

room, fire and brimstone scorching the wood-work.

It always rains, doesn't it, at the best funerals? Maxwell approved. Matilda Goodacre, with the unmistakable panache of a born actress, had pulled out all the stops. Two glossy black horses, their manes and tails hogged and flowing, stood steaming in the grey drizzle from the west. Their heavy, long-haired hooves clattered and splashed down the slope that led to St Wilfred's. And tall men in top hats lifted the gilded coffin that bore the mortal remains of Gordon Goodacre from the glass-sided hearse and into the tiny porch of the oldest church in Leighford. All that was missing from the black, Victorian magnificence of the occasion was the forest of ostrich feathers that once crowned the hearse, the stallions and the hats of all the mourners. The RSPB had galvanised themselves into action and ostrich was something it was rumoured they put into upmarket burgers in supermarkets in the Nineties but the feathers, you just couldn't get. It was the way of the world – Maxwell, like everyone else, had to accept it.

Leighford had moved. Just as Old Sarum, the accursed hill of the Saxons, had become Norman Salisbury, so the centre of gravity had slipped from the little river that leapt and sparkled through the heather and the dunes to the sea. It spread and sprawled, from its fishing village and its Domesday Mill, to its Sea Front, its Candy Floss and its Kiss Me Quick hats. No Regency opulence for Leighford, no namby-pamby Jane

Austen wandering the Shingle in search of inspiration. Just the spur of the Southern Railway Company slicing through the landscape as the Victorians discovered a new word – Tourism. And townies came from miles away to gawp at the sea and paddle in it, trousers rolled up daringly and hankies tied to their heads. They took strolls along the Promenade, had their photos taken by dodgy men in straw boaters and buried their children, temporarily of course, in the sand.

Only St Wilfred's stayed where it was – the little chantry chapel of the medieval monks had grown as far as it was going to by the end of the fifteenth century, and now it would accept the soul of Gordon Alan Goodacre.

Peter Maxwell did his best to blend with the crowd of mourners. Few of them, perhaps, had known Gordon. But all of them knew Matilda, serene and stately as a galleon. Some he recognised from the Arquebus – Ashley Wilkes in a long, dark coat, his face pale, his mood quiet. Patrick Collinson, fussy, crimson-faced, ever-solicitous, checking that all was well and everyone knew what to do. Maxwell vaguely recognised others, one or two minor celebs from the world of yesterday's telly; that bloke who played the serial killer in one of the *Taggarts;* the woman-who-looked-as-though-she-might in *Flambards;* Bev from the car ads. One by one, they kissed Matilda Goodacre, held her, whispered all the empty words of condolence that well-meaning people do at moments like that.

They sang the hymns, heard the poetry delivered in a stentorian tour de force by a luvvie

Maxwell couldn't quite place. The vicar, bloody nice fella, shook their hands solemnly at the graveside as the descendants of Hamlet's people lowered Gordon Goodacre to the flowers.

'Ashes to ashes...' came and went on the wind that suddenly whipped from the north. Fallacy had never been more pathetic than this. A clap of thunder and a jagged lightning fork would round it all off nicely, but it never came. Just Mad Max standing by the horses, stroking the soft, warm muzzle as the bits jingled and the hoofs stamped. For the most fleeting of moments, he was waiting in the Valley of Death for Louis Nolan to arrive with his fated order.

'Mrs Goodacre,' he extended a hand as the widow passed him with her entourage. 'Please accept my condolences.'

'Mr ... Maxwell.' She took it. 'It's good of you to come.'

'I ... er ... I'm afraid I had something of an ulterior motive,' he said, gazing into the steady, cold grey of the woman's eyes, shrouded under the monstrous sweep of her hat.

'Really?'

'May I call on you, perhaps in a day or two?'

'Of course,' she said. 'But what...'

'In a day or two,' he smiled. 'Thank you.'

And they swept by him, to the waiting cars and the baked meats and all the tragicomic reminiscences that mark the passing of a life.

Henry Hall hadn't gone to Gordon Goodacre's funeral. He was in two minds about releasing the body for burial at all. Something didn't sit right

217

about this man's death; all his experience told him so. But Jim Astley was adamant. There was no evidence of foul play. The forensics pointed to one of those futile accidents that occasionally make Christians doubt the existence of God and atheists talk of the lottery of life and statistics. So, he'd relented and Matilda Goodacre had her day in widow's weeds, centre stage where she loved to be.

The groundlings stood before the DCI now, in the neon-lit Incident Room he'd been forced to set up in Tottingleigh, west of the Arquebus and a little south of the Flyover.

'Where are we on Dan Bartlett?' Hall wanted to know.

'Well, he wasn't as well off as we thought he was, guv.' Gavin Henslow was the one with A-level Maths; he always got the financial aspects of a killing.

'Go on.' Hall settled back in the uncomfortable chrome chair with his coffee cup crumpled in its plastic nastiness beside him.

'Ask yourself,' Henslow rather enjoyed the limelight, even among this most critical of audiences, his own oppos, 'why a bloke whose family is supposed to have owned half of Sussex is living in a poxy little bungalow.'

'Wasn't *that* poxy,' Bill Robbins felt he had to counter. 'Damn sight bigger than mine.'

There were heartfelt grunts all round.

'Alimony.' Jane Blaisedell provided the woman's touch.

Henslow clicked his fingers. 'What she said,' he nodded. 'If you ask me, Mrs Bartlett was bleeding him dry.'

218

'We *are* asking you, Gavin,' Hall said, straight-faced as only he could be. 'I don't want assumptions, lad.'

'No, sir.' Henslow might have got A-level Maths, and a degree in Social Sciences, but he wasn't a total ignoramus. He recognized a knuckle-rap when he felt it. 'These are the figures according to the dead man's bank account. But he may have had offshore.'

'*May* have had?' Hall queried.

'His High Street bank said they couldn't shed any light, guv.' Henslow realised now how empty that sounded. When he'd been face to face with the pretty Polish teller, commiserating with her lot in life, that sort of stonewalling seemed entirely reasonable; now, he wasn't so sure.

'Midland?' Hall wanted to know.

Henslow nodded.

'Tomorrow morning, Gavin, you will go back to the premises of the Midland HSBC in the company of DS Walters here. And he will stand over you, or hold your hand, whatever it takes – until we have those offshore details. Are we at one on this, Gavin?'

'Yes, sir. Of course.'

'Good. Anything on forensic follow-up, Giles?' Hall scanned the tired faces in front of him.

'No prints in Bartlett's house have produced anything meaningful, guv. Nothing on central computer. Ditto in Brighton and Hove records.'

'We do have a possible sighting, guv.' Tom O'Connell was pounding his cigarette butt into submission in an ashtray by his PC.

'When was this?' Hall was all ears.

219

'On the night in question. A girl, well, woman, I guess. Mid- to late twenties.'

'Whose sighting?'

'Neighbour.' O'Connell was tapping keys, flicking images across his screen. 'A Mrs Wilkins. Lives at number 86, diagonally opposite the Bartlett house, but some way away.'

'What did she see?'

'Bartlett arrived home at some time in the evening. Mrs Wilkins wasn't certain of the time. He had this woman with him.'

'What did Bartlett drive?'

'Toyota,' Dave Walters chimed in. 'Soft top.'

'So,' Hall crossed to the street plan in the corner, on the third of the hastily erected whiteboards. 'Where's this Mrs Wilkins live?' He was tracing the area with his biro tip.

'There, guv.' O'Connell talked him through it. 'No, south. That's it.'

'Did Mrs Wilkins say which direction Bartlett drove in from?'

'West, guv,' O'Connell was sure. 'Leighford.'

'Could be the theatre.' Jane Blaisedell, like everybody else there, was going through the route in her mind.

'Could be,' Hall nodded, scanning the options in front of him. 'There again, it could be any of the discos in the High Street or the pubs west of the river. Bartlett goes cruising – we know from his wife he had a penchant for that – and picks somebody up. They go back to his place. Night-cap. Whatever.'

'And he's made a bad choice.' Henslow was with him. 'Gets a psycho, a night stalker.'

'Or somebody who just wouldn't play along.' Jane was there with the woman's angle again.

'Did you get the impression,' Hall asked her, 'from Mrs Bartlett that her husband was into anything odd? Kinky?'

'She was a bit coy about that,' Jane told him. 'Said it was all a long time ago. They had been separated for some time.'

'Eight years,' Hall put something finite into it. Cross tees and dot eyes and you catch murderers. 'What's wrong with the night stalker scenario, Gavin?'

The DCI had sauntered back to his chair. The DC had the spotlight again and he wasn't sure he liked it any more. It made him feel vulnerable, alone. 'Umm...?'

'Anybody?' Hall switched the spotlight off and Henslow breathed again.

'MO.' O'Connell was already reaching for another ciggie.

'How?' Hall chased him.

'If he picked up a casual for a one-night stand and suggested something she didn't want to play or maybe refused to pay her, she'd ... what? Grab the poker, a bottle, some *objet d'art.*'

'Precisely,' Hall said, glad his team were still thinking, wrestling with it. 'The frayed flex is pre-meditated, remember. It was the work of some-body who knew the layout of Dan Bartlett's house. Knew the wiring. Knew his habits, too. His bath time. Now who would fit that description, hmm?'

Hall said nothing else. But he saw it all. For Gavin Henslow to fall short was one thing. He

221

was new, green, over-ambitious. The rest of his team were experienced detectives; and they were missing things, perhaps vital, perhaps not, but missing them nonetheless. And that Henry Hall didn't like.

'Let me put one over-riding question to you all,' he said. 'What made Dan Bartlett get out of his bath and walk, wet and semi-naked, along the corridor? If we can get a handle on that, we might just have our killer.'

Chapter Fifteen

'Pizza, mate?'

'Hawaiian, easy on the pineapple, anchovies and olives?' The man with the wiry hair peered round the door at him.

'No,' the delivery man frowned, looking instinctively down at the box in his hand although he knew perfectly well what was in it.

'Just checking,' Maxwell smiled and passed him the cash. 'Keep the change ... Ralph.' He was reading the name on the van.

'No, mate.' The delivery man felt he had to put his deranged customer right. 'Ralph was four managing directors ago. I'm Liam.'

'Of course you are,' Maxwell winked, wondering anew why a beautiful Celtic name was always given to idiots, the rather large Mr Neeson excepted, of course. 'Thanks again.'

He turned with a dexterity surprising in a man of his years and took the stairs of 38 Columbine two at a time, hurtling through the lounge and into the kitchen, careful to keep his box level.

'So, Signorina,' he lapsed into his Italian waiter routine with an almost legendary smoothness. 'Pizza Napolitana – without the odd bits they put on a *real* Neapolitan pizza – we bigga Italian boys, we knowa what you Englisha girlsa like.'

'Wine?' Jacquie held up the bottle, an amusing little Chianti from the south side of Tesco's.

Maxwell obliged of course with a high-pitched nasal intonation that had the Count flexing his claws in the lounge next door. It was trite, it was corny, but it was all part of Mad Max and his lady and neither of them would change it for the world.

She poured for them both as Maxwell unpacked and bisected the pizza with an expert hand, only a few mushrooms going wild. 'Oops,' he apologised. 'Just dropped yours.'

She raised her glass while he threw the salad together, having inadvertently watched a Jamie Oliver programme once. *And* he did it fully clothed. 'Here's to Sonny Jim,' she smiled.

'Sonny Jim,' he clinked his glass with hers. 'May all his bills be little ones.'

'Amen to that,' she said. 'I heard from Jane today.'

'Oh?' He sniffed the dressing and thought better of it. 'How is she?'

'Still scared shitless, by the sound of it. It's too bad of Henry to pass the buck to her like that. She's not up to it.'

'She always struck me as being quite resilient,' he said, burning his tongue on a piece of salami.

'Oh, sure,' Jacquie agreed. 'On the outside. In the Incident Room, brief and debrief, she'll be as cool as a cucumber. Inside, she's falling apart.'

'Tell me about psychics, then.'

Jacquie took a large gulp of her Pellegrino; the Chianti was for Maxwell. 'I thought we'd had this conversation.'

'That was for Jane's benefit,' he said. 'There comes a time when the bullshit has to stop.'

'Well, talking of bullshit, the idea comes from America, of course – psychics helping police, I mean. According to Jane, it's all the Chief Constable's idea – that dickhead Slater – he must have been on a course. Who knows, he might come out with something *really* cutting edge like fingerprints next.'

'Ah.' Maxwell wagged a wedge of Napolitana at his love. 'But as Leviticus tells us, "Do not turn to mediums or spiritists, do not seek them out to be defiled by them. I am the Lord thy God."'

Jacquie smiled benignly at him. 'I don't doubt that for a moment, my darling,' she said. 'Anyway, how do you know all this stuff?'

'Leviticus?' he sighed. 'Well, let's see. When I was a lad they hadn't invented computers or skateboards. I had yet to discover the dizzying world of women and drink. So I hunkered down with the Good Book. Actually, it wasn't all that good – I guessed who'd done it by Deuteronomy.'

'May you be struck down, Peter Maxwell.' She tutted around a particularly obstinate piece of lettuce.

'More importantly, *anima divina mea,*' he stabbed a particularly recalcitrant bit of salami, 'who is next to be struck down at the Arquebus?'

'You'll have to ask this Magda Lupescu,' Jacquie suggested.

'The wolf,' he mused, half to himself.

'Sorry?'

'Lupescu in Wallachian – er, Romanian – means wolf.'

'God, Max, are we into vampire country now? This is all getting a bit weird.'

'Wolfcoats.' Maxwell leaned back, masticating. 'The undead wandering graveyards wreathed in mist. Ms Lupescu comes from the most vampire-haunted country in the world. But I'd be even more worried if she came from California. The West Coast has more Goth and Visigoth weirdos per square inch than you've had takeaway pizzas. They make dear old Vlad the Impaler look like a choirboy. But, stick to the point, Woman Policeman, and tell me about psychics,' he repeated. 'Allowing for the Chief Constable and his course.'

'Well,' Jacquie leaned back on Maxwell's woodwork. It had to be said, her bump was causing her more than a little gyp today and judging by his wrestling skills, Sonny Jim didn't appreciate Napolitana and Pellegrino. Maxwell had already predicted that his offspring was more of a steak and kidney pie man, if indeed he was to be of the masculine persuasion. 'Usually, of course, psychics are brought in by the back door by some desperate, hick sheriff in the Boondocks whose case is going nowhere.'

'And that's not true of this one?'

'Max,' she pointed to the slowly gyrating Sonny Jim. 'It may have escaped your notice, but I'm not actually down the nick at the moment. I've no idea how far Henry's got.'

'No, no.' Maxwell cradled his glass in both hands. 'But you've worked on dozens of cases with the man. You know how his mind works. How's he going to use the Madame Arcati of Sighisoara?'

'That depends on what kind of psychic she is,' Jacquie explained. 'Some use physical objects, from the crime scene. Er ... the paintbrush that

226

Gordon Goodacre was using, the blanket wrapped around Martita Winchcombe, Dan Bartlett's towel. Mind you, that buggers up crime scenes pretty comprehensively and the whole chain of custody thing becomes a complication.'

'How?'

Jacquie never knew when Maxwell was being patronising. Was he putting her through her paces to make her feel useful, she whose brain was already addled with domestic boredom? Or was he thick as a parrot?

'Chummy kills Martita Winchcombe,' she patronised right back at him, using his own Fifties police jargon too. 'Person unknown, motive un-known. He – or she – covers her body in a blanket – reason unknown. Whose dabs are on the blan-ket?'

'Miss Winchcombe's, if Chummy wore gloves.'

'And if Chummy didn't?' It was like drawing teeth.

'Chummy's too.' Maxwell was coming along like a copper.

'SOCO will handle it with every non-con-taminant known to man, so will the lab. If we give it to Magda Lupescu, that's another set of gloves, dabs. At very least, it'll cause confusion in court. Chummy's brief will get him off on a careless tech-nicality. Anyway, that's not Lupescu's method.'

'Jane said she just walked about, didn't she?'

Jacquie shrugged. 'Seemed to,' she said. 'But Jane's really frightened, Max. She obviously thinks the woman has genuine powers.'

'Uncle Tony,' Maxwell remembered.

'Yes.' Jacquie risked leaning forward and incurring the wrath of her little bundle. 'Whatever that's all about. Of course, it's important to the investigation that she believes.'

'Is it?' Maxwell was on a learning curve, a rare experience for him.

'Anybody who's anti – any copper, I mean – shouldn't work with them. I imagine that's why Henry didn't get involved directly. Their negativity can block the psychic's energy. Allegedly.'

'Yes, indeed,' Maxwell smiled, 'but aren't they supposed to get results? That Peter Hurkos bloke back in the Fifties was pretty impressive, if memory serves.'

'Psychics? Yes. But since my own profession's clear-up rate is only running at twenty-three per cent at the moment, I'm not sure league tables should be the name of the game.'

'Wash your mouth out,' he growled, wide-eyed with mock fury as he topped up her glass with fizzy water and his with still wine. 'I don't want to hear the LT. phrase mentioned again in this house. Savvy?'

She chinked her glass against his. 'What'll you do when Sonny Jim's taking his GCSEs?' she asked. 'What'll you do about LTs then?'

'I shall be dead,' he laughed.

Very quickly, Jacquie's face darkened. And she started to cry. Out of a blue, cloudless sky. Maxwell scurried around the table to hold her, cradle her head, kiss the tears away.

'Hey,' he whispered, lifting her tear-streaked face. 'You know I've got a picture of myself in the attic,' he said. 'Along with the lads of the Light Brigade. And haven't we always promised ourselves, when the time comes, that we'll drive to Brighton and beyond and go off Beachy Head together, hand in hand?'

She nodded, sniffing, trying to smile through the tears. 'Don't say that again, Max,' she pleaded. 'Promise me. Promise me you'll never say that again.'

He didn't have to ask her which phrase she meant and he promised her.

Jane Blaisedell was on the phone to Jacquie Carpenter for nearly an hour the next day. It was her lunch break and she was psyching herself up for what was to come. And what was to come was night and Magda Lupescu.

'Tell me.' The Romanian woman stood just inside a dead woman's front door. At her request, no one turned on the lights.

'About Martita Winchcombe?' Jane was at her elbow, watching, waiting, her heart thumping under her ribcage. Jane had Martita's house-keys in her hand and had turned the heavy lock in its rattling hole. Ahead lay the hall, lit only by the fitful moon from the skylight over the door, and the deadly stairs rising to the left.

'No, no,' Magda said quickly. 'The boys who found her.'

'Er ... well, they're fourteen-year-olds, go to the local comprehensive school. They were out to burgle.' Jane was more rattled than ever now. What did this mad bitch want to know about the boys for? How relevant could those little bastards be? Unless ... but that didn't bear thinking about.

'They didn't come in the way we did.' Magda

229

jerked her head behind her to the heavy, Victorian front door.

'No. From the kitchen. Straight ahead.' Jane could have kicked herself. She was doing what fairground fortune tellers relied on, giving too much information. Well, in for a penny...

'They've both coughed.'

'Coughed?' Magda frowned.

'Confessed,' Jane clarified. 'Told us everything.'

'Their names?'

'Is this relevant?' the detective asked, snapping at last. 'I mean, we have rules in this country about minors.'

'It is relevant,' Magda assured her. She had that annoying habit of Eastern Europeans on unfamiliar ground; she didn't smile. Jane found herself wondering anew about Henry Hall's antecedents; was the bland bastard from Romania too?

'Er ... Anthony Wetta and George Lemon.'

'Wetta is the thief,' Magda said, 'the professional. This Lemon, he is the ... fall-guy, hm? Went along for the ride?'

Her English was clearly learned from some mid-Western university Stateside.

'Probably,' Jane nodded. 'That would be my reading of it.'

'There.' The Romanian pointed to the base of the stairs. 'That is where she died. Her neck was broken.'

'That's right.' It was happening again. Jane had seen the SOCO photographs, the sprawled corpse wrapped in a blanket, the weird angle of the head. Jane had seen these. Magda had not.

The psychic crossed to the stairs and knelt on one knee, tracing the ghastly swirl of the hall carpet with her fingers. 'Pain,' she frowned, her face a living mask in the half light of the stair windows. 'She felt pain here.' She was running a hand around her throat. 'And another...' She slid upright, using the banister as a counterweight and almost slithered up the stairs, gripping the smooth, worn wood as she went. 'Another, here. Her ankle. She tripped...' She was on the third stair from the top now, looking up into the total blackness of the landing.

'Don't you want some light?' Jane asked. She'd had enough of the darkness, fear lying like a cold mask over her face and creeping down her neck onto her shoulders.

'Not yet,' Magda said. She knelt down on both knees on the top stair, head bowed, back straight, hands extended and touching the wall on her left, the banister on her right. 'She's cold. It's night. "What do you want?"'

Jane Blaisedell froze, the hairs on her arms and neck standing upright. Two days ago, she'd heard the woman barking in a man's voice. A voice that ended in a scream. Now she was quavering like an old woman, the voice this time high and brittle. "What are you doing in my house? You've no right to be here. No right. I've told you. You're wasting your time."'

It was a bleary-eyed Peter Maxwell who cautiously opened the door. Minutes ago, he'd been asleep. Then he'd heard the doorbell, shattering his dreams, insistently forcing him to the here and now. It was gone midnight, the witching hour when demons stalked the earth in the shape of black and white cats. And his eyes hadn't quite acclimatised to recognise the shape beyond the glass of his front door. It was Jane Blaisedell and she was crying.

'Oh, Max!' She threw herself into his arms. 'Max! For God's sake...'

He caught her with a dexterity born of a lifetime of coping with fainting girls and boys and he bundled her inside. 'It's all right,' he said, patting her head and bearing the weight of her quivering body as he half-carried her up his stairs, trying to find a way of doing it without grabbing her breasts. After all, he *was* a public schoolboy.

Jacquie was at the top of the stairs, struggling into her house coat and doing the soft-shoe shuffle in her mules. 'Jane.' She reached out and together they helped the girl to the settee.

'The dead,' Jane was whispering, clinging to them both as though she daren't let go. 'The dead are all around us. Did you know that, Jacquie? Max; Max, you're the cleverest man I know – did you know that? Magda sees them. All the time. Gordon Goodacre with his skull stoved in. Martita Winchcombe with her neck snapped and her spinal cord severed. She can *see* them, like I can see you. Oh, Jesus!' and the girl fell sobbing into Jacquie's comforting arms.

'Brandy, Max.' The policewoman in Jacquie Carpenter took over now. Last time, it was Maxwell who did the honours, said the right things, calmed the girl down. Now, it was her turn. 'And ring Jane's mum and dad, can you? Their

232

number's in my phone book. She's out of it now.'

'Jacquie!' Henry Hall got up at the woman's entrance. A lesser man would have beamed to see his favourite DS back for a visit, kissed her even, hugged her with the pleasure of just saying 'Hello'. Henry Hall just got up. 'I thought I'd have heard more of a welcome outside.' He nodded to the ante-room where his team were up to their eyes in depositions, leads and cross-references, heads down, foci engaged.

'I didn't come that way, guv,' she said quietly. 'I nipped in by the back door. This isn't exactly a social call – I just wanted a word.'

'Have a seat.' He slid the hard, upright chair out for her. 'Can I get you a coffee? Is there a problem?'

Henry Hall and Jacquie Carpenter went back a decade. They'd faced death together – murder up close and personal. You develop a bond in those circumstances like no other.

'It's Jane,' Jacquie said, looking her boss straight in the glasses. 'Jane Blaisedell.'

'I thought it might be.' Hall leaned back.

'I know I'm out of this,' Jacquie said. 'And it's none of my business.' She'd been wrestling with this all night. Jane had sipped her brandy, blurted out the whole story and gone home with her mum and dad, something she hadn't done for years, and they'd put her to bed. Like she was a little girl again, hoping that Uncle Tony wasn't going to call.

'Jane's been sucked in, hasn't she?' Hall asked. 'And she's in over her head.'

233

'A psychic, guv? What's it all about?'

Hall shrugged. 'Just one initiative too many,' he said. 'An experiment on somebody's record sheet, a tick-box ticked.'

'That's fine for somebody,' Jacquie said. 'What about Jane?'

Henry Hall looked at the woman. She'd grown a few yards since they'd seen her off with jibes interlaced with their blessings. Their Jacquie was going to have a baby. The Maternity Unit would call it a senile pregnancy; after all, Jacquie Carpenter was thirty-four. Now, she was back. And she'd changed. Perhaps it was that new life inside her, the new responsibility. It was the she-wolf defending her cub.

'What about Jane?' Hall clasped his fingers together in front of him and looked steadily at his DS. 'How is it with her?'

'You've put her with this nutter,' Jacquie almost shouted. She suddenly saw Henry Hall as outsiders saw him, cold, aloof, using people to get results. And she didn't like what she saw.

'Psychic consultant,' Hall corrected her.

'The devil,' she growled, 'is in the detail. The woman goes into trances, speaks in tongues. Even her face changes to look like the corpse she's investigating.'

'Jane told you this?'

'She's *seen* it, guv, heard it. She was there, for Christ's sake.'

'And she doesn't want to be there,' Hall nodded. 'What do you think?'

He leaned back again, assessing the situation. 'Did she send you, Jacquie?'

'No, of course not.' It was Jacquie's turn to lean back, easing off, echoing her boss's posture. She'd come on too strong, behaved like a bull in a china shop. 'I came on her behalf, guv. She can't handle it.'

'Can you?'

'What?'

'Can you do what Jane can't? Stand in dead men's shoes?'

Jacquie blinked, licked her lips. This had thrown her. She'd expected blandness, political correctness. Possibly, if she rattled his cage enough, fireworks. What she hadn't expected was a job.

'I'm on Maternity leave, guv.'

'"Five o'clock,"' Hall seemed to be remembering something. '"Fed the chickens and ploughed the Lower Meadow. Eight o'clock was delivered of my fifth child."'

'I'm sorry?' Had the guv'nor flipped too? The whole place had become a madhouse since Jacquie had gone on leave.

'Your Peter Maxwell would recognise that,' he said. 'I don't know why it stays in my mind. It's from the diary of a pioneer woman in Oklahoma in the 1880s.'

'Well, with respect, Chief Inspector,' Jacquie was even beginning to sound like Peter Maxwell, 'I am not a pioneer woman.' She struggled to her feet. 'I just hope you can live with yourself,' she said, pale-faced and iron-jawed. She saw herself out.

'That'll be a no, then,' Henry Hall murmured.

There was water dripping from an oar, the blade dipping through reeds that rustled and whispered as the dawn came creeping over the misty meadow. He lay cold and dead in the boat, his hand trailing in the black of the water. She knelt over him. And she cried.
  Her love, her life, had gone.

Chapter Sixteen

'You know Ellen Terry once played the Arquebus?' Matilda Goodacre asked, tracing her fingers over the sepia photograph of the great actress. 'Of course, it was a real theatre then, where the Nat West stands today.'

'Yes.' In telling Peter Maxwell all this, she was probably talking to the wrong person. 'She was Ophelia to Irving's Hamlet. They were on a tour of the south coast. Nice to think dear old Leighford was at the cutting edge of culture in those days.'

'It still is, Mr Maxwell.' Matilda Goodacre seemed to grow three or four inches whenever she climbed on her high horse. 'You know Anthony Minghella saw my Eleanor of Aquitaine last year?'

'Really?' Maxwell raised an impressed eyebrow. 'That must have been a privilege for him. For you both.'

'Tell me,' she swept imperiously across her lounge. 'You said you wanted to talk to me – I take it that it was not about the theatre.'

'Just about the Arquebus Theatre,' he said, accepting her offer of a chair. Matilda's home was rambling, a little down-at-heel perhaps, along Mock Tudor row as Maxwell called it, just south of the Pitch and Putt and within a golf-ball thwack of the Boating Lake.

She fixed him with the look of Eleanor, of Blanche du Bois, of St Joan. 'You have something of a reputation as a sleuth, Mr Maxwell,' she said.

'I dabble.' He was suitably humble, buried in opulent chintz as he was.

'How does that work, exactly?' she asked.

He shrugged. 'It just does,' he told her. 'I ask questions. And like the old, not very savoury joke, I get some rebuffs. I also get some answers.'

'But how do the police react to all this?'

'Badly,' he confessed. 'Oh, it's fine in fiction, isn't it? Dotty old Jane Marple is related to the copper in charge of the case. Impossibly irritating Hercule Poirot is a buddy of Chief Inspector Japp. Poor old Gregson/Jones/Lestrade, whichever tec Conan Doyle was using, go cap in hand to see the Monstrous Ego of Baker Street. But in practice ... well, I think our boys in blue are wonderful – and most of them would like to give me a good smacking.'

'And you believe my Gordon's death was not an accident.'

'Martita Winchcombe didn't think so,' he told her.

Matilda sat upright, blinking behind her chained spectacles. 'Martita Winchcombe talked to you about this?'

'Briefly,' Maxwell nodded. 'Before the tide of modern living tore us apart.'

'What did she mean?' Matilda asked.

'Murder, Mrs Goodacre,' he said.

She whipped off her glasses, letting them dangle, and turned dramatically to the window. 'Do you know how that makes me feel?' she said.

'I can't imagine,' he said. 'I'd be furious.'

'Furious?' She turned to face him.

'If my nearest and dearest died in suspicious circumstances, I'd move heaven and earth to find the person responsible.'

'And I suppose *you* are heaven and earth?' she asked, straight-faced.

'Mrs Goodacre.' He rose and stood beside her. 'I've just told you – I don't know how I get involved in these things, but I do. Three people linked to the Arquebus have died suspiciously in as many weeks.'

'The coroner's verdict was that Gordon's death was misadventure – an accident.'

'Coroners have been wrong before,' Maxwell told her. 'Their job is to speculate on evidence placed before them. If the evidence isn't there...'

'Then the police must investigate.'

It was Maxwell's turn to spin away. He could match Matilda Goodacre move for move and he crossed to the window. The lawns fell away to a neat hedge and beyond that the chiselled gardens of the West Ground, laid out in the Hungry Thirties to provide work for the unemployed, hope for the hopeless. Beyond that was the sea, endless and with no horizon. 'Do you know Henry Hall?'

'The chief inspector? Yes, I've met him.'

'So have I. He's a good copper. By the book. Honest, bright, efficient. But he doesn't have a nose for these things. He'll go by the coroner's verdict. There'll be stones left unturned.'

'Whereas those stones will be turned by you?'

'I know where to find them,' Maxwell said.

239

'I don't understand.'

'How long had you and your husband been married, Mrs Goodacre?'

Time for another theatrical move, regal, imperious, St Joan condemned at Rouen, Eleanor leaving Chinon for the last time. Years of playing deranged French women had given Matilda Goodacre a legendary quality, an aura of the untouchable. 'Thirty-three years,' she told him. She picked up a photograph of the dead man, the only one in the room that wasn't of her. 'I shall miss him.'

'That's a thirty-three-year advantage you have over me, Mrs Goodacre. I never knew your husband. An awful lot of stones gather over thirty-three years.'

She looked at Gordon again, smiling at her from the silver confines of the frame. Then she looked at Peter Maxwell. 'I understand from the children working at the Arquebus that they call you Mad Max. Is that right?'

'Among other things,' he smiled. 'In the Seventies, I was the Blue Max, courtesy of George Peppard in the film of the same name; in the Eighties Max Headroom. Mercifully, dear old Mel Gibson came to my rescue, roaring through some ghastly Australian Future Neverland, or I might be called Pepsi by now.'

'All right,' she smiled. 'Mad Max. What do you need to know?'

'Everything,' he said. 'Everything you can tell me about the man who was Gordon Goodacre.'

'Gordon Goodacre.' Graham Larter kicked his

swivel chair across the flotex to reach a filing cabinet. 'Yes. Yes. Tragic.'

Peter Maxwell had skived off his last two lessons at the great centre of excellence that was Leighford High. He had no lessons and the looming nearness of the Oxbridge UCAS entry deadline could loom for a day or two yet. Thingee One, the switchboard operator newly promoted to doing the day's cover, had tried to pass him one of the ominous green sheets that meant that Maxwell had to babysit a Chemistry lesson. He would normally have just raised an eyebrow and consigned the sheet to the bin, but Thingee was new in post and the job carried more opprobrium than that dished out to traffic wardens and Conservative MEPs, so he had the courtesy to give her an explanation of why he couldn't do it. He could have told her he'd rather die than enter a Science lab. He had a *degree* for God's sake, in History! He had allergies to the smell of Something or Other Phosphate and he'd come out in hives. His sciatica wouldn't stand the backless torture of the lab stools. And the vertigo! Dear God!

As it was, he just said, 'Thingee, darling. Find somebody else, there's a good girl.' And he threw the sheet into the bin. Game, set and mismatch.

So here he was, still cycle-clipped from his hurtle across town that Wednesday afternoon, sitting in the MD's office at Ampleforth Components. The MD looked about six, longing for the day when his acne would leave him and he could have his first shave. But he had a plastic name on his desk and an air of being in control. For the moment, Maxwell would go with that.

'What exactly is your interest, Mr Maxwell?' he asked, lifting out a manila folder with a dead man's name on it.

'I am here on behalf of Mrs Goodacre,' Maxwell told him.

'Ah, yes.' Larter was the soul of concern. 'How is she? I wasn't able to attend the funeral, I'm afraid.'

'She's suspicious,' Maxwell told him.

'Sorry?'

'Not happy with the coroner's verdict. Asked me to step in.' Technically, this was Maxwell's script, not Matilda's, but would a six-year-old Managing Director of a company that made components be aware of that?

'So you're a private detective?'

'Such a dramatic term, don't you think?' Maxwell smiled. 'Smacks of Philip Marlow, Sam Spade, guys in trench coats with broads and attitudes.' He'd lapsed into his best Bogart.

Larter looked oddly at him. Yep, he was six. Nope, he wasn't aware that Maxwell was running the show. 'This,' he held up the file, 'is, of course, confidential.'

'Of course,' Maxwell nodded. 'Do you know Henry Hall?'

'Who?'

'Local DCI based at Leighford nick. He's about to re-open enquiries.'

'Is he?' Larter asked. 'Into what?'

'The murder of Gordon Goodacre.'

'Murder?' Larter blinked.

'Oh, damn,' Maxwell clicked his tongue. 'There

I go again. Sorry. Death. Death of Gordon Goodacre.'

'How do you know?' The six-year-old suddenly looked four in the grey afternoon light.

Maxwell drew back, crossing one cycle-clipped leg over the other. 'How do I know the police are about to launch a new inquiry, Mr Larter?' he said. 'That's an irrelevance, really, isn't it? What do you actually make here at Ampleforth Components?'

'Components,' the MD told him, increasingly nonplussed by this interview.

'And you have a fine reputation in the area.'

'Well, we like to think...'

Maxwell held up his hand. 'Now, now, Mr Larter. This is no time for false modesty. The name of Ampleforth Components is known the length of the south coast. Didn't I hear dear old Declan Whatsisface give you a plug on *Breakfast* last week?'

'Did you?' Larter was astounded. 'I didn't know...' His PR people were letting him down big-time.

Maxwell waved him aside. 'And then this nasty business with Gordon. Well, it's a shame.' And he stood up. 'Give my regards to Henry,' and he flipped his shapeless tweed cap onto his head and turned for the door. 'When he arrives.'

'Wait,' Larter shouted, on his feet too. 'Wait.' Calmer now, trying to smile. 'Isn't there some way out of this? I mean, can't we keep the lid on things?'

Maxwell sighed, frowning, thinking it over. 'I don't really see how,' he said. 'I mean, they'll

243

want access to all your records. Personnel, audit, tax, sales. They're quite clinical, those forensic accountants. Still, it's in a good cause.'

'No, no.' Larter was fumbling at the door as Maxwell opened it. 'Look, er ... what do you need?'

'Me?' Maxwell asked, bewildered. 'I'm sorry, Mr Larter, I got the distinct impression that you couldn't help me.'

'No, no.' The MD's smile was as broad as it was brittle. He suddenly looked like Tony Blair on Election Night, a rabbit in the headlights of a fading majority. 'All I meant was, this dossier on Gordon ... well, it's confidential to the firm. Delicate. I can't just give it out to... Can you divert the police? I mean, is there a way...? Perhaps a word from you?'

Graham Larter knew when he was beaten. He hadn't been MD long and had only got the job because it was his daddy's firm anyway. And daddy would be furious if he thought great hairy coppers with their size elevens were trampling all over his creation. And against Maxwell? Well, AVCE Business meets History Honours, 1st Class, Cantab. Done and done. 'What do you need?' he asked.

'That folder.' Maxwell pointed to it lying on Larter's desk. 'For five minutes.'

'All right,' Deena Harrison shouted through the darkened auditorium. 'Take five, everybody.'

It wasn't going badly tonight. Alan Eldridge had almost got Seymour's words right and Andy Grant, the dangerous dentist, was warming to the essential psychopathy of his part. The Tendrils crashed into varying positions of gratitude around the auditorium. Their ra-ra skirts, black lacquer wigs and Fifties platform shoes were all in place by now and were combining to kill them.

'Miss Harrison.' Ashley Wilkes padded down the auditorium steps to where the director was lighting up. 'You *are* aware of the No Smoking nature of the theatrical tradition?'

Deena flicked off the lighter. 'God,' she sighed. 'Mr Wilkes, I am *so* sorry. It's been a long haul.'

He smiled. 'OK.'

'Oh, Ashley.' She followed him into the darkness. 'You don't mind if I call you Ashley?'

'No, of course not.'

'Could I have a word?' And some of the cast couldn't help but notice that she had a gentle hand on his shoulder.

Would you Adam and Eve it? White Surrey had a puncture. *And* it was pissing down with rain. But Peter Maxwell had once been a Boy Scout, with an armful of badges for proficiency in everything from Woodcraft to tying a knot in his granny. So such reversals held no terrors for him. Had he got a puncture kit? No, of course not. He just belted Surrey a few times *à la* John Cleese in *Fawlty Towers* and pushed the battered old thing along the edge of the Dam, squeaking and rattling as they went, and out towards the Flyover. He would have been late anyway, because all evening, over a particularly challenging baguette of gargantuan proportions, he and Jacquie had been wrestling with the quickly photocopied con-

245

tents of the late Gordon Goodacre's dossier. The boy MD had winced as he'd watched him do it, smarming around his Girl Friday, but the whole thing was – literally – out of his hands now.

Gordon himself had been Personnel Manager at Ampleforth Components for nearly sixteen years. In that time, he'd hired and fired his share of people, from shop floor machine operators to Board Room execs. Maxwell focused on the fired, that list of the damned whose faces hadn't fitted, whose time-keeping was suspect, whose hands were in the till. Any one of them could have hated Gordon Goodacre. Peter Maxwell had never known the pain, the despair, the hopelessness of redundancy, the curt order to clear your desk, the ignominy of being escorted off the premises. But in the real world beyond the halcyon existence that was teaching, such things happened. And sometimes, people didn't get mad; they got even.

'My money's on this one,' Maxwell had said, as another spring onion shard got right up his nose. 'Martin Lincoln.'

'What about him?' Jacquie had hoped their conversation would drown out the gurglings from her stomach, Sonny Jim on the rampage again.

'Lost his job at Ampleforth's two months ago. Something dodgy in accounts. I'd chanced my arm getting Goodacre's file from Larter. I thought asking for somebody else's was pushing it a bit.'

'You should send that lad of yours,' Jacquie had suggested. 'Whatsisface? Anthony Wetta. See if he can break in and burgle it for you.' She had stolidly attacked her prawn mayo wrap.

'Do I detect a note of disapproval in your usually dulcet and supportive voice, Woman Policeman?' Maxwell had asked.

'This is very naughty of you, Max,' she had scolded him. 'You had no right to see this file. You bullied the man into it.'

'Careful, Woman Policeman,' the Head of Sixth Form had warned. 'Your training's showing. To me, the rules don't apply.'

She had blown a raspberry at him. 'So what'll you do with the information, now you've got it?'

Maxwell had scanned the notes he had made. 'Find this Martin Lincoln,' he had said. 'See where he was on the Night in Question.'

'Max.' Jacquie had become serious about then. 'You know all this is flying in the face of reason, don't you?'

'Maybe,' Maxwell had nodded, looking laughingly into the steady grey eyes of the girl. 'But at least it's flying.'

'Hello?' He rattled the theatre's side door along Bakewell Street, where it turned its sharp angle to curve towards the river. The rain had stopped now, but Surrey was wet and heavy as Maxwell leant the clapped-out creature against his bum. 'Bugger!' he muttered as he realised he'd missed the whole shooting match. All was locked and barred and no one was tying a dark red love knot into her long, dark hair. He hoisted Surrey to the upright and trudged off into the darkness. Squeak. Rattle.

They lay in the back of his Mondeo, blowing

cigarette smoke to the roof.

'Isn't this where I come out with another cliché?' Deena Harrison asked. 'Asking how it was for you?'

Ashley Wilkes laughed. 'And if this was television, you'd get up with an entire sheet wrapped around you as if I'd never seen your body before.'

She ran a hand down between them, cradling his manhood and smiling. 'Not bad,' she mused.

'I beg your pardon?'

'For a man of your age, I mean.' And they both burst out laughing.

'I'd better get you home,' he said.

'I'd rather go to yours.' She began moving her hand backwards and forwards, stroking his stiffness again.

'Uh-uh.' He removed her fingers reluctantly. 'Not tonight.'

'Mrs Wilkes?' She looked up into his face.

'Mrs. Wilkes departed the scene a long time ago,' he told her. 'By mutual consent. Exit stage right. She was only ever a bit player. What about you? Anybody in your life?'

Deena's face darkened, even in that darkened back seat with its steamed-up windows. 'Not any more,' she said solemnly.

'Well, it happens.' Wilkes reached across to stub his cigarette out.

'Suicide? Yes, I suppose it does.'

'Suicide?' Wilkes repeated.

'It's nothing...' and she extinguished her cigarette too.

'No.' He stopped her, cradling her left breast as she lay there. 'No, it's not nothing. Tell me.'

'It was – like you – a long time ago.'

He laughed softly. 'Deena. How old are you?'

'I'm twenty-two,' she told him.

'So,' Wilkes nodded. 'How can anything be a long time ago? Tell me – please.'

She shrugged, snuggling down into his embrace. 'I knew a boy at Oxford. His name was Alex. He was tall, dark and handsome. There we go with those clichés again. A little vulnerable, perhaps. A little … other-worldly, really. He came from the country, from the south-west. His wild, singing county, he called it. He wrote folk songs. A bit retro, really – sort of John Denver meets Neil Young. Something of an ingénu, I guess. Well … I fell for him big-time.'

'He was reading Drama?'

'No,' she smiled fondly. 'No. Alex wasn't an extrovert. He'd never actually perform the songs he wrote. He was reading Chemistry. We loved each other. Oh, we had such plans. You know how it is.'

Ashley Wilkes couldn't remember when he'd had plans of the kind Deena Harrison was talking about. Had he been that blind, once? That young? That hopeful?

'But Alex had his problems,' Deena sighed, nuzzling into Wilkes' naked shoulder. 'I didn't see it at first; couldn't see it. He found people difficult. He hated college. There's no privacy, of course. Endless hall dinners and coffee at so-n-so's. I was into the party scene. We Thesps, you know?'

This time Wilkes did know. He hadn't been sober for six years between his undergraduate days and landing the Arquebus job. He knew all about that.

'Alex got worse,' Deena remembered. 'He'd dipped out of parties, was too busy to go punting. Just stayed in his rooms, twanging the guitar. Eventually, he started missing lectures. Couldn't handle the pressure.'

'It must be a hothouse at Oxford,' Wilkes commiserated. 'There were moments at Manchester... What happened?'

The girl was gripping his arm until her knuckles were white. 'In the end, he started avoiding me. I felt crushed. Left out. All at once, I was just "people" as he called all his old friends. We'd talked marriage, kids, the whole nine yards. One day...' her voice trailed away.

Wilkes lifted her face. It was sweet and smooth and soft and streaked with tears.

'One day,' she struggled on, 'I found him in his rooms at Balliol. He'd ... taken an overdose. I thought he was asleep at first. He was lying on his bed, his face turned to the window, staring at the sky. The window was open. I remember hearing the birds singing. I just ... just sat on the bed. Our bed. I sat and held him. They say I was still talking to him hours later when they found us both.'

'You poor darling.' Wilkes kissed her forehead, his own problems forced into perspective by the dazed, broken girl in his arms. 'How can you get over a thing like that?'

And she nuzzled under his chin. 'I'll let you know,' she said.

Chapter Seventeen

'I have to say, Mrs Elliot, you were a little difficult to trace.' Henry Hall was standing in her hotel lounge as the morning sun lit it, throwing strange September shadows across the magazine racks and the tourist posters that offered so much from sunny Leighford.

'Was I?' The woman looked a little more relaxed than when she and Henry Hall had parted last, looking down at an old woman, dead on a mortuary slab. 'In what way?'

'In the way that we didn't know where you were,' Hall felt obliged to explain.

'I didn't care for my first hotel,' she explained. 'Too many draughts. And the room service was abysmal. No wonder people go abroad these days. Well, now you've found me – what progress on the murder of my aunt?'

'Were you in regular touch?' Hall asked, watching an old boy wandering through in search of his morning paper.

'Aunt Martita and I?' Fiona sat back in the snug fit of the Lloyd Loom. 'Not until very recently.'

'How recently?' Hall asked. 'I have your address here as West Bromwich.'

'Since last week,' she told him.

Hall blinked, but behind those bland glasses' lenses, who could tell? 'But your aunt died two weeks ago.'

Fiona Elliot closed to the detective. 'She has been in touch from the Other Side.'

'The other side?' Hall echoed.

'The Other Side,' she confirmed.

'I'm afraid you'll have to explain that one, Mrs Elliot.'

'My husband and I have been members of the Christian Spiritual Church for several years.'

'I see,' Hall said. 'And your aunt has been in touch...'

'I wouldn't expect you to understand,' she snapped. 'Well, we're used to it, God knows. The arrogance of little men, with their rationalism and logic, their earth-bound science. How often have you heard some over-qualified, over-paid idiot on the television say that there can be no life on other planets because those planets do not contain carbon? And, of course, all life contains carbon. Bunkum and hogwash! I have *seen* dead men walk, Chief Inspector. That's why I wanted to see my aunt.'

'I don't follow.'

'Her neck was broken,' Fiona Elliot explained, 'but her legs were intact. She was able to come across.'

'Across?'

'From the Other Side.' The woman was incredulous. 'How can you be so blinkered? The newspapers said you were using a psychic on this case. I can't tell you how overjoyed I was to hear you say that. Sense at last. I thought you'd go down in history as an enlightened liberal, with an open mind and deep respect for the spirit world. Instead, I find you're a myopic idiot, with all the

252

prejudices of your calling.'

'My mind is as open as anybody's, madam,' Hall told her. 'I'll try any avenue to catch a murderer. Right now, I'm concentrating on the here and now. This Side, so to speak.'

'Very well,' she sighed.

'Other than ... very recently ... when were you in touch with your aunt last?'

'Oh, let me see.' The woman stared out across the Sea Front and the gardens where the grey sea rolled high and menacing beyond the peeling paint of the hotel's portico. 'Two, two and a half years ago.'

'You say she lived alone?'

'Yes. She had some sort of companion, an older woman, a few years back. I understand there was some sort of falling out and the woman left.'

'Was she, from what you know, self-sufficient?' he asked. 'I mean, did she have a cleaner, shopper, any help from the neighbours?'

'I believe she coped by herself, by and large,' Fiona said. 'Like all us Winchcombes, Martita was a stalwart. Came from a long line of copers. My great-great-great grandmother was with her husband through the siege of Lucknow, you know.'

Hall didn't know, but he wasn't sure it had much bearing on his case.

'One or two of the theatre crowd used to help her occasionally,' Fiona said. 'You know, shopping on line, that sort of thing.'

'Anyone in particular?'

'You'd have to ask them,' Fiona said. 'But I understand that Daniel Bartlett was one such.'

'Daniel Bartlett is dead,' Hall told her.

'I have read the papers, Chief Inspector,' she assured him. 'What are you telling me? That someone killed my aunt and then killed Mr Bartlett because he was kind to her? That would seem to be taking spite to extremes.'

Hall's eyes narrowed. 'Is that what we're looking for, Mrs Elliot?' he asked. 'Someone with spite in them?'

'After tomorrow night,' she said, leaning back and folding her arms over her ample bosom, 'I shall be able to tell you who you are looking for. You can judge their spite for yourself.'

'Tomorrow night?' Hall repeated. 'I don't understand.'

'Clearly.' She pursed her lips. 'Tomorrow night, we are holding a séance. Aunt Martita will tell us what you want to know.'

He was only a blur at first, bits of leaf and twig flying in the air. And Maxwell heard him rather than saw him. One of those tractor jobbies that the Council use for their playing fields was rattling its way across the turf of the Francis Chichester Centre, ripping shit out of a hedge.

In a gentler age, Maxwell told himself, there'd be an old hedger standing there in the mad, unstable changeability of the weather, a little nut-brown man with hands and face of leather, leaning for a moment as he sharpened his hook and caught his breath. He'd toil all day under an English heaven, in his gaiters and waistcoat, wiping the sweat from his forehead with a navvy's scarf and laying the most immaculate hedge, weaving the saplings into a pattern that would last for years.

Now, the tractor with its murderous blade fitment was hacking branch and root and stem, great filches of ground bouncing and flying as it took the crest of the hill. Maxwell stood like an ox in the furrow and waved him down. The driver considered evasive action, but thought better of it and switched his engine off, hauling on the brake and tilting up his visor

'Mr Lincoln?' Maxwell called. The man didn't *look* like an ex-rail splitter with Marfan's syndrome, but you couldn't have everything.

The tractor driver wrenched the earmuffs off and sat in his saddle, glaring down at this interruption.

'Mr Lincoln?' Maxwell asked again.

'I'm Martin Lincoln,' he nodded. 'Who are you?'

'Peter Maxwell.' The Head of Sixth Form held out his hand. 'Wrongful Dismissal Claims.' He'd been careful to leave his scarf and cycle clips at home.

'What?'

'Sorry.' Maxwell rummaged in his jacket pocket and produced his Teachers' Countdown card. 'Social Services. Legal Department. We're investigating cases of wrongful dismissal.'

'I've never heard of that,' Lincoln told him.

'Well,' Maxwell closed to him, popping the card away quickly. 'Strictly between you and me, it's a bit of a sop.'

'Is it?'

It was difficult to gauge Martin Lincoln's age in the earmuffs and the County overalls and the grime of oil hanging round him like a shroud.

Maxwell moved closer still, braving the heat of the machine's engine and the overwhelming smell of diesel. 'One of the criticisms of the government just prior to the last election. It's all about targets, isn't it? We're having to move fast, fulfilling a few manifesto promises, if you catch my drift.'

'Drift caught,' Lincoln said, wiping his forehead with a grubby towel on the tractor's controls. 'Why are you talking to me?'

'Well, our records show that you recently lost your job with Ampleforth Components?' Maxwell pretended a certain vagueness. He'd met jobsworths before. They were about as interested in details as in flying to the moon.

'That's right,' the tractor man nodded. 'Two months ago, now.'

'Can I be absolutely frank?' Maxwell asked. He risked the old joke in reply, but all he got was a nod. Disappointing, really. 'We have reason to believe that a Mr ... Gordon Goodacre...' he was carefully reading his shopping list from his other pocket, 'may have been, shall we say, a little overzealous in his hiring and firing.'

'Gordon?' Lincoln blinked. 'Never. Er ... you know he's dead, don't you?'

'Dead?' Maxwell decided to play a hunch.

'About two weeks ago now. Tragic accident at the local theatre.'

'No! What happened?'

'Seems a ladder fell on him. There's a certain irony there, of course.'

'Is there?'

'Well, Gordon was personnel manager.

256

Sedentary occupation if ever there was one. And he's killed by a ladder. Here I am, accountant of sorts and I'm doing one of the most dangerous jobs known to man.'

'Accountancy?' Maxwell was surprisingly good at playing the idiot. It must be the people he worked with.

'Tractor driving!' Lincoln realised he had a bright one here. 'Do you know how often these things turn over?'

'Just once, I guess,' he said, but Lincoln wasn't in a responsive mood. 'But to get back to Gordon Goodacre.'

'*Nice* bloke,' Lincoln concluded.

'Even though he fired you?'

'Look, Mr ... er ... Maxwell. I know you've got a job to do and so on, but really, this is a no-no. All right, so Gordon called it wrong. He thought my bookkeeping was less than immaculate. I disagreed. But I didn't bear him any ill will or anything. To be honest, Ampleforth's and I had reached about the end of our run anyway. No, I'm freelancing now, building up my own client base. Oh, it'll take time, of course. Hence this bit of groundsmanship. It's marvellous, really. I just went down the Job Centre, filled in a few forms, did a few circuits on this thing and here I am. It's quite therapeutic. I recommend it. You ever leave the rat race of the fake claims world,' he slapped the tractor, 'this is the life. I've never felt so well.'

'So ... you didn't bear Mr Goodacre a grudge, then?'

'Good Lord, no. Matter of fact, I had a drink with him, only a couple of days before the poor bloke bought it.'

'You did?'

'Yes, at the Sword and Buckler. Mind you,' Lincoln frowned at the memory of it. 'I must say he didn't seem himself that night. Not himself at all.'

'So who did he seem, Count?' Maxwell's hands were clasped behind his back as he lolled back in his modelling chair. 'Well may you ask.'

The great black and white beast appeared to be dozing in his time-honoured place on top of the basket in Maxwell's inner sanctum under the eaves at 38 Columbine, his War Office. He *appeared* to be but, actually, one eye was open. It was a subterfuge many an ex-rodent had fallen for.

'It seems that our Gordon was quietly petrified in his own suburban little way. Ever seen *Night of the Demon*, Count? It's occasionally on TCM, quite late, but I appreciate you're often out on your rounds by then, so you may have missed it. Poor old Dana Andrews, of all people, is the recipient of a curse, a mere slip of paper that prophesies that the demon of the title is on its way to get him. It's based on a short story by that creepy old bugger late of my own university, MR James. From what Martin Lincoln told me, Goodacre was afraid of something in the theatre. Or perhaps the theatre itself.'

Maxwell let his chair rock forward and uncoupled his hands to pour himself another Southern Comfort. 'What do you think of all this, Count? The supernatural, I mean. Things

258

that go bump in the night. Happens to you all the time, I suppose.'

The cat flicked an ear. The only things that went bump in his night were the mice he flicked across the kitchen floor in what would prove to be their last ever game of footie.

'There are some people,' Maxwell said, 'who believe that evil can lurk in a building. That something happened in a place, so appalling that it's somehow imprinted in the very stones, the very fabric of the building itself. Let's see, the Arquebus has been on that site for ... what ... a dozen years or so. Before that, warehouses. Derelict. Abandoned. Great happy hunting ground for you, I shouldn't wonder, as a kitten on the quays.' He glanced at the cat. 'No, you can't use that one, it's copyright P. Maxwell. Eat your heart out. It was like that for ever, if I remember rightly. Let's see.' He lolled back again, talking to the cat and the air and watching the dark clouds scudding across the moon through his skylight. 'I came to Leighford in '75. Maggie Thatcher became the new leader of the Tories that year, ousting the best band leader of our times, Edward Heath. King Faisal was killed by his mad nephew and the then unknown Jack Nicholson made *One Flew Over the Cuckoo's Nest*. And what, I wonder, was happening – or had happened – at the warehouses along the Leigh? What do you think, Count, a local history project for Year Eight or should I wait till Hell freezes over?'

He took a sip of the amber nectar and glanced at the open trap to his left. 'On the other hand,' he murmured, 'I know a woman whose investigative skills are second to none. And she's not doing very much at the moment...'

She heard the voice as if far off in the echoes of her mind, down the labyrinthine tunnels which offered no escape, the endless dark twists of her own fear. 'How are you feeling now?' the voice asked, over and over again. It was cold. It was mocking, and it didn't really want an answer.

'Max?' Patrick Collinson was peering over the balustrade to the auditorium below, leering, like dear old Charles Laughton's Quasimodo, at the crowd below. 'Max, can I have a word?'

'Sure.' Rehearsals were over for the week and the cast of *Shop of Horrors* had been given the weekend off for good behaviour. And because they were all knackered, falling prey to that eternal disease of school plays the length and breadth of the land – cold feet. What had seemed a rattling good idea when Angela Carmichael had bullied Geraint Horsenell into it last year, was everybody's worst nightmare now that Opening Night loomed. Horsenell had wanted to do *The Threepenny Opera*, complete with unplayable music and a plot more lifted than Zsa Zsa Gabor. It was time to take stock. Time for a rest. Psyche up. Focus. Focus.

'Are we ... er ... are we alone?' Collinson had padded down to Maxwell's level via the back stairs, his shadow positively Hitchcockian on the wall.

'I believe so,' Maxwell said. 'I was just off

myself.' He was rummaging for his hat and scarf.

'Yes, sorry.' Collinson looked around him, easing his collar. 'I won't keep you. I only wanted a word.'

'Yes?' Maxwell waited.

'Well, this is … ah … a little awkward, really. I had a … well, let's just say, incident earlier. With Deena Harrison.'

'Incident?' This was déjà vu country for Maxwell. For seven years he heard similar laments in the staff room at Leighford High.

'A moment.' Collinson tried to find the right words. 'A *cri de coeur* if you will.'

'What sort of *cri?*' Maxwell asked. The déjà vu, when the name of Deena Harrison was on everybody's lips, crept up his spine and parted his hair.

'Well, it was earlier this evening. Before anyone had arrived. As you know, it was my turn to unlock and lock up tonight. She came up to me and threw her arms around my neck.'

'Did she now?' Maxwell had been here before too.

'She made an allegation, Max. And I don't really know what to do about it.'

'An allegation?' Maxwell repeated. 'What sort of allegation? Against whom?'

Collinson sighed sharply. 'I find all this rather distasteful,' he muttered. 'Deena made an allegation against Ashley Wilkes. She claims he raped her.'

'All right, boys and girls.' Henry Hall clapped his hands together. It wasn't his best Mad Max impression, but it got the attention of the Incident

261

Room, an ever more motley crew of professionals whose enquiries were going precisely nowhere. 'Nobody goes home tonight until we've talked about telephone calls. What've we got, Gavin?'

'Daniel Bartlett's telephone calls.' Henslow had the stage as the neon strip nearest him popped and spluttered. 'On the day he died, he made a call to Ralph's Express Pizza at six-thirty-four. It lasted nearly two minutes.'

Everybody looked at everybody else.

'Sorry, guv.' Tom O'Connell didn't mind admitting, 'I don't follow.'

'Tell him, Gavin.' Hall had been over this already. It didn't exactly have breakthrough written all over it, but it was *something* at least.

The golden boy beamed. This was his call. He could see promotion and the George Medal staring him in the face. 'I paid a visit to Ralph's Pizzas this afternoon,' he said. 'Spoke to Liam.'

All eyes were still on the ambitious little shit. Presumably this *was* going somewhere?

'Liam assured me,' Henslow went on, refusing to be rattled by the icy silence, 'that he had an order for pizza from a Mr Bartlett at about half past six.'

'So?' Walters couldn't see what cause the lad had to smirk.

'So, Mr Bartlett was most insistent that the pizza was delivered at ten-thirty.'

They all waited.

'That is the time,' Henslow couldn't believe how slow his colleagues were on the uptake, 'that we assume Dan Bartlett was in his bath. Now, who orders pizza for a time when he's in the bath?'

'A forgetful bugger?' Bill Robbins suggested.

'A screaming poof who wants an excuse to flash at a pizza delivery man?' Dave Walters was too long in the tooth to start worrying about political correctness now. He could have been Peter Maxwell's time twin.

'Not exactly, Dave.' Henry Hall stepped in to give the earnest lad a fraction of a chance against these old cynics. 'Who orders pizza for a man in the bath? The same person who has carefully doctored the house's wiring system and knows his victim will get out of said bath to answer the door. Unwittingly, Liam is an accessory to a murder. He duly arrived at ten-thirty, as instructed. It was his last order of the night and he was on his way home. He rang four or five times but didn't get a reply. What he did get was annoyed. He saw the lights go out and thought the occupant was having a laugh. In fact the occupant was dying in that instant, two hundred and forty volts going through his body. Liam wasn't remotely aware of this, of course, and continued to ring and knock, but the place was locked up. He was all set to go back there the next day and settle the payment, but he caught the item on the local lunchtime news and recognised both Bartlett's name and the house. Now, everybody,' he walked out from behind his desk, 'this is not the end. It's not even the beginning of the end. But let's hope it is the end of the beginning. Go home. Get some sleep. Tomorrow, I want Dan Bartlett's place turned over again. And this time, I want some answers.'

He caught the girl's eyes as she switched off her VDU. 'Jane,' he said. 'Can I have a word?'

Jane Blaisedell had gone home to Mum and Dad, exhausted, broken. She who'd never told them about Uncle Tony and his disgusting, wandering hands, still couldn't tell them now. That was because Uncle Tony had been cleaning his car one day on that steeply sloping drive of his. He'd been working on the rear number plate when, quite suddenly, the handbrake had slipped and the vehicle rolled backwards.

There had been a dull thud as the car's weight hit Uncle Tony's head and slammed him backwards like a puppet, to crush his pelvis against the garage wall.

And Jane could never tell her parents all about that, now could she? That she'd been sitting in the car at the time. And if anybody else should ask, in the years ahead, she'd tell them that Uncle Tony had been a strange one and had hanged himself because he couldn't live with his guilt. Jane was learning to live with hers.

So she'd made some lame excuse about needing a couple of days' break and a spot of R and R. And now, she was back, words unsaid, business that she thought was finished, suddenly unfinished. Unspoken thoughts made vivid and vocal by a strange, gaunt woman who knew things ... things she couldn't possibly know.

'Jane?' Henry Hall said again. 'Are you all right?'

Chapter Eighteen

She drove out along the Flyover as the darkness gathered. The lights of the Front shone in the dying days of the season, although the Factory Fortnight was an institution fast disappearing in the world of extended 'sickies' and stress-related holidays. She felt awful. It wasn't just the problem of squeezing behind the wheel of the Ka these days, or indeed of where she was going and why. She really felt awful because she hadn't told Max about any of this. And Max was half her soul as she was his. They'd made no vows as such. No plans for a wedding with bells, books and candles. Not even a brief fifteen minutes with some dotty old Registrar. No rings, no twining knots of true love. There was a time when, perhaps, they'd both wanted that, when they were younger and brighter-eyed and bushier-tailed. Now, it was just quiet understanding and the touch of hearts by the electric firelight. But it was real nonetheless and it was true. And Jacquie hated herself because she hadn't told Max.

There was the house she'd heard about through the garbled snippets she'd got from an increasingly hysterical Jane Blaisedell. Quite smart as bungalows went, but a bungalow nonetheless. Laying aside Max's endless tirade against the tastelessness of bungaloid growth, it was not exactly the sort of house you buy if Bill Gates occasionally rings you up for a loan. Jane had told her that Dan Bartlett's wife had said the dead man was loaded, rich as Croesus. It didn't show.

She parked the car round the corner, a habit born of years of police experience and earlier, furtive meetings with Max, neither of them wanting to put the other on the spot. The night air struck cold after the warmth of the Ka and she pulled her coat tighter round her. The night sky was a purple haze with a pale moon already making a mystic appearance; bad moon rising. She heard the rising breeze rustle the privet leaves as she negotiated the hedge; it would be a windy night. There was a fence to her right, a low wall and the privet to her left. Dan Bartlett's love nest was quite secluded, for all it was on the edge of an estate. Anyone could have come and gone after dark without causing any fuss whatsoever. Various neighbours had seen people come and go and had reported it to Henry Hall's team. But who had they missed, behind the privet and the Cotswold stone?

She heard her feet crunch on gravel. A silent approach wasn't an option, unless there was a way in from the back. She tried that next, while there was still enough light in the sky to let her. A lawn, rather less neat probably now there was no one to mow it. Flower beds. But the fence was unbroken. There was no back gate; no other way in that might have masked the arrival of a murderer. Chummy, as Max would no doubt call him, must have arrived by the front.

It was as she turned back to the squat blackness of the house that her blood froze. Like that scene

266

she hated in one of Max's favourite films, *The Innocents*, a gaunt woman stood in the half shadows, like Quint's dead mistress in the waving reeds where she died.

'I'm Jacquie Carpenter,' she said, hoping her own voice would inject normality into the situation. 'Are you Magda Lupescu?'

'What are you doing here?' the woman asked. She was still in the shadow of the house and had not moved.

Some psychic, thought Jacquie, but she didn't want to sour their relationship from day one. She walked forward, holding up her warrant card and the little torch with it that she always carried for moments such as these, identification in the dark. 'I'm with Leighford CID,' she said. 'Jane Blaisedell's replacement.'

'Why is Jane not here?' Magda wanted to know.

'She's not well. DCI Hall has asked me to take over for her.'

Magda looked the woman up and down. 'You are expecting a child.'

Wow, thought Jacquie. Perception upon perception. She clicked her tongue. 'One little mistake,' she said.

'You do not want this baby?'

Jacquie was already fumbling for the house keys, but stopped and looked hard into the woman's eyes. 'Yes, I do,' she said firmly. 'Very much. But that's enough about me. I need you to tell me what you can about the last days of Daniel Bartlett.'

'One moment.' The psychic stopped her. 'May I hold the key?'

It was Jacquie's experience that *something* held

the key in every case, but she already knew two things about Magda Lupescu. She was weird and she had no sense of humour whatsoever. She passed it to her. The woman held the Yale in her hand, then closed her eyes and pressed it against her forehead. Then she passed it back.

Jacquie waited for some meaningful pronouncement, but Magda said nothing, so she unlocked the door and in they went.

'No,' Magda said as Jacquie fumbled for the lights. 'We don't need those.'

'Well, I do,' Jacquie said, flicking out her pencil torch again. 'As you so rightly surmised, Miss Lupescu, I'm pregnant. And for Sonny Jim's sake if not my own, I'd rather not fall over anything, thank you all the same.'

Magda stood inside the front door. Ahead of her, the corridor ended in darkness. The dim light from the hall window formed a backdrop to the darting rays of Jacquie's torch, bouncing off hall tables, mirrors and a hat stand draped with coats. The psychic started here, running her bony pale hands over the Barbour, the long, affected scarf, the little Roman Polanski cap. 'He is unhappy,' she said. 'Disturbed.'

Jacquie hadn't moved. All the way over here from Columbine, indeed ever since Henry Hall had asked her to take some work leave from her maternity, she'd decided to play it this way. Jane Blaisedell had played it wrong, let the moment and this woman get to her. She wasn't going to be sucked in. This was just a house. It was new, for God's sake. Miss Winchcombe's place may have been old and creaky and spooky, and the

Arquebus Theatre had been a warehouse since God knew when. Such places had a right to ghosts. But there was nothing other-worldly about an Eighties bungalow on the south coast. She would keep some perspective. And the woman in front of her, frowning now as if in pain, was just ... what? at best, just an expert witness; at least, a meddling old fraud. And it was inconceivable that such people could ever be used in court. What would happen? The defence would bring in their medium to rebut the prosecution's medium and pass the Tarot round the jury while the judge gazed into his crystal ball? She shook herself free of the image.

'There's something else,' Magda was saying. Her eyes were closed, but she was walking ahead. Jacquie went with her, training her torch on the woman's face. Her eyes were closed the whole time, yet she was negotiating furniture like a sleepwalker, she who was wide awake. 'There's trouble here. A woman.'

'From what we know, there were lots of women in Dan Bartlett's life,' Jacquie told her.

'Not like this one.' Magda stopped, cocking her head to one side, listening. 'This one's different.'

'Who is it?' Jacquie was used to ID parades, witness statements, depositions. No time for nonsense. Cut to the chase.

Magda was moving along the corridor now, running her fingers over the woodwork of door frames, sliding her hands over the chunky furniture. Jacquie knew that the SOCO team had been all over this place already, at least once. If she knew the DCI, he'd be sending a team back any day now to double-check, not the forensics this time, but all the little ways a man's life could be pieced together – the contents of his computer, his freezer, the personal shorthand he'd scribbled on his kitchen calendar, his taste in books, music, films. All of it was there, the residue of a life that might leave a clue about the death. But what this strange, silent, compelling woman was doing was something different, something else.

'There was someone here,' Magda said, standing in the middle of Dan Bartlett's lounge, silhouetted like a ghost against the window. 'On the day he died. She sat here.'

'Who?' Jacquie persisted. 'Who are we talking about?'

Magda had dropped suddenly and silently to the settee. Again, her eyes were closed. Her hands were roaming over cushions, the arms, the window ledge behind her, like a demented spider spinning its web. 'She is troubled. I see water now. A boat.' She stood up just as quickly, frowning. Her eyes were open. She was shaking her head violently, as if a wasp was buzzing around her, threatening, deadly. She left the room, Jacquie in her wake, relying again on the torch now that they were in the total darkness of the corridor. To the right lay the kitchen and Magda seemed to have no inclination to go there. They turned the curve of the corridor, snaking to the left. Jacquie hadn't seen the plans of the place as Jane had and Henry Hall had not been forthcoming. There would be blow-ups in the Incident Room at Tottingleigh, photographs of each room, SOCO's telltale note-lets fluttering from the white-board, measurements, links, speculation, guesses even – but all of it rooted in reality. In the dead man's house, both women were, in all senses, in the dark.

Magda shrieked, leapt back, her hand against the wall; Jacquie's heart was pounding as she watched the woman recoil. She flashed her torch at the floor. Charred carpet. This is where it happened. Where Dan Bartlett died.

'There is a ringing,' Magda moaned, as though struggling through unspeakable pain. 'A doorbell. He was on his way to answer the door.' She stood bolt upright, fists clenched. Then she felt her cheek. 'Were there marks?' she asked Jacquie. 'Here, on his face?'

'I don't know.' Henry Hall had been at his wheedling best when he'd rung Jacquie at home, but he only half expected her to go through with this anyway, given her condition. When she'd said yes, he'd metaphorically fallen off his chair and hadn't given her all the detail she needed. Or perhaps that was deliberate. You never could tell with Henry Hall.

'He felt pain,' Magda continued, 'before he died. Pain and ecstasy. Perhaps they were one.'

'Who was with him?' Jacquie pressured her. 'Was someone here when he died? When the doorbell rang? Was he alone?'

'Fucking bitch!' Magda snarled, rounding on Jacquie in the darkness of the corridor. But it wasn't her voice. It was a man's. And her face was odd, hard and distorted.

'Why?' Jacquie could feel the hairs standing on her head, her whole body cold and rigid. The torch was dangling uselessly in her hand, illuminating the carpet in little circles of light. She was terrified. She knew exactly what Jane had experienced and she wanted to run. To get out of that house and be running, Sonny Jim or no. Get out and back to Max, to the man she loved with his cat and his soldiers and the heart he wore on his sleeve. She wanted to tell Henry Hall where to stick his bloody favour. And his bloody job. She understood now the tears and the terror from Jane. But she was a copper. Tried. Tested. And if ninety-nine per cent of her being told her that Magda Lupescu was a con woman, that shaky one per cent couldn't let it go. 'Why am I a bitch?'

'You know why,' the man's voice goaded back. 'Kicking a man when he's down. And you've got it. You've got it all.'

'What have I got?' Jacquie asked, her heart thumping somewhere under her chin. 'What is it that you want? Magda? Are you Magda? Who are you?'

But Magda was sliding down the wall, the strange light gone from her eyes, her features softening, her own voice returning in a whisper. Jacquie went with her, as far as her bump would allow, and checked the woman's pulse. Then her eyelids, flashing the torch into the tiny black dots that were her pupils. She'd fainted. And Jacquie blew all the breath that she could muster, feeling the goosebumps ripple up her arms. She could have got some water, slapped the woman around the face to revive her. Instead, she struggled upright and switched on the lights, first in the corridors, then in the kitchen. She rummaged in Dan Bartlett's cupboards for Dan Bartlett's tea and put on the kettle. She'd let Magda come to in her own good time and in the meantime she went through the calming, routine ritual of a housewife; doing the basics, returning to normal. There was nothing amiss really. In the hallway outside, a psychic was lying in a heap, having turned into a dead man in front of her. Just one of life's little trials.

While the kettle noise grew into bubbling life, Jacquie opened her coat and the blouse underneath. She couldn't help smiling at the bump that met her, the skin stretched and shiny, with the bugging wire across it, the one Henry Hall insisted she wore. She hauled out the mini tape recorder from under her armpit and pressed replay. It was faint, distorted, but it was there. An inrush of air, then, 'I'm Jacquie Carpenter. Are you Magda Lupescu?'

Jacquie found herself staring at the contraption. What was the matter with the bloody thing? Henry's boffins had sold her a pup. All she could hear was a sort of ... sighing. Then, loud, crackling, as though directly into her ears. 'Look, who's there? I've had enough of this.' Silence. A click. The tape had ended. Jacquie pushed buttons, rechecked. The tape had minutes to go yet, but the bloody machine had switched itself off.

The kettle bubbled to boiling point behind her and she heard a low moaning from the corridor. Magda was back.

'That was a helluva drinkie with the girlies last night,' Maxwell said through a mouthful of toast. 'What time did you get in?'

273

'Late,' Jacquie told him. 'I slept in the spare room – didn't want to wake you.'

'You thoughtful old thing,' and he chucked her 'neath the chin. 'Was Jane there?'

'Jane – er ... no.'

Maxwell took the toast out of his mouth and looked at Jacquie. She looked pale, a little fragile. 'Are you all right?' he asked her. It had been a long time since Peter Maxwell had had a pregnant woman in his house. He'd forgotten the symptoms.

'I'm fine,' she smiled. 'What's today?'

'God knows,' he sighed, stuffing books into his already bulging briefcase. 'Monday, I think. That must mean – ah, yes, History teaching. You?'

'I'm having lunch with Jane, all being well. You know Henry's taken her off the case.'

'Has he?' Maxwell slurped some coffee. 'Common sense at last.'

'Well, at least the psychic part of it.'

'Ah, yes. Madame Arcati. I'd love to meet her.'

'Would you?'

Again, Maxwell stopped, wiping crumbs from his bow tie. 'Darling,' he closed to her. 'Are you sure you're all right?'

'Just tired,' she said. 'Some days – Sonny Jim, you know. You should try it some time.'

'D'you know,' he winked, 'I think I might. I'll have a word with dear old Doc Shipman and see if I can get the op on the NHS. But in the meantime, hey nonny-nonny. See you later, darling heart,' and he kissed her and was gone.

She watched him from the lounge window as he led Surrey out down the garden path. He'd fixed the puncture now and the contraption's chrome sparkled in the weak October sun. He raised his shapeless hat to Mrs T., forever clipping the other side of their communal hedge. He turned to wave as he wobbled out into the road, doffing his cap to her and bouncing low in Surrey's saddle. She smiled and loved him all over again. Mad as a tree.

'Look after yourself, Peter Maxwell,' she whispered. She went to the bathroom and mechanically turned on the taps. Then she looked in the mirror. 'God, Jacquie,' she heard herself saying. 'Not only do you feel like shit, you look like it too.'

While the Stress Relief bath pong spread bubbles in the water and the steam coated mirror and window, Jacquie rang Leighford nick. 'Dave?' She recognised the desk man's quiet, calming tones. 'Jacquie Carpenter. Put me through to the guv'nor, will you?'

'This,' Peter Maxwell had halted temporarily on his way into Leighford High that morning, wheels spinning on the gravel as his laser eyes caught sight of an erring child, 'is what I believe the working classes call a football.' He was spinning the thing in his hand. 'That, not ten yards from it, is a plate glass window. The oldest known in Western Europe was made for General Lucius Lucullus so he could look out and enjoy his stupendous garden in bad weather. Know what happens, Joshua, when one meets the other at several miles an hour?'

'Er ... it smashes.' Joshua was doing GCSE

275

General Science. Eat your heart out, Einstein.

'Indeed it does.' Maxwell was impressed. 'And?'

'Sir?' Joshua was looking up at the Great Man. He hadn't heard the hiss of Surrey's tyres behind him and not until Maxwell grabbed the ball had he realised he was there at all. Staff in cars he could spot half a mile away, but sneaky old bastards on bikes were a different matter altogether.

'The inevitable corollary is that I cuff you round the ear and a whacking great bill is sent to your mum and dad. Do you get the picture?'

'Yes, sir.' Joshua's middle name could have been contrition.

'Good. I'm glad, because the ball you haven't got. Pick it up from my office at the end of the day.'

'Aw, sir, that's not fair...'

Maxwell checked his stride on the school's front steps. 'You're right. The punishment must fit the crime,' he said. 'Justice must not only be done, but be seen to be done. Let's make it the end of tomorrow.' And he was gone.

A mass of tangled, greying hair appeared around the sliding hatch door of Thingee One, already fielding phone calls from the hapless bunch of incompetents who called themselves parents. 'Thingee, light o' love – you've changed your hair.'

'Last term, Mr Maxwell,' Thingee replied resignedly. 'Had it done to go on holiday.'

'Right.' Maxwell clicked his fingers, remembering their conversation intimately. 'Barbados. Weather was lovely.'

'Lanzarote,' she corrected him. 'It rained.'

'Excellent. Tell me, do we have a current address for Deena Harrison?'

'Deena?' She ferreted on her computer screen. 'Yes, I think so. 14 Delaware Avenue.'

'Brill! Oh,' and he threw the football at her, gently of course. 'That's Joshua Fairbrother's. I've told him I've got it, which is a lie, so he'll probably check with you four or five times during the day, to see if you've got it. Just tell him you haven't seen it since Mr Maxwell stuck a compass point in it and threw it in the school skip, all right? Oh, Thingee. I'm out of school for a while. No cover required Lessons One and Two. And make sure nobody pinches my bike space, will you?'

'But Mr Maxwell,' she called after him as he hurtled out of Reception like a bat out of Hell. 'I've put you down to cover Mr Holton's Science, Lesson One.'

'Give it to Mr Ryan,' he waved back through the front door. 'He only teaches five periods a week and desperately needs the practice.' He stared back at two wandering girls who were staring at him. 'Yes?' and they scurried away. Madder than ever.

'And that's it?' Henry Hall sat in his Lexus on the slope of Staple Hill. The new yet-to-open golf course tumbled away below him and the sky was astonishingly cloudless for an October day at the height of the Global Warming Season.

Jacquie Carpenter sat next to him, glad to release the seat belt from her bump. 'That's it,' she said. 'The rest of the tape's dead. As if it never recorded. Or refused to work after a certain point.'

Hall nodded. 'I've never liked these things,' he said, pushing buttons in a futile attempt to make the gadget behave. 'More trouble than they're worth. It's just that when I couldn't get much sense out of Jane, I thought this might be useful. I should have had her wired too.'

'You'd probably have got the same result,' Jacquie said.

He looked at her, his favourite detective sergeant. She didn't look too well today, he thought. Pregnancy affected women in different ways. His Margaret had been healthy as a pig all three times, but it didn't always go like that. 'Are you OK?' he asked solemnly.

'If you mean was I scared shitless by that dodgy woman and her circus act ... yes, I was. It's been a long time since I didn't sleep at all.'

'This voice...?' Hall was pointing to the tape recorder.

'If it's her,' Jacquie said, 'doing one of her impersonations, it wasn't something she said last night. Believe me; I'd remember. Do you recognise the voice?'

He shook his head. 'No.'

'Could it be the tape?' she asked him, still trying to make sense of it. 'Some defect?'

'Could be,' Hall nodded. 'It's a new tape, as far as I know, but I'll get it checked. See if the lab can come up with anything.'

'You might want to check for background noise too – the white stuff. It sounded pretty weird to

278

mc last night. Not...' she looked into her twin reflections in his lenses, 'not of this world.'

'Why did you want us to drive, Jacquie?' he asked her. 'You could have given me this at the nick.'

'It's Max,' she told him, gnawing her lip and looking out of the window to the bare horizon and its single pine tree, the sea a peacock blue beyond. 'He doesn't know about any of this.'

'I see.'

'And I don't like that.' She turned back to him. 'I don't like having to lie to him.'

'Nobody's asking you to,' Hall told her. 'You could have said no.'

'Could I, guv?' she asked him. 'You've seen what a wreck Jane Blaisedell's become. Do you think I could leave her like that?'

'What you tell Max is up to you,' Hall said, 'and I seem to remember we've been having this conversation on and off for years.'

She smiled. 'On and off is right,' she reminded him. 'Sometimes it was "Don't you dare tell Maxwell a bloody thing".' That was an unfair characterisation; Henry Hall hardly ever swore. But he acknowledged the sentiment anyway.

'Do you think she's a con woman, Jacquie?' he asked her, switching track with a suddenness that pulled her up short. 'Magda Lupescu? Do you think she's pulling our collective chains?'

Jacquie stared ahead, out of Hall's tinted windscreen. 'Somebody is, guv,' she said. 'I just wish I knew who.'

Chapter Nineteen

Teachers rarely know where their kids live, let alone ex-kids. If they're sensible, they'll buy a house out of the catchment area, because even if they're popular, they'll be met with a barrage of ''Ello, sir!' ''Ello, Miss!' every time they go out. If they're not popular, they'll have shit through their letterboxes.

So Peter Maxwell had had no clue where Deena Harrison lived, until Thingee had found the address for him on the school computer. He'd then rung her on her mobile and invited himself over. It was a Monday lunchtime and with Lesson Five being free, he'd just have time to pedal like a thing possessed along the Front and up into the high country above the Shingle, before dropping down into Tottingleigh and the Littlehampton Road. A more determined trencherman would have grabbed a Ginsters on the way and risked a few minutes' wobbly handlebars to slake his morning hunger pangs. As it was, Mad Max pinched a chip off Slobbo Allen in Eight Eff Two as he left the building.

'Thanks, Slobbo!' he called.

''Ere!' Slobbo didn't take the theft too kindly. 'I'll have the law on you, Mr Maxwell.'

'If you made a complaint today,' Maxwell was swinging his good leg over White Surrey's crossbar, 'thank a teacher.'

And he was gone, down the plantain-bordered highway, out into the world of freedom and adventure that was Leighford, West Sussex. He ran a red light at the intersection of Wilding and Albemarle like the road hog he was, cut through the pedestrian precinct area outside Boots as old men with sticks roared at him about the insolence of the youth of today. He was Marlon Brando in *The Wild One,* a delinquent after his time. Then it was rubber to the pedal and the snarl of synchromesh as he took the rise with the great, grey sea sparkling on his right and the gorse-strewn heathland of the South Weald above him to his left.

He could see the little cluster of police cars in the car park of what had once been Tottingleigh Mixed Infants School and now doubled as a Day Care Centre and occasional Incident Room. Henry Hall would be there, he knew, wrestling with the same problems that Maxwell faced, worrying them in his own police procedural way; worrying them to death. He had a fine mind, did Henry, but he also had a manual, one by which he had to live. Peter Maxwell didn't have a manual at all.

What he did have was a new problem now, one that might become Henry Hall's in the fullness of time. He eased Surrey's brakes and the noble machine's rear wheel hissed and skidded on the gravel. The Harrison house was large, solid, Edwardian with tall hedges to keep out the prying world. If Maxwell remembered aright, Deena was a singleton. All this would be hers now; a property owner at twenty-two. Still, it would, no doubt, not be the way she would have wanted to inherit.

281

'Mr Maxwell?' A puzzled face peered round the door.

He swept off his hat. 'Deena,' he said. 'I was sorry to be so cryptic on the phone. May I come in?'

'Cryptic indeed,' she said. 'Please.' The girl wore her hair piled up in an untidy tangle on top of her head. A large, floppy jumper hung off one shoulder and there were once-fashionable designer tears in her jeans.

She led him into a large, elegant hall with heavy oak furniture and a hat stand. It was like something out of *Flog It* and he half expected a deliriously excited Paul Martin to leap out of a cupboard in his enthusiasm any minute. Mock Rennie Mackintosh panels lit the Edwardian gloom, all pale pinks and greens, until they reached the living room, which was strewn with mags and coffee cups that reminded Maxwell of his own rooms in those far-off Granta days. He had been the only student in Cambridge not to have a Che Guevara poster on his wall. Asthmatic medical student drop-outs had never impressed him much.

'Have they let you out?' She tidied the worst of the Cosmos into a neater pile.

'Ticket of leave only, I'm afraid,' he said, shaking a leg at her. 'This damn tag on my ankle itches to buggery.'

'Can I get you anything?' she asked. 'I don't do lunch any more – call me faddy if you like – but I can make you a coffee.'

'No, thanks, faddy.' He smiled and sat upright in one of her armchairs to wait until she sat down too. 'Look, Deena ... there's no easy way to say this. Patrick Collinson had a word with me last night.'

'Really?' Deena chirped. Then her face fell. 'Oh, God, there isn't a problem with the show, is there? I mean, the cast haven't...'

'No, no, it's not the show, Deena. It's you.'

'Me?' The girl sat forward. 'What do you mean?' She wasn't as chirpy now.

'Ashley Wilkes,' Maxwell said quietly.

Deena blinked, frowning. 'Mr Maxwell, I'm afraid I haven't the faintest idea what you're talking about.'

Ever had times in your life when everybody's singing from a hymn sheet and so are you, but you're on the wrong page? Peter Maxwell felt a little like that. 'Deena.' He leaned forward, cradling one hand in the other, choosing his words carefully. 'Patrick told me that you told him Ashley Wilkes raped you.' He was Head of Sixth Form again, quiet, patient, loving in his old grammar school sort of way.

For a second, Deena Harrison sat bolt upright, a frozen look of horror on her face. Then she crumpled and fell back in hysterical laughter. When she'd finished, the tears running down her cheeks, Maxwell hadn't moved. He was still looking at her with the utmost concern, the utmost solemnity. He'd talked to raped girls before, but he had to admit he'd never known a response quite like this one. Slowly, Deena pulled herself together, drying her eyes and clearing her throat.

'Oh, I'm sorry, Mr Maxwell,' she said, still trying to stifle her giggles. 'It's just that I've never heard anything so preposterous. When ... when did Mr Collinson say this conversation of ours took place?'

'At the Arquebus,' Maxwell said, 'last night. I missed the whole rehearsal because I had a puncture and didn't get there until you people had gone home. He didn't go into details, but he was quite sure of what had happened.'

Deena was frowning again. 'This is downright peculiar,' she said, looking into the middle distance as though wrestling with a problem.

'What is?' Maxwell was more confused than ever.

'Ever heard of Paul Usherwood?'

'I don't think so,' Maxwell shook his head.

'Paul was my professor at Oxford. He was quite a dish and very kind. One of the youngest professors in the university in fact. And when ... my parents died ... well, he sort of took me under his wing. Literally. Or tried to...'

'I'm sorry,' Maxwell said. 'I don't follow.'

'I'm not saying Paul raped me,' she said, shaking her head, 'but he certainly, shall we say, took advantage of my vulnerability. But I've never told anyone about that. Until now.' She reached out and touched his hand. 'I suppose, what with everything else, I just put it to the back of my mind. He was going through a bad patch at the time. His marriage was on the rocks and I was ... needful, I suppose. These things happen, don't they? And they don't all make the *News of the World*. It wasn't violent or anything. But as for Mr Collinson, I don't know what he's talking about.'

'So you and he never had a conversation about

Ashley Wilkes?'

'No, of course not,' she chuckled. 'Why would I confide in a man I hardly know? If anything had happened, Mr Maxwell,' she tightened her grip on his hand, 'I would have come to you.' She eased herself forward so that their knees were nearly touching and she held his right hand in both of hers. 'I will always come to you, if you'll let me.'

He stood up. To check his watch would have been rude and clichéd, but he really did have to get back. Time, tide and Eleven Bee Nine would wait for no man. They'd be tearing off his Derry Irvine wallpaper and swinging from the Rococo chandeliers in Aitch Eight. You couldn't turn your back... 'I'm sorry, Deena,' he said. 'This is some sort of sick joke. And I'm afraid it's on me. I'm sorry to have bothered you.'

'Mr Maxwell,' she held his arm. 'I'm sure Mr Collinson meant no harm. He seems a nice old boy. Don't be hard on him.'

'Do you have an appointment?' Patrick Collinson's secretary was still asking as Peter Maxwell crashed through his office door. Patrick Collinson worked from home. And it was quite a home. Out beyond Staple Hill where the Weald began and serious money held sway. The lawns were trimmed after the summer's croquet and the whole place oozed opulence. As an accountant, Collinson had achieved the impossible – a fortune from sitting on his arse. And, as Rod Steiger's Napoleon said of Christopher Plummer's Wellington in *Waterloo*, Maxwell was going to move him off it.

Collinson looked up in some alarm as the be-scarfed whirlwind hurtled across the deep shag of his carpet, reached his desk and slammed his fist down. Computer and papers jumped along with the accountant.

'We're going to be brutally frank with each other in a minute, Patrick. Do you really want your secretary to witness you picking up your teeth?' The woman hovered in the doorway, her hands flapping as if her fingers were on fire.

'Er ... it's all right, Doris.' Collinson was patting the air with his left hand, trying to calm everybody down, not least himself. The other hand hovered near his desk drawer. For an instant, Maxwell wondered whether he had an alarm button connected to the nick or a Magnum .357 tucked away like most accountants did.

'Shall I call the police, Mr Collinson?' Doris asked, dithering between her boss's would-be assailant and the land line. If truth be told, Maxwell hadn't taken the time to suss her out as he barged his way past her desk, but she didn't have the look of a seventh dan, so he'd probably be all right.

'No, no,' Collinson blustered. 'I'm sure whatever grievance Mr Maxwell has, we can sort it out.'

'But...' Doris was not convinced. She'd seen various degrees of raised dander before, but nothing quite like this.

'Thank you, Doris.' Collinson was firmer with the loyal old girl than perhaps he intended to be, but it did the trick. She closed the door quietly, but hovered just outside, just in case, trying to

286

memorise Maxwell's features and appearance for when he was on the run for murdering her employer.

'Max...' Collinson spread his arms in a gesture of innocence and bewilderment.

'Deena Harrison wasn't raped by Ashley Wilkes, Patrick,' Maxwell told him levelly, 'so why did you tell me she was?'

The accountant who doubled as theatre secretary blinked and dithered. He began to say something, but thought better of it and just sat down.

'Well?' Maxwell was looming over him, leaning on his knuckles, arms straight, legs braced. Many was the homework-forgetter who'd had a similar view.

'Max,' Collinson gabbled. 'I just don't know what to say... I...' and he shook his head.

Maxwell straightened, giving the man some space. Clearly, he was rattled, put out, confused. He'd give him time, let him breathe. 'I was wondering on my way over here why you'd invent a thing like that. I saw Deena at lunchtime. She found it astonishing that you'd spoken to me about something that never happened. I worried about it all afternoon, while casting historical pearls before teenaged swine. Had you misunderstood, I wondered? Misheard, perhaps? Hardly. So that left me with two choices – either you've got some vendetta against Ashley Wilkes that I don't know about or this is all part of a delusional fantasy in whatever sick world you inhabit. Put me out of my misery, Patrick: which is it?'

'Neither,' Collinson bleated. 'I mean, this is nonsense. It happened just as I told you. Deena was at the Arquebus last night, distraught. Ashley Wilkes had raped her. I was on my way to the police when I shut up shop for the night.'

'Were you?' Maxwell stood, drumming his fingers on Collinson's desk. 'You'll forgive me if I find that a tad unlikely.'

'As God is my witness, Max,' Collinson pleaded. 'I'm not some sort of pervert who goes round inventing lurid stories about young girls.'

'But you didn't go? To the police, I mean?'

'No.' Collinson looked a little crestfallen.

'Why not? If she told you and you believed her...'

'Well, that's just it. As for Ashley Wilkes, I'll admit he's not my favourite theatre manager, but that doesn't mean I'd swear away his reputation in a court of law on what is patently a lie.'

'Why is it patently a lie? When you told me about it, you believed her.'

'Didn't you?'

'She didn't tell *me!*' Maxwell bellowed.

'Dan Bartlett now.' Collinson changed tack. 'That wouldn't have surprised me at all. If Deena had come to me with a tale about him, well...'

Maxwell sat down in the huge leather chair alongside Collinson's coffee table. Either this man was one of the best liars he'd ever met – to rival Ben 'Pinocchio' Williams of Ten Bee Seven – or...

'What did Deena say?' he asked, calmer now, trying to make sense of it all. *'Exactly.'*

'Exactly? God, I can't remember. I'm a bachelor, Max, tried and tested. When a young girl starts sobbing on my shoulder, well, I must admit, I was a little out of my depth. I mean, I've barely exchanged pleasantries with the woman, and here she was, pouring her heart out.'

'Details,' Maxwell persisted.

'Now who's having delusional fantasies?' Collinson demanded to know.

Maxwell leaned forward ominously. 'I am a Western buff, Patrick,' he said quietly, patiently. 'And in a lot of Westerns in the Fifties, the hero – that's me, by the way – was so lost for words at the appalling behaviour of the villain – that's you – that he grabbed said villain by the shirt, yelled, "Why, you..." and proceeded to knock seven kinds of shit out of him. That's more or less where we are now, bad screenplay or no. And please don't think I'd worry about the lawsuit you'd inevitably bring, because your teeth on the carpet would be well worth it. I've put up with thirty very odd years at the Chalk Face, which has now mysteriously not only turned white but is interactive. It would be rather ironic, wouldn't it, if all that pent-up fury was unleashed not on some behooded moron it is my misfortune to have to teach but on a respectable pillar of the theatrical community. Details!'

Collinson took off his glasses and threw them down on the desk. Then he remembered the old adage about not hitting a man with glasses and quickly put them back on. 'If I remember rightly,' he said quickly, 'she told me with much sobbing and sniffing, you understand, that Ashley had invited her out for a drink. He insisted on taking her home and on the way, pulled into a lay-by where he assaulted and raped her.'

'That's it?'

'Isn't that enough?' Collinson asked.

'I mean, is that all she said or are you being coy because we don't know each other very well?'

'You have my word, Max,' Collinson insisted. 'That's all she said. No times. No places. Not even the make of car, although I happen to know that Ashley drives a Mondeo. She swore me to secrecy, however.'

'She did?'

'Yes. As I've said, I've no experience of this sort of thing, but I have read the more salacious Sundays in my time. It makes women feel dirty, doesn't it? A sexual assault, I mean. Used? It's understandable.'

'Why did she talk to you?' he asked.

'Hmm?'

'Deena. Why did she unburden herself to you, a virtual stranger?'

Collinson sighed, still coming to terms with the bizarreness of the situation he had been in and the very different one he was in now. 'I really have no idea,' he said. 'Wait a minute.' An odd smile crept over his face. 'That's what this is all about, isn't it? You're pissed off because she didn't come to you?'

'No,' Maxwell shook his head. 'She might have come to me when I was her Year Head, maybe even when I was her History teacher. But not now. That's not how it works. You want your teachers to remember you at your best, winning cups and scoring goals. You don't want them to know you when you're down.'

'Parents, then?' Collinson suggested. 'Why didn't she turn to them?'

'Because they're dead,' Maxwell told him. 'Killed in a car crash a couple of years ago.'

'Oh, dear. Well, then, I'm simply at a loss, Max. Do you think … do you think she's entirely well? Emotionally, I mean?'

Maxwell stood up, sliding back the accountant's leather chair and striding for the door. 'Are any of us?' he asked.

In the outer office, Collinson's loyal secretary stood with a cast iron doorstop in her hand. Loyalty and a sense of survival had driven her to it. 'You can put that down, Doris,' Maxwell said. 'I've decided to let your lord and master live – for now. And whatever you're paying this woman, Patrick, it isn't enough. You two have a nice day, y'hear.' And the psychopath with the Cambridge scarf and the deep Alabama drawl had gone.

'Max.'
  Silence.
  'Max.'
He heard his name whispered, as though far away. In the super eight reels of his dreaming, he was chasing the wind across the heather. An altogether younger Maxwell, not yet Mad, not yet cranky. No cycle clips in those days, no black and white cat ignoring his every word. No sadness. No sorrows. Just sun in meadows of lavender and the drone of bees. Bright eyes and laughter.
  'Max.'
  'Hmm? What time is it?'
  'Um … time we talked.'
Maxwell jolted himself awake. The liquid green digits of the bedside clock answered his question

291

more accurately. It was three thirty-eight. The witching hour when his bladder usually drove his dreams away anyway and he'd find himself padding along the passage in search of the little teacher's room. Jacquie was sitting upright, cradling her raised knees with her encircling arms, crying softly to herself.

'Darling.' He struggled up alongside her, wrapping her in his gentle grip. 'What is it, sweetheart? Bad dreams?' and he recited the mantra he used to recite to his little girl long, long ago. 'Dreams, dreams, go away, come again another day.'

'It's no good, Max,' she sniffed. 'I've tried to keep it all to myself, but I just can't.'

'Darling?' Maxwell was fully awake now, frowning and turning her gently to face him. 'Darling, what's the matter? Is it the baby? Anything wrong?'

'No, you soppy old thing.' She smiled through her tears. 'The baby's fine. I'm fine. I'm ... just a little scared, that's all.'

'Now, now.' He smoothed her hair, pale in the dim light of the master bedroom at 38 Columbine. 'I know a baby's a pretty scary thing. The responsibility and so on. But I've been *in loco parentis* now for nearly four hundred years. We'll manage, really we will. We'll have the little bugger up chimneys earning his keep before you can say Climbing Boys Act.'

'No, Max,' she sniffed and he let her wipe her nose on his pyjama sleeve. Greater love hath no man... 'There's something else. Something I should have told you a week ago.'

He waited, unsure whether to be flippant or

grave. He opted for the latter, saying nothing, and that rattled her even more. After what seemed an eternity, she broke the silence. 'I've gone back to work,' she told him. 'Only on a part-time basis.'

'Back to work?' he repeated. 'Don't tell me you're bored already.'

'Henry asked me.'

'Henry asked you?' Maxwell frowned. 'Is he really that short-staffed?'

'It's nothing to do with him,' she sniffed, feeling her lip tremble again. 'I did it for Jane.'

'For Jane.' There was already a chill realisation in Maxwell's voice, there in the darkness.

'She can't handle the whole psychic thing,' Jacquie said. 'You have to be strong.'

'And you are,' he said. It wasn't a question. It was a statement of fact.

'I thought I was,' she said, fighting the tears still. 'But now ... I'm not so sure.'

'Tell me,' he said, holding up her face by the chin and looking into her tear-filled eyes. 'Tell Uncle Max all about it.'

'We went to Dan Bartlett's house,' she told him. 'The nasty little bungalow on Haslemere Road. Magda was ... confused.'

'Confused?'

'Look, I didn't want to believe it, Max; any of it. I told myself, I told Henry, I'd be detached. Cool. It wasn't quite like that.'

'What happened?'

'She...' Jacquie was trying hard to focus, to rationalise the whirlwind in her head. 'Magda registers pain. She feels heat. Cold. Fear. Joy. She recounts – don't ask me how; I've no idea – actual

293

conversations with the dead.'

'Like a séance?'

'No, no, I don't mean that. It's as if she ... like Jane said, she *becomes* the dead. Her ... oh, Jesus.' Jacquie shuddered at the memory of it, her scalp crawling in the darkness of the bedroom; even here where she used to feel so safe. 'Her voice changes. Hardens. Becomes male. Her face ... I just can't describe it.'

'What did you hear?' Maxwell asked.

'A male voice. I assumed it was Dan Bartlett's.'

'But it wasn't?'

She looked deep into his eyes. 'Brace yourself, Max,' she said. 'I was wired.'

'You were?'

She nodded. 'Henry insisted on it. To give us some sort of record of what Magda's MO actually is. All the poor bastard's got is some ludicrous edict from on high. The Chief Bloody Constable belongs in a straitjacket. He left it to Henry to work out the how of everything. Jane's garbled accounts were of no help, really. I've read them; you've heard them, from Jane herself. Wait till he reads mine.'

'And?'

'And the tape didn't work properly.'

'Doesn't surprise me,' Maxwell said. 'Electronics are about as useful as a chocolate teapot.'

'No,' she sniffed. 'No, you don't understand. The machinery worked. It's just that, somehow it picked up words I didn't hear spoken. And in a voice I didn't know.'

'But you don't know Dan Bartlett's voice,' Maxwell reminded her.

294

'No. Agreed. But what was recorded on the tape was not the voice I had heard coming from Magda minutes before. One was Dan Bartlett. The other wasn't. Another place. Another time. Christ, Max,' she let out a long sigh. 'I don't want to do that again.'

'You won't have to,' he said firmly. 'Henry Hall, Jane Blaisedell. They can sort out their own problems. Jacquie,' he held her face firmly between his hands. 'It's over, Jacquie. You're on maternity leave now, remember? You are never, ever to work with this Lupescu woman again. Are we on the same page on this? The same line?'

She looked at him, tears breaking over her eyelashes and tumbling down her cheeks. 'Yes, Max,' she blurted. 'The same line. Exactly the same line.' And she cried into his shoulder like she hadn't cried since she was a little girl.

Chapter Twenty

Henry Hall and Magda Lupescu looked at each other across his desk in the Tottingleigh Incident Room – the bland leading the bland. It would be difficult to find two people less capable of showing their emotions. And that would be for the same reason – that neither of them dared; they had both seen too much.

The team watched her as she walked across the uneven floorboards of the old school. No one quite knew who she was, walking like a ghost alongside the bulky form of Sergeant Dave Walters; no one except Jane Blaisedell, who shrank down in her chair, hoping the computer screen would hide her. It didn't. The most fleeting of smiles passed over the pale, gaunt face of the visitor, but Magda didn't acknowledge her. Then she was gone through Hall's glass-panelled door and the WPC watched as he got up and they shook hands.

'Don't let her touch you,' Jane found herself thinking. 'She can see into your soul.'

'Well,' Hall broke the ice. The woman had already refused coffee or tea and sat bolt upright in her chair. 'You've visited all three of our murder sites. I have the reports of DC Blaisedell and DS Carpenter here in front of me.' The folders were manila and already dauntingly thick.

'They do not help,' Magda said, reaching into

her handbag. 'Is this place no smoking?'

'This office, yes,' Hall said, 'but I think in your case we can make an exception.'

'Why?' she snapped. 'Because I am a woman or because I have the power?'

'Because you are a civilian,' Hall told her, 'and a guest.' He ferreted in the desk drawer and slid a glass ashtray across to her, one somebody had pinched from a Met convention a few years back. She lit up, her hollow cheeks flaming for a moment in the match light. Her eyes narrowed and her nostrils flared and she crossed one slim leg over the other.

'You are confused by these reports.' It was a statement, not a question.

'Yes, frankly,' Hall said. 'What I have here is my officers' perceptions of what happened. Now I'd like your version.'

'You English have a phrase that I have learned,' she smiled. 'It is the organ grinder and his monkey, no?'

'Something like that,' Hall nodded. If Magda Lupescu was waiting for a smile in return, she would have to learn another English phrase. It had to do with Hell and freezing over. 'Tell me about Gordon Goodacre,' he said. 'At the theatre.'

Magda frowned, closing her eyes and blowing smoke down her nose like some contemplative dragon. 'He was working late. Painting.' This much Hall knew already. 'He did not like the place.' Her head was on one side now, her eyes still closed, as though she was listening. 'He felt its presence.'

'Presence?' Hall repeated.

Magda's eyes flashed open. 'What you would call ghosts,' she said, looking into the strongly reflective lenses of the Chief Inspector.

If Hall had been a laughing man, now would have been the time. 'Miss Lupescu,' he said. 'I have been a policeman now for more years than I care to remember. And I have gained experience from colleagues with more experience still. I have never, in all that time, heard of a murder committed by a ghost.'

Magda looked at him, then stubbed out her cigarette. 'And that is why you will never know what happened to Gordon Goodacre,' she said. 'I can only tell you what I felt.'

'All right.' She still had his attention.

'He heard voices,' she told Hall. 'I cannot say what. I only know what I heard.'

'Which was?'

'A man hanged.'

'I'm sorry?'

'In your country, judicial hangings,' she explained. 'You take a man to the scaffold, no? You place his feet on a trap door. The hangman binds his ankles, his wrists. He places a ... what you call ... hood over his head and the noose around his neck. The hangman pulls a lever. Smack!' She brought the flat of her hand down sharply on Hall's desk so that the ashtray jumped. 'The bolts on the underside of the trap door slide, the trap opens and a man twists in eternity. That's what I heard. Not once, but several times. The snarl of the iron bolts, the thud of the trap, the breath as it leaves the body, the creak of the rope

298

taut and swaying with its weight. Is that what Gordon Goodacre heard just before he died? I do not know.'

'We haven't hanged anyone in this country for forty years, Miss Lupescu,' he told her.

'That is not my concern,' she said.

'So... What are you saying? That someone was hanged at the Arquebus?'

She uncrossed her legs and smoothed down her skirt. 'It has not always been a theatre,' she said.

'No,' he confirmed. 'It was originally a warehouse, I believe. Storing ... I don't know ... grain, cotton, whatever.'

'There would have been ... what is it you call them? Er ... jousts?'

Hall blinked. 'Joists?' he suggested.

'Joists,' she clicked her fingers. 'They are used to pull up the goods from the boats, *yes?*'

'I believe so,' Hall nodded. Just for a moment, too fleeting to register really, he wished that Peter Maxwell was at his elbow, with his infuriating historian's grasp of the nuts and bolts of these things.

'Men can be hanged from those. Like the children's game at school. Hangman, yes?'

'Yes,' Hall said, grim-faced.

'He was on the stage. Gordon Goodacre,' Magda went on. 'He heard a sound – the bolts, the trap, the sigh? I do not know. It was coming from the right.' Her eyes were closed again and she was frowning, shaking her head. 'I do not like that place, it is dark. Cold. Gordon ... he did not like it either.' She opened her eyes suddenly. 'But he's an Englishman.' She smiled wistfully. 'Like you. Stolid, hmm? No imagination. His instincts told him he was not alone. He was right.'

'There were ... presences?' Hall asked.

'Of course,' Magda said. 'But a living person too.'

'In the Arquebus?' Hall checked. 'At the time of his death?'

'I do not know when he died,' she shrugged. 'But when the ladder fell, he was not alone.'

'Who?' Hall sounded a little over-eager perhaps, and consciously relaxed, drawing himself back. 'Who was it?'

'Evil,' Magda told him flatly. 'Hurt. Broken. I felt it again at Daniel Bartlett's bungalow.'

'The same presence?'

'In my world, Chief Inspector,' the psychic explained, 'the distinction between the living and the dead is not so clear. We are not talking about life in terms of a beating heart or inhaling and exhaling lungs. We are talking about what survives all that. What stays.'

'Miss Lupescu...'

'I know.' She held up her hand. 'You cannot debate the other world with me because you do not have the time or the interest.' She leaned towards him. 'But it is, in fact, because you are frightened by it. They are all around us, you know. All the time. As we speak.'

'Really?' Henry Hall leaned back in his chair.

'That corner,' she pointed to his left, beyond a green-fronted filing cabinet, 'there is much sadness there. I see a little boy. He's there now. What is he ... five? Six perhaps? He is crying. He has a pointed cap on his head. Is this some sort of ritual? He has been punished. And not for the first time. He is as afraid as you are.'

The Chief Inspector wasn't going to give the psychic the pleasure of looking to his left. He knew what he'd see – a green-fronted filing cabinet. Jane Blaisedell, even Jacquie Carpenter, might have fallen for this woman's party tricks; but not him. He was made of sterner stuff.

Magda began to look around her. 'This is a school,' she chuckled, with a sudden happy realisation. 'They are still here, the children. The boy in the corner, he hated this place, but he cannot leave. The others loved it. They do not want to leave. They are confused...' she closed her eyes and cocked her head again. 'They want to know why you are here. This is their school. They do not know what you are doing.'

Hall let out a sigh. 'That makes several of us,' he said. Though Magda Lupescu didn't realise it, it was the nearest thing to a joke she was likely to get from Henry Hall.

'Whatever was at the theatre watching Gordon Goodacre was not like these children. Except the one in the corner. It was quite like him. And that one was alive.'

'Thank you, Miss Lupescu.' Hall was on his feet, hand extended.

'We have not yet spoken about Martita Winchcombe or Daniel Bartlett,' she reminded him.

'Another time, perhaps,' he said. 'Can you reschedule for this time tomorrow?'

'Yes,' she said. 'But my findings will not be any more comfortable to you then. You are disturbed.'

301

'I am?' Hall cleared his throat, on the spot, on the back foot. It was not a position he enjoyed.

She got up slowly and placed her cold, bony hand briefly in his. 'You know you are,' she said.

And Henry Hall waited until she'd left the room before he glanced, briefly, to his left. There, in the shadow, just below the window, stood a green-fronted filing cabinet.

'A chap can get frostbite,' Maxwell called across the Tottingleigh car park. For the last hour, he'd wandered about beyond the Victorian wall of the old school as Leighford rush hour had disgorged its Lowrie people along the Flyover, hurrying east and west and north into the chill of the October evening. He'd stamped his feet, wrapped his Jesus scarf around his nose and stuffed his hands into his pockets. A degree or two colder and his breath would be snaking out and winter would be here.

'Max.' Jane Blaisedell shouted back. 'You've gone blue. Can I give you a lift?'

'At least.' He tried to smile, but was afraid his cheeks would crack. 'But what I'm really after is a cup of your legendary cocoa.'

She laughed and clicked open her four-by-four. He clambered in beside her, fumbling for the belt.

'What's going on, Max?' she asked, her hand nowhere near the ignition.

'*Que?*' It was a masterly Manuel, the scurrying little Spaniard of *Fawlty Towers*.

Jane looked ostentatiously round. 'No Jacquie,' she said. She glanced down into the well where his feet used to be attached to his legs before the cold had got to him. 'No Surrey. Otherwise you'd be wearing cycle clips. And if you had Jacquie, you wouldn't need Surrey. And vice versa.'

'Anybody would think you were a woman policeman.' He clicked his tongue. 'I'm impressed.'

'Which means,' she checked her watch, 'you left Leighford High nearly two hours ago...'

'One,' he corrected her. 'Pastoral meeting. I can show you the agenda if you like. It's not the perfect alibi, though; I was asleep through most of it, even though I was in the chair.'

'...and you probably caught the 109 from Eagle Street.'

'You've got me.' He held up both hands. 'I used my OAP bus pass for the Hell of it.'

'Why?'

'Because I can.'

'Don't bullshit me, Max,' she said flatly. 'I've had a bitch of a day and I'm not in the mood for your eccentricities. What do you want?'

'I want to know about Uncle Tony,' he said.

Jane turned away from him sharply. 'Get out,' she growled.

'Jane...'

'Fucking get out!' she shrieked.

He leaned across to her. The tough little Cockney from south of the river was losing the hard-nosed shell she built and rebuilt around herself with every reversal in her life. 'Jacquie's putting her sanity on the line for you,' he said.

'What?' The girl was blinking, staring into the face of this old mad man.

303

He leaned back, giving her space. 'You didn't know.'

'I still don't. For fuck's sake, Max, what are you talking about?'

'Henry's taken you off the Lupescu thing, hasn't he? You couldn't handle it.'

She turned to him, her face white with rage. 'No,' she snarled. 'I couldn't handle it. I wake up shitting myself every bloody night. You know that. I'm not proud of the fact. I cried all over both of you. Isn't that enough? How much more humiliation do you want?'

'No,' he told her flatly. 'No, it isn't enough. Henry asked Jacquie to take your place.'

He heard the girl's intake of breath. 'Jesus!' she whispered. 'Oh, that's terrible.'

'Potentially, yes,' he nodded. 'Jane, are you on tablets? Getting counselling?'

'Both,' she said. Suddenly, she was a very little girl, crouched behind her steering wheel, lost, alone.

One by one, her colleagues were scattering to their cars, giving the pair odd glances. She noticed and tried to smile.

'Bastards!' she hissed through the tears. 'They're loving this.'

'I've got colleagues like that,' he nodded, taking in their leering faces. 'Can you drive this thing? Or did we give you people the vote all those years ago for nothing?'

She sniffed defiantly and kicked the ignition into life, jamming the stick into gear and roaring out of the gateway in a flurry of gravel.

'Stuff 'em,' said Maxwell, waving at Gavin

304

Henslow with a winning smile. 'Let 'em think we're having a torrid affair.'

She looked at him, scowling through tear-filled eyes. 'I'm having counselling, Max,' she said. 'But I'm not that far gone.'

'Atta girl!' And he nudged her knee with his fist, in the most fatherly way he could.

'She knew about Uncle Tony.'

'What?' Jacquie hadn't seen Maxwell all day. He'd been off at the crack of eight o'six, pedalling like a banshee – and you know how they can cycle – along Columbine to fight the good, underpaid, outnumbered fight. Then he'd chaired his wretched pastoral meeting, hearing himself drone on about academic mentoring and target setting and all the other revisited ideas that Educationists kept recycling every decade or so. He'd stopped off for a bite at that centre of world-renowned cuisine, the KFC in Mortimer Street, asking the terminal acne case behind the counter just what was a Zinger exactly; and on to the Arquebus, where Deena Harrison was notable by her absence and they'd run through a couple of scenes and gone home. It was late now, the October night enfolding sleeping Leighford in its arms, the sea a wild, grey thing searching hungrily for its prey in the darkness.

'Jane's Uncle Tony,' Maxwell said. 'Magda Lupescu knew about him.'

'No.' Jacquie shook her head against the padding of the bed head. 'You've lost me a few times in the years I've known you, Max; there, I've admitted it. But now I'm as lost as...'

'The lost Dutchman mine,' he smiled, remembering the magical cowboy books of his childhood, where board games lay back to back with articles on how to make your own lariat and understand smoke signals. 'Think back, heart of darkness. Remember when Jane came to see us in that dreadful state after her experience with Lupescu at the murder site?'

Jacquie remembered. How could she forget? She'd been there herself.

'She said, between her tears, that Magda even knew about Uncle Tony. Then she clammed up. I asked her about it.'

'When?' Jacquie frowned.

'Between my pastoral meeting and the culinary apogee of *my* entire life.'

'Max,' she sat as upright as her bump would allow, 'you didn't tell me.'

'No,' he agreed. 'That's what I'm doing now. See – watch my lips. I'm talking about today.'

Jacquie was appalled. 'You pried into my friend's private life.'

'You bet your sweet bippy I did.' Jacquie was too young for Rowan and Martin's catchphrase from the Sixties, but a little generation-leaping had never fazed Mad Max. 'Three people are dead and the woman who is carrying my child is frightened to death. I feel a little prying is in order, don't you?'

'So who is Uncle Tony? Jane certainly doesn't talk about him.'

'That's because he molested her when she was ten. Then he killed himself.'

'My God. She told you this?'

'It took a while,' he said. 'I was late for rehearsal as a result. Look, Jacquie, I wouldn't have done any of this without good reason, you know that.'

She did. Peter Maxwell was the kindest person she knew. He would never hurt anyone. Oh, unless it was Dierdre Lessing, the Kraken of Leighford High. Oh, or Bernard Ryan, Lord of the Flies. But they both had it coming. 'It's not uncommon, I guess.' The policewoman in Jacquie kicked in. 'Most sexual cases against children are perpetrated by a family member. What happened?'

'It started shortly after her tenth birthday,' he told her, folding his pyjamaed arms over the quilt cover. 'Just cuddling at first, then it got a bit sweatier. I suppose you don't have to groom kids if you're related to them. Apparently, he tried full intercourse...'

'Bastard!' Jacquie hissed.

'But had an attack of the consciences. They found him a few days later. He'd hanged himself.'

'Hanged?'

Maxwell nodded. 'The point is, Jacquie,' he said, 'that Jane has never told anyone about this until me, earlier tonight. I think she feels better for it now.'

She looked at the familiar face, the bright, sad eyes. 'I'm sure she does,' she said. 'But why did you need to ask her in the first place?'

'Because,' he turned to her, 'I need to know whether this Lupescu woman is a fraud who gets lucky sometimes or whether there's anything in her.'

'And?' Jacquie's face had darkened. Darkened

307

because she didn't really want to know Maxwell's answer.

'She knew about Uncle Tony.' Maxwell was repeating himself, and Peter Maxwell never did that lightly.

Chapter Twenty-One

'Paternity leave, Max?' Legs Diamond swept off his specs in the manner of great headmasters throughout time. Except that Diamond wasn't a great headmaster; come to think of it, he wasn't even a headmaster, on the grounds that he'd never mastered anything.

'I'm shocked you haven't heard of the concept, Headmaster.' Maxwell's eyebrows had nearly reached his hairline. 'You being of the post-modernist persuasion and all.'

'Well, yes,' Diamond flustered. 'Of course I've *heard* of it. It's just that, well ... you?'

Maxwell took in the plastic, grey-suited idiot sitting in his plastic, grey office. 'I don't know which aspersion you are casting in my direction, Headmaster; whether I lack the physical capability of fathering a child or whether I am so appallingly insensitive and chauvinist that I would not contemplate even launching such a request.'

'No, no, Max.' Diamond was well and truly wrapped up, as usual. 'I didn't mean either, I assure you.'

'So it's settled, then.' Maxwell was already on his feet. 'I'll see Paul Moss about my cover on my way out.'

'No, that's not how it works,' Diamond called. 'It's like maternity leave, Max. From date a to date b.'

'Ah, that's maternity leave, Headmaster,' Maxwell patronised. 'Paternity leave may be *like* it, but it is not it. Physiological differences demand different considerations.'

'So what do you need?' Diamond was confused, as he often was, in fact, in the presence of his Head of Sixth Form.

'A couple of days should do it,' Maxwell smiled.

'A couple of days?' Diamond blinked.

'Starting this afternoon.' He stopped in the doorway. 'Did anyone ever tell you what a brick you are, Headmaster? It just isn't true what the others say.' And he was gone.

Maxwell was still pedalling home when Jacquie came back from shopping. From the bushes beside the front door of 38 Columbine, a yellow-eyed killer watched her every move, his nostrils quivering, his ears pricked. He saw her struggle out from that appalling machine, the one with the roar and the smell, though it had a nice warm bit he liked stretching on in the cold weather. She was carrying those white plastic things again, the ones he knew carried food. This was a good sign. Chicken, perhaps? Or steak? Metternich was a surf 'n' turf man as any self-respecting maritime feline should be. He yawned and stretched, easing the claws from their hoods. A startled sparrow screeched, flapping skyward from the ground yards away. Still got it, Metternich, old boy.

'Hello, dear.' The unmistakable chirrup of Mrs Troubridge caught Jacquie as she reached her front door. The little square by Mrs Troubridge's vestibule had to be the most gardened four inches in Tony Blair's Britain.

'Hello,' the policewoman smiled. 'How are you?'

'No, no.' The old girl appeared through the gap in the privet, the one carefully crafted by years of nosiness. 'That's what I should be asking you.' She pointed with her trowel to Jacquie's bump. Jacquie had never seen Mrs Troubridge without a gardening implement in her hand.

'I'm fine,' Jacquie told her, grateful to rest the shopping bags against each other on Maxwell's step. 'Over that ghastly morning sickness, thank God.'

'Oh, good, my dear.' Mrs Troubridge nodded. 'Dreadful. Dreadful. Those men don't know what they put us through, do they? Do they know who killed that appalling Winchcombe woman yet?'

Jacquie was expecting a little more balance in the question, perhaps, a little more getting round to things gradually, but Mrs Troubridge *was* a gardener, used to calling a spade a spade, and she'd clearly dispensed with the small talk. 'Er... I don't know,' she said.

'But you're in the police, my dear.'

'Not at the moment,' Jacquie reminded her, patting her excuse.

'Oh, yes,' Mrs Troubridge shrilled. 'But you can't plead the belly for ever, you know. Besides, your rather bossy friend, what's her name? Jane? She keeps you ... what do you young people say? Up to pace, hmm?'

'You are very well informed, Mrs Troubridge,' Jacquie said, narrowing her eyes at the old girl

311

and making a mental note to watch her like a hawk in future.

The neighbour poked her gently with her trowel, gripped in a pink rubber hand. 'My dear,' she smiled softly. 'I'm an old woman. I've lost my husband and God didn't bless us with children. I don't have any family and most of my friends have shuffled off this mortal coil. What I do have is an insatiable interest in what goes on around me.' She closed to the younger woman. 'Did you know, for instance, that that snooty bitch at number 30 is on the game?'

'Really?' Jacquie's eyes were wide.

Mrs Troubridge leaned even closer. Her nose was now nearly in Jacquie's cleavage. 'And Mrs Wickens, in that ghastly Mock Tudor monstrosity on the corner, used to be Charles Williams, a steel fabricator of Hove?'

Jacquie's speechless response said it all.

'Exactly.' The old girl tapped the side of her nose. 'No, I knew no good would come of Martita Winchcombe. I could have predicted she'd meet a sticky end ever since she fell pregnant.'

'Hardly *that* terrible,' Jacquie smiled, having fallen pretty far herself.

'Oh, my dear,' Mrs Troubridge chuckled. 'How times have changed. You and Mr Maxwell make a delightful couple, for all you're living in sin and he's old enough to be your father. But I'm talking about the Forties. Yes, I know, there was a war on and we all thought we'd be blown to bits any minute and those ghastly Americans were over-paid, over-sexed and over here, but *some* of us retained our principles. I happen to know Mr

Troubridge was a virgin when we wed and him in the navy for five years. No, in some places, back then, they still put girls ... like that ... into institutions, you know?'

'Did they?'

'The news was all over Leighford. We didn't have abortions on the NHS in those days. In fact, we didn't have an NHS. Martita passed out one morning at my very feet. We all knew why.' Mrs Troubridge bridled quietly. 'She had to go away – to have the baby, I mean. When she came back, well, no one said anything of course. She'd been on a scheme, as the Canadians called it then. Had the little bastard adopted.'

'You seem to know an awful lot about it, Mrs Troubridge,' Jacquie commented.

The old girl chortled. 'I have to confess my insatiable interest in what goes on around me is not something that developed with maturity. I've always had it. Little boy, apparently. Brought up in Cheltenham, so the story went, by very respectable people. Martita never set her cap at anyone after that.'

'Whereas ... before?' Jacquie ventured.

A shadow came over her neighbour's face and Mrs Troubridge turned back to her gardening. 'I told Mr Maxwell,' she said. 'Venetian blinds. You'll forgive me, my dear, if I don't elucidate.'

Henry Hall was slumped in his office back at the nick. A less professional man would have run out of the Incident Room screaming long before that wild, wet Wednesday night. The rain hit his window like machine gun bullets, the wind hammering in vicious gusts from the north. He was still swilling the dregs of his coffee around the bottom of the plastic cup in his hand, poring over the paperwork that comes with murder. His computer was switched resolutely off, as his back and his eyes and his mouse finger told him he'd done enough of the superhighway for one day. He toyed for a while with jacking in his police career and making a fortune by inventing computer pop-ups that said 'Tiredness Kills. Take a Break'. But there was probably a copyright clause somewhere, so it was back to sleuthing.

Everybody was on his back on this one. The Fourth Estate, those gallant, sensitive and helpful gentlemen and ladies of the Press, had done little but ridicule Hall and his entire investigation ever since the leak about psychic detection. At least they did not have the name of Magda Lupescu – yet. But it could only be a matter of time. Fiona Elliot may have been trusting of messages from the Other Side, but she seemed particularly keen that the terrestrial police from This Side solve her late aunt's murder and pdq. And the grating Carole Bartlett was almost a daily visitor, demanding to know what had happened to the missing copy of the Sheridan play and how long it would be before her husband's entangled finances were sorted out.

Jane Blaisedell was flaky. Jacquie Carpenter was better. But that was another odd thing for Henry Hall: not that Jacquie had agreed to act as Jane's stand-in – he knew instinctively that she would – but that Peter Maxwell hadn't gone ape-shit about it; he knew instinctively he'd do that too. In the silence and the solitude, Henry Hall allowed himself the teensiest of smiles. Peter Maxwell would go ape-shit, all right; it was just that, with Peter Maxwell, you could never be sure exactly when. And many was the kid, and the colleague and the copper, who had rued the experience.

Christ Church meadow lay wreathed in the October mist as Jacquie's Ka purred past, grateful to be off the A338 and gliding past the Thames.

'Isis,' said Maxwell, apparently dozing beside her, slumped in the passenger seat with his tweed hat over his face.

'Hmm?'

'The Thames becomes the Isis when it goes past Oxford. Christ knows why. Pure snobbery, of course.'

'You don't like this town, do you?' she smiled, vaguely aware that the number of cyclists whizzing around her had trebled in the last few minutes.

'Oh, it's all right.' He stretched. 'Nobody lives here now, of course, after all those serial killings in the Morse series. Entire population's been wiped out. It's a ghost town. Rumour has it there's a university here somewhere.'

'Which college did you say you wanted?'

'Corpus Christi,' he told her, straightening up and pulling the cap off his face. 'That's body of Christ to you non-Classicists.'

'Bollocks!' she snorted and hung a right. They were in the High now – Oxford students for generations apparently being congenitally unable to pronounce the word 'street'.

315

'Founded in the year of Our Lord 1517.' Maxwell was giving Jacquie the guided tour. 'The same year in which Fr. Luther upset everybody in Christendom with his ninety-five theses pinned to the door of Wittenberg cathedral. God, I had trouble just doing one. There are twenty-seven sundials in Front Quad, topped with a pelican pecking out its own heart; like you do. Corpus is the only college to have its original founders plate. All the others gave theirs to Charles I for his war effort. So...'

'So?' It had been a long time since Jacquie Carpenter had done the Tudors and Stuarts.

'So either the college was tight as a gnat's chuff or they were secret parliamentarians. Like I said, they're a dodgy lot in Oxford. Next right.'

'How do you know?' She jammed on the brakes to avoid yet another cyclist. 'All these buildings look alike.'

'I have a nose for Academe.' Maxwell duly tapped it. 'That's Merton, with the oldest library in England – after mine – built in the 1370s. Didn't start out too well mind. Even Geoffrey Chaucer had more books than they did and he was a bloody customs officer. Here we are.'

She stopped the Ka. 'There's nowhere to park.'

He smiled. 'Welcome to Oxford.'

On his way up the stairs, Peter Maxwell tossed a coin.

'Heads,' Jacquie said, steadying herself on the banisters. She'd been here before, not Corpus Christi College, Oxford, but wheeling and dealing with Mad Max.

316

'Sorry, heart,' he consoled her. 'It's tails. My way, then.' His Sinatra was perfect. Flat and heartless.

'Thank you, Frank,' she grinned. 'I just hope it works.'

As they reached the door, he leaned to her. 'Trust me, lady, I'm a Cambridge man.'

In the lobby, a grey-haired woman in a starched white blouse appeared to be a leftover from the days of Gibson girls, with an upswept bun of a hairdo and a pearl-clasped choker, longing for the day when they invented brassieres and gave girls like her the vote.

'Good morning.' Maxwell swept off his hat and beamed. 'I wonder, is Professor Usherwood in?'

The Gibson girl looked over her pince-nez, sizing up the pair. Effete, over-the-top gent with his pregnant daughter. She looked a little long in the tooth for someone hoping for a place, but the Gibson girl had known stranger attempts to get into Oxford, circumventing little things like A-levels and University Applications procedures. Usually it was fathers and pushy mothers who claimed they'd gone to the college in their day and surely, there was some obscure little bursary...

'Who wants to know?'

Rather churlish riposte, Maxwell thought, the sort of comeback he'd expect on Leighford Sea Front of a Saturday night, but it merely confirmed what he'd always maintained about Oxford. 'I am Peter Maxwell,' he told her. 'This is Ms Jacquie Carpenter. An old pupil of mine suggested if ever I were in Oxford, to look up the Professor.'

'Really?' The Gibson girl rose and crossed to the counter on which Maxwell lolled. 'And who may this pupil be?'

'Deena Harrison,' Maxwell said.

The Gibson girl looked vacant. 'Don't know her,' she said.

'How long have you been at Corpus, Mrs...?'

'For two years,' she said. 'And that's Miss.'

'Yes, of course it is,' Maxwell smiled. 'Well, Deena came down this summer – the one that's just gone, I mean. She was reading Drama.'

'As I said,' the Gibson girl was standing her ground. 'I have never heard of her. You must have the wrong college.'

Maxwell was about to launch into Plan B when a warrant card flashed into the air inches from his nose.

'Detective Sergeant Carpenter, West Sussex CID,' Jacquie said, looking the woman straight in the eye. 'You are?'

'Helen Burden,' the Gibson girl blinked, taken off guard. This was an *unheard* of way to get into Oxford.

'Is Professor Usherwood in?' Jacquie was in work mode. The ground shook.

'Yes, yes of course. I'll tell him you're here.'

'Thank you.'

The secretary hurried to her intercom and pressed it. 'Professor, there are some police officers to see you.' A pause. 'Do go through. First door on the left.'

'Looks like I should have won the toss after all,' Jacquie whispered out of the corner of her mouth. 'We wasted three or four minutes there.'

318

'I've got to get one of those.' Maxwell pointed to the warrant card disappearing into Jacquie's handbag and did a double take at the door. 'Oh.'

Professor Paul Usherwood sat in his oak-panelled study, decorated with wall-to-wall leather volumes that Laurence Llewellyn Bowen would not have remotely understood. He was seventy if he was a day and he was sitting in a wheelchair.

'Police,' the man was beaming. 'How very exciting. Do, please, have seats.' He pressed a button on his intercom. 'Coffee, please, Helen. Now, how may I help?'

It had taken Gavin Henslow nearly three weeks to sequester the bank records of the late Daniel Bartlett. The Nat West had been forthcoming; so, astonishingly, had Lloyds TSB. Jowetts were a little more obstructive, muttering pompously about client confidentiality. How tin-pot little firms like these had survived the Bank Charter Act of 1844 men like Peter Maxwell didn't know. Men like Gavin Henslow, for all his fast-track insidery had never heard of the Bank Charter Act of 1844. The Swiss banks, all of them allegedly run by gnomes, were silence itself, until the oddly quick-witted Henslow breathed the word 'Interpol' in his phone conversation, and then they thought they might just be able to find a way to cooperate.

'He's skint, guv,' was the financial whiz-kid's summation of his enquiries. 'Next time his wife comes in asking who's nicked that bloody Sheridan copy, the answer is likely to be nobody. He hocked it himself.'

Henry Hall nodded, trying in his own mind to see how this related to anything. 'So what's he spent it on?' he thought aloud.

'If you mean the paltry sum he paid me in alimony, yes, I suppose it was enough, just.' Carole Bartlett had indeed called in again, late that afternoon, to check on how Hall's team were pursuing their enquiries. She was sitting in Hall's Interview Room Number One. And she hadn't even mentioned the Sheridan when the DCI was asking questions of his own. 'But don't let the amount fool you,' she snarled. 'The bastard owed me every penny for the mental cruelty he put me through.'

'You took him to the cleaners,' Hall observed.

Carole Bartlett was, momentarily, stuck for an answer. 'I hope that's not some sort of chauvinist rallying of the ranks,' she said eventually. 'The financial arrangements I had with my husband are no one's business but our own.'

'Normally, I would agree with you,' Hall said. 'But murder has a habit of publicising a lot of things that would ordinarily remain private.'

'I see.' Carole Bartlett was needled, pursing her lips and flashing daggers at Hall and the squat figure of Jane Blaisedell who sat beside him. 'So having made no progress at all on this case, you are now falling back on the tired old nonsense about spouses being the most likely killers of their husbands, hmm? Tiresome and hardly progress.'

'The statistics lean that way,' Hall nodded. Such things were his bread and butter.

'I would hardly kill the golden goose, would I?' the woman snapped.

'That's just the point,' Hall said. 'Your husband wasn't golden anymore, was he? There are other motives for murder.'

Carole Bartlett was on her feet, the tape still whirring in the corner. 'Are you sitting there, in your bare-faced incompetence, and accusing me of murdering my husband?'

'No, no.' Hall shook his head. 'There is a form of words for that, Mrs Bartlett, and rest assured, had I intended to charge you, I would already have used them.'

'That's outrageous!' she blurted. 'You will be hearing from my solicitor.'

'Can't wait,' said Hall. 'Could you see yourself out?'

'Floosies.' Carole Bartlett stopped in mid-fume. 'The many little trollops who have crowded, inexplicably, into my husband's bed. *That's* where his money has gone. You mark my words.'

As they heard her heels clatter away down the Leighford nick corridor, Henry Hall turned to Jane Blaisedell. 'Have we marked her words?'

Jane was getting back to something approaching normal now. She still had nightmares when the night came cold and gusting from the north. And she still didn't like flat, dimly-lit areas because they reminded her of the stage where Gordon Goodacre died. And soft, padded carpets scorched black that marked the end of Dan Bartlett and the old lady smell of the house of Martita Winchcombe. But worst of all she didn't like the bad breath of middle-aged men and their sweaty fingers...

'Jane?' Hall noticed, and not for the first time, the faraway look in the girl's eyes.

321

'Sorry guv,' she flustered. 'What was the question?'

'Floosies.' Hall repeated the widow's words. 'How many of Dan Bartlett's little trollops have we found to date?'

Chapter Twenty-Two

Geraint Horsenell's musicians moved into the Arquebus that night. If anything, Ashley Wilkes was a little more heartened by this lot than he was by Deena Harrison's cast.

'Girls with cellos, eh, Geraint?' Maxwell beamed at his colleague, unwrapping himself of scarf and hat.

'Don't knock it till you've tried it.' The Head of Music winked, struggling at the theatre's side door with a bass drum.

'Are you talking about the cellos now or the girls?' Maxwell asked.

'You dirty old bastard,' Geraint snorted. As heads of Music go, Horsenell was one of the more congenial. In Maxwell's experience, they were either up-themselves no-hopers, bitter because they were not concert pianists and with egos the size of the Albert Hall, or they were social misfits who thought that bashing the furniture with bits of wood passed for percussion. Mercifully, Geraint Horsenell was somewhere between. Besides, he was refreshingly human, told a darned good knock-knock joke and mixed Martinis drier than his native west Wales used to be in the Good Old Days of a Sunday. 'This is nice.'

He was looking at the orchestra pit, streets ahead of the corner of Leighford High's hall where they usually put him and his motley crew,

323

to punctuate passably good drama with a bit of terpsichore.

'Christ, is that Benny Barker?' He caught sight of the techie flashing past in the dim light swathed in cables.

'Hello, Mr Horsenell,' the lad waved.

'I've lost count of the microphones that bastard buggered up for me at school. Not to mention the PA system lovingly bought by the Friends of the School when we all thought we were going to perform at the Dome.'

'Ah, heady days,' Maxwell remembered. 'Still, I'm sure he meant well.'

'Don't tell me somebody's let him loose in the real world? God, the place will be devoid of apparatus by Christmas. Talking of which...'

'No.'

'Oh, come on, Max.'

'No, Geraint.' The Head of Sixth Form was adamant, helping Davinia Whatserface up the steps with her French horn. He knew exactly what was coming and refused to give an inch.

'But your Twelve Days of Christmas are legendary,' Horsenell pleaded, arms outstretched.

'Agreed, and that's *is* legendary, by the way. It's a single piece. Let one of the youngsters have a go, Geraint. Christ, man, I shall be ninety next birthday. Why don't you make the Christmas concert more modern this year? What about this new sound? What's it called? Jazz?'

'Oh, hah! Murphy, will you watch it with that bassoon? I assume you know, from the hunted look on your father's face in the car park just now, how much these things cost. Well,' Horsenell became conspiratorial, whispering in Maxwell's ear, 'is she here?'

'Who?'

'Who, he says. Who? Deena Harrison, that's who. I couldn't believe it when Diamond told me she was directing *The Shop*. One or both of you must be barking.'

'Are you talking about me and Diamond, now? Or me and Deena? Either way, you may have a point.'

The cast were in the Green Room, along the corridor and down the stairs from the stage. Only David Balham was in the wings, emoting inside the full size Audrey II and pulling cords like a maniac to get the thing to open its throat and swing its tendrils. Nobody told him when Mrs Carmichael did the casting that he'd need muscles like Arnie Schwarzenegger for the role. The night they brought the band in was always a break in service in any production. The orchestra had to acquaint themselves with the lighting, the seat distribution, the acoustics of the theatre. It took over an hour for Geraint Horsenell to set up the speakers and his own podium and he felt sure that Benny Barker was fighting him every inch of the way, with insucks of breath and tuts and 'Well, I don't know, Mr Horsenell. *You're* the expert, of course.'

Of Deena Harrison, there was no sign. And that was a pity, because Maxwell particularly needed to speak to her.

'Mr Wilkes.' The Head of Sixth Form had left the squabbling musos to it and bearded the Theatre Manager in his lair, the sound-proofed control box high above the gods. From here, Maxwell could see Audrey II's tendrils vibrating as David Balham got into his stride and Geraint Horsenell fussing like the old Welsh hen he was, clucking from one muso to the next, endlessly pandering to their little peccadilloes. These were the pampered few, the last of a dying breed – the children of grammar school children, to whom the piano, along with elocution, ballet and the gymkhana, were still the arbiters of breeding. Everything else was a sop to the masses, the great unwashed.

'Oh, evening, Mr Maxwell. It's coming on, I see.' Wilkes was nodding to the scene below.

'Indeed,' Maxwell nodded, finding a swivel chair alongside an instrument panel that appeared to have been borrowed from NASA. 'Talking of coming on, how are things with Deena?'

'I'm sorry.'

'You might well be,' Maxwell nodded. 'Many of us might be, in all sorts of ways.'

Wilkes hauled the headphones from around his neck. 'What are you talking about?' he asked.

Maxwell was gazing around him. 'You've got some woofers and tweeters here, haven't you? Do your own wiring? I mean, you are familiar with electrics?'

'Maxwell.' The 'Mr' had gone. It's always the first thing to disappear when people are rattled. 'I think you'd better explain what you're talking about.'

Maxwell leaned towards his man. 'About you raping Deena Harrison.'

The theatre manager blinked, swallowing hard.

'What do you mean?'

'Violation, Mr Wilkes, the taking of virginity in some cases, compromising a lady's honour. I could be more graphic, but I went to a good school and I'm sure you get the drift.'

'It was consensual,' Wilkes blurted. 'The lying little bitch...'

'You needn't bore me with positions,' Maxwell said. 'But I will need other details.'

'Details?' Wilkes frowned. 'You fucking weirdo. That's what this is all about, isn't it? That's how you get your kicks. *Hearing* about things. I've read about teachers like you. Well, I'm not playing your perverted games.'

'Oh, there's nothing perverted about catching a murderer, Mr Wilkes.'

'A m– Now, wait just a minute...'

'What happened with Deena?' Maxwell was shouting. Wilkes licked his lips. The odd man in the bow tie and the tweed jacket was staring at him. There was no escape, no compromise, no middle ground. Just Peter Maxwell, the one the kids called Mad.

'She ... came on to me.' The theatre manager was calmer now, trying to compose himself. 'Giving me a sob story about how messed up her life was.'

'And you took advantage of her?' Maxwell's voice was steady, like the turns of the rack. Regular. Slow. Relentless.

'No, I ... well, I suppose, in a way. Look, Maxwell, we're all human. She's an attractive girl, for God's sake. We're consenting adults.' He stopped for a moment, thinking. 'Is she saying I raped her?' His voice was rising again.

'She is,' Maxwell nodded, 'to some people. And yet not to others.'

'What? You'll have to pass that by me again.'

'She told Patrick Collinson you raped her. She told me you didn't.'

'Then why...'

'Because there's something wrong with Deena, Mr Wilkes. And I had to be sure before I go further.'

'Be sure about what?'

'That what she told Collinson wasn't true. And what she told me was.'

'So you believe me?'

Maxwell let the man sweat a little before nodding. 'Yes,' he said. 'I think I do. About Deena, I mean.'

'So what's all this about murder?' he asked.

'Ah, well.' Maxwell was on his feet, making for the door. 'That's the sixty-four thousand dollar question, isn't it? If I were you, Mr Wilkes, I'd make very sure I wasn't alone with Deena again.'

Where was Anthony Wetta when you needed him? Actually, it was just as well the lad wasn't with Maxwell that Thursday night. After all, it was one thing to shop him to the law for his night-breaking activities – that was merely what a responsible and caring teacher would do, impossibly pulled as he was between duty to his charges and duty to society. But to encourage the boy to hone his skills on the Harrison household, with said charges pending, might have been considered criminal conduct unbecoming.

Maxwell leaned Surrey against the hedge and peered in through the darkened windows. He'd been here before, of course, but only once and it took him a while to get his bearings. He rattled locks and checked window catches at the front, well screened as he was by the high privet. Thank God for the Englishman's obsession with his castle and the privacy it brought. He was wearing the hoodie and trainers he'd worn in his little night raid with George Lemon. He'd half-inched them from Lost Property at school. Not only did he look the part of a congenital waste of space; he smelt like one too.

'Shit!' He stubbed his toe on a roller someone had left lying about behind the house. Hard, aren't they? The garage to his right looked deserted, abandoned. No Deena. And he needed to talk to Deena. The kitchen door was locked too and none of the ways in had those little catches he knew how to force. If he wanted entry this time, it would be an elbow through the glass or a brick against pane. And anyway, what could he learn? Nothing he didn't already know, thanks to the nice man from Oxford, the one in the wheelchair. He checked his watch by what light there was. Half-ten. His Jacquie would be asleep now. She'd have waited up as she always tried to do, but would be quietly snoring in the crook of the sofa. Time to bounce ideas off his other companion of a mile. The black and white one.

'Now, you're not going to accuse me of anything, Max, are you?' Patrick Collinson held up both hands in something approaching alarm. He was sitting in his office again, Doris primed for action in the ante-room as before.

Maxwell laughed. 'I think I've made enough of a fool of myself for a while,' he said. 'I was hoping you had a minute.'

'As it so happens,' Collinson said, 'my ten o'clock cancelled earlier. Just as well; he doesn't need an accountant, he needs a miracle worker. Grab a seat.'

Maxwell plonked himself down in Collinson's comfortable armchair. The man was doing all right for himself, despite the rather ghastly wallpaper – still, there was no accounting for taste.

'What can I do for you?'

'Martita Winchcombe,' Maxwell said.

'Ah, yes.' Collinson's face fell a little. 'Tell me, are the police making any progress?'

'If they are, none of it's come my way,' the Head of Sixth Form said. 'You must have known her quite well. What sort of woman was she?'

'I thought you were concentrating on Gordon Goodacre.' Collinson leaned back in his chair behind the enormous desk.

'I was,' Maxwell admitted. 'But the trail's gone a little cold there. If there was a trail at all, of course.'

'Meaning?'

'Meaning, what if Gordon were just an old-fashioned accident, after all? Nothing to do with what happened to Martita?'

'Helluva coincidence, isn't it?' Collinson frowned.

'It happens,' Maxwell said. 'Remember when Jill Dando was killed?'

Collinson did.

'She was on the front cover of the Radio Times the previous week. And on the back of said magazine was an ad for whodunits, some book club or other. The word at the top, in bold red type, was "Murder". If you opened the mag out and read, as we Europeans are wont to do, from left to right, the sentence was a clear instruction. "Murder Jill Dando".'

'My God,' Collinson muttered. 'So you mean, that was some sort of divine message for a nutcase?'

'No.' Maxwell shook his head. 'I mean it was a coincidence. You want another one? Seven Seven. Suicide bombers on London streets. The Number Thirty bus in Tavistock Square. Know what was advertised on the side?' Collinson didn't.

'"The Terror",' Maxwell quoted. '"Bold and Brilliant".'

'Well, I didn't see anything bold or brilliant behind that. Act of appalling cowardice.'

'That's because you aren't a Muslim fanatic with jihad on your agenda and paradise in your sights. Let's get back to Martita. How long had you known her?'

'Ooh, let's see. Ever since I moved to Leighford.'

'When was that?'

'Twenty years ago – give or take.'

'You knew her via the theatre?'

'Not at first, no. She was a client.'

'Was she?'

'Uh-huh,' Collinson wagged a finger at Maxwell. 'I'm not going to lecture you on client

331

confidentiality. Let's just say the old girl's house was in order.'

'Did she have any family?'

Collinson shook his head. 'No,' he said. 'Nobody.'

'I heard there was an indiscretion years ago,' Maxwell said.

'Indiscretion?' Collinson repeated. 'Martita? Ooh, how juicy.' He was chuckling.

'And the indiscretion led to a child, a son.'

'Well,' Collinson sighed. 'There's nothing in the old girl's paperwork to that effect. I've shown the police, of course. They do seem to be quite thorough.'

'Who did you have?'

'Hmm?'

'Who interviewed you?'

'Oh, Lord,' Collinson frowned. 'Now you've asked me. They all look alike, don't they? In our day, Max, a copper was about forty with shoulders like tallboys. Now they're children who weigh about six stone dripping wet. Look ... I don't want to labour the point – about Deena I mean. But I don't mind telling you, that whole business shook me up a little. I even confided in Doris, I was so shook up. I mean, why would she invent things like that?'

'Why indeed, Patrick,' Maxwell smiled. 'Why would someone stretch a piece of wire across Martita Winchcombe's stairs? Why would someone carefully fray Dan Bartlett's wiring system?'

'My God.' Collinson's eyes widened. 'You think it's the Harrison girl, don't you?'

Maxwell looked at his man. 'When she was

eleven, she set fire to the toilets at Leighford High. She'd just celebrated her twelfth birthday when she threw a little boy called Oliver Wendell down some stairs.'

'Good Lord.'

'In your double life, Patrick, as Chartered Accountant and Theatre Secretary, have you come across many serial killers?'

'Er ... I should hope not,' the man chuckled.

'Well, you probably have,' Maxwell said, matter-of-factly. 'But they don't always stand out. It's well known among the psychiatrists who study them, that most of those who go on to serial slaughter exhibit three tendencies as children. They call them the Triad. The first is an obsession with fire. They love nothing better than to see things burn. The crackle of flames, the flare, the panic it causes – it excites them. Deena and the toilet block – sounds like one of JK Rowling's earlier, little-known efforts. The second is a compulsion to torture animals. Now, it's unpro-fessional of me, I know, but young Oliver Wendell could easily have been mistaken for an animal – and Deena threw him down the Physics Lab stairs, his head bouncing on all six; count them. The third tendency? Well, that's rather a delicate one, really. The third tendency is wetting the bed. Perhaps we should ask Ashley Wilkes?'

She lay in the darkness, listening to the dog barking somewhere to the west and the stray growl of a passing car. When she sat upright, her head against the cold metal of the bedstead, the room was bathed in light, bright, painful. Why didn't they switch it off? Why, even though she knew it was the wee, small hours, didn't they let her sleep?

She could see them looking at her through those holes in the walls, their eyes bright and leering. And she could hear them laughing, laughing at her pain, her torment. She, who had borne so much, must bear still more.

'Mrs Sanders?' Fiona Elliot peered down the red-lacquered passageway. The place looked like a knocking shop in downtown Amsterdam. Not that Fiona Elliot had much experience of those.

'Rowena,' the woman said, opening the door. 'You're Fiona, aren't you?'

'Yes. Is this a good time?'

'It is always a good time in the spirit world, Fiona, you know that.'

'Yes,' the large woman said. 'Yes, I do. And that's a comfort.'

Rowena Sanders was a little, bird-like woman with spiky, orange-tipped hair and a mass of cheap jewellery. Had Peter Maxwell been at her house in Acacia Grove, the one that had been the vicarage, he'd have assumed she was rehearsing for the Leighford Carnival. She led Fiona into a small room, its aggressive squareness softened with long, low, padded furniture, scatter cushions and throws. There was an indefinable smell in the air which would have had Henry Hall reaching for his truncheon and the tons of paperwork consistent with an arrest for possession of illegal substances.

'Sit here, Fiona,' Rowena said. She had a soft sibilance that was soothing to a woman who had spent the last three weeks battering her head against the brick wall of police officialdom. Rowena held both her hands and sat cross-legged on the cushion opposite her. She closed her eyes. 'Sadness,' she said. 'I feel sadness. But at the same time, an anger.' She opened her eyes. 'Someone close to you has passed over.'

'Not all that close,' Fiona had to admit, although the anger was fair enough.

'We all become close on the Other Side,' Rowena said, almost intoning. 'You seek closure, don't you? An explanation. Answers.'

'Yes, I do,' Fiona told her. 'And I want to arrange a séance.'

Rowena let the woman's hands go. 'A séance?' The voice was harder.

'A full séance,' Fiona went on. 'As soon as you can arrange it. You *do* have the expertise?'

'Oh, yes.' An odd look flitted across Rowena Sanders' face. 'Yes, I have the expertise.'

'Will it be here? In this room?' Fiona wanted to know.

'No. Not here. Across the hall. I could show you.'

'No.' Fiona shook her head. 'Not now. There will be time enough.'

Chapter Twenty-Three

'Well, obviously,' Jacquie was freshening Maxwell's coffee, passing him the sweeteners as he poured his own milk, 'Patrick Collinson knows nothing. Martita Winchcombe's got no family, indeed! What about Fiona Elliot?'

'What indeed?' Maxwell was dipping his digestive until it had just the right amount of dunk. 'Who's Fiona Elliot?'

'According to Jane...'

'...and where would we be without her?' Maxwell raised his mug in salute.

'Amen to that,' Jacquie agreed. 'Fiona Elliot is the old girl's niece.'

'Ah,' Maxwell mused. 'Do I smell inheritance?'

'You're just a crabby, suspicious old git,' she told him, in the nicest possible way.

'Fill me in, my darling. My paternity leave ends today and Ten Aitch Three are yearning to hear my war stories.'

'Oh?' Jacquie raised an eyebrow. 'Which war is that, then?'

'Take your pick,' Maxwell shrugged. 'Anything from Hannibal onwards, really. I remember 'em all. Don't get me started on them now. Fiona.'

'Yes.' Jacquie leaned back gratefully in Maxwell's, now their, kitchen. She'd be the last to admit it, but getting around was getting harder these days, the rounder she got. And sitting in

336

one position with a miniature David Beckham inside you was pure murder. Not that she used the analogy in front of Maxwell. To him, it was more likely to be Jonny Wilkinson. After all, he'd gone to a good school. 'Well, Jane told me...'

'That was last night's four-hour phone marathon?'

'It was barely twenty minutes,' Jacquie corrected him. 'But last night, certainly. Jane told me that Fiona Elliot is pretty rabid in the pushing things to a conclusion stakes. She's told Henry she wants action.'

'Not unreasonable, I should have thought.'

'But rumour has it she's calling in the Spook Squad.'

'The what?'

'The Spiritualist circle. There's one in Leighford apparently.'

'Along with the synagogue, the mosque and the Church of Christ Skateboarder; yes, I know.'

'Be serious, Max,' she scolded him. 'They've been going for years, apparently.'

'A hundred and forty-nine to be exact. They were founded by Jedediah Urwin, whose wife used to do manifestations.'

'You what?'

'Phantasms,' he explained, reaching for his last biscuit. 'Ghosts. It's all in the Museum archives. Mrs Urwin'd go into a cubicle, draw the curtains; Mr Urwin'd ask if anyone was there and lo and behold, da-daa, a glowing mass of ectoplasm that looked extraordinarily like Mrs Urwin in a lump of cheesecloth.'

'Fake, then?'

'They all were,' Maxwell told her. 'And the extraordinary thing was how readily everybody fell for all that, back in the good old days. Physicists like Sir William Crookes, philosophers like Henry Sidgwick, doctors like Arthur Conan Doyle – they all bought into the table-rapping bit hook, line and sinker. It was a more gullible age, the faking Fifties and beyond.'

'Well, be that as it may, Jane says the rumour is that Fiona Elliot wants to set up a séance.'

'In the hope that Aunt Martita will pop round for a go on the planchette?'

'The what?'

'Spirit writing. The medium sits with a slate on her lap – or used to in Victorian times, anyway – and the spirit would move in her, so to speak. Hey, presto, a text message from the Other Side.'

Jacquie leaned forward again as Sonny Jim caught her a sharp one in what felt like her chin. 'But this will be no ordinary gathering. She wants everyone connected with her aunt to be present – Ashley Wilkes and Patrick Collinson from the theatre. Magda Lupescu, whose work – and I quote from Jane – "she values highly", the medium herself, Rowena Sanders and Deena Harrison.'

'Deena?' Maxwell sat up. 'I don't think, knowing what we do, that's a very good idea, do you?'

'I don't think *any* of it is a good idea, Max,' Jacquie said. 'I've seen too many kids go off the rails playing with Tarot cards and Ouija boards.'

'It's all in the mind, dear heart,' he smiled, shaking his head.

'So's murder,' she reminded him. 'And there's

one other name on the list.'

'Oh? Whose?'

'Henry Hall's,' Jacquie said. And they both collapsed into fits of hysterics.

'I'm going round and round on this one, guv,' Bill Robbins had to confess. It was a dull, wet Friday morning and he hadn't seen his family for three days. The bed in the Incident Room was not exactly his idea of home comforts, but as Gavin Henslow reminded him in one particularly bitter exchange, it was better than the station house any day of the week.

'Talk to me, Bill.' The DCI lolled back, his jacket slung on the chair behind him, his hands behind his head, looking across the desk to his sergeant. 'It can help sometimes.'

'OK,' Robbins began. 'We've identified five women who have been seen in the company of Dan Bartlett in the last six months. Two of them were one-night stands. Lorraine Cusiter from Tottingleigh – Bartlett picked her up at the Last Man Standing disco on Bayer Street at the end of August.'

'Form?' Hall asked, although he'd read the reports himself and knew the answer.

'Hardly, guv. Just left school. The disco was a celebration of her A-level results.'

'One of Maxwell's Own, eh?' Hall was half talking to himself. 'Better not tell him. I sense his nose up our collective arses as it is. Anything useful on the girl?'

'Bartlett took her home and got into bed with her. She'd had a skinful and couldn't remember

339

much of it.'

'Not exactly Don Juan, then?' Hall commented.

'She was a bit pissed off when he expected her to walk home the next morning. What with it pissing down and her in a thong and fuck-me shoes. And not knowing quite what she'd say to Mummy and Daddy.'

'Life's a bitch,' Hall nodded. 'Who's the other one-night stand?'

'Andrea Reed.' Robbins checked his notes. 'Works in Top Man in the High Street. Last Man Standing again. September 6. At least this time he gave her the taxi fare home.'

'Is there no end to this man's largesse?' Hall wanted to know. 'Either of them could have swiped his Sheridan, I suppose, the heirloom most coveted by the winsome Mrs Bartlett?'

'They could,' Robbins agreed. 'But I doubt whether either of them would know it was a book, let alone a valuable one. No, I'd put my money on one of the others.'

'Ah,' Hall nodded, leaning forward and picking up his pen. 'These are what you might call the long-term relationships?'

'Well, it's all relative,' the sergeant sniggered. 'I think we can safely say when it comes to Mr Bartlett, the only person whose company he really liked was Mr Bartlett's. Relationship number one was Pearl Reilly.'

'Pearl?' Hall frowned. He'd read the name too and couldn't really believe it. 'Named after the harbour, do you think? I thought Carole Bartlett said he liked them young.'

'She was only twenty-three, guv,' Robbins explained. 'Just that her parents must have been a bit retro, that's all.'

'Links with Bartlett?'

'They met in a Pizzeria. One of his weaknesses, apparently, pizza. And nothing posh and Italian, either. Just your bog-standard dough from the High Street. They went out a couple of times, or should I say stayed in, but according to Ms Reilly she's very adventurous in bed and dear old Dan didn't live up to expectations.'

'I trust you had a WPC present when this interview took place, Sergeant Robbins.'

'Better than that, guv,' Robbins winked. 'I had *Mrs* Robbins with me. You can't be too careful.'

'Long-term relationship two.'

'Well, I saved a bit of leg work here, guv. Long-term relationship two quickly merged with long-term relationship three. Laura Pettingell, something in sales at Leighford Garden Centre, and Susan Ledbetter, a teller with HSBC. Mrs Pettingell was first – Bartlett was buying some garden furniture to make a "room", whatever that is, by his pond. Nice girl, Laura...'

'Oh?' Hall's left eyebrow appeared over the top of his glasses frame.

'She remembers being a bit suspicious of Bartlett when they first met because his cheque bounced.'

'Did it now? How much was it?'

'Er...' Robbins checked his records. 'Three hundred and forty-four pounds. There was a special deal on.'

'When was this?'

'July. Bartlett explained there was – and I quote Laura – "a silly mix-up at the bank". And the bank in question...'

'...was the HSBC.' Hall finished the sentence for him.

'Got it in one, guv,' Robbins smiled. And he and Hall went back far enough for the sergeant to risk, 'You should have been a copper.'

Hall, of course, wasn't laughing.

'Bartlett seems to have been two-timing them throughout late July and August, but by the end of that month, they were having threesomes. "Theatre Artistic Director Gets His Leg Over – Twice" as the *Advertiser* might have said had they known.'

'You very definitely had Mrs Robbins there for *that* interview,' Hall checked.

'No, guv,' Robbins laughed. 'I just keep playing the tape over, you know. Pick up a few pointers.'

'Was all this still going on at the time of Bartlett's death?'

'No.' Robbins was adamant. 'First of all, Mr Pettingell got wind of it and threatened to put Bartlett's lights out. Bearing in mind he's a body-builder with more attitude than I've recorded juicy interviews, Bartlett got the message and dropped Laura like that proverbial hot potato. Susan – she's a nice girl, too – hung on in there, but the bank got wind of it. Now, there's no actual law against employees having it away with clients, but the manager there is a born-again Christian and he takes a dim view. So Susan backed off – a position I believe she often assumed when the ménage was at full throttle.'

'So,' Hall was trying to tie in all the disparate ends. 'Am I right in assuming that all these women's DNA, prints, whatever, have been found in Bartlett's bungalow?'

'Yes, guv. Along with others, of course. We've had no luck tracing anybody else's yet. Of course, it's early days.'

'No, it's not, Bill.' Hall shook his head. 'The clock's ticking. And did you, in all your over-zealously close questioning of these young ladies, discover whether any of them was a dab hand with electrical wiring?'

There was no Deena Harrison at the Arquebus again that night, so Maxwell had put on his Trevor Nunn meets Kevin Spacey act and directed like there was no tomorrow.

'Dentists are by definition unpleasant people, Andy,' he had to remind the *Shop of Horrors* psycho. 'I want to feel the pain the first time you appear on stage. I want to hear that high-pitched whine, smell the acrid pungency of burning nerve-endings and feel the ghastly sense of drowning with that gurgling thing down my throat. Unless the audience feels that, you just won't convince. Now, from the top, just one more time!'

He sat down in the darkened auditorium and shook himself. All he had to do was put his hands on his hips and he'd actually *become* Deena Harrison.

There was a deep stillness as Leighford approached the witching hour. Private William

343

Pennington was all but complete now, sitting his bay charger in fifty-four millimetre splendour and waiting for the off. Peter Maxwell had no idea – nobody did – exactly in what position Pennington rode the Charge, so he placed him in B Troop, diagonally behind the impossibly petulant Lord Cardigan before the difficult old duffer decided to pull the 11th Hussars back into what would become the second line to ride down the Valley of Death. Maxwell had put a little book into the soldier's right hand as though he was rehearsing for a part on some stage – perhaps Leighford's all those years ago. It was artistic licence and the book wasn't likely, but if you can't take a few liberties with the subject that is your *raison d'être,* what can you do?

Maxwell smiled. Another one completed. He liked it when a plan came together. Then he turned to his other plans and topped up the level of his Southern Comfort in the lamplit shadows of his Inner Sanctum under the eaves. He eased himself down into his modelling chair and slowly and methodically cleaned his brushes.

'A séance, Count?' He glanced at the black and white beast watching him from the top of the old linen basket. 'I thought you'd never ask. Once upon a time there were two little girls, the Fox sisters, who lived in Hydesville, New York State. This was in 1848, when your Lord and Master was a mere stripling applying for his first teaching job, and the girls claimed to be able to communicate with the spirit of a dead drummer – that's travelling salesman to you and me – whose body had been stashed under the floorboards in their home many moons previously. Are you taking notes, by the way? I shall be asking questions later. All this not unnaturally caused a bit of a stir in Hydesville – I suppose it was a bit like Leighford without the slot machines. Folks came from far and wide and when the investigators held the knees of the girls – and we won't ask why it occurred to them to do that – the mysterious rappings by way of communication with the spirit world abruptly ceased.'

Maxwell took a languid sip of the amber nectar. 'Well, it's obvious why, Count, if only you'd give it a moment's thought. Listen.' He pressed his toes against his shoe and produced a clicking sound. 'One knock for yes and two for no,' he said. 'I'm just doing that with my feet. The Fox sisters could apparently dislocate their knees at will to make a similar noise. I know – makes your eyes water, doesn't it? The point is that spiritism as it was called should have died the death there and then. Two silly little girls faking it to gain attention – how often have I seen similar ploys in my own legendary career, I hear you ask. Deena Harrison, for instance... Anyway, back in 1848, it was *au contraire*. The craze caught on and spread to France and England. It got more exotic — table-rapping, essentially what the Fox girls did, became table-tilting, spirit writing with the planchette, levitation and finally, full blown manifestation. There's barely a house in England that hasn't got some sort of ghost.'

He stood up, stretching, looking at the pale sliver of moon that shone on the silent sea now that the rain had stopped and the clouds had broken. 'Oh, you and I know it's all bunkum, Count, but we're men of the world, educated, refined, sophisticated. Some people are afraid of their own shadows. In fact, shadows are what ghosts are all about. All right, so you've got twenty-twenty vision and can hear a dormouse fart three fields away. But how often have you caught sight of something, oh, just fleeting, just now and again and thought to yourself 'What the Hell was that?" And then, you see, Count, unlike you feline types, we humans have this wretched thing called imagination. And we *like* to be scared shitless. That's why we watch video nasties. That's why the hapless heroine in a spooky old house after dark never switches on the lights. What would be the fun? Hand-held cameras wobbling jerkily in Minnesotan woods; Japanese girls crawling, silent and hideous, out of wells; that drowned, rotting corpse that gets Harrison Ford in *What Lies Beneath;* we just love it.'

He sat back down again, hanging the forage cap on its peg. 'So, a séance is just an extension of all that really. It's people sitting in a circle, some of them sad, some of them silly, trying to do the impossible and reach the Other Side. Except there is no Other Side. Life's a beach and then you die.'

He caught sight of the photograph of Jacquie on the shelf above him, smiling at a party with a copper's helmet tilted over her left eye. 'Well,' he smiled. 'Perhaps not so much of a beach after all. And as for dying,' he sighed, finishing his glass, 'not just yet awhile. Now,' he clambered to his feet and switched off the lamp, 'be off with you

346

and reduce the Leighford rodent population, there's a good chap. It's past my bedtime – you won't mind if I don't wait up?'

Chapter Twenty-Four

'What's all this about, Ashley?' Patrick Collinson was perplexed. He stood in the Committee Room at the Arquebus with a letter in his hand.

'Surely, final tax demands don't hold any night terrors for you, Patrick?' The Theatre Manager had not had a good day and it wasn't yet lunchtime. On Saturday mornings, the Little Extras playgroup took over the Arquebus and although the entire Committee agreed that it was admirable, in theory, to encourage the next generation of players and playgoers, the reality was altogether different. And the reality hit Ashley Wilkes every week. They arrived with pushy mothers, each convinced that their little darling was the next Shirley Temple, Jodie Foster, Nahum Tate or Dakota Fanning, depending on their taste in Hollywood stardom history.

The little darlings were all over Wilkes' theatre now, squawking and squabbling in the auditorium, stuffing crisp packets down the backs of seats, scattering Smarties in all directions. The Little Extras' leaders were of the limp-wristed, pinko-liberal persuasion. Secret lefties to a man and woman, they had no concept of control and resorted to so many countdowns to silence that the concept became meaningless. Only half an hour to go, so Wilkes was prepared to grit his teeth for a while longer.

'Tax demands be damned,' Collinson roared. 'I've been invited to a séance.'

Wilkes blinked at him. 'You too?' he said, grim-faced.

'What?'

The Theatre Manager rummaged in the debris that was his desk. 'Snap, I suspect,' and he held up a letter of his own.

Collinson snatched it, comparing the pieces of paper. Identical. From an address in Acacia Grove. Good address. Word-processed. And signed by the same hand. 'Who is this Rowena Sanders?' he demanded to know.

'Some local medium,' Wilkes told him. 'You know, tea leaves and "You'll meet a tall, dark, handsome man, dearie. Cross my palm with silver".' For a non-actor, Ashley Wilkes could turn out a mean characterisation when the mood took him.

'That's a fortune teller, Ashley,' Collinson said. 'I suspect this Sanders woman would take serious umbrage at you mixing the two.'

'What does it matter, Patrick?' Wilkes said. 'It's all a load of bollocks anyway. I can't see why you're upset.'

'I'm not upset,' Collinson retorted. 'But we're all busy people. And I find it quite bizarre.'

Wilkes turned to face him, ignoring the scream-ing coming from the stage. 'Don't you want to know who killed Martita?' he asked. 'Dan?'

'Of course I do,' Collinson said, flinging him-self down into his usual chair around the Com-mittee table. 'But I'd prefer it if twelve jury people decided that after due deliberation and the process of law carried out by a competent police force. Some fairground faker mumbling and swaying from side to side isn't going to do it.'

'Well,' Wilkes shrugged. 'No one's going to force you, Patrick. It's still, despite ominous rumours to the contrary, a free country. You can have your own chair of course.'

'Chair?' Collinson looked confused.

'The séance is being held here.'

'What?' Collinson was on his feet. 'How do you know? It doesn't say that in the letter.'

'No,' Wilkes agreed. 'I had a phone call from Ms Sanders this morning – on that very phone, spookily enough – asking if we could hold it here.'

'And you said yes?' Collinson was incredulous.

'Too right I did. And I'm charging the mad old biddy.'

'This is a Committee matter, Ashley.' No one had a higher horse than Patrick Collinson when he chose to saddle up. 'We must all discuss hiring policy.'

'Policy, yes,' Wilkes corrected him. 'Not day to day operations. That's my job.' He held up his hand against Collinson's further blustering. 'It's a done deal, Patrick. Lighten up. If you don't want to join us tomorrow night, you don't have to. I'll let you know who dunnit.'

Collinson fumed, but inwardly this time. He knew Wilkes was right. 'Do we know who else is joining this charade?' he asked.

'A séance, Henry?' Margaret Hall had heard some pretty bizarre things from her husband over the years; most recently, the hiring of Magda Lupescu. It went with being a copper's wife and the mother of a copper's kids.

'That's what the letter says.' Hall was trying to concentrate on his newspaper.

'You're not going?'

He looked at her. Darling Margaret, honest, good, dependable. She could always be relied upon to bring in that hint of common sense when everything else seemed to be falling apart. 'Is that a question?' he asked her, 'or a statement?'

'Well,' she sat down across the kitchen table from him, 'are they legal?'

In the safety and sanctity of his own home, Henry Hall smiled. 'Oh, yes,' he said. 'A lot of people laugh at them. Some people are unnerved by them. Say they tempt fate. Open the gates of Hell, depending on how rabid your religion is.'

'Do you know this Rowena Sanders?' she asked him.

'No,' he said, folding away the paper, since clearly he wasn't going to get much chance of reading it. 'But I know the woman who's set the whole thing up.'

'Who's that?'

'Unless I miss my guess, it's Fiona Elliot, the niece of the dead woman. She's into spiritualism. Seems to think we can get some words of wisdom from Martita Winchcombe on the Other Side.'

Margaret snorted. She couldn't help herself.

'Snigger away,' Henry said quietly, looking into her eyes. 'But about now, I'll take all the help I can get.'

They were still looking at each other, locked in

the silence of their different perspectives, when the phone rang. Margaret got there first, with the speed born of long years of things that go ring in the night.

'Hello, Tom,' she said resignedly. Didn't that bloody place *ever* give her husband some time to himself? She passed the cordless. 'Tom O'Connell.'

'Tom?' Hall said. 'What's up? Hmm. Really? All right. Wilkes. Yes. And Collinson.' A pause. 'Really? Well, that *is* interesting. Do we have an address? Right. Bring her in.' He checked his watch. 'I'll see you at twelve. Interview Room One. Don't let her make her call before I've had a chance to talk to her. And don't let Jane Blaisedell anywhere near this one. Thanks, Tom. Good work.'

And he hung up.

'A breakthrough?' Margaret asked. In all the years they'd known each other, PC Henry Hall hadn't given too much away; DC Henry Hall had said even less; DS and DI Hall were positively monosyllabic and the DCI in front of her today sometimes took a Trappist vow. But when *that* moment came in a case, then Henry Hall could be positively garrulous.

'Could be,' he said.

'Well, it took a while, guv,' Giles Finch-Friezely said. 'As you know we fingerprinted everybody connected with the Arquebus, except ... er ... Mr Maxwell and his kids from Leighford.'

'Just as well.' Hall was getting outside a coffee in his office at Leighford nick. Peter Maxwell would have invoked every civil liberty since Magna Carta to explain why the taking of fingerprints was an option and that Englishmen had never bowed to arbitrary arrest, suspension of habeas corpus, deforestation or the levelling of hedgerows without a bloody good reason. Perhaps even Peter Maxwell would concede that murder was reason enough, but Hall didn't want to go there unless he had to. 'Hit me with it.'

'We've got Ashley Wilkes' and Patrick Collinson's dabs all over the Winchcombe and Bartlett houses.'

'No surprises there,' Hall nodded. 'They all work at the Arquebus.' He riffled through the pile of depositions on his desk. 'Both of them admitted to visiting both places on several occasions. Tell me about the others.'

'Partials,' Finch-Friezely admitted, 'but clear enough for our purposes. In the kitchen, lounge, bathroom and bedroom at Bartlett's bungalow and Deena Harrison – the saliva on the glass. No question.'

'Deena Harrison,' Hall repeated. 'Any link with the Winchcombe house?'

Finch-Friezely shook his head. 'Not a dicky bird, guv. I'd stake my reputation on it.'

Hall looked at the lad, earnest, dedicated, hardworking.

'You may have to, son,' he said. 'So,' he took a sip of the ghastly stuff that passed for coffee, 'what was Deena doing in Dan Bartlett's house? And more importantly, when? When that great day dawns when science gives us that little advance, Giles, you and I can hang up our truncheons and go home. Any word from Tom?'

Tom O'Connell slammed his fist down on the roof of his car. He snatched the walkie-talkie out of the open window and patched through to the nick.

'Guv? Tom. I'm at the Arquebus. There's no sign of Deena Harrison at her home. Place looks kind of shut down to be honest. I've tried the theatre. The Manager says he hasn't seen her for days. She's done a runner. Yeah. Sure. I'll probably find one in the house somewhere. Yeah. Right. OK. Sorry, guv. All points it is.'

The phone rang at 38 Columbine a little after lunch. Jacquie was out shopping, insisting she still had the use of her legs, had some spotty kid to help her pack and if, indeed, her waters were to break, what better place than Tesco's? Spillage in Aisle Fourteen.

So Maxwell sat at home, worrying and only half concentrating on the load of old tat produced by Nine Eff Three in lieu of a decent piece of home-work. Like a bullet from a gun, he was out of his chair and bounding across the room. The cat called Metternich raised one exhausted eyebrow. What *was* that all about, that ludicrous ritual? A shattering and repeated ringing and humans talking into white plastic things. It defied belief.

'War office,' Maxwell said.

'Max. It's Jane.'

'Hello, darling.'

'Is Jacquie there?'

''Fraid not. Can I help?'

A pause. Jane Blaisedell had spilled a lot of beans to Peter Maxwell over the last few days. Surely, one more couldn't hurt? 'There's an all points out for Deena Harrison,' she told him. 'You haven't seen her, have you?'

'No,' Maxwell told her. 'Not for a few days. I wanted to talk to her myself, as a matter of fact.'

'Oh, why?'

Jane Blaisedell may have spilled beans to Maxwell, but in the bean-spilling department, he was rather more circumspect. 'About the show,' he said. 'We're on in a couple of weeks and it's all getting a bit fraught about now.'

Jane knew that feeling.

'Why are you looking for her?' Maxwell asked, although he was fairly sure he knew the answer.

'Sorry, Max,' Jane said, her voice hard, her demeanour professional. 'That's classified.' And the brrr told him she'd gone.

It started just before nine o'clock. Jacquie had tracked down a DVD of the ever-elusive *Seventh Seal* as a treat for Maxwell and they were just about to settle down to watch a very young Max von Sydow playing chess with chilling Death when there was a ring of his bell and shouts in the night.

Maxwell crossed the lounge in a couple of strides. His front lawn was obscured by a crowd of people, men and women, looking up at his windows and muttering. All they needed was flaming torches and they could have been the extras from the village marching on Franken- stein's laboratory to stop his hellish experiments.

355

'Come on, Maxwell!' he heard one of them shout. 'We know you're up there. Come on down. We want some answers.'

'Max?' Jacquie was alongside him. 'Who are they?'

'Well,' Maxwell frowned. 'It could be the new style Ofsted inspection,' he said. 'We were warned there'd be a new approach. Little advance notice. A more direct attack. That sort of thing.'

'Max!' Jacquie screamed at him as they thumped his glass partitioned door again. 'Be serious.'

'Seriously.' He moved her away from the window. 'The one with the mouth is Mr Spall, father of my leading lady – oh,' he caught the fear in her face, 'after you, of course, sweetness.'

'Max, you're not going down?' She gripped his arm.

'Just think of it as an ad hoc parents' evening,' he told her. 'A sort of proactive PTA.'

'Max, this is dangerous,' she said.

He knew that perfectly well. Parents didn't normally arrive in a body at a teacher's house. 'Dinna fret yoursel,' he said. It was a perfect Mel Gibson as William Wallace.

'I'm calling for back-up,' she told him, snatching up the cordless and thumping buttons.

'I'm not sure how much use Legs Diamond, Dierdre Lessing and Bernard Ryan are going to be in a crisis,' he chuckled. 'But try them anyway. And you,' he pointed to her. 'You stay here, Woman Policeman.' And there was iron in his voice.

He took the stairs slowly, one by one, listening

356

to the babble outside. As he wrenched the door open, it stopped and the gaggle stood there, staring at him in their parkas and anoraks. Some faces he knew. Some he didn't. He was John Wayne. He was Robert Mitchum. He was Dean Martin. In any of the remakes of *Rio Bravo* you care to name, defending the jail against the rowdies bent on freeing the baddies. Except that this was Leighford. West Sussex. England. And the people in front of him were mums and dads. And they were more scared than he was.

'Ladies and gentlemen,' Maxwell said quietly. 'How good of you to call.'

'What's going on, Mr Maxwell?' the mouthy Mr Spall wanted to know. 'In the theatre. People are dying and our children are in the middle of it.'

Cries of 'Hear! Hear!' and a sudden cacophony of agreement. Maxwell held up his hand. He'd been expecting this for days. The great British public is slow to anger, slow on the uptake, but once they're roused... They were oxen in the furrow, she-wolves defending their cubs.

'How did you know where to find me?' he asked.

'You're in the bloody book, Maxwell,' a burly man snarled. 'It ain't rocket science.'

At last. A ringleader. Maxwell's target. The Head of Sixth Form stepped out to stand with his nose inches away. 'No shit, Sherlock,' he said.

'You're in charge of this crap,' the thug said. 'It's your fucking responsibility.'

Maxwell stepped even closer. 'By "this crap", I assume you mean the forthcoming production of

Little Shop of Horrors, Mr ... er...?'

'Grant,' the man grated, slightly taken aback. 'Grant's my name.'

'Ah, yes,' Maxwell smiled. 'Father of Andy, the psychotic dentist. He's not bad, but, having met you, I'd have thought he'd be better.'

'You what?'

'Get this!' Maxwell shouted so that they could all hear. 'I don't know what all this vigilante nonsense is all about or why it's taken you brave people this long to get your respective acts together. But there is a procedure for all this, you know. If you'd care to ring Leighford High School at nine o'clock on Monday morning, the delightful young lady on the switchboard will be only too pleased to make appointments for each and every one of you to meet me and voice your complaints.' The smile vanished. 'But for those of you who haven't the first idea of how to conduct yourselves, let me summarise my response to such a discussion. Between nine and four for thirty-nine weeks of the year, come rain, come shine, I *am* you. We teachers call it *in loco parentis* – in the place of parents. I've wiped your kids' noses, listened to their whinges, kept them on the right track for ever. That's what I do.' He wandered along their front, less united now than it had been. 'That's what I'm doing still. In rehearsals, at the Arquebus, at school – it doesn't matter where. Your kids are safe, people. There's nothing to see here.'

'Mr Maxwell.' Another father stepped forward, a little shame-faced. 'We ... we don't mean any disrespect. We're scared, that's all. For our kids.'

'I know, Mr ... Reynolds, is it?' The Head of

Sixth Form was looking straight into the eyes of Mushnik senior, who had come over to Ellis Island in the hopes of a fresh start, according to Deena Harrison. The man nodded. 'Three people are dead,' he told him and the rest of them, 'and the youngest of them was pushing fifty. I don't pretend to know what's happening at the Arquebus – not yet – but this much I can promise you. Your children are safe. Now, go home, people.'

One by one they broke away, couples huddling together, shuffling, shame-faced. One woman reached out and touched Maxwell's sleeve, mouthing 'Sorry' as she left. They weren't a baying mob any more, they were mums and dads, confused, bewildered, desperate.

'I ain't satisfied.' The dentist's dad had not moved. He was standing legs apart, fists locked, the muscles in his jaw jumping. He could take Maxwell out, no trouble.

'Satisfaction's not his job, friend,' a female voice called out. Strictly against orders, Jacquie had waddled down the stairs and was standing alongside Maxwell.

'Oh yeah?' Grant sniggered. 'And who the fuck are you? Mrs Maxwell?'

'Yes,' Maxwell interrupted. 'And if you use the f word again, you thick shit, I'll be scattering your teeth over the pavement.'

'You what?'

That warrant card was in the air again, inches from Grant's nose as he tried to focus on it. 'I'm sure you'll have seen one of these before, Mr Grant,' Jacquie said. 'Now, you get on home, sir.

'Cos if you don't, three things will happen. First, I will arrest you for threatening behaviour and disturbing the peace. Second, I will turn a blind eye while Mr Maxwell here carries out his threat. And third,' she held up her hand and placed it behind her ear. 'Let's reverse that order, shall we? Hear that siren? That's my colleagues coming to the rescue.'

So it was. The sound of sirens. Blue lights flashed at the end of Columbine and clanging police cars shot, white and terrifying, along the quiet street, dispersing knots of parents scurrying into their cars. When Jacquie turned back, the dentist's dad was history, hurtling away into the darkness as she and Maxwell applauded the arrival of Jacquie's colleagues, the boys in blue.

'What kept you?' she laughed at Dave Walters, first, as always, on the scene.

'It's no good,' Maxwell said, shaking his head. 'I've got to get one of those.' He was pointing at her warrant card.

'Max,' she turned to him, suddenly serious, suddenly afraid. 'Please don't do that again. Play chicken with nutters.'

He smiled lovingly at her, quoting the Duke of Wellington – sort of – 'I don't know what you do to the enemy, Police Woman Carpenter, but, by God, you terrify me.'

Chapter Twenty-Five

There was a raw wind rising the next morning as Peter Maxwell put sole to pedal. Sunday, bloody Sunday. The gentlefolk of Leighford paced their living rooms, desperate for the supermarkets to open or the papers to arrive. The younger generation, anybody under thirty, was still driving them home in the snoring department.

Mrs Troubridge would ordinarily have been up and pruning. She didn't sleep so well these nights, so dawn clipping was no hardship for her. Today, however, one of those erratic, temperamental gusts might blow her over, so she stayed indoors and demolished an illicit bacon sandwich.

Metternich the cat watched Maxwell go, pedalling down Columbine like a demon, his cycle clips flashing in the early light, his scarf flying in the wind. Metternich the cat got back to his breakfast, founder member of the Pigeon Fanciers' Club as he was. The trouble with that mad old bastard on the thing with wheels is that he didn't appreciate the finer things in life.

The wind was against Maxwell – it wasn't just his paranoia – it was an easterly and it took him a little longer than usual to reach the Arquebus. He recognised Ashley Wilkes' car in the car park along the river bank as the ducks quacked at him, annoyed by the wind ruffling their feathers. Then he was in at the front door, dashing up the stairs to the man's office.

'Mr Maxwell.' The Theatre Manager was in his shirt sleeves, shredding cables with a Stanley knife and not a little skill. 'You're early. I thought we said five.'

'We did,' Maxwell told him. 'But something's come up.'

'It has indeed,' Wilkes responded. 'I was about to ring you.'

'Oh?'

'There's been a double booking.'

Maxwell frowned under the rim of his tweed. Ashley Wilkes seemed to be reading from his script. 'There has?'

'Yes, look.' The Theatre Manager got up from the job in hand. 'This is all a bit embarrassing, really. I mean, I know you guys have your technical rehearsal tonight – hence my wiring – but ... well, I've had a request.'

Maxwell never did requests, but he was older school than Wilkes.

'A Mrs Elliot has booked the stage this evening.'

'For a séance,' Maxwell nodded.

Wilkes blinked at him. 'How the Hell did you know that?'

'"I'd be a fine soothsayer if I didn't!"' he snarled, bulging his eyes and throwing his arms in all directions; but his Zero Mostel on his way to the Forum was lost on Ashley Wilkes. 'I've been invited too.'

'You have?'

'I came over to ask you to reschedule. I was wondering how we'd all squeeze in.'

'Why you?' Wilkes was suspicious.

'Why here?' Maxwell countered.

'Gordon,' the Theatre Manager explained. 'Apparently this Rowena Sanders woman was going to use her place, but one of the invited is Matilda Goodacre and she insisted, since her late husband is potentially going to be there, that we hold it at the spot where Gordon died, i.e. down there.'

Both men looked at the stage, deserted now save for three differently-sized incarnations of an altogether terrifying carnation, Audrey II, the man-eating plant. An apparition wandered across it, draped in cables.

'Is that Benny?' Maxwell peered through the gloom. 'I need to have a word. Remind me of the time again, Ashley.'

'Eight,' Wilkes told him.

'Do we have to bring anything?'

'An open mind, apparently,' Wilkes shrugged.

'Well, that's a bit of a tall order,' Maxwell smiled.

'You've said it,' Wilkes agreed. 'I've got to make a few calls. I couldn't get through to all your kids yesterday – hence Benny this morning.'

'No reply from Deena, I suppose?' Maxwell checked.

Wilkes' face fell. Needling from this man was something he didn't need. 'No,' he said. 'No reply.'

Maxwell beamed broadly and bounced down the plush-carpeted stairs to the ground floor and the auditorium. 'Benny Barker as I live and breathe.'

'Morning, Mr M.' The lad peered round an outsize speaker system.

Maxwell rested his elbows on the stage and his chin on his folded arms. 'Tell me, Benjamin: are you familiar with the Scottish play?'

Maxwell was a little late for lunch that day. Jacquie didn't scold. After the night before, they'd lain awake for hours, each afraid for the other, neither saying so. Parents' evenings weren't normally quite so scary.

Her chicken was, as usual, splendid, but neither of them was much in the mood and they drove their veg around their plates for a while before giving up with a shake of the head and an inane grin.

'There's an all points out for Deena Harrison,' Maxwell said as he pushed his plate away.

'I know,' she nodded. 'The guys were talking about it last night.'

'In view of that,' he said, 'and in view of what we discovered in Oxford, don't you think you ought to have a chat with Henry?'

Her eyes widened. 'I thought you told me I had to stay away.'

'I know,' he sighed. 'And I hate to have to change my mind, but Henry needs to know what he's up against.'

She nodded. 'I think he's got a pretty good idea already,' she said. 'But I'll have a word.' And she got up, fumbling for her keys and her coat.

'Aren't you going to call?' he asked.

Jacquie looked at him. 'No,' she said. 'Some conversations you've just got to have face to face.'

At the top of the stairs, she stopped and turned, waddling back to him and cradling his head as he sat there. 'Max,' she said. 'This séance tonight. You will be careful, won't you?'

He got up and held her, kissing her forehead. 'We have room,' he said, 'for a few ghosts.' It was pure Charlton Heston in *El Cid*, but Jacquie wasn't listening to the characterisation. She just heard the word ghosts. And it frightened her.

They came in ones and twos under the over-hanging span of the Flyover, solemn, silent; the only noise the clatter of their feet on the tarmac.

Then the hiss of tyres as the last one arrived – the uninvited. They acknowledged each other briefly in the portico, where the great and not so good of Leighford's am dram over the years smiled down at them from tired posters. The crimson carpet was reflected in pools of light and the double doors to the auditorium were thrown wide open.

'Welcome.' Ashley Wilkes met them there and ushered them into the theatre itself. It struck cold here after a day's emptiness, with that indefinable mustiness that theatres acquire when they have been warehouses and places of death, dramatic and real.

The Theatre Manager had followed Rowena Sanders' instructions to the letter. Centre stage in a dim pool of blue light stood an oval table and around it eight high-backed chairs. One by one, they trooped down to the front, divesting them-selves of their outdoor clothes. With a natural sense of leadership, Rowena Sanders began pointing to the chairs, arranging the arrivals for what was to come.

'No.' The imperious Matilda Goodacre was having none of it. 'First, I want to know who these people are,' she said, along with St Joan and Blanche du Bois and Eleanor of Aquitaine.

'That is not the way,' Rowena said, frowning. 'The spirits know everybody.'

Matilda fixed the little woman with her terrible stare, the one that she usually used to curdle the milk. 'Balderdash!' she roared. 'I am not a spirit and I am going no further with this nonsense until I know who I am sitting down with.'

'You have already changed the venue,' Fiona Elliot spat back at her. She was only an inch or so shorter than the Dame of the Arquebus and nearly as wide; in a cat fight, it could go either way. 'Let that be enough.'

'My husband died up there!' Matilda snapped, gesturing with her right hand in a way that Maxwell had often seen Hitler do in the old newsreels. He hoped the woman had no plans to invade Poland.

'And my aunt died in her home!' Fiona bellowed back. 'It is vital to the spirits to come together on neutral ground. You've probably ruined everything already.'

'OK!' A man's voice brought the proceedings to an abrupt halt. They all turned to the tall man in the grey three-piece and the glasses. 'Let's do it. I am Detective Chief Inspector Henry Hall, currently conducting police inquiries here in Leighford. I have a wife and three sons. And I must confess I don't quite know what I'm doing here.'

366

Fiona crossed to him. 'Do you *believe*, Chief Inspector?' she asked him levelly.

'I'm a policeman, madam,' he told her. 'I believe what I can see and hear. I have to deal in reality.'

'Please, Chief Inspector,' Rowena said. 'Take a seat on the far left, can you?'

Hall looked around the assembled group, not a little surprised to see the latest arrival, the one in the scarf and cycle clips. Everybody else he could put in the context of the case. But the uninvited? You never knew what he was doing there. But he *was* there, nonetheless.

'Ashley Wilkes,' the Theatre Manager announced. 'I run this place. Acting background, currently divorced.' He managed a weak smile.

'Thank you, Mr Wilkes,' Rowena was in the driving seat again. 'Next to the Chief Inspector, if you please.'

'Patrick Collinson.' The crimson man reached the bottom of the steps. 'Theatre Secretary. My day job – which I can't afford to give up – Accountancy.' No one but Collinson tittered at the weak joke and he waited patiently to be placed next to Hall, on the opposite side from Wilkes.

'Carole Bartlett.' The widow of the late Artistic Director could hardly be more of a contrast to the widow of the late set painter. She was wearing a skimpy pair of jeans a couple of sizes too small and twenty years too young for her and a man's shirt tied around her midriff, in the navel of which jewellery sparkled. 'My husband was Daniel Bartlett, of anything but blessed memory. All this,' she gestured at the table and chairs, 'is

367

just so much bullshit. It's like those corny old movies where a bunch of misfits agree to spend the night in a creepy old house. But that's usually for money. What's in it for us, eh?'

'The truth perhaps.' Fiona Elliot was walking up the steps. 'Martita Winchcombe was my aunt. I have been a member of the West Bromwich spiritual circle for many years. And,' she glanced at Rowena, 'I know exactly where to sit.' And she placed herself next to Collinson. That was actually the seat that Carole Bartlett had intended to take, and she flounced around the table to sit opposite Hall.

'Not there!' Rowena snapped, then gentler, 'that's reserved for someone else.'

'You already know who I am.' Matilda seemed to float onto the stage. 'Life chairperson of the Arquebus Theatre Committee, widow of Gordon Goodacre, may his soul rest in peace.'

'Amen,' said Rowena softly. Then she was looking at the gaunt, angular woman who stood next in line. 'I didn't expect to see you again,' she said as if neither meeting, this one nor the last, had been much of a pleasure. 'You know where to sit.'

'I am Magda Lupescu,' the woman said in her rich, dark voice. 'Just think of me as an interested bystander.'

'No,' said Fiona. 'That won't do. You are more than that, Ms Lupescu. You are legend.'

'Very well,' the woman smiled. 'I am legend. Let's leave it at that, shall we?' and she sat with a strange silence next to Matilda.

'Er...' Rowena blinked at the man in the scarf

and the cycle clips. 'I don't believe you're on my list,' she said.

'Oh, now, don't you believe it,' Maxwell chuckled, pinging the clips into his pocket and draping his scarf over the seats. 'I'm always on *somebody*'s list. I'm Peter Maxwell, Head of Sixth Form at Leighford High. I've been teaching for a little over two centuries and have a passing acquaintance with History.'

'No.' Rowena stopped him on the steps. 'I mean you weren't invited.'

'Oh, I'm sorry.' Maxwell beamed at her. 'I thought I'd explained.' He looked directly at Ashley Wilkes, then Henry Hall. 'Deena Harrison couldn't make it. She asked me to come instead. Ah,' he glanced down at the seat between Magda and Carole Bartlett, 'the siege perilous.' And he sat down, his back to the auditorium, uneasily aware that the late James Butler Hickok was sitting thus at a card table in downtown Deadwood when somebody blew out the back of his head. All right, so that was a saloon, but the analogy was close enough.

Rowena Sanders was still staring uneasily at Maxwell as she took the last seat, opposite Hall at the other end of the oval table, stage right. 'I am Rowena Sanders,' she said, 'of the Leighford Spirit Circle. For those of you unused to such gatherings, I would like to explain what will happen. First, Mr Wilkes,' she looked at him, 'is the theatre locked?'

'As per your instructions,' he told her. 'No one can disturb us.'

That was just as well, thought Maxwell; most of

369

them around the table were disturbed enough already.

'We are going on a journey,' Rowena said, placing the tips of her fingers together, 'to the Other Side. Who we will meet there, I have no idea. I would ask you all, whatever happens, to stay in your seats. On no account must you leave the stage. You may feel cold. You may ... hear things. See them. Smell them even. But remember, we are seeking our loved ones and we are seeking the truth. As long as we cling to that, nothing can harm us. Now,' she closed her eyes and tilted her face upwards, 'let us place our hands palms down on the table so that our thumbs are touching and our little fingers are touching the little fingers of those next to us.'

She waited until everyone had shifted.

'There,' she smiled. 'Can you feel the presence? The circle is complete. Breathe with me. Softly now. That's it. In ... out...'

Maxwell had been here before. He habitually had to remind Year Seven how to breathe. And the Advanced Classes, by the end of the Summer Term, included chewing gum too. As for the rest, very clever auto suggestion. Tell someone they'll feel cold, see things, hear them and smell them and some of them will. Fiona Elliot, for a start. It was the cleverest media April Fool's joke he could remember – a cooking programme from the Seventies advertising Smell-o-Vision and inviting television viewers in their own homes to get down on those knees and smell the lowest fifty of the four hundred and five lines on the screen. Hmm, smell those onions!

'Let us close our eyes,' Rowena said.

Now, this was a challenge. It was one of the Great Games of childhood. Prayers of a sultry afternoon in Infant School. 'Hands together and eyes closed,' the mantra dear to the heart of every teacher – another day done. And Peter Maxwell, long before he was Mad, used to keep one eye open, just in case... And in case of what, he never knew. So, here he sat, in a hushed and darkened theatre where at least one man had died, holding hands with perfect strangers and with one eye open. To his right, Magda Lupescu's eyes were shut; so were Fiona Elliot's and Matilda Good-acre's. Wilkes' eyelids were fluttering a little, as Maxwell expected. Rowena's were closed and he couldn't see Patrick Collinson. As for Henry Hall, behind those damned glasses, who knew?

A low, keening sound was coming from Rowena Sanders to Maxwell's left. He kept one eye trained on her, watching for all the telltale signs of the Victorian fakers: the Gladstone bag, the fake wax hands, the yards of luminescent cheesecloth. All of it was mysteriously absent. Rowena began to sway, her hair swirling as if in slow motion around her face. Her eyes were still closed. There was a shuddering, a rattling of the table under their hands, as if someone was drilling deep under the stage.

'Don't be alarmed,' Magda Lupescu's un-mistakable voice was saying. 'Stay where you are.'

'Who's there?' Rowena's head was cocked on one side, listening intently, a frown on her pale, flat face.

'Is it Aunt Martita?' Maxwell saw Fiona Elliot

371

leaning forward in her chair.

'Gordon,' Matilda Goodacre insisted. 'If it's anybody, it'll be my Gordon.'

There was a rattling of the door far across the auditorium, and instinctively, everyone turned. Somebody screamed, although to his dying day, Maxwell never knew who. And they looked up at the low rake of the empty seats and the solitary figure approaching the stage.

'Hello?' a voice called. 'Is anybody there?'

It was Dan Bartlett, come to visit.

Chapter Twenty-Six

'Jesus!' Ashley Wilkes was the first to react to the shattering sound of glass and the roar of flame. What sounded like a bomb had gone off in the theatre's foyer, and for a moment Dan Bartlett stood silhouetted by fire, that indefinable colour curling and billowing down the aisle towards the stage and bouncing in burning debris onto the seats on either side.

'Fire!' Wilkes bellowed, which had to be one of the most obvious statements any of them had ever heard. But he was the Theatre Manager. Health and Safety was his stock-in-trade and instinct took over. 'This way!' he commanded as the sitters, already standers, were now running towards the wings. All, that is, except Peter Maxwell, whose stare was riveted on the lighting and sound box high above.

'Maxwell!' Wilkes yelled at him. 'This way. The side door. Come on.'

'Get the others out,' Maxwell shouted back. 'There's someone up there.' And he was gone, hurtling up the other aisle where the fire had not yet caught hold, making for the stairs that led to the upper floors.

'Police business now,' Henry Hall said to Wilkes. 'Do as he says and get the others to safety. You've got a mobile?'

Wilkes nodded. He was already punching

buttons as the theatre's wailing alarm system kicked in and sprinklers showered the whole place. He turned back to shepherd the others out of the side door, kicking open the bar with his foot while Patrick Collinson steadied the fainting Carole Bartlett. Henry Hall had disappeared into the smoke.

The DCI reached the stairs in the foyer. Wilkes had locked the front doors, whose giant glass panes flashed fire with reflected flames. Hall had seen this before and as soon as he heard the sound he knew what it was. Officially an incendiary device. To his grandparents it was a Molotov cocktail. A petrol bomb. And whoever had thrown it had tossed it into the other entrance to the auditorium, beyond the ticket office, itself now alight. The sprinklers were beginning to cope with the flames at ground level, but fire had leapt upwards with its terrifying speed, engulfing the joists overhead and spreading outward.

Thick, choking black smoke was filling the auditorium now and Hall coughed and spluttered his way along the landing. He knew the auditorium and stage had to be below him, to his right, but he couldn't see it for the smoke and the incessant downpour of water. Wilkes would have got the others out by now and the fire engines would be on their way. But where the hell was Maxwell and what had possessed him to go this way? Into the jaws of death. Into the mouth of Hell.

Glass shattered to Hall's left as the front of Ashley Wilkes' sound and lighting box blew out. It felt like a thousand needles and the DCI was flung sideways, cracking his ribs against the

374

balustrade. Blinded and bleeding, in agonising pain whenever he breathed, Hall managed to crawl forward, inch by painful inch, keeping the flames and smoke above him, looking for the other stairs.

But the other stairs had gone and he heard the appalling crack of timbers as the floor beneath him began to give way. A column of flame shot towards him, jerking him backwards as it defied the water jets in its unstoppable thirst for oxygen and the night sky.

Then Hall felt himself grabbed by the wrist, the elbow, the shoulder and he was being lifted bodily, slung like a trophy over somebody's shoulder. And that somebody was carrying him back the way he had come, crunching on broken glass, batting aside burning debris. And the last thing Henry Hall remembered, head down, bouncing along with every cough that jolted and seared his lungs, was the thought, 'Aren't our firemen wonderful?'

'We know all about it, Deena,' Peter Maxwell said, easing himself down on the sloping ground under the concrete girders of the Flyover. The scene below them was chaos. The Arquebus' fire was out now, but smoke still rose from windows where the glass had gone and the fire engines stood at crazy angles to each other, along with ambulances and police cars, the whole place a mad fairyland of flashing lights and water and people trying desperately to be British and to stay calm.

Maxwell's face was a mask of blood, where the flying glass had ripped him moments before he'd

375

dragged Henry Hall to safety. Fancy him remembering how to do a fireman's lift after all these years. That's what being a Boy Scout does for you. When all this insanity was over, he made a mental note to ring Akela and tell him all about it. He'd have a word with Henry Hall too. The curmudgeonly bugger could do with losing a few pounds; he'd been unconscionably heavy on the turns of those stairs.

'Are you all right?' the girl asked. The fire had burned her parka hood and her hair smelt singed.

'I will be,' he nodded, sniffing in the damp, smoky October night air. 'You?'

She looked at him, at her old Year Head and History teacher, unrecognisable under the blood. 'No,' she said, suddenly cold. 'I'm not all right. And I'm not sure I ever will be.'

'Tell me about Oxford,' he said, looking into her cold, dead eyes.

'Oxford,' she tried to smile, 'was so twelve months ago.'

'No, Deena,' he shook his head sadly. 'It was more than that. You haven't been to Oxford since halfway through your very first term. Where have you been since?'

Her face said it all and it all came flooding back like the worst nightmare, the one from which she couldn't wake up. Candles fluttered in front of Maxwell's face until she couldn't see him any more and there was a sigh, half-human, half-not. There were shadows on the wall. A man's voice. Then a woman's. A sigh, slow, long-drawn-out. From nowhere a light flashed across her eyes, sharp, white, blinding. She wanted to scream but she couldn't and she was grateful for the sudden darkness.

'They never turned the light off, you know,' she said softly.

'Why, Deena?' Maxwell asked. He was gentleness itself. 'Why didn't they turn the light off?'

'I don't know,' she shrugged, the tears near. 'They wanted to study me, I suppose. Watch me all the time.' Her eyes suddenly flashed up at him, briefly lit like the flames in the theatre that would roar and dance and leap in Maxwell's memory for ever. 'And they talked about me. All the time, talking about me. Do you know what that's like?'

Maxwell shook his head.

'Tell me,' he said.

'How did you know,' she asked him, smiling now, 'that I didn't stick it out at Oxford?'

Maxwell's gaze fell. 'We don't need to do this, Deena,' he said.

'Oh, but we do,' she laughed. 'That philosophical debate – remember? I said we'd have it one day – that or a fuck.' She suddenly frowned. 'And that wouldn't be right, would it?'

'No,' Maxwell said. 'That wouldn't be right.'

'So tell me.' She reached out and tapped his arm, sitting as he was, cross-legged in front of her. 'How did you know about Oxford?'

'The red carnation,' he said.

'What?'

'Before we started work at the Arquebus, I said to you, "So you're a red carnation woman now". And it was obvious you didn't have the first clue what I was talking about. Now, I went to the

Other Place, Deena, as you know, but at Oxford there's a tradition that finalists at the end of their third year, especially very able people like you, wear red carnations in their buttonholes in the last exam. You didn't know about it because you never sat that final exam. Or any exams.'

'You're right,' she nodded, like a kid caught with her hand in the cookie jar. 'When Mummy and Daddy died...'

'Mummy and Daddy didn't die, Deena,' he told her. 'There was no fatal crash, no death visitant. That was all in your head, wasn't it?'

'What are you talking about?' she blinked, bewildered now and afraid.

'I went to see your old professor,' he said. 'At Corpus. Paul Usherwood. He was a nice man, Deena, a very nice man. At the time you claimed he seduced you, he was sixty-seven years old, paralysed from the waist down. His secretary had never heard of you – that's because the woman had only been at the College for two years and you'd already gone by then, hadn't you?'

'Yes,' she nodded, her dark eyes bubbling with tears. 'When Alex – that was my fiancé – killed himself...'

'He didn't kill himself, Deena.' Maxwell reached out to hold the girl's trembling hands. 'He drowned, in a punting accident on the Isis. Before I left Oxford, I checked the back copies of the local paper, just to confirm what Professor Usherwood had told me. It was one of those silly, student things. We did them all the time on the Cam but perhaps the Isis is a less forgiving river. Alex couldn't swim, could he? And you,' he wrapped his arms around her narrow shoulders, 'you couldn't live with the loss. You had a nervous breakdown. Your world fell apart. And that world had always been fragile, darling, hadn't it? We remember, don't we, you and I, the fire in the toilet block at dear old Leighford High? Ollie Wendell on the Science block stairs? The water fight when you were in Year Twelve? Oh,' and he looked down at the aftermath of the blaze, still smouldering and scorched below the slope, 'and, of course, the fireworks.' He put his blood-dried face close to hers, staring into those dark, frightened eyes. 'The people talking about you,' he said. 'A man's voice? A woman's?'

'How... how do you know?'

He shook his head. 'I know people,' he told her. 'I know how the system works because I'm part of it. My guess would be the people in your nightmares were your mum and dad, distraught, desperate to help you in the only way they could. Doctors, educational psychologists, specialists. Between them all, they kept you on the straight and narrow, didn't they? But then, with Alex at Oxford ... then it was the whitewashed rooms, the lights they never turned off. Broadmoor?'

She looked back at him. 'Rampton,' she said. 'But I hadn't *done* anything, Mr Maxwell. Not really.'

'It was what you might have done, Deena,' he said, looking down at the theatre. 'What you might be capable of.'

She dropped his hands, struggled out of his hold. '*They*,' she was on her feet, pointing at the Arquebus, '*they* had it coming. Just like Ollie

Wendell. He called me a fucking bitch. Just like that. No reason for it. So I threw him down the stairs. And that lot – that simpering bitch Sally Spall, that freak Andy Grant, that no-hoper Alan Eldridge – all of them, whispering about me, sniggering. Carrying on behind my back. They even went to the Head of Sixth Form about it. Can you imagine? Mad Max? What's he got to do with any of this?'

Maxwell saw the two uniformed men scrambling up the grassy slope towards them. 'What indeed?' he sighed. And that sigh, to Deena, was half-human, half-not.

'Max, oh, my God, Max.' Jacquie didn't know whether to laugh or cry. Maxwell was sitting on the tailgate of a squad car, swathed in blankets. His face was black with blood and it looked as if he'd been crying. 'Max, thank God.'

'There, there, Woman Policeman,' and he kissed her, stroking her hair as she clung to him, sobbing her heart out.

'What happened here?'

'Deena.' He tried to smile. 'Deena Harrison happened. I should have listened to Sylvia Matthews. She warned me about Deena from day one, but I wouldn't have it. Well, next time,' and he winced as a thousand pin pricks pierced his face again, 'no more Mr Nice Guy. How's Henry?'

'What?' She was fussing round him, using her handkerchief to dab away the blood, trying to see in the floodlit darkness how bad it all was. 'Oh, he's fine. The lads who fetched me said he was OK. Couple of broken ribs apparently. Lots of

glass damage. Bit likc you, I should imagine.' She
was sniffing now, choking back the tears, glad to
be busy, doing stuff. There was a churning in her
stomach. 'Not now, Jim,' she hissed.

'No,' Maxwell growled. 'Thank you, but Henry
Hall is *nothing* like me. Wash your mouth out.'

'Mr Maxwell,' DS Tom O'Connell was at their
side, helping Maxwell up. 'I'd like to shake your
hand, sir,' he said. 'I wasn't exactly pleasant when
we first met. Goes with the territory, I guess. Anyway, I understand you saved the guv'nor's life.
That was brave. You'll get a medal, I shouldn't
wonder.'

'Yippee,' said Maxwell flatly, unable in his
present state to even *think* of a smile. 'And as for
saving Henry's life, I was under the impression
he was trying to save mine.'

And O'Connell helped the pair, the old crock
and the pregnant one, into the ambulance.

'At least,' he said as he closed the door on
them, 'we can wrap this one up.'

'What do you mean, Detective Sergeant?' Maxwell was grateful to be lying down.

'Well, the murders.' O'Connell frowned at the
man. The old bastard must be in shock. 'Deena
Harrison.'

Maxwell lifted himself up on to his better elbow.
'Deena Harrison no more committed these
murders than this good lady here.' He reached
out for Jacquie's hand. 'And believe me, I shall be
asking her a lot of questions on the way to the
hospital.'

Chapter Twenty-Seven

Dierdre Lessing was at her conspiratorial best that Monday morning. The menopause was not being kind to her, turning her into even more of a withered old prune than she had been erstwhile. As always, the Sir Mordred of Leighford High was fawning around his Morgana Le Fay.

'You've heard about that business at the Arquebus last night,' she said. It was a statement, nothing more.

'I have,' Bernard Ryan said. 'Deena Harrison, I understand.'

'Doesn't surprise me at all.' Dierdre was nibbling her wafer thins. 'I don't know what possessed James to take the girl on. I think we all told him.'

'I think we all did.'

'Of course,' Dierdre leaned slightly across Ryan's cluttered desk. 'You know who was behind the whole thing, don't you?'

Ryan did, but he'd like it confirmed.

'Peter Maxwell,' she bridled. Dierdre Lessing bridled every time she heard – or spoke – Peter Maxwell's name. 'He's off today, of course.'

'Hurt in the fire, I understand,' Ryan nodded.

'The only thing of his that'll be hurt is his pride. And to think he's got that girl pregnant. Well, it's just nauseating.'

'He's your age, isn't he, Dierdre?'

But the Senior Mistress of Leighford High School had already left, her coffee unfinished, her wafer thin crumbled on Ryan's paperwork.

'Oh, my God.' A startled Rowena Sanders peered around her vicarage door at the apparition in front of her.

'Forgive me, Mrs Sanders,' the apparition said. 'Under all these bandages, I'm Peter Maxwell. One of your companions to the Other Side last night.'

'Yes,' she faltered. 'Yes, I know who you are.'

Peter Maxwell looked like the Invisible Man. Only his eyes, his nose tip and his mouth were uncovered. Everything else was National Health Service white. 'I came to apologise,' he said. 'And to explain.'

'Perhaps you'd better come in.' And she checked up and down the road before she closed the door. Many were the oddities who had crossed that threshold, but none *quite* so odd as Peter Maxwell. 'Er ... the room on the right,' she said.

There was an oval table in the room's centre and seven chairs around it. Maxwell took it in immediately. 'So we were one chair too many last night,' he said. 'Is that why it went wrong?'

'It went wrong because you made it go wrong, Mr Maxwell. You weren't even invited. Oh, God!' Rowena sat down suddenly, on a settee below the window. Maxwell was standing behind one of the upright dining chairs, his back to a large, solid Victorian fireplace. 'Maxwell,' she said, her eyes wide at the sudden memory of it. 'You've been here before.'

'No,' said Maxwell, frowning as well as he could, what with the cuts and the bandages. 'No, I don't think so.'

'Yes, yes.' Rowena was intermittently closing her eyes, then glancing at Maxwell. 'Tall.' She'd got that right. Maxwell was nearly six-one in his co-respondent shoes. 'Dark.' That too she could tell by the thatch, now greying, that sprouted out on top of the bandages. 'Not handsome exactly...'

'Oh, thanks,' Maxwell murmured.

'But with a certain roguish charm.'

'Aw, shucks,' Maxwell was giving Rowena his best Jed Clampett impression. 'Ah bet yuh say that tuh all yuh travellers tuh the Other Side.'

'I held a séance, here in this room,' Rowena gabbled. 'I can't remember when – five weeks ago, six? You were here. Oh, not in the flesh; I don't mean that. In the spirit. You were talking to me,' she looked at him, her grey eyes ever wider, popping out of her head. 'And you are going to die.'

'Well,' said Maxwell after a pause. 'That's one thing you clairvoyants will always get right.'

'I am not a clairvoyant, Mr Maxwell. I am a conduit. A guide for travellers. No more. That was a cruel trick you played on Mrs Bartlett last night.'

'Cruel?' Maxwell repeated. 'Yes, perhaps it was. But not as cruel as fastening a trip wire across an old lady's stair or shooting a few hundred volts through a wet carpet. We're talking ends and means here, Mrs Sanders.'

'Well, then,' she breathed to compose herself. 'You said you had come here to explain. And please move away from that fireplace. It ... it disturbs me.'

Maxwell sat alongside the medium on her settee and took up the tale. "Daniel Bartlett" was my idea,' he said. 'I rather lost touch with everybody when the torch went up last night or I'd have come clean then. I hope you weren't too hard on poor old Benny.'

'Benny,' she repeated. 'He was the lad in the disguise?'

'That's right. He's one of My Own at Leighford High, although to be honest, he's not exactly a regular. No, his love is woofers, tweeters and all the rest of the theatrical backstagery that means a show will go on. He moonlights – or, in Benny's case, daylights – at the Arquebus. I needed him to do a Banquo, Mrs Sanders.'

'The character in *Macbeth*?' the medium checked.

'The ghost at the feast,' Maxwell nodded, 'whom only the guilty Macbeth can see. There, I admit it – I pinched an idea from the Bard; how often do you see that done? The Scottish play's the thing wherein I intended to catch the conscience of the king. And it damn near worked.'

'But Mrs Bartlett told us, and she's hardly a believer,' Rowena said, 'but just for a second, she thought the boy *was* her late husband. How did you do it?'

'It was a bit of luck that Benny was about the right build for Bartlett. Actually, I think he's nearly three inches shorter, but in the dark and in the charged atmosphere you had helped create, I didn't think anybody would have a tape measure. The coat and cap were borrowed from the Arquebus' wardrobe department. As for the voice ... well, modest to a fault though I am, that was me, pre-recorded and set off by Benny with some sort of timing mechanism from the theatre's sound-box. I've got to hand it to the boy – it worked a treat.'

'But the fire...'

'Ah, well,' Maxwell shook his head, 'the best-laid plans of mice and men. *That* wasn't supposed to happen.'

'So what did you achieve?' Rowena wanted to know. 'You terrified us all and what is worse, you tried to make light of my powers and the genuine need of Mrs Elliot to find closure in the death of her aunt.'

'If I terrified you,' Maxwell was on his feet, 'I'm truly sorry. And if your powers are genuine, Mrs Sanders, they won't be diminished by a little subterfuge of mine. As for Mrs Elliot, her closure can only be achieved by catching her aunt's killer. That's what I achieved last night.'

'You did?' Rowena was staring at him. 'But who...?'

Maxwell paused in the doorway and risked tapping his bandaged nose. 'Someone at that table,' he said.

Jacquie had been right. Maxwell should have stayed in the ward they put him in, not just over-night but the next day too, and he certainly shouldn't have been cycling all over the town.

Apart from his own cut, singed and shocked condition, she reasoned, what about the motorists swerving at the sight of the Invisible Man on his bike? But Maxwell wasn't having any. He resisted her concerned fussing and positively forbade her to follow him. He also refused to carry his mobile, the umpteenth one she'd bought him so that he could keep in touch. 'If the Good Lord had intended us to have mobiles,' he often said to her, 'then there was something wrong with his grand design.'

So he eased himself off the saddle in the drive of Patrick Collinson's house, the one that doubled as his office, and dragged himself up the steps.

It was a wary Doris who sat, riveted, at her desk in the outer office. When Maxwell had called last, she'd been uncertain whether she should call the police. Now, she faced the same dilemma, except that this time perhaps she should call the men in white coats too.

Jacquie paced the living room, tidying his sixth form essays into a neat stack. Then she busied herself in the kitchen, rattling cups and wiping surfaces. Then she turned to take the stairs, carrying a couple of towels to the airing cupboard. She was filling time and it lay heavy on her hands. Time passing. Clock ticking. Time wasting.

Then she took the second set of stairs, the wooden ones to the attic, to the Inner Sanctum below the eaves. Only her head appeared above the parapet and the black and white killer in the corner lurking there had smelt her long before.

She didn't see him at first, crouched as he was on the old linen basket.

Lord Cardigan's Light Brigade sat their horses in the centre of the room, the diorama that Maxwell had been working on for so long. It had filled the hours of his loneliness, framed his thinking as he wrestled with his problems – how to teach Seven Zed Four or how to catch a murderer. She couldn't crouch any more to see their detail at eye level – Sonny Jim wouldn't let her. He was just too big now and too boisterous, although he was particularly quiet that morning. She walked around the end of the table where Cardigan and Lucan sat with the impetuous Captain Nolan, his arm flung out behind him, pointing down the wrong and fatal valley with the careless and deadly words – 'There is your enemy, my lord; there are your guns.' Less than two-thirds of the Brigade would ride back.

'Well, Count.' Jacquie lowered her head to look the animal in its green, smouldering eyes. 'Time for a reckoning, don't you think? You see, it's not just your Lord and Master now. It's me too. And soon,' Sonny Jim failed to kick on cue, 'a third party. The days of the bachelor club are over. Can you handle that, you murderous bastard?'

Metternich stretched, his claws extending in the morning light, and yawned, his eyes closing, his teeth bared – all the apparatus of the perfect killing machine. Then, he did something he hardly ever did to Peter Maxwell. He reached up and planted a lipless kiss on Jacquie's nose. I can handle that – thanks for asking.

'Who's there?' Peter Maxwell was standing on the Arquebus stage. He had just clambered over the still wet debris in the foyer and picked his way carefully down the shallow steps of the auditorium's aisle.

'It's me, Max; Patrick Collinson.'

'Patrick,' the Head of Sixth Form hailed him. 'Thank God.'

'My God!' was the accountant's riposte.

'Yes, yes, I know.' Maxwell was attempting a chuckle. 'It's worse than it looks. Where the Hell are we on insurance on this lot?'

'Oh, we'll be all right,' Collinson told him. 'And for all it looks terrible, it could have been far, far worse. Shame about *Shop of Horrors* though.'

'Oh, we'll put that on at Leighford High,' Maxwell told him. 'Back to Plan A, I suppose.'

'The firemen told me that mad girl had used two fire bombs,' Collinson said. 'What had she got against the place, Max?'

'Paranoid schizophrenia is the official term, Patrick,' Maxwell said sadly. 'But in layman's terms, God knows. They just let her out into the community too soon, that's all.'

'She could barely have known Gordon Goodacre.'

'Gordon?' Maxwell blinked. 'I didn't think she knew him at all. She told me...' and he thought of chuckling, but it was taking too much of a toll. 'I was going to say she told me she started here days after his death, but then she told us a lot of things, didn't she, which bore no relation to the truth.'

'That's right,' Collinson sighed, wiping his

sooty hands on a cloth. 'No, she joined two days *before* Gordon died. She obviously slipped the chains on the ladders and pushed them over while he was working.'

'Obviously,' Maxwell nodded. 'But how did she get access to Martita Winchcombe's place? That's the one I can't work out.'

'Well,' Collinson gave it some thought. 'She was plausible enough. Had me believing all sorts of things about poor old Ashley, for instance. I daresay she befriended the old girl and wormed her way into her confidence. In the case of Dan Bartlett now ... what *was* all that about, Max? With the fire and everything, that little piece of play-acting went rather out of the window. But when we talked to that lad of yours – Benny, is it? When we talked to him after the fire was under control, he said *you'd* put him up to it.'

'Did he?' Maxwell was appalled. 'Well,' he tutted. 'There's loyalty for you. You were saying – "In the case of Dan Bartlett..."'

'Hmm? Oh, yes, well, I wouldn't be at all surprised to find that he lured her into his bed. The old lecher had no scruples whatsoever. He upset her somewhere, I suppose, and she snapped. We all saw her in action last night. Absolutely terrifying.'

'Terrifying indeed,' Maxwell agreed. 'But not guilty, nonetheless.'

'Not...? Oh, come off it, Max,' Collinson chuckled. 'I mean, I know she was one of yours and you want to be loyal and all...'

'There you go again, Patrick,' Maxwell tutted. 'That word loyalty. Yes, I like to think I'm loyal.

But then, so are you. So is Doris.'

'Doris?' Collinson was frowning.

'Oh, didn't I tell you? I've just come from your place. She told me you were here.'

'Well,' Collinson was chuckling again. 'Yes, I suppose that's an example of loyalty. Although in the case of some clients, I'd rather they didn't know where I was every minute of the day.'

'Indeed,' Maxwell nodded. 'Minutes of the day is what the whole thing is all about, isn't it? Made everything very neat and easy. And it all began with Gordon.'

'I'm sorry.'

'The only thing you're sorry about, Patrick,' Maxwell eased himself carefully down onto a theatre seat, one of the few unscathed by the fire, 'is the death of Martita Winchcombe.'

'Well, yes,' Collinson conceded. 'I was rather fond of the old girl.'

'There was a kindness about that killing,' Maxwell said. 'Or rather its aftermath.'

'I don't follow,' Collinson told him.

'Yes, you do, Patrick. You follow all too well and even now you're hoping to lie your way out. But I'm afraid it's rather too late, old man. Gordon Goodacre's death was exactly what it appeared to be, what it says on the tin, an accident. He probably caused it himself with a moment of sheer carelessness. But that was the trigger, wasn't it? The trigger that set Dan Bartlett off on his little murder spree.'

'Max, Max,' Collinson's laugh was brittle. 'That flying glass must have done more damage than you thought. You're talking nonsense.'

'No, I'm not, Patrick,' Maxwell shook his head with difficulty. 'That's why I set young Benny up with the disguise and recorded my Dan Bartlett impersonation, just to see the reaction. I knew Henry Hall wouldn't buy it. Rowena Sanders, Fiona Elliot and probably Magda Lupescu would believe the whole thing. I wasn't interested in Carole Bartlett's response. No, it was down to you and Ashley Wilkes. You see, I invented body language, Patrick. I know all the signs – fear, panic, guilt. Ashley Wilkes reacted like a Theatre Manager. You reacted like a murderer. Dan Bartlett had lived high off the hog once – family money and so on. But he'd spent it – alimony, girlies, the gee-gees, unwise investments, who knows? So he went cap in hand to the Arquebus Treasurer, a slightly dotty old duck who was absolutely loaded. Big house, cash in the bank, more money than you could shake a stick at. And she turned him down. She had two loves in her life, did Martita Winchcombe – one was the Arquebus Theatre and she intended to leave all her worldly goods to that. That was because the other love in her life was financially secure and didn't need the handouts. Did you, Patrick?'

'Max...'

'That's where dear old Doris comes in. We got talking, Doris and I, about you; what a good, understanding employer you are and your passion for the theatre and your generous bonuses ... and the fact that you moved here from Cheltenham.'

'Is that a crime?' Collinson felt obliged to ask.

'I have a neighbour,' Maxwell went on, 'a Mrs Troubridge. Nice old duck, and terribly helpful

392

in the local history stakes. Knew Martita Winchcombe long years ago. Knew about her little spot
of bother. She got herself in the family way, did
Martita, at a time when doing ... that sort of
thing without a husband was frowned upon by
polite Leighford society. So she went away for a
while. To have the baby. She went to Cheltenham
and the little boy was christened Patrick. Tell me,
Patrick, when you first discovered Martita was
your mother.'

'Twenty-one years ago,' Collinson said, slumping down into a seat across the aisle from Maxwell. 'I did some sleuthing – I'm nearly as good
as you are, Maxwell – and I traced her. I was
petrified when I came to see her, already a
middle-aged man with a life and a successful
career of my own. She just ... wrapped her arms
around me on the threshold of Dundee and that
was it. I had come home, the Prodigal, the long-
lost son. Except, she still didn't want it known. It
must be our secret. And so we kept it, until now.'

'And Dan Bartlett?' Maxwell asked.

'You were right,' Collinson sighed. 'He was
worming his smarmy way into my mother's affec-
tions – or so he thought. One day, he asked her
outright. Would she leave everything to him?
Think of him as the son she never had. She
refused him, told him to get out. Never to call on
her again.'

'But he did?'

'Oh, yes. I was driving over to see her one night
– the night she died. I saw Bartlett's car leaving
the drive. I have a key of course so I let myself in,
although she had a habit of forgetting to lock the

back. I found her.' Collinson's eyes filled with tears. 'Lying at the bottom of the stairs. He'd... I don't know ... lost his temper, decided to punish her. Something. I think Gordon's death – the whole accident thing – made him choose the method he did. A tripwire I believe the papers speculated. All I know was that my mother was lying dead at the bottom of the stairs.'

'So you covered her up?' Maxwell checked.

'I put her blanket over her, yes,' Collinson sobbed quietly. 'I couldn't leave her like that.'

'Why didn't you just call the police?' Maxwell asked. 'You'd seen Bartlett leave. You knew he was pressurising your mother financially...'

'And achieve what?' Collinson shouted. 'They haven't caught me, have they, for Dan Bartlett's murder? I couldn't rely on that bunch of no-hopers. And anyway, even if they got their act together and the case went against him in court, what then? Fifteen years? Ten with good behaviour? Colour telly and ping-pong with Internet access? No, Max, no. It wasn't enough.'

'So it was revenge then, on the son Martita never had by the son she did?'

Collinson nodded. 'You were right,' he said. 'It was all about minutes of the day. Bartlett was a push-over because he kept a rigid routine. Even when he was seducing someone he was checking his watch behind their back. That and his obsession with pizza. All of us on the Arquebus Committee had keys to each other's houses by mutual agreement – that's how Bartlett would have got into Dundee should the unlikely have happened and mother locked the door. I knew he wouldn't be in his ghastly little bungalow in the early evening so I made a call, booking a pizza delivery at ten-thirty, when I knew he'd be in the bath. That way, his phone records would merely log that a call was made from his place and, everyone would presume, by him. I've been around theatres long enough to know how to make wires lethal, so I set to. With dry feet, you'd get away with light charring, but wet from the bath ... well. Curtains!' Collinson sat upright, defiant, even proud. 'I'm just sorry I wasn't there to see it.' He blinked, looking at the bandaged sight in front of him. What happens now?' he asked.

'Now...' Maxwell sighed, but he never finished his sentence.

'Max!' Jane Blaisedell was hurtling down the aisle, leaping over debris as she ran, crashing through rubbish. 'The baby. It's Jacquie. Thank God I found you. The baby.'

Chapter Twenty-Eight

They let Henry Hall out of Leighford General a few days later and with a little help he staggered back to his office in the Incident Room at Tottingleigh. He had a murderer to interrogate, paperwork to finish, tees to cross and eyes to dot.

He didn't quite know whether to include Magda Lupescu's work in the official report. And he was still wrestling with the problem, when something caught his eye, a sudden movement to his left as he sat at his desk. He turned and there, crouching behind the green-fronted filing cabinet, was a frightened little boy, with a dunce's cap on his head.

And when Henry Hall looked again, he'd gone.

Maxwell held his baby boy in his arms. Little Nolan, named for the hot-headed officer who brought the fatal order to the Light Brigade that long-ago October day. It was November now, crisp underfoot and wreathed in mist. It would be a long, hard winter, Global Warming notwithstanding.

He carried the pink bundle up the wooden stairs to his Inner Sanctum, his War Office.

'This,' he said to the boy, pointing to the plastic soldiers, 'is your namesake, Captain Louis Edward Nolan, 15th Hussars. Next to him, James Brudenell, the Seventh Earl of Cardigan... I hope you're listening, Nolan, 'cos I shall be asking questions later.'

He caught the light in the picture frame to his left and broke away from his Brigade, to look at the photo. His Jacquie. And it all came flooding back; that day that they arrested Patrick Collinson, the day Jane Blaisedell had come to tell him that the baby was early, the baby was here. He remembered the clanging of the police car siren, the flashing light. There were complications, Jane was gabbling, with Jacquie. But she'd be all right. Wouldn't she? Jacquie would be all right.

Maxwell looked at the girl. And the boy they'd made together. He had her nose, all right. Maxwell felt his eyes fill with tears. 'Well, kid,' he nuzzled against the baby's cheek, 'it's just you and me, now.' And he turned back to the Light Brigade.

'Max!'

'Up here,' he called, frowning.

Her head popped up on a level with the floor.

'I thought you were going to your mother's,' he said, confused.

'I was,' she said. 'Then I thought about my boys and thought "She'll keep". I rang her to cancel before I'd got to the bottom of the road. Fancy a coffee?'

'In a minute,' he smiled at her. 'In a minute, Woman Policeman. Your son and I have a little Charge to ride.'